# PATRICK EASTER

# Cuckold Point

First published in Great Britain in 2015 by Quercus Publishing Ltd
This paperback edition published in 2015 by

Quercus Publishing Ltd
Carmelite House
50 Victoria Embankment
London EC4Y 0DZ

An Hachette UK company

A CIP catalogue record for this book is available
from the British Library

PB ISBN 978 1 78087 767 9
EBOOK ISBN 978 1 78087 766 2

This book is a work of fiction. Names, characters,
businesses, organizations, places and events are  either the
product of the author's imagination or used fictitiously.
Any resemblance to actual persons, living or dead,
events or locales is entirely coincidental.

10 9 8 7 6 5 4 3 2 1

Typeset by Jouve (UK), Milton Keynes

Printed and bound in Great Britain by Clays Ltd, St Ives plc

For Zak and for Thomas – in the springtime of their lives

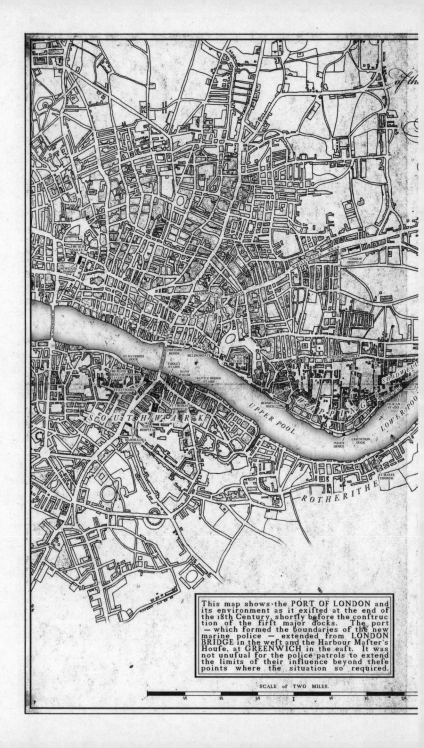

This map shows the PORT OF LONDON and its environment as it exifted at the end of the 18th Century, shortly before the construction of the firft major docks. The port — which formed the boundaries of the new marine police — extended from LONDON BRIDGE in the weft and the Harbour Mafter's Houfe, at GREENWICH in the eaft. It was not unufual for the police patrols to extend the limits of their influence beyond thefe points where the situation so required.

SCALE of TWO MILES.

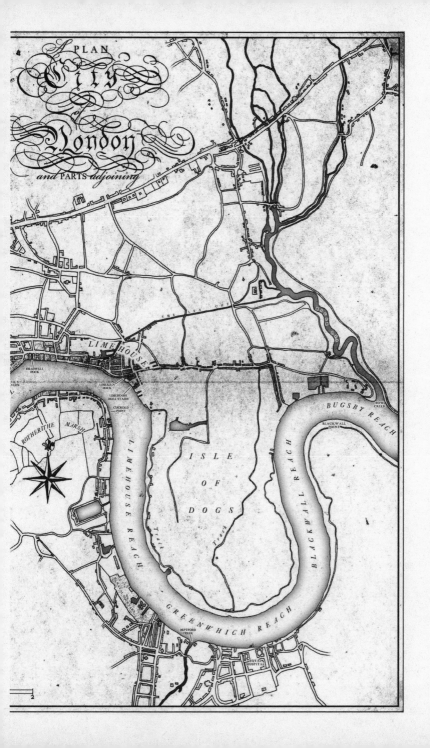

# PROLOGUE

*September 1799 – Paris*

Fear gripped every part of Antoine Flauhault's anatomy as he descended the stairs of his apartment on rue de la Verité. At the street door he hesitated and looked up and down the deserted boulevard, still damp from the night's rain. He knew he no longer had a choice. It was a question of when, and not if, he was caught. He stepped across the threshold and walked to the waiting caleche, glistening in the pale light of a crescent moon. The next hour would be the most dangerous. The risk of being stopped and searched by one of the ragbag patrols that had become such a feature of the city, would lessen once he had left the capital behind.

Flauhault, aide-de-camp to the general officer commanding the Garde du Directoire, nodded at the driver and settled back into his seat as the carriage rumbled forward. At the junction with rue Saint Martin, they turned south towards the Seine, the black outline of the Palais de Justice visible through the gloom. He leaned forward and stared out of the window at the silent streets. It would have been safer travelling by day. He would have been one amongst many and his reason for being on the road more plausible. But he didn't have the luxury of time. He dropped his hand to the hem of his coat and felt for the document that had been sewn into the lining. It would be safe there from all but the most determined of searches.

Soon they had crossed the river into the rue de Faubourg. There was still no sign of a patrol. Flauhault began to breathe more easily. To the right, the tall rectangular shape of the Observatory signalled the beginning of open country.

A sudden shout. Angry. Aggressive. From somewhere up ahead.

The caleche slowed to a halt and a bearded face appeared at the carriage window, a red, white and blue rosette pinned to the hat perched on his head, a belligerent look in his eyes.

'Your papers, *citoyen*, if you please.'

Flauhault removed a parchment from his pocket book and handed it over, hoping the man couldn't read. If he could, he'd realise the parchment was his appointment to the Garde du Directoire and not a passport to travel. With luck the wax seal and ribbon would be enough to convince the guard to let him pass. An anxious two minutes passed. Then he was through.

Countless days and sleepless nights followed as Flauhault fled south. He had little doubt that by now his flight from Paris had been noted and a search for him instigated. The authorities would be somewhere close behind.

He rested by day, always in remote hamlets and farmsteads, away from the highways he might have been expected to take. Several times he came close to capture; pursuing troops fanning out across the countryside in search of him. Exhausted almost beyond endurance, he often considered giving up, yet each time he continued for what he believed was the greater good of France.

He reached Lourdes and the foothills of the Pyrenees at the

end of the month to find the town overrun with gendarmes and troops. Every house was being searched. To remain meant certain capture and death. Yet a return to Paris was also an impossibility.

'Destroy the caleche,' he said to his driver. 'Leave one of the horses for me. You take the other one and return home. They are not looking for you.'

That night he made his way to the coaching inn on the edge of the town, to the room where he had arranged to meet the Spanish merchant who was his contact with the outside world.

'You have it?' asked the Spaniard, after they had spoken for a little while.

'Take care of it,' said Flauhault, handing him the tightly folded sheets of paper. 'And of yourself, of course. Now I must go. It is not safe here.'

An hour later, the unknown Spaniard left his room. He knew his way around the town and the mountains behind. He would not be seen. In a short while he would slip across the border and disappear. He made his way downstairs and out through a side door, into a darkened alley. At the corner of the main street, he stopped. On the opposite side he could see a large group of armed men carrying torches. They were gathered round something and shouting excitedly. He waited, curious as to the reason. Suddenly, an officer appeared and the crowd parted. In the centre, a man was kneeling on the ground, his head bowed.

It was Antoine Flauhault.

# CHAPTER 1

*October 1799, Erith, Kent, by the River Thames*

Mary Cox was never to see her husband again. She stood at the window and watched him walk quickly down the lane towards the pier. She had no reason to fear for his safety, except that he'd been behaving oddly these last few days. It was as though something was troubling him, something he had refused to discuss with her, much though she'd tried to engage him on the subject. She struggled to dismiss the concerns from her thoughts. In all probability it was something to do with his work as the sailing master of a hoy. It would soon resolve itself. It always had done.

She continued to look out of the window long after her husband had disappeared round a bend in the road. Then she walked into the back room. She had plenty to keep her occupied. He would be home in three or four days, a week at the most. His work took him to London where he might have to wait for a day or two for a new load to become available. Then he'd transport it to Sheerness or Chatham before returning home. It was a good job, even if it didn't bring in much money.

She stopped by the back door, her hand resting on the latch, and gazed out over the Thames, to the broad sweep of the Essex marshes on the far side. She knew she wasn't being honest with

5

herself. Her husband's problems were a deal more serious than she'd been prepared to accept. He had, in an unguarded moment, hinted as much. She remembered the two men she'd seen talking to him at the front gate, a week since. They lived in the village but she'd never cared for them although her husband had seemed oddly pleased by their visit, as though a weight had been lifted from his mind.

She closed the back door, the room suddenly gloomy. She preferred it that way. The absence of light hid the black soot that covered the wall above the fireplace, the threadbare rug in front of her husband's chair and the cracks in the small windowpanes through which the winter gales would blow. There was little point in thinking about what needed to be done. After the food was bought, what spare money there was had to be spent on wood for the fire and the other essentials of daily life. Worrying would make no difference to all that.

She stood still for a moment, drained of energy and in need of some rest. Her three daughters were still at the village school and it would be some time before they returned home for their midday meal. She climbed the steep, narrow stairs to the single bedroom she and her husband shared with their children. Later, she would get up and see to their needs.

But not now. Not for the moment. She thought again about her husband and wished he'd told her about whatever it was that was troubling him.

Daniel Creech, a sailmaker in the parish of Whitechapel, to the east of London, leaned his short, stocky frame against the bar of the Royal Oak, Rotherhithe, and watched the man's arrival with more than usual interest. The rumours had been circulating for a day or two and he was anxious not to let the opportunity they presented slip through his fingers. He knew that what a dozen men were aware of today, three times that number would know by the end of the week. And that would unnecessarily complicate matters.

He was, above all, a practical man who perfectly understood the minds of those who lived and worked on the river and the streets round about. For him, guile and physical strength went hand in hand. What could not be achieved with one would be dealt with by the other. His natural inclination tended to the latter course, and he enjoyed the thrill of seeing pain and fear in another man's eyes. There was something deeply pleasurable, almost sexual in the excitement that coursed through his forty-five-year-old veins in the moment of physical violence. Even with advancing middle age and the appearance of the first strands of grey in his otherwise pitch-black hair, he had lost none of the satisfaction that such occasions gave him.

'All right, Coxy?' Creech smiled in what he imagined was a friendly sort of way, his narrow, almost aquiline face scarred by smallpox, his coal-black eyes without a trace of warmth. He'd heard about Cox's recent difficulties. Gambling was a mug's game, in his opinion. The scrub should never have become involved. He was surprised he had.

The fellow had always struck him as a man he could do business with, the sort of cully who'd do what he was told and keep his mouth shut. Of course he'd do his own bit of thieving here and there. It was what everyone did and was as much a part of their lives as the air they breathed. But Coxy was in danger of forgetting the point beyond which it would be dangerous for him to go. As far as Creech was concerned that territory was reserved for men like him, men who knew how to ensure the profitability of what they did, and who didn't mind who got hurt in the process. He would have to bring Coxy back into line. All gentle, like.

'Drink?' he said, raising his eyebrows. 'On me, like.'

'I'll have a beer, since you're asking.' Rob Cox, sailing master of the hoy, the *Sisters*, leaned an elbow on the bar and tipped a sweat-soaked sou'wester onto the back of his head. He was not a fit man. Overweight and approaching his half century, his body bore the hallmarks of a lifetime spent out of doors, battered by all that nature could throw at him.

'You look all in, mate. Everything all right?'

'Aye. Just knackered.'

Creech glanced round the near-empty room. 'I hear you might've got a job what's worth a bob or two,' he said.

'Oh, aye?' Cox looked up sharply. 'Where did you hear that, then?'

'Here and there. You know how it is.' Creech held up his hands in mock surrender.

Cox looked over his shoulder. When he turned back, his eyes had narrowed. 'What's it to you, anygate?'

'Folk round here tell me you need money. Lots of it. And quick.'

Cox shrugged his shoulders but said nothing, a look of defeat in his exhausted eyes.

'As it happens I might be able to put some money your way, if you're interested,' said Creech.

'What's that all about, then?' A faint gleam of hope sparked briefly in Cox's eyes.

'You tell me about this job I've been hearing on and after that your old mate Creech will take care of all your troubles.'

There was a long silence while Cox seemed to wrestle with his thoughts. Finally, he said, 'I don't know, Creech. I don't want no trouble.'

'You ain't been listening to me, me old cock.' The smile had gone from the sailmaker's face, his mouth now twisted into a snarl, his eyes narrowed into mere pinpricks of anger. 'I ain't asking you, Coxy. You is going to tell me what I want to know about a certain ship what's got a handsome cargo just begging to fall into my lap.'

'I didn't mean no disrespect, Creech. Only—'

'Yeah, well, there's enough scallywags what's heard the story and I ain't about to let none of them get the best of old Creech. And you, my son, is going to help me.'

'What can I do, Creech? I ain't got the job yet. And without the papers, they ain't going to give it to me, neither.'

'I ain't stupid, cock,' said Creech, reaching across and gripping the unfortunate Cox by the throat. 'You're going to make sure you get the job, all legal, like. I want the silk what's in that ship. You understand me? You do that and I'll take care of the rest, never you fret.'

Cox nodded mutely.

'That's a good man. When will you know?'

'Maybe tomorrow,' said Cox, rubbing his neck in short, nervous movements. 'Maybe the day after. All depends on me guv'nor.'

'Don't piss me, Coxy,' said Creech, leaning in close, an unpleasant edge to his voice. 'You know how that upsets me.'

# CHAPTER 2

It was another week before Rob Cox brought the *Sisters* to a mooring buoy in the Galley Quay Road, close to the Custom House in the Port of London, and made her fast. The regular journey up from Sheerness had taken longer than expected and he was ready for his bunk. Tomorrow he would visit the hoy's owner and see if he'd been given the job of collecting the silk. The last time he'd asked, he'd been sent away with a flea in his ear.

He'd not, as he'd promised he would, been back to see Creech. There'd been no point – not until he knew whether or not he was to collect the silk. A shiver passed up his spine. It was never a good idea to ignore Creech, however good the excuse. Yet the more he thought about it, the less enamoured he was with the prospect of throwing in his lot with a villain of Creech's reputation. It wasn't that he had any moral concerns about what was being proposed. But he didn't much care for the idea of stealing property for which he was personally responsible. The chances of getting away with it were next to none. On the other hand, it did offer him a way out of his financial woes.

He thought of his wife and children. The gambling debt had been like a lead weight hanging over their lives. The risk he'd taken had been appalling. It wasn't as if the money had even been his. It wasn't. He could see all this now, in hindsight, but at the time his actions had seemed to promise a better future for them all.

He looked down the length of the Pool and across the Isle of Dogs towards an unseen cottage on the outskirts of the village of Erith, twenty or so miles to the east. His wife and daughters would be sitting round the table for their evening meal. If they were lucky a neighbour would have brought them a rabbit for the pot. If not . . . Cox shut his eyes, unwilling to think about it. There was no one to blame but himself. His earnings had been barely enough to feed them even before his fall from grace. He thought again of what Creech had said: *You tell me about this job . . . your old mate Creech will take care of all your troubles.*

'Cox?' The voice made him jump. He looked over the starboard rail. A skiff was approaching. There were two men on board, both of whom he knew, and wished he didn't. 'A word in your shell-like?'

Cox felt his stomach tighten. He doubted if either Gabriel Marr or Joe Gott would take no for an answer. Reluctantly, he waved them in.

'We's been talking to Creech,' said Gott, a dour, heavily built man, his thick, muscular arms and broad shoulders an odd contrast to his bald minuscule skull that seemed to have been fashioned almost as an afterthought by the Almighty on a bad day. 'He's very disappointed in you, Coxy. Seems you didn't want to accept his generous offer of help. That ain't very friendly. What d'you think, Marr?'

'It ain't friendly at all,' said Marr, turning a pair of ice-blue eyes in Cox's direction. Shorter and less powerfully built than his companion, he was, Cox already knew, prone to acts of violence even more extreme than his paymaster, Daniel Creech.

'Thing is, Coxy,' said Gott, 'Creech wants to see you.'

'Now?' Cox was finding it difficult to breathe as he watched first one and then the other of the two men climb onto the deck of the *Sisters*.

'What d'you think?' sneered Gott, his face close to Cox's. 'Of course, now. Get in the boat. We ain't got all night.'

Tom Pascoe, a river surveyor with the marine police institution at the Wapping police office, gazed longingly at the row of beer barrels set against the far wall of the Harp public house on Harp Lane, in the City of London. A tall, good-looking man in his late twenties, with a thick mane of yellow hair tied at the nape, his life was at something of a crossroads.

Four years ago, he'd been a recently promoted master and commander in the King's Navy, the proud captain of a sloop of war and the supreme authority over all that he surveyed. But within months he, like many of his brother officers, had been put ashore on indefinite leave by their Lordships of the Admiralty, his beloved sloop handed to someone with a deal more influence than he could muster. In need of an income he'd been obliged to accept a position as master of a West India barque until that, too, had ended rather more abruptly than he might have wished. Once more without work, he'd been offered his present role with the newly formed marine police based at Wapping, in July last year.

Tom wrenched his gaze away from the beguiling view of the beer barrels. Several times in the last half-hour he'd risen to his feet, intent on ordering himself a quart pot of Hammond's. And each time he'd sat down again, overwhelmed by a feeling of inadequacy.

He'd not ventured into any liquor shop in over a month; had thought himself free of the demons that had hounded him since Peggy's death. He moistened his lips and glanced out through the doorway of the cubicle in which he was sitting. The taproom beyond was crowded, as it usually was, whatever the day or the hour, the air heavy with the smell of tobacco smoke and human sweat. The sudden desire for that sense of oblivion, into which he had so often descended in recent times, was in danger of overwhelming him. Only one thing kept him in check. He felt in his pocket and drew out a crumpled sheet of paper. Carefully, he laid it on the table in front of him. It was a letter from his mother.

My dearest Tom, pray do not, I beg, think ill of me, but your brother, William, is growing quickly and has, for some time now, expressed a wish to see London and to meet you, of whom he has heard so much. I confess I do not care for the notion and have worried about what would become of him in that vast place if he were to have his wish. But he is determined and I no longer have the strength nor the will to stand in his way. If only you will agree to receive him and take care of him for a little while, my mind will be eased. He is a good boy, anxious to learn and obedient. I am sure he will cause you no alarm or distress.

The letter had arrived more than a month ago, but Tom had not replied immediately, putting off the moment when he would have to do so, afraid of what he had become, of what would be expected of him. He'd never seen the boy, had been at sea when his own father had died and his mother had married again. Later she'd written to him with news of the arrival of a new brother but in spite of that, he'd not returned home. The lad would be ten now. Tom stuffed the letter back into his pocket. For better or worse he'd finally replied to her letter and agreed to look after the lad. He clambered to his feet and stumbled blindly towards the door.

'Well, if it ain't Master Pascoe,' said a voice from the door of the cubicle. 'Didn't expect to see you in these parts, your honour. You stopping for a drink?'

Tom turned to see a pair of protuberant eyes squinting up at him from under a curtain of matted hair, its face pale, almost sickly, a gnarled fist clamped round a drinking pot. For a moment Tom wavered. Just one drink. It couldn't do any harm. With an effort, he looked away.

'No, thankee, Joseph. I was just leaving.' He adjusted the battered blue and white uniform coat that he still wore from his Navy days, and started for the door.

'Thing is, Master Pascoe, I was hoping to find you.' Joseph Gunn, a lighterman and regular guest at London's houses of correction, waved his half-empty pewter mug in Tom's direction. 'I've been hearing things what you might be interested in.'

'Outside, then,' said Tom. He knew he ought to be paying greater attention to the man. The fellow was one of his more reliable informants. But he could feel a headache coming on, probably exacerbated by the struggle he was having with his desire for a drink. He led the way out into Harp Lane where he paused for a moment, trying to clear his head.

'What is it you wanted to talk to me about?' he asked, suddenly wishing he'd stayed where he was and had the drink he so desperately wanted.

'Not here, Master Pascoe,' said Gunn glancing over his shoulder. 'Somewhere more private, if it's all the same to you.'

'Over there, then,' said Tom, pointing down the street. A minute or so later they had reached the junction with St Dunstan's Hill and were standing opposite a church. 'In there. We'll not be disturbed.'

The heavy oak door of St Dunstan's-in-the-East was not locked, and the two of them went in and sat on one of the pews. The smell of damp diffused with that of polish reminded Tom of the church in Bamburgh on the Northumberland coast to which his parents had taken him each Sunday, all those years ago. St Aidan's was not so different to this place – exuding the same sense of peace and tranquillity that he remembered so well and which had been largely absent from his life since he'd left home.

He stared up at the high altar draped in heavy damask and wondered if he would ever again experience that peace. The crushing weight of Peggy's demise had defined his waking hours and seldom did an hour go by when he did not blame himself for what had happened. For a while, his drinking had dulled the pain, but he'd known it couldn't continue. It was affecting his ability to think and act as he had once done. Perhaps more to the point, it was threatening his future within the river police, an organisation he had grudgingly come to admire since its formation in the summer of '98.

'What did you want to tell me?' he said, forcing his mind back to the present.

'Like I told you, Master Pascoe, I've been hearing some of the lads talking. Seems there's a large cargo of silk bales what's just arrived aboard a brig. Some of the boys is showing an unhealthy interest in it.'

'Where did you hear this?'

'I overheard some scallywags as I ain't seen before, Master Pascoe. They was in the Harp, not a day since.'

'Did they say when this was going to happen?' said Tom, his mind less than wholly attendant on what the man was saying.

'Not as I heard.'

'And the brig? What's her name? Where's she lying?'

'Don't know more than that, your honour. There was a lot of noise and I couldn't rightly hear everything. Is it any good for you, your honour?'

'Thankee, Joseph.' Tom tried to sound enthusiastic. He fished a couple of pennies out of his coat pocket and tipped them into the man's outstretched hand. 'I'll have a nose round and see what I can find out. Let me know if you hear anything else.'

Tom waited for his informant to leave, his gaze travelling round the empty church, its medieval walls hung with exquisite wood carvings. The information he'd been given was of the sort that swilled round the waterfront on a daily basis; the idle chatter of those with too much time on their hands – or a score to settle. He doubted if it was worth the effort required to pursue it. The arrival of a consignment of silk through the Port of London was hardly an unusual event and even if it had been, where was he supposed to start looking for it?

He got up and walked out into the autumn sunshine. Joseph Gunn was shambling down St Dunstan's Hill towards the river. Perhaps he owed it to him to make some sort of an effort. The thought quickly passed, replaced by another as the desire for a drink forced its way to the forefront of his consciousness.

# CHAPTER 3

'That snout of yours, sir. D'you believe him?' Sam Hart stood at the first-floor window of the police office in Wapping, watching a couple arguing in the street below. He turned back into the room and crossed to a chair where he sat down opposite Tom, his left arm held stiffly across his chest as though he were in pain.

'Who? Joseph Gunn?' said Tom. He caught sight of Sam's laboured movements. He knew the reason. The bullet had, after all, been meant for him, rather than Sam. His mind flashed back to the moment it had happened. He could see the Frenchman approaching them, his pistol cocked and ready to shoot. He'd barely had time to register the scene before the gun had seemed to explode, a tongue of fire spitting from its muzzle. No more than a heartbeat later he'd felt the quiver of air and heard the low hiss of the bullet as it shaved past his head. When the smoke had cleared, he'd seen Sam lying in the road, clutching at his chest. In that moment of blind anger and fear for his friend's life, his own pistol had spat out its message of retaliation, killing the Frenchman outright.

Tom had known he should not have done it. André Dubois had already thrown down his pistol, and the knife that had replaced it. His arms had been raised in surrender. He had often wondered, in the weeks that followed, if his actions on that day could have been attributed to his drinking. The subsequent coroner's inquest had, much to his relief, issued a verdict of lawful killing and made no mention of the state of his mind at the critical moment. It had, nevertheless, been a sharp reminder of his own limitations, his view of humanity seen through the narrow prism of experience, his words, thoughts and actions defined by the harsh and unforgiving reality of naval life where failure meant instant retribution. He knew he had to change, to put behind him the mind of the warrior, the attitudes forged in the heat of battle. It would not be easy. His shortness of temper would surely see to that.

After the shooting he'd taken Sam Hart to the accident hospital in the Whitechapel road and waited anxiously for news of his condition. 'The hurt is not, of itself, serious,' the physician on duty in the Receiving Room had eventually told him. 'The bullet struck a small but thick book of some kind that your friend was wearing in a pouch around his neck. I say it's not serious but we'll have to wait and see if the shock of the impact gives rise to the fever. If it does, then we must pray that he is strong enough to survive it.'

The fever had come that night, reaching its crisis in the small hours of the following morning before leaving Sam, weak and exhausted, as the sun rose on a new day.

Several days were to pass before Sam was fit enough to be released and be given his certificate of discharge by the hospital authorities. It was a further week before Tom was to discover the nature of the book which had been instrumental in saving his friend's life.

'It's the *siddur*,' Sam had explained as he'd tucked the battered volume of Jewish prayers into a new pouch around his neck. And that had been that. He had said no more by way of explanation and Tom had not thought to pursue the matter. Within days, Sam had insisted on returning to the police office, regardless of his inability to pull an oar, still less involve himself in the violent surroundings of the port.

'Sir?'

Tom looked up blankly.

'Sorry, Sam, I was thinking of something else. Do I believe my informant?' Tom hesitated, conscious that he'd done little to check Joseph Gunn's story. 'It's not a question of believing him or not. It's a question of whether we can do anything about it even if I did believe him. We can't search every ship in the port. Not without a lot of help. At the moment the information is just too vague.'

'What about Lloyd's, sir?'

'Yes, I've been there and had a look at the Register Book. It didn't help.'

'So what now?'

Tom expelled a lungful of air and looked up at the ceiling. He wasn't sure he knew the answer. He found his thoughts straying to the half-empty bottle of gin under the bed in his room. It had lain there, untouched, for several weeks. But . . . With an effort, he pushed the image from his mind.

'Put the word round with your snouts,' he managed at last. 'Get John Kemp and Jim Higgins to do the same with theirs. See what you can dig up. If there's anything to the story, somebody will know . . . What's the matter?'

'I completely forgot to tell you, there's a young lad what's asking to see you. Says you'd know what it were about. He's in the entrance hall.'

'Grief, Sam, how long's he been waiting?' said Tom, leaping to his feet and heading for the door. 'I warrant that's my young half-brother.'

Tom saw him from the top of the stairs, an untidy mop of fair hair above a face that so closely resembled his mother as to bring a lump to Tom's throat. The boy was standing by the front door of the police office, staring wide-eyed at the coming and going of people attending before the magistrate. His clothing was freshly washed, Tom noticed, though ragged and patched.

'William?' Tom ran down the stairs and held out his hand. 'I'm Tom. Have you eaten? No? Come, we'll dine at the Ramsgate. We can talk there.'

Scooping up the boy's meagre belongings, Tom led the way out through the main door, along the passageway and down into Wapping Street. Within minutes they were turning in through the door of the Town of Ramsgate tavern and climbing the stairs to the first floor where a long, deal table was already occupied by a rowdy group of seamen. Finding a space at the far end, Tom sat his brother down and slid in next to him.

'First things first, a pot of small beer for you, William. Nothing for me, I regret,' said Tom, looking longingly at the barrels lined up behind the bar, their polished brass hoops seeming to tease him. He summoned the pot-boy and delivered his order. Then he turned back to his brother. 'Tell me all about yourself, and your ma, of course. How is she?'

It was a while before the young William relaxed sufficiently to talk about himself and the family that Tom hadn't seen since he himself was a boy. But gradually the shyness slipped away, aided no doubt by a large bowl of jellied eel and thick slices of white bread and butter, not to mention the small beer.

Tom stared at the surface of the table listening to the boy's chatter and trying to make sense of the passing of the years, of the choices that had kept him away from home. He'd been about twelve when he'd felt the call of the sea and left to join a collier tramping between Newcastle and London. After that had come his years before the mast on one of His Majesty's sloops of war, gradually climbing through the ranks to be rewarded with the single epaulette of a master and commander. In the hurly-burly of his life there had never seemed to be enough time to make the journey north to the tiny coastal hamlet of Seahouses, lying in the shadow of Bamburgh Castle; not the time to see his father before he died, or to comfort his mother in her grief and loneliness. They were decisions that had, in the intervening years, often haunted him. Yet he had still not gone.

He looked down at the tousled head now drooping close to the table top, the eyes barely open. The reality of his new responsibility was only now beginning to dawn on him.

'It's time you slept, young fellow,' he said, picking the boy up and carrying him out into the street. 'Tomorrow we have to decide what you're to do.'

'Who's the nipper, Master Pascoe?' Tom looked up. A man was shuffling towards him, his head tipped back as though looking into the night sky. In his hand he carried a stick with which he was tapping the road ahead of him.

'Hello, Jack. Your ears will be the death of you one day. Don't miss a thing, do you?'

'Not me, Master Pascoe. Not old Blind Jack. He don't miss nothing, and that's the truth.' The man chortled, the sound mocking and unpleasant. 'I could tell 'ee a thing or two as what would make your innards tremble. But that's for another time. Who's the young'un, Master Pascoe? That's what old Jack wants to know.'

'Since you ask, Jack, he's my brother. He's come down to stay with me for a while.'

'Then best you take good care of him,' said the blind man, lowering his voice. 'There ain't no telling what some folk might do with a nipper like him, once they know who he is, like.'

'They won't know unless you tell them, Jack. So best you keep it to yourself.'

'Anything you say, Master Pascoe,' said the man, seeming to fix Tom with one white, sightless eye. 'But you mark my words, is all.'

Tom watched him go, disappearing amongst the shadows as surely as if he'd never existed, the tap-tap-tapping of his stick fading into the night, his footsteps as steady and as sure as that of a sighted man.

'How did that man know I was with you, Tom?' asked the sleepy voice of his brother. 'Weren't he blind?'

'Aye, he's blind right enough,' said Tom. 'Been that way for years. But he can hear things beyond the limits of ordinary men. He would have heard you even though you weren't speaking and would have known you were a youngster.'

'He frightened me. I don't think I liked him.'

'Pay him no heed.' Tom tried to sound convincing. 'There's no harm in Blind Jack.'

They walked on over the bridge at Hermitage Dock, past the Goodwyn brewhouse and on towards Burr Street. They were almost there before William spoke again.

'What did that man mean when he said there was no telling what people might do to me?'

'I don't think he knew himself, William. It was just talk. No more than that.' Tom wished he could believe his own assurances. The waterfront was an often violent place, particularly towards the weak and vulnerable and those who didn't understand its ways. 'We'll be home in a jiffy and you can get some sleep. We'll talk again in the morning.'

They walked on, Tom still thinking about their meeting with Blind Jack. He wanted to believe it had been a chance meeting but he doubted if that were true. Little happened in this part of London but that Blind Jack got to hear about it, sooner or later. All knowledge was a form of currency in his world, there to be made use of, to barter with and exploit to his advantage.

Tom felt an anxious twinge in his stomach. He couldn't always be at his brother's side.

# CHAPTER 4

A thick mist had settled over the river by the time Cox and his minders came in sight of the Royal Oak tavern on Bridge Yard, on the south bank of the Thames. The old timber building hung precariously over the edge of the embankment, supported by a number of heavy stakes that had been sunk into the grey mud. A flight of wooden steps led up from the river and joined a passageway close to the side of the building. It was towards this point that the boat now headed.

Drawing closer, Cox caught sight of a skiff moored beneath the overhanging building and, at first glance, out of reach to anyone wishing to make use of it. Passing close to the vessel, he looked at the underside of the tavern floor and saw a kind of trapdoor through which a man might pass on his way to or from the boat.

'Catch hold of the pole and make her fast, damn ye,' said Marr, giving Cox a hard shove in the back. The skiff had turned up into the tide and was slowing. Ahead of them a mooring pole loomed out of the darkness. Cox waited a moment and then, leaning forward, attempted to pass the line round the pole and back into the vessel. It should have been second nature to him, something he did almost every day of his life. But not today. He had leaned forward too early and too far. He scrambled to save himself, narrowly avoiding a ducking. He tried again, and again he fumbled his opportunity, his mind on his impending meeting with Creech. He knew what to expect, had long known of the scrub's reputation for unpredictability and savage ill humour. He remembered the frightening speed with which Creech's supposed camaraderie had evaporated the last time they'd met. He'd known, even before that, of the raw anger of which the villain was capable.

'What's your bleeding problem, Coxy?' rasped Marr, pushing him aside and taking the line. Passing it round the pole he looped it into a hitch on the short wooden stump in the bows of the skiff.

'She's fast,' he said, looking contemptuously at Cox. 'Now get out.'

The three men stepped ashore and climbed the slime-covered stairs to the alley. About halfway along Marr stopped and knocked on a door to the side of the tavern. It was opened by an elderly woman who led them along a corridor smelling of decaying wood and stale tobacco. At the far end she stopped and pointed to a second door, through which they now passed, entering a small room with a window overlooking the river. On a table in the centre of the room was a single candle whose faint yellow glow provided the only light. Two chairs, set against the wall, made up the remaining furniture.

'All right, Coxy?' Creech's voice reached out from a corner of the room furthest from the light. Cox spun round and watched the sailmaker climb to his feet and amble towards him. It was difficult to see his face or to read the tone of his voice. Cox doubted his welcome would be friendly. 'I were worried about you. I ain't heard from you the best part of a week. I were beginning to think you didn't want to talk to your old mate about what we was discussing.'

'I've been down to Sheerness, Creech.' Cox fiddled nervously with the rim of his hat. 'Ain't had no chance to talk to you, see?'

'You got the job yet?'

'No. Not yet. I'll see my guv'nor tomorrow.'

'You having a laugh?' Creech leaned forward, his face less than an inch from Cox's, his breath smelling of stale beer. 'You'll be telling me next you still ain't been told where the ship is.'

'Honest, Creech. Nobody knows. Not the guv'nor, nor me, nor nobody. Won't know until we get word from the revenue. It's on account of them thinking someone might plunder what's in the hold. All I know is what some cullies told me. They said there was this brig what had this silk on board.'

Cox felt a stinging sensation to his left cheek and realised that he'd been slapped. He hadn't seen it coming. He raised a hand to his face. It was beginning to throb and his eyes were watering. He knew not to look up, still less to say or do anything that might further antagonise Creech. Behind him, Marr and Gott had stepped closer, their fists clenched as though scarcely able to contain themselves. He closed his eyes, afraid to look. Hot, stale breath touched his mouth. Creech was speaking, his voice hardly above a whisper.

'I'm warning you, Coxy. You ain't here tomorrow morning telling me you got the job, then best you keep running 'cos I'm going to be looking for you. You got me? Now piss off afore I change me mind.'

Cox stumbled out of the tavern. He had to get the job. There was no alternative. Somehow he had to convince his employer to give it to him. But his employer owned other barges and employed other sailing masters, any one of whom could be dispatched.

What had begun as no more than an idea, a way out of his financial woes, had spiralled out of his control. Cox felt the blood drain from his face as he considered the probable outcome should he fail to win the job. He stopped and leaned against the wall of the tavern, a frightened man.

The next morning, Cox shivered in the cold, autumnal air as he walked back from his employer's house on Cinnamon Street, Shadwell. A white hoar frost covered the ground and the withered branches of the few trees that he passed along the way. He glanced at the bundle of papers his employer had given him. They were his authority to take possession of twenty-one bales of raw Valencia silk, the property of Master Miles Butler, a merchant of Union Street, Spitalfields, and a trunk of ostrich feathers belonging to a certain Master Abraham Cohen, a merchant residing at Bread Street, Cheapside. Both items were, according to the documents, presently in the possession of Captain Forsythe, master of the brig *Velocity*, now lying at anchor in Stangate Creek, off the River Medway.

Cox was not sure if he was relieved or not. The job offered a way out of his money problems and the chance to begin again. There could even be a little left over to ease the family through the rest of the winter. But there was another part of him which regarded the whole enterprise with deep foreboding. His life was at risk whichever way he turned. If he went through with it and was caught, he'd almost certainly hang. But if he pulled out now he faced the certain prospect of a knife in the throat from Creech or one of his bully boys.

It started to snow, small wet flakes driven before a wind that came bowling out of the north-east, soaking through his thread-bare jerkin to the skin beneath. He blew into his cupped hands and pushed them under his armpits. It made little difference, the wind nipping at the tips of his ears and the end of his nose as he crossed the Thames and descended the slope from Tooley Street to the Royal Oak on Bridge Yard.

'I got the job, Creech,' he said as soon as he'd caught the sailmaker on his own. 'Been told to pick up the stuff three days from now.'

'Come out the back.' Cox felt an iron grip take his hold of his arm and propel him through to the same room they'd occupied the previous evening. 'Show me them papers.'

'It's the order in council from the commissioners, Creech, that's all.'

'Show me.'

Cox dropped the packet onto the table and stood back as Creech scanned the documents that would allow the master of the sailing hoy, *Sisters*, to take possession of the silk and ostrich feathers and deliver them to the King's Beam on the Custom House Quay, hard by London Bridge.

'It says here that all the bales of silk is marked MH and some numbers. What's that all about?' said Creech, a suspicious frown on his face.

'Them's the initials of the agent, Mr Michael Horton. On account of it makes sure he gets the right goods,' said Cox, and then, under his breath, 'If he's lucky.'

'And the numbers?'

'The first one shows the number of bales in the consignment. The second is the running total. So the figure 21 followed by the figure 3 means there is twenty-one bales in the consignment and this is the third bale.'

'Where's the ship lying?' said Creech, after a short pause.

'Stangate Creek, off the Medway.'

'Tell me exactly what happens when you get there.'

'I goes alongside and I gives the captain the order in council what he keeps. The silk and the other stuff gets brought up and put into the *Sisters*—'

'Anybody watching what's going on?'

'Well, there's the gangmaster what's in charge of the lumpers.'

'Anyone else?'

'Aye, there'll be two officers from the revenue. They check all the bales and give me the bill of lading what shows what's been given to me. Then there's two more tide waiters what come with me to the Beam.'

'So you're watched all the time?'

'Aye.'

'How many crew on board?'

'Don't rightly know, Creech. Twenty-five maybe. Could be less if they got caught by the press gang. You ain't thinking of going aboard and nicking the stuff, are you?'

'Might've been,' said Creech, stroking his chin with the back of his hand. 'Cut you out, that way.'

'You can't do that, Creech,' said Cox, his voice rising. 'It were me what told you about the job.'

'I can do as I please, Coxy.' A cold smile crossed Creech's face. 'You go down to the ship on Friday like what you're supposed to. Me and the boys will follow you.'

Cox nodded, his face paling. 'What you got planned?'

'Never you mind. I've got some thinking to do. I'll tell you what I want you to do before you go.'

Daniel Creech stood at the bottom of Spring Street, Shadwell, and looked at the grim procession of dilapidated dwellings stretching north along either side of the road, away from the Thames. If he noticed the thick coating of soot that covered the buildings or the stench of discarded offal rising like a miasma in the afternoon light, or the barefooted children playing amongst this detritus of daily life, he gave no hint of it. His own home was at number thirty-four where he shared a first-floor room with his wife and six other people.

'Who knows about this?' he said, his arms folded, his face twisted into an angry scowl as he leaned against the wall of one of the houses. He would have preferred to conduct this conversation in the comparative warmth of his room, but that was impossible. What he had to say was not for general consumption and it was more trouble than it was worth tossing the others out onto the street.

'There's a few,' said a subdued Marr, an abandoned cart between him and his inquisitor. It was seldom an enjoyable experience bringing bad news to Creech. 'Blind Jack maybe.'

'Blind Jack? How did that villain find out?'

Creech had always known the story about the silk would do the rounds. He just hadn't anticipated it would be so widely talked about before he could take advantage of the situation. If he wasn't quick, things could become messy. And he wanted to avoid that. He ran through the names of the half-dozen or so men who might be expected to try their luck with *Velocity*'s cargo.

None of them would stand aside without a fight. He felt the skin over his knuckles tighten as he clenched his fists.

'Don't know how he knew, Creech,' said Marr. 'He said it were a pity no one had thought to go and get it. Then he tapped his nose, like he knew we was planning something.'

'I'll stop that villain's mouth up for good if he ain't careful. You tell him if I hears another word out of him, it'll be his last. D'you hear?'

'I'll have a chat with him,' said Marr. 'Blind Jack won't talk no more.'

'Good. Where are the others?'

'They're waiting round the corner,' said Marr. 'You said you'd call them when you wanted them.'

'Aye, so I did. Go and get them. I don't want to stand here in the bleedin' cold any longer than I have to.'

Creech watched as, a minute later, three men rounded the corner and approached him, their faces pitted with coal dust, their ragged clothing stained by sweat, their distrustful eyes probing the open doorways of the houses they passed.

'You wanted to see us?' said the first of the newcomers.

'Aye. Got a job for you. Make rich men of you,' said Creech, tapping the top of the cart with his index finger. 'You in?'

'We're in, Creech.' There was a general nodding of heads.

'Right then, this is what we got . . .' Creech quickly outlined the bare essentials, withholding both the name of the vessel carrying the silk and its present location. There was no point in telling them more than was absolutely necessary. 'The goods will be put onto a hoy what is supposed to take it to the Custom House Quay. But she won't make it that far on account she's going to stop for us. It's all arranged. When she stops, we go aboard and that's the last time they see their precious cargo.'

'You ain't planning on doing this in daylight, is you, Creechy?' said the newcomer who'd previously spoken.

'When d'you bleedin' think we was going to do it? Of course it's going to be daylight,' said Creech.

'I don't think so,' said the same man. 'You want to get us all hanged? And what about the revenue what'll be aboard? We going to fight them, too?'

'What's the matter, Haynes? Lost your balls, have you? Who said anything about a fight? No, my son, we won't be fighting no one. It's all taken care of. We put the revenue and the crew below deck and keep them there. After that the cargo gets put into a skiff and rowed ashore. That's where you come in, Smiley. I want you and your boys ready with some carts. As soon as you get the stuff, you take it to the place what I'll tell you about. You'll be expected.'

'When's all this happening?'

'Three days from now. The hoy what's picking up the goods will leave the Galley Quay Road at six o'clock on Friday morning. I want you all at the east end of the quay an hour before that. You all got that?'

# CHAPTER 5

Sam Hart felt a spasm of pain in his chest, where the bullet had struck. He steadied himself against the wall of the police office and waited for it to pass. As far as he was concerned, the only good thing about his injury was that the man who'd inflicted it was dead.

'Serves the bastard right,' he muttered.

He levered himself upright and walked gingerly down the steps and into Wapping Street where he turned towards the distant synagogue at Duke's Place. He didn't often go there. Had hardly done so since the death of his mother and father some years ago. In his childhood they had dragged him along to the local synagogue in Poland where the family had lived until he was about fourteen. Yet, of late, he had begun to think about the ancient beliefs of his forebears and what they meant to him. He raised a hand to the pouch containing the *siddur*, and offered up a silent prayer of thanks for his life.

It was strange how things turned out. Had he not begun to think about his faith, he would not have been carrying the *siddur*, and if he had not been carrying it . . . He shook his head and walked on. It was the first day of the feast of Sukkot and he needed to hurry. There was a man he wanted to see there, someone whose conversation he'd overheard. It had meant nothing to him at the time. But in the last hour or so it had assumed a significance that he could not have imagined.

Less than an hour later, he crossed Duke's Place to the synagogue occupying the bottom left-hand corner of the square. Mounting the front steps, he passed through the wrought-iron gates guarding the main entrance.

'*Shalom*,' said an attendant, offering him a white tasselled shawl and a *kippah*, the small black skullcap he was expected to wear. Putting on the cap, he draped the shawl over his shoulders and walked into the building's cavernous interior. He found a seat near the back and sat down. A few yards away, a young man stood on a raised platform, reading aloud from the Torah, a short stick in his hand seeming to dance along the lines of the text. Sam tried to concentrate, but struggled with the Hebrew. He'd forgotten most of it and could now only understand a word here and there.

He gave up and let his eyes sweep along the rows of prayer shawls and skullcaps occupying the seats in front of him, searching for the man he'd assumed would be here. It felt an impossible task. He'd only ever seen him once or twice before and wasn't even certain he worshipped here. He was beginning to regret coming. The injury to his chest had started to ache.

A white-haired elderly man in a long kaftan shuffled up the central aisle towards him. Suddenly he stopped, and Sam had the sensation of being stared at. He turned and looked at the gaunt face and deep-set eyes that seemed to bore right through him.

'Is there something I can do for you, sir?' asked Sam.

'You do not recognise me, Master Sam?'

Sam looked at the man for a moment, recognition slowly

dawning. 'Why, Master Isaac, to be sure I did not recognise you.' He glanced at the raised platform. The young reader had turned and was looking at them. Sam raised a hand in apology and eased himself out into the aisle, beckoning the old man to follow.

An unusually cold north wind was blowing as he emerged into weak sunlight and descended the steps to the square. He stopped and waited for the old man to catch up. Isaac Weil was a tall, bearded man who walked with a pronounced stoop as though embarrassed by his height and anxious to present a smaller pro-file. Sam had not seen him in many years but remembered him as one of his father's friends who would occasionally visit the family. A *schnorrer* by occupation who had honed his begging skills to an art form, the old man was more usually to be found plying his trade outside the ghetto theatre in Goodman's Fields or doing the rounds of his clients as a synagogue knocker. Sam had once heard him defending this lucrative role as necessary if the pious were to be roused from their beds in time for the morn-ing services.

'What brings you to this part of London?' said Sam. 'As I remem-ber, you always worked further north.'

'Aye, so I did, Master Sam. But now I mostly go between South-wark and Sheerness. There are many of us Jews down there. It's safer amongst our own people. But you? You've grown into a man since I last saw you.' He paused and looked quizzically at Sam. 'I've not seen you here before. I thought perhaps you had left the faith – no?'

'I don't often come,' said Sam, embarrassed by his admission. 'I wanted to speak to a man who worships here. That's all.'

'What, pray, is his name?'

'I know him only as Jacob.'

'Jacob?' Isaac thought for a moment, a frown of concentration on his brow. Suddenly, his face cleared. 'Can you mean Jacob Emden? He does not worship here, Master Sam. He is a Sephardi. You would do better going to Bevis Marks. I sometimes see him there. What did you want him for?'

'Nothing important,' said Sam, suddenly wary. There was little to suggest Jacob Emden's involvement in any wrongdoing but that didn't matter. The merest hint that Sam might want to question him would be enough to stop the old man talking to him.

Sam bid the old man goodbye and left Duke's Place, armed with the information that the Jacob he sought had a shop somewhere along the north side of the Aldgate. Beyond that, and the fact that he was a dealer in old clothes, his informant had been of little use. Almost every shop in the street – and there were many – dealt in old clothes, the ragged stock hanging on nails on either side of the entrances or suspended on butchers' hooks above shuttered openings, their owners standing at their doorways, anxious that no potential customer should be lost for want of attention.

Sam walked slowly along the broad thoroughfare, buffeted by a shuffling throng of tangle-bearded men dressed in black, ankle-length gabardines and broad-brimmed hats that reminded him of the Berlin ghetto of his youth. Others begged at the roadside, holding out their hands for such alms as might be given to them, their faces bearing the woebegone expression that was the hallmark of their occupation.

Sam sympathised with their plight as he did with the pedlars who, if it were possible, were even more numerous than the beggars. He'd never been able to ignore those who earned their living in this way, prolific and rudely persistent though they were. They reminded him of his own father and the daily abuse that he'd been forced to endure at the hands of an uncaring world. The experience had left a mark on the young Sam which he'd never forgotten. He sometimes wondered if it had, perhaps subconsciously, led him to cut himself off from the rabbinic faith and those who practised it.

He peered in through the open doors of the shops, searching for a face he had seen only briefly. If he was lucky, Jacob Emden would be able to tell him more about the rumours relating to a quantity of silk expected to arrive on the market in the days ahead. The chance was a slim one. The little he'd overheard of the conversation had hardly been enough to persuade him that his search for information was nearing its end.

The number of shops began to dwindle and finally petered out. Sam stopped and looked back the way he had come, as certain as he could be that he'd checked every premises he'd passed. The shop had to be on the other side of the street. He crossed over and began to walk back towards the city.

He hesitated as the sight of a man standing at the entrance of what appeared to be a private dwelling, his black kaftan bulging over an expansive stomach, a pair of dark brooding eyes set on either side of a large Coptic nose.

'Master Emden?' he asked.

'Yes, I am he,' said the man, staring at him intently. 'Who is it that is asking?'

'My name, sir, is Samuel Hart,' said Sam. His memory was of

someone less rotund. He put the thought behind him. 'I've seen you from time to time at the synagogue in Duke's Place.'

'Now I remember,' said Emden, one hand scratching at the tufts of black hair sprouting from an olive-like face. 'What brings you here?'

'As it happens, I was looking for you. I'm with the marine police.'

'Ahey, I'd heard there was a Jew at the police office in Wapping. Is it permitted to ask why you wished to see me?'

'Is there somewhere we can talk?'

'Please.' Emden swept an arm in the direction of his front door and stood back for Sam to precede him.

'I was told you was a dealer,' said Sam, nodding at the near-empty room into which they had stepped. He hadn't known what to expect. Perhaps a little more evidence of his trade. But there was nothing except a rude shelter made of rough pieces of timber with a roof of pine branches that seemed to have been thrown together in a hurry. It looked oddly out of place.

A long-forgotten memory sidled into his brain, a picture of a similar shelter his own parents had made in their room at about this time of the year. They had told him it was a *sukkah*, used for the seven days of the feast commemorating the Jews' flight from Egypt.

'Yes, I'm a dealer. But not as you imagine. It's many years since I was compelled to buy and sell rags.' Emden paused and met Sam's gaze. 'But what is it you wanted to speak to me about?'

'I hear a shipment of silk is expected to become available in the next week or two. I'm hoping you might be able to tell me more about it.'

'Shipments of silk arrive almost daily from India, from China and from elsewhere. You will have to be more specific, Master Sam.'

Sam strolled to the back of the room and gazed down at the *sukkah*. 'You were overheard talking in the synagogue about a quantity of silk which might become available at a special price. Do you recall that conversation?'

'I am a busy man, Master Sam. I talk to people all the time about matters of business. They approach me and sometimes we do business, sometimes we do not. I regret it extremely but I cannot remember the occasion you refer to.' Emden sounded suddenly impatient, anxious to be rid of his visitor.

'We know of a plot to steal a large quantity of silk from a ship recently arrived in this country,' said Sam, carefully. He was acutely conscious of the social order which separated the two of them. Emden belonged to the Sephardic tradition of the Judaic faith and would, unquestionably, consider himself superior to the Ashkenazi roots to which Sam belonged. He would need to tread with care if he hoped to get anywhere with his inquiry. He pressed on. 'We also know that once the silk is stolen, it will be necessary to find a buyer. You were heard talking about it. Please think carefully. What do you know of the matter?'

'Stands it not written in the Talmud,' said Emden, spreading his arms wide, 'that he who shames another, spills his blood?'

'I have not shed your blood, Master Emden,' said Sam. 'I have asked you a question. No more.'

There was a long pause as Emden seemed to wrestle with his thoughts. Finally, he said, 'You are not a true son of Israel, but I will tell you what I know. I was approached by a man I did not know. He told me he was a Sephardi, like myself, and knew of a quantity of silk that was expected to become available. He asked me if I was interested.'

'And were you?'

'Does a Jew turn his face from a profit?'

'You would do business with a man you did not know?'

'What? I should not trade with men I do not know? How should I make a profit if I do not trade?'

'Did he tell you how much silk was on offer?'

'About two thousand pounds in weight.'

'Did he show you a sample?'

'No, he told me the goods are not yet available.'

'What is the name of this man?'

'You ask me this?' said Emden, a stony look on his face.

'When he returns with a sample, will you tell me?' asked Sam, suspecting he already knew the answer.

'Ahey, ahey, what are you asking? Do I look like a *moser*?'

'Tread carefully, Master Emden.' Sam wagged his finger. 'You would not enjoy life in Newgate. When do you expect to see this man again?'

'Soon,' said a reluctant Emden.

'This week?'

'Perhaps.'

Sam heard a rustle behind him. A door had opened and a female face appeared.

'Father?' She was hardly more than a child, perhaps eighteen or nineteen, her raven-black hair tied back with a single white ribbon, her dark oval face smooth as silk. 'Mamma says your dinner is ready.'

'Thank you, Adina. I shall be there directly.' Emden hesitated and looked from his daughter to Sam and back again. 'Adina, this is Master Samuel Hart. Master Hart, this is my daughter Adina.'

'Your servant, miss.' Sam bowed, not daring to meet the girl's eyes, blood rushing up through his face. He turned back to face the girl's father, aware of feelings coursing through him that he'd not experienced in a long time. He thought of Hannah, the girl he'd planned to marry. She had been dead for over eighteen months, but it made no difference. The pain of her loss was still there. For a long time he'd thought his life at an end, the whole purpose of his existence devoid of meaning. And although the bitterness of those early days had now largely disappeared, he still didn't feel ready to let go of her memory, still less to feel the attraction of another woman. It didn't seem right, somehow. But it had happened.

He heard the door close softly behind him. His anguish seemed a punishment for the hope that had suddenly bloomed. For the hope had no future, no prospect of fulfilment. Adina was a Sephardi, as far removed from him as it was possible to be. Her father would never agree to their friendship. Sam pushed the longing to the back of his mind and tried to remember where he'd got to in his questioning of the girl's father.

'Did your visitor tell you where this silk had come from?' he asked, his heart still pounding.

'No, he did not. Master Hart . . .'

Sam looked up and met the other man's gaze. 'Yes?'

'You don't know what you are meddling with. My new acquaintance warned me about the men concerned. He said they are dangerous scoundrels who it would be unwise to cross.'

'Who are we talking about? Do you have their names?'

'He would not tell me, sir, and I did not ask.'

Tom gazed round the dingy surroundings of the Chapter Coffee House on Paternoster Row, a dish of steaming hot coffee cradled in his hands. The place was packed with merchants, bankers and those seeking to escape the bitter autumnal cold for an hour or two. He glanced out of the nearest window. A swirling grey-white fog had descended on the capital and looked set to remain for the rest of the day. He leaned back in his chair and looked across the table at Sam.

'He wouldn't tell you the name of his contact?'

'No. It's contrary to rabbinic law to act as an informer. The penalties are severe.'

'Yes, you've mentioned that before,' said Tom, yawning. He'd not slept well the previous night. Young William had developed a slight fever which had kept them both awake. He'd left the boy with the promise that he would see him later in the day. Beyond that he'd given little thought to the lad and his future. 'What d'you suppose he meant about you not knowing what you were meddling in?'

'It was strange. He clearly didn't want me to ask any further questions. It was as if he was frightened of something although I can't imagine what. Unless, of course, he's involved in some way or another.'

Tom looked pensively at his friend. If Sam's reading of the encounter was accurate, there might be more to this case than he'd originally suspected. Then again, the informant, Emden, might simply have been trying to put a stop to questions that he felt unqualified to answer. Either way, it was almost certain that others would hear of the larger than usual consignment of silk. It was always the same. Those involved would talk, partly because they needed to and partly because they couldn't resist the temptation. And as soon as they did, the news would spread, the circle of those who knew getting larger and larger. Eventually, someone within this swirling pool would be willing to talk to the police.

'What about Higgins and Kemp? Have they heard anything?' asked Tom, hoping the other two members of his crew had had more luck with their inquiries.

'Only the usual chatter, sir,' said Sam. 'They said they'd done the rounds of every villain they could lay their hands on. Apparently, they've promised, threatened and bribed them with the Lord knows what and still got nothing we didn't already know. What d'you want us to do now? We've not got much time.'

Tom gazed at the ceiling, the drone of conversation mingling with the chink of crockery and the occasional peal of laughter barely registering in his conscious mind. He thought of what Sam's informant had said about the men involved in this case: *You don't know what you are meddling with . . . They are dangerous scoundrels.*

There was nothing unusual in that. Most of the people he dealt with were, to a greater or lesser extent, dangerous, his daily life a series of ugly confrontations that too often ended in injury or death. He smiled in spite of himself, recalling his years of war. Compared to that, nothing counted. Yet the dangers that lurked in the shadows of the port could not be dismissed, their random nature and casual brutality a reminder of the fragility of life. Tom shook his head, his thoughts returning to the present.

'No, we haven't got much time,' he said. 'I want you and the other two to have another nose round the taverns, coffee houses, early breakfast stalls and anywhere else you can think of. If this job is as big as people think it is, there'll be a lot more talk than we've managed to turn up. I don't suppose anyone's going to be able to tell us the whole story, but that doesn't matter. We can put the bits together if enough people talk to us. While you're doing that I'll have a look round Spitalfields. It's about time I found out a bit about the silk trade.'

'What about William, sir? Didn't you say you'd promised to call in on him?'

'Yes, I'll see him on the way.'

# CHAPTER 6

William Pascoe rolled off the bed he shared with his older brother and ran across to the window. It was getting dark. Tom had promised he would look in during the morning when the two of them would go out for something to eat, but he hadn't come and now the day was nearly over. He felt his stomach rumble. He was hungry.

He opened the window and gazed out over rooftops of St Catherine's to the River Thames, where the ships' lights twinkled in the darkening shadows of early evening. He shivered and pulled the window closed. The thrill of seeing the Thames and the ships lying at their moorings more than made up for the sense of apprehension he'd experienced when the coach from Newcastle had deposited him in the middle of Fleet Street the previous evening. He remembered stepping down into the midst of what seemed to him a vast crowd, and being compelled to ask for directions to Wapping. Nobody had seemed to know where the place was until a jolly man had pointed him in the right direction. Yet it had still taken him until after nightfall before he'd found his way to the police office.

Turning away from the window, he picked up the knotted handkerchief his mother had given him when he'd left. Inside were some pennies she had given him for the journey down. 'It's for you, pet, in case you feel a little peckish on your way to the big city,' she had said, kissing his forehead as he'd got ready to climb into the southbound coach. He remembered catching sight of a glisten in her eyes and, young as he was, he'd felt the sharp prickle of his own tears as she had turned and walked quickly away.

He sat on the edge of the bed for a moment, wishing he was back in the only place he'd ever called home, in the little house set on a grassy knoll overlooking the fishing boats and the men working on their nets, the raging sea kept at bay by the encircling arm of the harbour wall.

He'd been down by the waterfront on the day his mother gave him the news he thought he'd never hear; that he was to go to London to be with his brother. In that single moment a feeling of exhilaration and fright, joy and sadness had swept over him, the prospect of what was to come amongst the smoke of the big city too much to take in.

He'd known about Tom, of course, a master and commander in the King's Navy who, with acts of derring-do, had fought for his country and been wounded in the process. William's face flushed with pride as he remembered the stories his mother had told him.

Now, as he sat on the edge of the only bed in the room, a sense of reality began to seep into his mind. He knew no one in London except Tom, and he didn't really know even him. The awareness of being alone in the world bore down on him like some heavy weight and he found himself wondering if the money in his hand was enough for the return journey to Seahouses.

Another rumble in his stomach reminded him he was hungry. The money might not be enough to get him home but it was surely enough for some bread and cheese and perhaps a dish of tea at the food stall he'd seen at the bottom of the street. He could be back in the room in less than ten minutes. Tom would never know. He found his boots under the bed, slipped them on and ran down into the street.

'Well if it ain't Master Pascoe.' William jumped at the sound of the voice close behind him at the food stall in St Catherine's Street. He looked round. Blind Jack was leering, if not quite at him, then in his general direction, the man's head tilted to one side, the white orb of his left eye appearing to stare at the sky, the other pointing off to his right. He shook the stick he was carrying, as though for additional emphasis. William wondered how he could possibly have known it was him. 'What's the young Master Pascoe doing all on his lonesome? Why, this ain't no place for a gentlemen like what you are, Master Pascoe, and that's the truth.'

William stepped back a couple of paces, his heart racing faster and harder than it had any right to do. Over the old man's shoulder he could see a few curious stares being turned in his direction. 'I . . . I's getting me victuals. How did . . . ?'

'How did old Blind Jack know it was you? Is that what you was asking?' A powerful hand reached out with lightning speed and gripped William by his shoulder. 'I told you afore, old Jack can hear things as you wouldn't believe. Why, I knows the sound of your tread like I knows me own. If you knew what's good for you, young feller, you'd not be out without your brother as is looking after you.'

With that the hand was withdrawn and Blind Jack turned to leave, his high-pitched, cackling laugh reaching down into William's soul and turning it as if to stone. For a moment or two he watched the old man shuffle along St Catherine's Street and listened to the sound of his stick beating a tattoo against the walls of the houses he passed. Then he looked round. The men he'd seen around the stall were still watching him, amused expressions on their faces.

A hot blush rose to William's cheeks. Dropping his breakfast of bread and cheese, he turned and ran.

Darkness had fallen by the time Tom got back to Burr Street. His trip to Spitalfields had been fruitless. By the time he'd got there, the merchants and silk weavers had already finished their business for the day and left for their homes – or their clubs. He'd been unable to find anyone with anything to say on the subject of the silk trade, let alone on the specifics of a shipment expected within the next few days.

It was then he suddenly remembered he'd promised to see his brother and take him out for some lunch. He strode in through the front door of the house and ran up the stairs to his room on the first floor, rehearsing his apology.

'William,' he called as he opened the door. There was a faint scuffling noise and he was in time to see the boy emerging from under the bed, a frightened look on his face. 'What on earth's the matter?'

'I saw the blind man.' William's voice was hesitant, his eyes looking beyond Tom to the door through which he'd come.

'Blind Jack? How? Was he here, in this room?'

William hesitated. Eventually, he said, 'No, he weren't here. I kind of saw him.'

'Where did you see him? Outside the house?'

'Sort of.' Another long silence. William stared at the floor, his hands hanging limply at his sides.

'Where were you, William, when you saw Blind Jack?' Tom could hear his voice rising, anger and fear punctuating his every word. 'Tell me the truth.'

'By the river.' William was whispering now, looking more frightened than ever.

'Good God, boy,' shouted Tom. 'What were you doing there? I thought I told you not to go out without me. Who else, apart from Blind Jack, saw you?'

William hesitated, remembering the other men by the stall. 'No one. I swear,' he stammered, tears beginning to fall down his cheeks.

'Tell me the truth, boy,' said Tom, still shouting. 'This is London. You're not in Seahouses any more. There are men here who wish your brother harm because of who and what he is. If they can't hurt me they'll come after you instead. D'you understand me?'

'You weren't here, Tom, and I were hungry,' William blurted. He wiped away a tear with the back of his hand and looked up at his brother. 'I didn't know where you were.'

'Did anyone follow you when you came back here?'

'Dunno. I don't think they did.'

'But you're not sure?'

Tom sank down onto his bed and covered his face with his hands, regretting his outburst. The fault was entirely his. He should have taken proper care of the boy. Then he wouldn't have needed to go out. He looked up. William's face was crumpled with tears. He got to his feet and put a hand on the boy's shoulder. William shrugged it off.

Tom turned away, smitten by the rebuff. He'd regretted his words as soon as they were out of his mouth. Could only watch the effect of them on the lad's tear-stained features. Yet he knew it wouldn't have been the first time a youngster of William's age had been set upon by the feral youths who roamed the streets of the waterfront or, worse, become the victim of those who sought revenge against the watermen constables who patrolled the river.

They had parted badly. Nothing Tom had said had succeeded in healing the boy's hurt. Now he stood on the pontoon at the bottom of the river stairs at Wapping and waited for his crew to settle into their rowing positions. Sam's injury meant he wouldn't be a great deal of use as an oarsman for at least another month, but he'd insisted on rejoining the crew and Tom had not had the heart to turn him away. He watched his friend shuffle into his warming straw-filled sack and tie it off around his waist. Behind him, the other two crew were doing the same.

Tom scanned the briefing sheet he'd been given by his late-turn counterpart a few minutes earlier. It contained the usual litany of offences reported to police in the previous twenty-four hours, a list of the West Indiamen recently arrived in the port, and some items of general interest that might lead to trouble in the coming hours.

One incident in particular caught his attention.

*About four o'clock this afternoon, in the Custom House Road, three men were seen acting suspiciously aboard the* Sisters *sailing hoy. When approached by police, two of the men absconded. The third was identified as Robert Cox of Erith. He stated he was the sailing master of the hoy. Cox,*

*who appeared frightened, further stated that the two men were friends*
*who had been assisting him. When asked for the men's particulars, Cox*
*refused to answer. A search of the hold showed it to be empty.*

On its own there was nothing unusual about the report. The
port was a rough place and people generally gave the police a
wide berth. The late-turn patrol who had dealt with the matter
had come to the conclusion that it was probably no more than a
dispute about whose turn it had been to go alongside one of the
legal quays. In any event the officers had taken no further action.
Tom put the matter to the back of his mind. If he had time he
might call on Cox and find out a bit more about what had happened. His story did not seem to ring true.

'All correct, your honour,' said Sam.

'Thankee kindly, Sam,' said Tom, stepping into the galley.
'You're looking pleased with yourself. You in love?'

Sam's cheeks reddened and he looked away as though confused.

Tom grinned, suddenly curious. He wondered who she was.

'Stand by to cast off,' he said.

A minute or so later the galley had slipped away from the pontoon and was heading upriver into the Upper Pool, its stern
lantern glimmering in the gloom as it swung to and fro to the
pull of the sweeps. There was still movement on the river – a few
skiffs, a late-running lighter or two – but mostly the men had finished their work for the day and would be doing their utmost to
forget the drudgery of their day. But the comparative quietness
didn't stop Tom looking for the unusual and the suspicious, his
eyes sweeping over the long lines of lighters and hoys moored
stem to stern in the various barge roads.

The fish market at Billingsgate on the north bank came and went. Next would be the Custom House followed by the solid edifice of London Bridge and the western limit of his responsibility. He would come about there and begin the tedious business of inspecting each of the West India ships whose captains had paid for the service. He thought again of his brother. He would have to do something about the boy; perhaps find him some work in a chandler's shop or as an apprentice with a master cooper or the like. Then he remembered that someone had mentioned a school on the south bank. Perhaps that was the answer. He'd give it some thought tomorrow or the day after – when he had more time.

'Over there, sir.' Kemp's West Country burr was hardly above a whisper. Tom's head swung round, his eyes staring in the direction that Kemp was pointing. 'See them cullies? Two of them.'

At first Tom could see nothing. Then a shadow moved on one of the sailing hoys, separated into two and moved again. He blew out the boat's lantern and altered course for the north shore, slipping through a gap in one of the barge roads. The two figures on the hoy would find it more difficult to see him with the buildings on the shore as a backdrop.

'Easy,' he whispered. The galley's forward motion slowed, its bow wave reduced to a trickle, the sound of the sweeps quietened. A barge lay in their way, obscuring his view. Tom swore quietly and manoeuvred round it. Now he could see the outline of the two men on the sailing hoy. Less than twenty yards separated them from the approaching galley. Tom watched them moving about the deck. They appeared to be searching for something – or someone.

'Way enough,' said Tom. Then, a moment later, 'Ship starboard oars.'

The galley was barely moving when it nudged alongside, its sudden arrival meeting with a loud gasp from one of the men on the barge, quickly followed by the sound of running feet. In an instant, Tom was on his feet and had vaulted up onto the hoy. Behind him Higgins and Kemp were following, racing across the swaying decks of the barges as only men familiar with them could do.

But they were too late. The shadowy figures had disappeared amongst the sacks and barrels that littered the legal quays on their way to one of the narrow lanes leading to Lower Thames Street.

'You want us to follow them, sir?' said Higgins, coming to a halt beside Tom.

'No, they'll be long gone by now. We'll have a look round. Make sure everything's all right on that hoy.'

'Your honour.' Tom heard Sam's voice calling from the police galley where he had remained.

'Yes, Sam, what is it?'

'Didn't you tell us about a hoy what's called the *Sisters*? You was going to see her master about something?'

'Yes, I was.'

'This is the one, your honour. It's the *Sisters*. Her name's on the side.'

'So it is,' said Tom, peering at the white-painted letters at the bow of the hoy. 'Those two scrubs were here for a reason. Be so good as to look at the hold, will you, Higgins? Kemp, I want you to check the crew's cabin and see what you can find.'

Five minutes later they were all back on the upper deck.

'Anything?' said Tom.

'She's empty, sir,' said Higgins. 'Ain't no sign of any damage to the hatch cover and when we got inside she were as clean as a whistle. I reckon she were unladed not more than a few hours since. Probably waiting for another load.'

'I wonder what they were after,' said Tom, running a hand over his head. 'Anything from you, Kemp?'

'Nothing, sir.'

'Odd there's no sign of the master or his mate. I'd have expected one or both of them to be on board. Could be out drinking, I suppose, but . . .'

He trailed off, remembering what the briefing note had said about the sailing master being frightened of something. The presence of the two men might have been a coincidence, but it seemed unlikely.

# CHAPTER 7

Creech paced up and down the back room of the Royal Oak, his fists clenched. He did not like being ignored. As far as he was concerned, anyone who ignored him had only himself to blame if he got hurt. He whirled round and faced Marr and Gott, both of whom were standing by the open door. 'Did Pascoe see you?'

'He didn't see nothing, Creech, and that's a fact. We legged it before he got too close.'

Creech shifted uneasily, clasping and unclasping his fists as though faced with an intractable problem. He was not easily frightened. He would not have reached his current position of influence within the port had it been otherwise. Yet this time it was different. This time Pascoe was involved. He bit his lower lip. The news was not what he'd wanted to hear. Ever since he'd first heard of the river surveyor and his reputation, he'd made a point of keeping out of his way. It was said of him that he was incorruptible, a man who, if he suspected you of any wrongdoing, would pursue you to the ends of the earth. Creech let the thought go. He had a more immediate problem on his hands.

'You're sure Coxy wasn't on the *Sisters*?' he growled.

'We had a squint down his cabin. It were empty. Didn't have time for the hold before Pascoe turned up, but it were battened down good and proper. It wouldn't make no sense for Coxy to get himself in there. Nor his mate neither.'

'You think he's done a runner?'

'Might have. He didn't look too happy when we saw him earlier and told him you wanted to see him again.'

'Where's he live? You been there?'

'Erith,' said Marr. 'He ain't there. If he was he'd have taken the *Sisters*.'

'He's right, Creech,' said Gott. 'He don't go nowhere without he takes the *Sisters*. We saw Blind Jack in the Highway. He said he'd heard Cox and his mate had gone over Southwark way for a draught or two. You want us to find him?'

'Yeah, I do,' said Creech. 'The scallywag needs to learn his manners.'

Robert Cox, sailing master of the *Sisters*, stood next to the boy at the northern end of the Bridge and scanned the Custom House Road for any sign of movement. It was difficult to see properly. The lights from the legal quays were not nearly bright enough for him to be sure. And the shadows were playing havoc with his mind. The longer he looked, the more difficult it became to separate the real from the imagined. He crept closer to the north bank of the river, stepping over the outstretched legs of those who'd chosen the Bridge for their night's rest.

Some hours had passed since he'd heard the scuff of feet and the muttered oaths of men approaching the *Sisters*. He'd barely managed to escape undetected before they'd boarded the hoy and begun to search for him. Cox shuddered. He'd known who they were without having to see them. He should have gone to see

Creech when he'd had the chance, but fear had got the better of him. And with good reason. He, like everyone else, had heard the stories about the fate of the men who'd crossed Creech in the past. Mostly, they had simply disappeared, their bodies turning up weeks later in the Fleet ditch or on the marshes, east of Limehouse. Nothing was ever said. There was no need. Only a fool could fail to understand the warning signs. Looking back it was easy to see that he, too, should have taken notice. He should never have agreed to help Creech with the silk. But he'd needed money and the sailmaker was in a position to give it to him. More than that, the villain had given him no choice in the matter.

Escaping from the *Sisters*, he'd made it onto London Bridge from where he'd watched Gott and Marr searching for him. A few moments later, he'd noticed the dark shape of an approaching galley, its sweeps entering the water in perfect unison, the white ripple of its bow wave caught by the lights on the legal quays.

Cox's pulse quickened as he thought back to that moment when the police galley had fetched alongside the *Sisters* and he'd seen the officers go aboard. He wondered if their arrival had been a coincidence or whether they had suspected something. He cast his mind back to the afternoon, when Creech's men had first paid him a visit. That, too, had resulted in the arrival of a patrol galley. They *had* to know he was involved with Creech. But how? He had done nothing; had broken no law. And yet there was no denying the police had come to the *Sisters* twice in the same day. The thought raced around his brain, gathering force and momentum. He felt giddy, gripping the bridge parapet for support, searching for a way out of his impossible dilemma.

He would have to meet with Creech. Tell him what had happened. He would understand. There would be a beating, of course. He fully expected that. But he might just avoid the worst excesses of Creech's retribution were he to take himself down to the Royal Oak and seek the cully's forgiveness. It was better than waiting for the return of the bully boys.

'What you going to do, Coxy?' The boy's voice interrupted his thoughts. Cox had almost forgotten he was there. He didn't answer for a while. He'd not told the mate of the *Sisters* everything about the events of the last few days; had not thought it necessary. But matters had moved on and young Stevie Lyons had a right to know what he was becoming involved in, of the risk he was taking in staying on as a member of the crew.

'Got no choice, lad,' said Cox, hoping the visit to the Royal Oak would be quickly over. 'Got myself into a spot of bother. Best you stay away. No point in us both getting hurt. We'll talk again tomorrow.'

He turned to walk away. He could not delay his meeting with Creech any longer.

Tom sat at a table close to the door of Old George's coffee house in Church Street, Spitalfields. From here he was able to see everyone who entered or left the place. A word with the head waiter had ensured he'd be given a nod as soon as one of the silk brokers known to frequent the establishment made an appearance.

'Shouldn't have long to wait, sir,' the waiter had said. 'If it isn't a broker it'll be a master weaver. Why, bless me, sir, they use this place as though it were a proper exchange. Always talking about prices and the like.'

Tom extracted a gold hunter from his coat pocket and flicked open the lid. He'd been here more than two hours and still hadn't seen anyone even remotely connected with the silk trade. If his information was accurate, he had until the end of the week – effectively, tomorrow morning – to discover the name of the ship carrying the silk, and her location. After that, the job of tracing the thieves would become a deal more difficult. He decided to give it another half-hour and then try Old Slaughters in St Martin's Lane, where silk weavers were also known to congregate.

He thought back over his morning and wondered how his brother was getting along. The incident the night before had finally persuaded him of the need to find the boy a school and he'd remembered someone recommending an establishment in Carter's Square, Rotherhithe. He and William had gone there this morning.

Mrs Jones, a widow, had met them at the door and shown them the front room of the house where she instructed her twenty-eight pupils in the rudiments of reading, writing and the Christian faith. For a small additional fee she would also provide her charges with lunch. The terms agreed, Tom had left a very cross-looking brother in her care and promised to be back to collect him at four.

'Table over in the corner, sir.' Tom looked up as the waiter returned to his table and nodded towards the back of the coffee house. 'The gentleman in the blue brocade.'

The man glided away, leaving Tom to work out which table he'd meant, the dark interior of the coffee house and the thick cloud of tobacco smoke making the task something of a challenge. An initial search revealed nothing resembling a blue coat. He got to his feet and walked the length of the room, glancing at each of the tables as he passed. At the far end, and hidden behind a solid oak pillar, he saw a ruddy-faced gentlemen in his early forties, whose coat fitted the description he'd been given.

'Forgive the interruption, sir,' said Tom, approaching the man. 'My name is Tom Pascoe. I'm with the marine police at Wapping. If you is at leisure perhaps I might take up a minute of your time?'

The man stared at Tom and then at the tipstaff he was holding, as though hoping to wake from a doubtful dream.

'Please,' he said at last, waving to an empty seat on the opposite side of the table. 'Is there something wrong?'

'Nothing that need be of concern to you,' said Tom. 'I understand you are connected with the silk trade?'

'Yes, I am a silk merchant, sir. My name is Craddock. What, may I ask, is this about?'

'I'm interested in a shipment of silk which is due to arrive in the Port of London sometime within the next day or so. I believe there will be an attempt made to plunder it.'

'Well, if I can help, sir, I should be happy to do so,' said Craddock. 'Where is the silk coming from?'

'That, sir, is part of the problem,' said Tom. 'I know nothing other than the fact that a quantity of silk is due in London.'

'Not the buyer, or the ship? Not even the country of origin?' Craddock looked disbelievingly at his visitor. 'I really don't see how I can be of any assistance to you, I—'

'If a large shipment were due, would it be known to your fellow merchants? And perhaps to others in the trade?'

'Without a doubt it would be of interest and would become

60

known in the course of conversation. We live in hard times, sir, and the competition for work amongst the weavers is great.'

'But you haven't heard of a recent shipment?'

'I hear of shipments of raw silk almost every day.'

'Raw silk?'

'Silk that has yet to be woven.' Craddock looked up sharply. 'I hope we are talking about raw silk. Bringing woven silk into the country not only deprives our people of work, it's illegal.'

'Thank you. I didn't know,' said Tom. 'But I've no reason to think the shipment is anything other than lawful.' He paused. 'When silk – raw silk – arrives in this country, what happens to it?'

'I'm not sure I understand the question.'

'I'm simply trying to understand the process. You mentioned weavers. Would they know about consignments of silk arriving in the Port of London?''

'I doubt it would be generally known,' said Craddock. 'Every merchant will have his own favourite master weaver to whom he is likely to give the bulk of his work. It's possible the merchant would tell him about an expected arrival of silk. But beyond that? The journeymen weavers, for example? No, I don't think so.'

'How would I discover the name of the merchant who ordered this consignment?'

'Without knowing whence it comes, or the ship carrying it? You can't. There are no records kept, aside from those of the individual merchants. Have you checked the List at Lloyds?'

'Yes, there was nothing there of interest.'

'Then, I suspect, I'll not be able to help you either.'

'Thank you for your time, sir,' said Tom, rising to leave. Then he turned back, the palm of his hand pressed to his forehead. 'Just one further question. Rumours concerning this shipment have been circulating for at least a week and perhaps longer. In my experience high value commodities such as spices, silk and so on are unladed immediately on arrival in port so as to reduce the risk of plunder. Why would you suppose this particular cargo is still aboard more than a week after its arrival?'

'I've no idea, sir, unless . . .'

'Unless what?' asked Tom.

'It depends entirely where the ship carrying this silk has come from,' said Craddock. 'But it's likely to have passed through the Mediterranean. If that's the case, the ship will have been kept in quarantine.'

'I see,' said Tom, frowning. 'But I regret that don't answer my problem. A vessel in quarantine would not allow anyone to get on or off. Even supposing "our" ship were in quarantine, it's difficult to see how anyone could have discovered what she was carrying.'

'Nothing, my dear sir, could be more simple,' said Craddock. 'It is a requirement at law that certain goods – amongst them, silk – should be opened and aired for at least seven of the forty days of any quarantine period. During that time, the silk would be on view to all and sundry.'

'Where are such vessels kept?' said Tom.

'Stangate Creek, off the River Medway, but . . .'

Tom checked his hunter. Nearly four o'clock. He might still make it. He jumped to his feet. 'You have been most kind, sir. Now, if you'll forgive me, I must go.'

# CHAPTER 8

Cox eased his aching body from the bunk in the *Sisters'* tiny cabin. The beating he'd taken from Creech had been worse than he'd expected. Three of them had taken it in turns to give him a kicking in the back room of the Royal Oak. There had been long moments when he'd thought he would die under the blows.

He tried to open his eyes but his face had swollen, almost blinding him, at least for the time being. He put a hand to his nose and gently wiped away the dried blood that had trickled down over his lips during the night. There was no question that the nose was broken. He didn't need to see it to know that much. And from the pain in his fingers it seemed likely that they had all been broken, too. What was less clear was the extent of his other injuries. Slowly, he placed his feet onto the ceiling boards and gradually increased the weight until he felt confident of standing. He opened his shirt and felt around his stomach and chest. It was painful to the touch. He remembered trying to protect his face and the front part of his body but the kicks and punches had got through anyway.

He sat down on his bunk and wondered if young Stevie Lyons would heed his advice to stay away. If the lad had any sense he'd never come anywhere near the *Sisters* again. Cox hoped he was wrong. He could use the boy's help. He knew he was being selfish, but his beating meant he'd find it almost impossible to navigate the hoy on his own.

He bent to the ceiling boards, slipped on a pair of ancient boots and fastened the buckles before making his painful way up on deck. Around him, he could see one or two of the other sailing masters moving about on their own barges. He squinted up into the sky. The morning was almost over.

'You all right, Coxy?' Cox turned to see Stevie approaching, a concerned frown on his face. 'Christ, is that Creech's handiwork?'

'Aye,' said Cox, hiding his pleasure at seeing the boy. He was determined to be seen doing the right thing by the lad. 'What you doing here, anygate? This ain't no time for you to be here. Get on home. I'll see you when I get back tomorrow.'

'You'll never make it, Coxy. Not in your state. What happened last night, anygate?'

'If you's coming, you best know the truth. Then you can make up your own mind.' Cox wiped the dew from a section of the hatch cover and sat down. 'Old Coxy made a mistake. That much I already told you. Now he's got to pay for it.'

'Go on,' said Stevie, taking a seat beside his sailing master.

'There's a brig on the Medway what's carrying a cargo of silk and some other stuff. I told Creech about it and—'

'He wants to nick it. Is that it?'

'I wouldn't care if that were all he wanted,' said Cox, dabbing at a fresh flow of blood from his nose. 'But it ain't. He wants me to get it off the ship and onto the *Sisters*. On the way back, he wants me to run the old girl onto the hard.'

'You can't do that.' Stevie's voice rose a note. 'Don't he know we'll have the revenue on board? You lose the tide and they'll know you've done it on purpose. My God, Coxy, we could all hang for that.'

'Aye, I know that right enough, lad. But what choice have I got? Last night were just a warning. If I don't do what he says, he'll put me to bed with a shovel. Worst of it is, I think Mister Pascoe, the officer, knows about it.'

A moment of silence fell between them. All around, the tightly packed barges bumped and ground against each other, the sound mingling with shouts and cries. From out in the channel they could hear the curses of the lightermen working their heavy charges round into the murmuring tide.

'So, you going to tell Creech? About the revenue and Mr Pascoe, I mean?' said Stevie.

'Won't make no difference to that villain. Don't suppose he'd believe me. He says he'll be following us. When we're on the hard, he'll come across with some of his lads and pretend to offer help. Once he's on the *Sisters*, he'll put us all in the cabin and batten the hatch.'

'Including the revenue?'

'Aye.' Cox glanced at his young mate and then up at the thin layer of cloud hiding the morning sun. The boy's face had become deadly pale. 'You don't want to get mixed up in this, Stevie. Stay away for this trip.'

'I can't let you go on your own, Coxy. It wouldn't be right.'

Tom could ill afford the fare for a chaise, but he'd worry about that later. Drawing up outside the Custom House in Lower Thames Street, he paid the driver and ran to the street door where he was stopped by an elderly doorman.

'Whoa, not so fast, young fellow,' said the old man, leaning heavily on a long stick. 'You can't come bursting in 'ere without what I know your business with their worships, the Commissioners of Customs and Excise.'

'I want information on vessels currently in quarantine,' said Tom, waving his tipstaff at the man.

'Well, let me see now. I reckon the man you need is young Morrissey, but I ain't seen him today. He's the one what keeps his eye on matters of quarantine.'

'Then name me someone else who can help.' Tom's patience was ebbing away.

The old man gazed at the floor for what seemed an eternity. 'Don't reckon there's anyone else what could help you. Come back tomorrow. Young Morrissey should be here at seven o'clock sharp.'

Tom breathed deeply and did his best to keep the frustration from his voice. 'It's important that I get the information now. Give me the name of anyone who might know—'

'You youngsters is all the same,' said the man. 'Ain't got no patience. It were different in my day. Why— You can't go there. Come back.'

Tom strode up a broad flight of steps and stopped on the first-floor landing. He could hear the drone of voices coming from the other side of a polished mahogany door a few paces from where he was standing. He guessed it led directly to the Long Room, a place he knew well from his days on the *Swansong*. It was where the routine work of the customs was carried out, the room to which he'd been obliged to come to declare his cargo and be billed for the duty payable. Now he hesitated, wondering if, in his haste to find the answers he sought, he might have come to the wrong place. He had always approached the room from the river side of the building. He decided to risk it. Pushing open the door, he walked in.

The room was aptly named. Stretching almost the entire length of the Custom House and overlooking the Upper Pool, it was presently occupied by lines of clerks bent over their desks, recording details of ships' cargoes. In front of each desk stood a queue of sea captains in varying stages of impatience. Tom wondered if things had improved since his day and the details of ships' cargoes any more accurate than they had been. Probably not, he thought. At the far end of the room was a raised platform on which were placed desks of a slightly superior size and quality. Only one was presently occupied. Tom made his way over.

'Good afternoon,' he said, coming to a halt before an ancient-looking clerk, crouched over an open ledger in which he was scribbling furiously.

'Yes?' The man did not look up, his right hand moving towards an inkwell. He dipped his pen and returned to the business of writing.

'Marine police,' said Tom, placing his tipstaff onto the desk and sliding it under the man's nose. 'What can you tell me about vessels undergoing quarantine on the Medway?'

'I beg your pardon.' The clerk's head moved slowly upwards as though any greater speed might result in it falling off. He stared at Tom over a pair of iron-rimmed spectacles, his lower jaw moving up and down, his lips pursed. 'I am a busy man. What is the nature of your inquiry?'

'I'm trying to trace a ship believed to be carrying a large

quantity of silk. I believe the vessel is currently under quarantine. Who can I speak to? And please don't tell me it's Morrissey. He, apparently, is not here today.'

'I regret Mr Morrissey is indeed the only person who can deal with inquiries of that sort. Come back tomorrow. Now, if you'll excuse me, I have work to do.'

Tom laid a large hand over the man's ledger. 'You will please do me the honour of attending to my inquiries, sir. It is of the utmost importance that I obtain the information I'm seeking. If you cannot help me with the name of the ship, at least tell me how many vessels you would expect to be under quarantine in Stangate Creek at this moment?'

'I don't know, sir,' said the man, startled. 'Perhaps thirty. Possibly more. They arrive daily while others leave. Morrissey will have the details. He deals with orders in council and so forth.'

Tom thanked him and turned away. He'd not expected that answer. Even thirty ships was too many for him to inspect in the time he had available. He needed the name of the ship. If Morrissey was the only man who could help him, then . . .

'Which is Mr Morrissey's desk?' he asked.

A tired pair of eyes dragged themselves off the desk and travelled up a soiled naval officer's coat until they came to rest on Tom's face. After a moment's pause, the clerk nodded at an empty desk on the other side of the room. 'He sits there.'

Tom checked his watch and looked despairingly up and down the room. 'Where does he keep his registers?'

'In his desk, but you ain't seeing them.'

'Thankee,' said Tom, crossing over to Morrissey's desk.

Tom was conscious of a shadow falling across the page of the register open on the desk in front of him. He looked up to see a rotund and bewigged gentleman of about fifty-five, a pair of pince-nez perched precariously on the bridge of his beak-like nose. Apart from a scarlet waistcoat, he was dressed entirely in black. On either side of him stood a couple of very large men with fists and broken noses to match.

'What, sir, is the meaning of this?' The gentleman's voice was surprisingly high-pitched. 'Who are you and what are you doing with that register? You will explain yourself this instant.'

Tom was aware of a dozen pair of eyes being turned towards him from the adjacent desks. He knew he'd overstepped the mark but this was no time to admit to such a trifling irregularity. Some half-remembered words of Napoleon that he'd once read popped into his head – *A man who speaks makes more noise than ten thousand who are silent.* The sentiment seemed apt. He got to his feet, removed his tipstaff from his coat pocket and placed it on the desk.

'As you see, I carry a warrant of authority issued by a magistrate. I have reason to believe a ship presently in quarantine in Stangate Creek is shortly to be attacked and plundered. I need the name of that vessel and I need it now.'

'I regret I cannot help you,' said the gentleman. 'The information you require is confidential to His Majesty's Commissioners of Customs and Excise and cannot be divulged except by order of a court. I suggest you go away and obtain that order. Then, sir, I shall be happy to oblige you.'

Blind Jack stopped at the corner of the street and struck the wall of a house with his stick. Cocking his head, he listened to the confused chatter of voices that filled the air around him, seeking some con-firmation that he was still on his chosen path. Then he moved on, his steps quick and confident, the stick tapping the ground in front of him as he went. Perhaps it was familiarity that guided him, or perhaps information gleaned from the cacophony of the surround-ing noise, but soon he had reached the front entrance of the Royal Oak tavern on Bridge Yard, a little to the east of London Bridge. He pushed open the heavy door, muttering to himself as he did so.

No one knew how Jack had come to lose his sight, although that hadn't stopped the speculation. There were nearly as many stories about it as there were people prepared to tell them. Cer-tainly the man himself had never spoken of it and there were few who were prepared to risk a thrashing from his stick for the priv-ilege of asking him. Now in his mid forties, he was rumoured to have come to the area from somewhere east of Limehouse, per-haps Barking or Bow or the wetlands beyond the Lea, but whatever the truth, he had been a fixture in the port for as long as anyone could remember, the beat of his stick on the surface of the road an early indication of his presence.

Jack stopped midway between the door of the tavern and his regular seat in the corner of the taproom. He turned his head towards one of the windows overlooking the Thames.

'Mornin', Creech,' he said, his long, narrow face breaking into a ghastly grin, his white, marble-like eye seeming to roll in its socket. 'Thought you'd be gone by now.'

'I reckon someone ought to have broke your head years ago, on account you don't mind your business, Jack,' said Creech, swill-ing his beer round his tankard. 'Where d'you suppose I should have been gone to, then?'

'Why, if you don't know then it ain't my place to tell ye. But you mark my words, I ain't the only person who knows.'

'Why damn you, you villain. Speak plain afore I clout you. What d'you mean, I ain't the only person what knows?'

Blind Jack made his way to Creech's table and sat down. 'Ever hear tell of a cully what's called Pascoe?'

'Aye, so I have. What of it?'

'He's been asking questions.' Blind Jack's voice dropped to little more than a whisper. 'I hear tell he knows the name of the ship what's carrying some silk. And it won't be long afore he gets to hear of the folk what's interested in taking it for their own, like.'

Jack heard a sharp intake of breath and the scraping sound of a bench being pushed back. He jumped to his feet and banged the table with his stick. 'Not so fast, Creech,' he said, a triumphant note in his voice. 'I were right, weren't I? It's you he wants, ain't it? You best be careful. He ain't nobody's fool, is our Master Pascoe.'

'You know more than what's good for you, Jack. There's some what would welcome the sight of you face down in the Fleet.'

Jack turned to go, suddenly aware of a light scraping away to his right, as though another bench were being pushed back. He listened as footsteps made their way to the tavern door. Two men, he thought. Odd they should have chosen that moment to leave.

# CHAPTER 9

The autumn sun had yet to rise over the rooftops of the houses to the east of the Custom House and the dull grey light of the pre-dawn still covered the quays. Yet even now the place reverberated with the noise and bustle of activity. A line of treadmills at the water's edge clanked, rattled and clicked as the men within them stomped and sang their way through the morning hours. Beneath them, carts rolled forward to receive the goods taken from the lighters while the general din of shouted orders, instructions and curses rendered the process of conversation all but impossible.

At the quay's eastern end, where a narrow lane led up to Lower Thames Street, two men stood apart from the general mêlée, stamping their feet and blowing into their balled fists in an effort to keep warm. There was nothing unusual about them in either their facial appearance or the manner of their dress, and the casual observer might have taken them for merchants or even passengers waiting to board one of the many ships in the Pool.

They had been there some time, no word passing between them, their eyes alternating between a hoy moored in the Custom House Road and a sailing barge on the opposite side of the river, close to Hays Wharf. Suddenly, the first of the two men stiffened. He nudged his companion and pointed to a group of five men shouldering their way through the crowd to the shallow flight of steps leading to the water's edge at the far end of the quays. Led by a short, stocky man in his mid forties, the group climbed into a waiting skiff and were swiftly carried to a sailing barge on Galley Quay Road.

'That were Creech,' said the taller of the two men, stepping back into the shadows. 'Shouldn't be long before Cox gets here.'

'There he is, sir. Over there. There's someone with him,' said the second of the watchers. A few years older than his companion, he had the appearance of someone used to the cut and thrust of life on the streets, his eyes sharp and knowing, his lips tightly drawn. And yet there was an aura of deference in his manner, a seeming acknowledgement of his companion's moral and temporal superiority.

'Aye, I see them now.'

The strangers watched as the hunched figure of Rob Cox, accompanied by the mate of the *Sisters*, emerged from the jostling throng, Cox's face heavily bruised and swollen round the eyes, his shoulders hunched. He seemed to walk with difficulty. The two reached the eastern end of the long quay and climbed down a ladder onto the first of several lighters lying alongside.

The watchers moved closer to the edge of the quay and waited for Cox and the boy to reach the *Sisters*. Minutes later, the hoy slipped its moorings and begun drifting down on the tide, waiting for her gaff sail to catch the wind.

On the far side of the Thames another barge separated itself from its fellows and followed in the wake of the *Sisters*.

It was time for the two watchers to be on their way.

*

An hour or two later, a rowing galley drew alongside the pontoon below Wapping police office. Tom got out and climbed the steps to the passageway at the top, still smarting from yesterday's refusal of the custom's official to allow him sight of the register of incoming ships. It irked him that the buffoon had been unable to see the urgency of the matter and the likely consequences of his decision to stand on the letter of the law. It had meant more time wasted while he returned to Wapping and arranged for Mr Harriot, the resident magistrate, to let him have a court order. It had not helped his mood to discover that Harriot was not in his room and could not be traced.

Nor was that the only thing on his mind. He'd only just remembered to collect William from his school in Rotherhithe yesterday afternoon and the stress of getting him there this morning was beginning to tell. He would have to think of some other arrangement for the daily task. It was too dangerous to leave the boy without an escort.

'It seems you've ruffled a few feathers at the Foreign Office,' said Harriot when Tom walked into his room, half a minute later. 'The Under Secretary of State wants to see you pretty damn quick.'

'Do we know why?' said Tom, his heart sinking. 'I was hoping to get down to the Medway. I think the silk I've been looking for is there but I need a warrant from you to let me discover the name of the ship concerned.'

'I regret it extremely, Mr Pascoe, but I gather it's in connection with the case that the Under Secretary wants to see you. Seems he's interested in hearing more about it. It would not be sensible to make him wait.'

\*

'Thank you for coming, Mr Pascoe,' said a young-looking John Hookham Frere, Under Secretary of State at the Department for Foreign Affairs. 'You must be wondering why I wanted to see you in such a hurry.'

'I'm certainly curious,' said Tom, glancing round the familiar room dominated at one end by an ornate marble fireplace over which hung a portrait of the King. He'd been here on a previous occasion and hoped this visit would be shorter and more productive.

'Do sit down.' Hookham Frere waved Tom to one of the comfortable-looking leather armchairs arranged in front of the fireplace while he himself walked round from his desk and sank into another. As soon as he'd settled, he said, 'One of our people has made contact with us. It appears you've been making inquiries about a quantity of silk recently arrived in the United Kingdom. The Secretary of State has directed me to find out the nature of your interest.'

'May I ask, sir, why the Secretary of State wants to know?' said Tom. 'You will doubtless appreciate that we do not, as a general rule, make known the nature of our inquiries before they are complete.'

'No, of course not. Forgive me, Mr Pascoe. All will become clear to you in a moment, but I wonder if you would be good enough to confirm that the silk you are interested in is recently arrived in the Thames?'

'That's my understanding, yes.'

Hookham Frere seemed simultaneously relieved and concerned by Tom's answer. He laced his fingers and leaned back in his chair, his pale green eyes fixed on his visitor. 'Am I also to understand that you have information suggesting the consignment is at some risk?'

Tom hesitated. He had the feeling of being pushed into a corner, of being obliged to answer questions without being made aware of the reason. If he was to get anything useful out of this meeting he would need to insist on a degree of reciprocity before too long.

'I would be able to help you better if I were to understand, sir, the purpose of your questions.'

'Very well,' said Hookham Frere. He was about Tom's own age, with a long, narrow face and a beak-like nose. He leaned forward and placed his folded hands on the desk. 'What I am about to tell you must go no further. It is, sir, a matter of the utmost sensitivity.'

He paused for a moment before continuing, as though to gather his thoughts.

'For some weeks now we have been expecting the arrival of a consignment of silk addressed to a merchant in the city. Secreted in the skeins is a document prepared by a highly placed source within the Directoire of the French revolutionary government. It is thought to provide some highly confidential information of interest to His Britannic Majesty's Administration. We believe it has the potential to materially affect the course of the war.'

He paused again and appeared to consider the wisdom of continuing. At last he seemed to reach a decision.

'How much, sir, do you know of the ongoing conflict between the French and the United States of America?'

'Only what I read in the papers,' said Tom. 'I understand there have been several skirmishes at sea, mainly confined to the Caribbean.'

'Quite so,' said Hookham Frere. 'For some time these engagements have threatened to develop into a full-scale war between the two nations, a situation with which we, in these islands, would not be unhappy. Unfortunately, some time ago, influential elements within the French administration began secret talks with the Americans with a view to avoiding such a war and drawing the Americans onto their side. I cannot overstress the seriousness of the situation. Should the Americans come in on the side of the French, it would almost certainly result in our losing the war. We now know the talks came to a sudden and unexplained end last year. We think the cause of the breakdown was a demand by the French foreign minister for a bribe to allow the talks to continue. Unsurprisingly, the Americans refused, and two of the three American diplomats involved returned home. The third, a man named Elbridge Gerry, remained behind, we think at the insistence of the minister, Monsieur Talleyrand, although for what purpose we do not know.'

Hookham Frere rubbed his face with both hands, looking suddenly tired. 'For a while not much happened and we think that the negotiations irretrievably broke down. Certainly the affair attracted a great deal of adverse publicity in the United States.'

'But if it's all over, how will this document you say is hidden in the silk skeins affect anything?'

'For two reasons. Firstly, the French continue to attack American ships trading with us and could, far from bringing the Americans in on their side, lead to war between them. Secondly, we believe that the whole affair has seriously weakened the ruling Directoire with consequences we can only guess at.'

'I see,' said Tom. 'And you're hoping the documents will give you a clearer idea of what's happening?'

'Yes.'

Tom stared down at his hands while he considered what the Under Secretary had said. 'May I ask how you come to know where the papers are hidden?'

'We don't. We only suspect that that is where they are. To make matters worse, there is a suggestion that the French may already be aware of the existence of the report, if not its precise contents. Certainly, there's been increased police activity along the Spanish border.'

Tom gave a low whistle. 'How d'you suppose they found out?'

'In the usual way, I'm afraid. We know one of our sources in France was arrested, almost certainly in connection with this case. We don't think he had any direct knowledge of what the document contained and was merely acting as a courier. The French will have tried to extract as much information as possible from him, including details of the person to whom he passed the papers. Fortunately, they were too late as the package had, apparently, already crossed the border into Spain and into the hands of another of our agents. At this point the story becomes a little hazy.' Hookham Frere drummed the desk with his fingers for a few moments. 'It seems no firm arrangements were made for the dispatch of the report to London, but the Spanish contact subsequently let it be known that it was on its way, hidden in a consignment of Valencia silk. The trouble is, we don't know the name of the ship concerned, let alone the date she sailed.'

'So you're guessing?'

'Not quite. Nearly all Valencia silk intended for this country is transported overland to Gibraltar from where it is loaded onto a ship. All we needed to do was find out the names of British ships passing through the Port of Gibraltar in the last six weeks. Unfortunately it is the nature of travel at sea . . .' Hookham Frere broke off and smiled. 'But of course you know about such matters. Anygate, it was only this morning that we were able to discover the name of the likely ship concerned. At the same time we learned of your own inquiries. As you might imagine, it caused quite a stir here at the Foreign Office.'

Tom sat bolt upright. 'What, pray, is the name of the ship?'

'Why, sir, I thought you knew. She is the *Velocity*, currently lying at anchor in Stangate Creek under a quarantine order.'

'No, I didn't know. It was the one piece of information that had been missing.' Tom paused and looked at the Under Secretary, frowning. 'I was recently at the Custom House where I was able to see the register relating to ships in quarantine. I saw the *Velocity* listed, although the name meant nothing to me at the time. The period of her quarantine expired at midnight last night and, if I'm right, she will begin unlading her cargo today. They have probably already started.'

Hookham Frere's face became suddenly grey. He leaned forward and buried his head in his hands. 'My God, sir, as like as not we're too late.'

Tom left the Foreign Office, crossed Whitehall and ran down the narrow passageway beside the Privy Gardens to where Sam and the others were waiting for him in the police galley.

'Our ship is on the Medway,' he said, sitting down on the arms' box and considering his options. As he saw it, he had just two. He could try to cover the thirty-two river miles to the Medway in the time available. Or he could wait in one of the lower reaches and hope his instincts were good enough to spot the villains as they returned, laden with their plunder. Either way he would be taking a risk. He made up his mind.

'We've not a minute to lose. Any villain with half a brain would have left London at first light this morning or, worse still, last night. Give way together. Handsomely, now. We have to reach the Medway before it's too late.'

The galley peeled away from the river stairs and swept round to face downstream, its bow wave creaming the water as it raced towards London Bridge and the Pool beyond.

Tom let his mind return to the interview with Hookham Frere, wondering who it was that had informed the Foreign Office of his interest in the case. 'One of our people has made contact with us. It appears you have been making inquiries about a quantity of silk,' Hookham Frere had said. There were only two people Tom could think of who might have passed on the information. One was the silk merchant, Craddock, from whom he'd sought information at Old George's coffee house in Spitalfields, the other was Jacob Emden, the Sephardi Jew Sam had spoken to in Aldgate.

Craddock's behaviour had, Tom thought, suggested a greater knowledge of the facts than he'd been prepared to admit. But then Emden had, according to Sam, been just as evasive and uncooperative. 'You should know what you are dealing with,' he had said.

The galley passed under London Bridge and was now amongst the swarm of lighters and wherries pushing their way to and from the legal quays. Tom slowed the pace and weaved his way through the heavy press. Once through there, the river would became a little clearer and the galley could pick up speed again.

'What?' snapped Tom, catching sight of Sam's questioning stare.

'Nothing, sir. I were just wondering what were so important about this job that we is going all the way to the Medway, that's all.'

Tom's eyes softened. He knew the last few months had been hard for his friend and the others on the crew. His fits of depression and irascibility brought on by his drinking had affected all their lives. He had, with the arrival of his young brother, made a determined effort to break the habit, but there'd been some testing moments along the way when temptation had beckoned and his moods had plummeted to new depths of melancholy. Yet it was at times like those when he'd most felt Sam's reassuring presence and his hand of friendship that he'd come to value so much.

'I'm sorry,' he said. 'But it seems there's more at stake than the plunder of a few skeins of silk. I'll tell you when we're clear of this lot. Suffice it to say it's going to be tight.'

'We'll see what we can do for you, your honour,' said Sam.

# CHAPTER 10

The flat land on either side stretched away into the distance as Rob Cox passed the Isle of Grain. Another few yards and he would begin his turn into the broad mouth of the Medway, the port of Sheerness nestling on its eastern shore. He could already see a scattering of brigs and snows lying at anchor in the approach roads to the harbour. On his port bow and close to the sandbanks of the Nore, a dozen line-of-battle ships of the King's North Sea fleet stood across the estuary, guarding the approaches to London and the naval yard at Chatham.

He still ached from the beating Creech had given him. Several times he'd considered asking Stevie to take over the tiller but hadn't. He glanced over his shoulder. Creech was still there, about a hundred yards behind him on the sailing barge he partly owned. The scrub had made sure he'd be seen, frequently standing in the forepeak and staring at the *Sisters*, like some predatory animal watching its prey. But at this moment it wasn't Creech who was the object of his attention; his eyes strayed beyond him to what lay behind.

He'd first seen the sloop as he'd rounded Blackwall Point into Bugsby's Reach, just outside the eastern limit of the Port of London. He'd taken little notice of it at the time. It had been one vessel amongst many in those crowded waters. But as mile had followed mile on the long journey to the Medway, he had grown increasingly conscious of its presence, now in sight, now hidden by a turn in the river or obscured by other vessels, but always a quarter mile or so astern, neither closing nor extending the distance between it and the barge carrying Creech. He had tried to dismiss his nagging concerns as no more than the product of a fertile imagination, yet the questions kept coming, demanding an answer. Who were they? What did they want? Were they, in some way, connected with him or Creech?

But this time there was no sign of the sloop. Cox searched the small inlets on the Kent side of the estuary. There was nothing. It was inconceivable the sloop would have made it to the north side of the river in the short time since he'd last seen it. Perhaps he had, after all, been mistaken. Perhaps it hadn't been following them. Cox ballooned his cheeks and waited for his pulse to slow.

'Take over, Stevie, will you?'

'You want me to follow them, Coxy?' The mate of the *Sisters* was gazing over the hoy's larboard quarter. Cox turned to look. Creech was overhauling them and heading for Sheerness. He watched the barge heel slightly in the freshening breeze and recalled Creech's words of the night before. *Don't be doing nothing foolish, you hear? I'll be watching you. You try anything . . .*

'No, take us into the Medway,' he said. He steadied himself with a hand on the gunwale as the *Sisters* began to bear round the eastern end of the Isle of Grain.

It was a further quarter of an hour before they passed Deadman's Island and swung south into Stangate Creek. The rays of the afternoon sun slanted down across the marshlands stretching away into the distance, burnishing the countryside in its golden light. Cox had been here many times before, occasionally to the creek but more often to the naval yards at Chatham or to the town itself, a mile or two further on. There had always been a need for his services, a need to satisfy the voracious appetite of the metropolis, to carry grain and wheat there and return with manufactured goods for the Medway towns.

It had been on one such visit that he'd learned of the existence of the skeins of silk in the hold of the *Velocity*. Two men – casual acquaintances of his – had come to his little cottage on the outskirts of Erith and told him about it. He remembered the meeting principally because his wife had wanted to know who the men were and the nature of their business. They had quarrelled over it, a silly, inconsequential spat, but he'd felt obliged to tell the men he wasn't interested in pursuing their proposal although, the Good Lord knew, he needed the money. Yet somebody must have talked. And somehow the chatter had come to Creech's attention.

Cox took in the busy scene before him. Long brick and timber sheds stood on the east bank of the creek. Their massive doors were open to the cold north wind, allowing an endless stream of men to pass in and out carrying tools or lengths of timber, copper sheets or coils of hemp. Still more could be seen in skiffs or hoys or sloops rowing out to the dozen hulks that lay on the still water, all of them in varying states of disrepair. Further along were some third- and fourth-rate men-of-war whose needs were being tended to by another army of shipwrights, coopers, armourers, ropemakers and the rest.

Cox paid out the hoy's gaff sail and let her run before the wind as he searched for the telltale yellow flags of the ships in quarantine. He found them close to the southern end of the creek, opposite Chetney Hill, an untidy heap of perhaps thirty vessels, all but one of which were displaying the required signal flag at their jackstaff.

'There's the *Velocity*,' said Stevie Lyons, pointing to the clean lines of a brig about a hundred yards ahead of them. 'The one what's got no flag.'

Cox waited for his mate to alter course and then close-hauled the mainsail as the wind veered to the north-east. A few minutes later they brought the hoy up into the wind and dropped the sail as she fetched alongside the brig.

'Coxy?'

'Aye, what is it, lad?' said Cox, making fast to the *Velocity*'s main chains.

'You seen that sloop? Over there, t'other side of that barque. Them two coves what's in it have been watching us these past few minutes.'

The view didn't have a great deal to commend it. Captain George Forsythe stood in his day cabin aboard the *Velocity* and looked out over the distant Deadman's Island to the flat featureless marshlands of the Kent countryside. There was a limit to the number of times he could admire the redshanks, terns and curlews that seemed to blacken the sky with their numbers. There were, he thought, better ways to spend forty days and nights, whatever the wonders of nature. He shook his head in irritation. The only reason he was here was because of the silk he was carrying in the hold. A late change of orders had seen him diverted to the Bay of

Gibraltar where he'd picked up the extra cargo. He'd had no say in the matter, but the end result was an additional forty days spent looking at – what? A few thousand seabirds, most of whom had seen fit to spend their time fouling the *Velocity*'s decks and rigging.

His face brightened as he remembered that his enforced period of inactivity had come to an end at midnight. He was beginning to wonder if the mate had remembered to strike the quarantine flag when a knock on the cabin door interrupted his musing.

'Come in.'

The door opened and the ship's mate sidled in and touched his forehead.

'Begging your pardon, sir, but there's a hoy alongside. The master reckons he's come for the bales of silk.'

'Thankee, Mr Alder. I've been expecting him. Ask him to present his papers. When he's done that, you may inform the revenue. Any sign of the tide waiters?'

'Not yet, sir.'

'Very well, I'll be there directly.'

Forsythe drained the coffee he'd been drinking and then followed the mate out onto the quarterdeck. A stiff, north-easterly wind was ruffling the surface of the creek, hurling small, white-tipped waves against the side of the ship. He drew his greatcoat closer about him and glanced in the direction of a group of men standing abaft the main mast.

'Mr Alder?' Forsythe waited for the mate to join him. 'Who are those men with the revenue?'

'The crew of the sailing hoy what's to take the silk, sir.'

Forsythe eyed them for a moment. Then he said, 'Still no sign of the tide waiters?'

'No, sir.'

'Very well. Do you have the orders in council?' Forsythe held out a hand for the slender sheaf of papers. 'While I read these, be so good as to inform the master of the hoy the reason for the delay. In the meantime, tell him to stand clear of the ship. To be on the safe side tell him he may return for the cargo in, say, four hours. That should be enough time for the tide waiters to join us, I think.'

Cox hadn't expected to see the sloop again. He'd felt an unpleasant lurch in the pit of his stomach when the mate, Stevie Lyons, had pointed it out to him. He'd managed to convince himself that its presence behind him in the Thames had been pure chance with no connection either to him or Creech. His eye scanned the eastern shoreline of Stangate Creek. There was no trace of it now – it seemed to have vanished. He turned and looked across the deck of the *Velocity* to the opposite bank. Still no trace. His hopes began to rise. He was worrying unnecessarily.

He stepped through the gateway in the ship's rail and followed Stevie down the companion ladder to the deck of the *Sisters*. He'd reached the bottom when he felt Stevie's hand on his shoulder. The lad was staring at a small, single-storey building standing a little further back from the water's edge than its neighbours. A solitary figure was leaning against one of the side walls, seeming to gaze at something in the distance. A moment later his head twisted towards the *Velocity* and he appeared to start before stepping back out of sight behind the building.

'If I'm not sadly mistook,' said Stevie, 'yon cully were on the sloop what were here quarter of an hour since.'

'Aye, I think you might have the right of it, lad,' said Cox, continuing to stare at the spot where the man had been standing. His mind was racing. He wondered about the wisdom of telling Creech what he'd seen. There was at least a chance he'd not be believed, that Creech would suspect him of making the whole thing up, of seeking a way out of his enforced participation in the theft of the silk. He shivered as a gust of cold wind sent white peaks of water prancing south. Soon it would be dark and all work would stop until the morrow. Creech would be waiting for him at Sheerness. He would at least have to tell him about the delay.

Cox thought it over. If there was someone else interested in the silk, he was welcome to it. There was a part of him that would savour the prospect of the silk being stolen by someone other than Creech, someone with whom he, Cox, could not be identified. True, he would receive no part of the booty, a booty he desperately needed to pay off his debts, but it would mean he need no longer fear the hangman's noose.

He shook his head. Creech would never believe him, would hold him responsible for the loss and require that he pay the price. Without question it would be short and bloody and he'd be unlikely to survive.

Daniel Creech followed the progress of the sloop as it passed in front of the harbour mouth at Sheerness and turned left into the Thames. He had the feeling he'd seen it before but couldn't quite place where. He was still looking at the fast-disappearing craft when he heard his name being called. He looked round. Cox was waving to him. The *Sisters* had slipped unnoticed into the harbour.

Creech sauntered over. 'What you doing here?" he said. "You got the silk, 'ave you?'

There was a pause and Creech thought he saw a flicker of fear in the other man's eye.

'Been a delay, Creech. I were told to come back later. The captain won't hand over nothing till the tide waiters get there.'

'What?' Creech stared in disbelief, recalling the conversation he'd had with Blind Jack and the warning that others, including Pascoe, were not far behind. He peered nervously in the direction of the Thames, half expecting to see his nemesis rounding the point. He looked back at Cox, anger flaring in his eyes, his mouth twisting into an ugly snarl. 'Get back to that brig and don't leave till you've got them bales. You understand me, Coxy? You tell that captain you got to deliver the silk to its owner by first light tomorrow without fail or he'll want to know the reason why.'

'There's something else, Creech . . .'

'What now? You's upsetting me, Coxy, and that ain't a good idea.'

Cox dropped his eyes. He was trembling. When he next spoke, his words came out in a rush.

'I've heard one of the tide waiters what will be on the *Sisters* used to be a fisherman.'

'You've lost me, old son. What's being a fisherman got to do with anything? And slow down, will you?'

'It means he knows the river as well as what I do.'

'You've still lost me.'

'It ain't possible, Creech. It ain't possible to run the *Sisters* on the hard like you want me to. He'd know straight away what I'd done.'

'Who would know, you death's head on a mopstick?'

'The tide waiter what I've been telling you about. He knows the river too well. He'd have me with a rope round me neck if I tried to run her aground.'

'That ain't my problem, Coxy. You just do as I tell you. You let me down, old son, and I warrant you won't need to wait for no rope. I'll see to you myself. Now get going.'

# CHAPTER 11

Tom cast a worried glance at the shoreline as the police galley rounded Coalhouse Point, not far from the beginning of the estuary. The falling tide had exposed a wide swathe of mud on which ships and barges lay stranded, their decks and masts tipped over at drunken angles. He wondered what was happening at Stangate Creek, whether the *Velocity* had begun discharging her cargo and whether the silk bales and the documents hidden within them had yet been unladed. If they had, where would they be taken? Sheerness and Chatham were both nearby. From either place, the silk could easily be transported overland to London.

Tom considered the possibility. From the little he already knew, those involved almost certainly came from London. They would not be familiar with either Sheerness or Chatham. Still less would they have the necessary contacts to arrange for carts, horses and men to transport the cargo overland to the capital. And why would they go to those lengths anyway? They had arrived by boat and could return by boat.

But not yet.

For the moment the state of the tide was preventing anything from moving up the Thames, a situation that would continue for a while longer. And after that? Daylight was passing, the sky already streaked with pink. Soon it would be dark. Few would choose to travel by night, and those that did, Tom would stop and search.

The police galley rounded up into Lower Hope Reach as the sun finally sank below the horizon and the tide halted its onward rush to the sea. Tom turned up the collar of his naval greatcoat and tucked his chin below the protective layer of barathea as a cold wind gusted down the estuary from across the Essex marshes. The galley pitched in the turbulent waters, sending spumes of icy water into his face. He leaned forward and lit the oil lantern, hanging it on a pole at the stern. Elsewhere, lights began to appear on the vessels stranded by the falling tide, first one, then several; tiny pinpricks of yellow against the black curtain of a sky suddenly overcast.

Tom spotted the lightship at the mouth of the Medway and the lights of Sheerness beyond. He'd seen nothing in the last hour to arouse his suspicions although he had to admit it would not have been difficult for someone to pass unnoticed in the broad sweep of Sea Reach, especially those who failed to show a lantern.

'Got far to go, sir?' Sam's voice sounded tired, as well it might. Even a man in full vigour would struggle with what the crew had achieved, and it was still not over.

'To the *Velocity*? No, we're almost there,' said Tom, his forehead furrowing in concern. He wondered if it had been wise to allow Sam to come with them. But there hadn't been much choice. Fit or not, his friend's contribution had been essential. 'But I'd be surprised if we see anything of the silk on board.'

'Where d'you think it's gone, sir?'

'I'll warrant it's on the *Sisters* or some other barge somewhere.

If it's passed us at all it will have been in the last half-hour. Any earlier and we'd have seen her. We'll have a word with the *Velocity*'s captain and find out what we're looking for.' Tom caught the resigned look in Sam's eyes, and stopped. 'Of course, we might need a short rest before we start back to Wapping.'

'Amen to that, sir,' grunted Sam.

It was the boy who saw it first: the dim flicker of a light, a solitary beam in a world of darkness, swinging gently from side to side and moving towards them along the Medway.

'Seen that, have you?' Stevie pointed over the bows of the hoy to the distant speck of light.

'Have I seen what?' Cox stopped what he was doing. There was a pause, then, 'Where did it come from, lad?'

Stevie shrugged his shoulders. 'I weren't looking. First I saw of it, it were about where it is now.'

There was something almost military in the precision of the boat's passage through the water. Even at this distance, Cox was able to make out the splashes of white where the sweeps entered the water. For a second or two he thought it might be a Navy cutter, but it was a little out of the way for that and anyway the Navy didn't use the randan rowing formation. His felt his heartbeat quicken. The only people he'd seen using that style were the marine police, the boys from Wapping New Stairs.

Cox stared at the approaching vessel, remembering the time he'd seen Pascoe's crew in action. It had been on the night Creech had sent his bully boys to bring him in. Cox had been expecting them. He'd left the *Sisters* and had been standing on London Bridge looking down onto the Custom House Road when Marr and Gott had arrived. Out of the corner of his eye, he'd seen a light in the centre of the channel moving silently through the water, white water spilling away from her stem. He'd watched her alter course and pass through a gap in the barge road to the shoreward side, its light suddenly extinguished. He'd known, then, what it was and where it was going, had been able to admire the practised ease with which it sliced through the black waters of the Thames.

He guessed the crew must have seen the two men on the hoy. Why else had they altered course? Why else had they extinguished their navigation light? Moments later the galley had fetched alongside the *Sisters* and he'd recognised the yellow-haired man in the naval coat vaulting onto the deck of the hoy. There weren't many people on the river who didn't know Tom Pascoe.

Cox continued to stare through the Kent night. It didn't seem plausible that Pascoe was here unless he knew about the silk. Cox felt suddenly cold, as though an icy hand had embraced him and touched his heart. He had long suspected that Pascoe might know, but he hadn't been sure. Not really. Yet if Pascoe did know, he was done for. Cox fought down the panic that was threatening to overwhelm him, and tried to think. The silk was lawfully in his possession. He had done nothing wrong. He had nothing to fear from the law. Not yet. But that was about to change. Soon he would become a party to plunder and liable for the consequences.

A thought slipped into his mind. He would tell Pascoe what he was being forced to do. Creech would be arrested and that would be an end to his troubles. He stopped in mid-thought. That wouldn't work, either. If he, Cox, hadn't yet committed any offence, then neither had Creech.

He looked round for the two tide waiters, then remembered they'd gone below. They would not have seen the approaching light. But time was running out. He had to decide what to do before the opportunity passed. He felt helpless, incapable of rational thought, a decision beyond his mental capacity. It had been like this for days. He'd barely slept since his first meeting with Creech. The whole scheme was, for him, a living nightmare that occupied his every waking moment.

He thought of home. It was close by. A matter of a few miles west of where he now was. He imagined himself stepping ashore from the long, narrow pier that jutted out over the mudbanks at Erith. In his mind's eye he was walking up the main street from the river, past the butcher's shop and the place next door from where old Peter Bowcock sold candles. Further up the street, on the left, was where Joe Spittle the blacksmith was hard at work. But he wouldn't get that far. There was a lane on the right, narrow and dusty, on which his cottage rested, a mile or so short of the wooded ridge, where stood the abbey at Lesnes.

He reached the junction and turned west, his eyes searching for the home he shared with his wife and young children. He knew he'd not be able to see it. Not yet. It was hidden behind a giant beech which grew in the meadow, close to the road, its long boughs drooping low over the lane. He hurried on, the old home gradually revealing itself through the dead foliage, its white-painted picket fence standing guard over the small patch of garden, forlorn at this time of the year, the stalks of the flowers wilting amongst a carpet of blackened leaves.

He was almost there when the fear overtook him, physical in its intensity. He slowed his pace, his feet weighed down as if with lead. In his mind he saw a rope dangling from a gibbet by the front gate. He was being led towards it, his hands bound before him, a nightcap on his head. A crowd had gathered and in it he saw Creech and Marr and Gott. He saw them pointing in his direction. They were laughing.

'Coxy? What's occurring?' The voice seemed to come from a long way off. He looked round and saw Stevie. The boy was staring at him.

'It's nothing.' Cox wiped the sweat from his brow and tried to quell the anxiety he felt. He needed to concentrate. The light was much closer now, the outline of a rowing galley just visible through the gloom, the backs of the crew bending and straightening in perfect unison. Their presence represented his only chance of starting again, of freeing himself from Creech's terrible embrace. He knew what he was planning was fraught with danger, but what was he to do?

He pushed the tiller bar to larboard and watched the bows of the hoy begin to turn. He wanted to pass as close as possible to the galley, to tell Pascoe everything he knew. He glanced over his shoulder and felt the blood drain from his face.

Creech was less than twenty paces astern and closing.

The *Sisters* veered away and crossed behind a tier of ships anchored off the harbour wall at Sheerness. Behind him, Creech had followed suit. He held his breath, waiting for the order to heave-to. He was sure Pascoe had seen them; would want to question what they were doing.

The thudding beat of the galley's sweeps grew louder as it raced closer. Cox could see the rush of the bow wave, its frothing peak sluicing down the length of the hull, tiny bubbles boiling on the water's surface. The waiting was unbearable. He fought down the urge to cry out.

Then, abruptly, it was over, the sounds fading on the night air, the silence returning with just the moan of the north wind to remind him of where they were. He felt strangely elated, as though he had cheated the gallows. The mood quickly passed. Nothing had changed. He was still expected to run the *Sisters* onto the hard. Creech had been blind to reason. No amount of argument had convinced him of the lunacy of his scheme.

Cox's heart was still thumping when he rounded the Isle of Grain into Sea Reach, the hoy's rust-coloured sails blending with the night. Of Creech he could see nothing, but knew he'd not be far away. He half turned towards the mate, his eyes fixed on the hatch leading to the cabin where the tide waiters were asleep, his mind made up.

'I've been thinking, Stevie lad,' he said, his voice hushed. 'We'll not be stopping between here and the Pool. Not with them revenue cullies aboard.'

'What about Creech?' said Stevie, his eyes widening. 'Have you told him?'

'No. Best we keep that between ourselves for the time being. He'll know soon enough.'

'What will you do when he asks you why you didn't put her on the hard like what he told you to?'

'Ain't much I can do. Nothing is going to satisfy that villain 'cept doing what he tells you. And sometimes not even then. Truth is I ain't prepared to hang for the scrub – not now, not never.'

*

Tom was aware of the captain's appraising eye running over his battered uniform coat as the two of them stood on the quarter deck of the *Velocity*.

'Police, you say?' Captain Forsythe had evidently completed his inspection. 'If I'm not sadly mistook, sir, that coat you're wearing is of an officer in the King's Navy.'

'Aye, so it is. But—'

'And that patch of blue on your shoulder, sir. Would I be right in thinking you was a master and commander?'

'Yes, but—'

'Let me shake you by the hand, sir,' said Forsythe, suddenly animated. 'Why, sir, there have been times when I've had just cause to thank the Lord for the sight of a King's ship on the horizon, I can tell you. Only three months since, I were—'

'Forgive me, Captain. The silk?' said Tom, anxious to be gone. 'How long ago was it taken?'

'Yes, yes, of course. It was, sir, handed over not above an hour ago. All quite legal. The sailing master produced the signed order in council directing me to hand over the silk and some ostrich feathers. I have the order here, together with a copy of the bill of lading showing exactly what was handed over. Would you care to see them?'

'Yes, thank you, I will,' said Tom. 'Did any customs officers accompany the cargo?'

'Yes, of course. Old hands, they were. I've seen them before.'

'See anyone else?'

'Only the mate. He came aboard with the sailing master.'

'No other vessels in the vicinity?'

'Not so as I noticed.'

'What was the name of the vessel you gave the silk to?'

'The *Sisters*, a sailing hoy. It's on the bill of lading. Why all this interest, sir?'

Tom ignored the question. He was in a hurry and in no mood to lose more time than was absolutely necessary. Whoever had taken the silk might have done so legally, but that didn't mean it was safe. He needed to find the *Sisters* as quickly as possible.

'You say she left not above an hour since?'

'Aye.'

'Thank you, Captain.' Tom strode to the larboard rail.

'You haven't told me what this is all about.'

'Nothing for you to concern yourself about, sir,' said Tom, looking back. 'But we may need to speak to you again in the future. In the meantime I must find this sailing hoy.'

He dropped down the ladder to the waiting galley and settled into the stern sheets. Moments later, the narrow clinker-built craft had curved away from the ship and was heading back down Stangate Creek to the Medway.

'The silk's gone,' said Tom after a few minutes of silent rowing. 'It's on its way to London in a sailing hoy. The *Sisters*, as it happens. She has legal possession of the cargo which means either our information was wrong or she's being followed and will be attacked somewhere between here and Greenwich. If that's the case, I want to be there when it happens.'

# CHAPTER 12

The Pool of London was bathed in the silvery light of a full moon, the buildings on either bank rising ink-black into the sky. The shadow of a sailing vessel made its way towards the Galley Quay Road, close to London Bridge. It carried no lights and made no sound as it fetched alongside a line of barges and was made fast. From her stern, Rob Cox peered aft through the gloom, a worried frown creasing his brow. There was no trace of the barge which had followed him upriver from the Medway. Its temporary absence meant nothing. He knew Creech was out there somewhere, searching for him.

Cox knew there'd be trouble when, eventually, Creech arrived. Cox had defied him.

'Don't make no sense to stay aboard tonight, Stevie boy,' said Cox, his face still turned towards the east. 'You get yourself home as quick as you fancy. I'll go and see Master Horton. He'll want to know the silk and the feathers have arrived all safe, like.'

'Who's going to look after the silk, Coxy?'

'That'll be safe enough with them revenue cullies below deck.'

'What you going to do after that? You ain't coming back here, are you?'

'Nowhere else for me to go, lad. Anygate, Creech ain't going to try anything while them revenue is on board.'

'Let me stay with you, Coxy. It would be safer that way.'

'No, lad. I'll be right, thankee. Now get going.'

Cox watched the mate step onto the neighbouring barge and from there to the next until he was swallowed up in the night. He was still watching when a shadow fell across the hoy's deck as though a cloud had covered the moon. He glanced at the velvet vault of the sky. There was no cloud, nothing to obscure the moon or the million tiny specks of light that lay scattered across the heavens.

'I want a word with you, Coxy.'

Cox spun round, suddenly conscious of dryness in his throat. Less than six feet separated him from the barge on which Creech was standing, a heavy cudgel in his hand.

He felt the urge to run, wished he'd taken his own advice to Stevie and gone. Now it was too late. What was done was done. If he tried to run he would be caught and the punishment would be greater. He saw a shadow move behind Creech's head. Gabriel Marr bent forward and looped a line round the *Sisters*' sternpost, drawing the two craft together.

'I ain't best pleased with you, Coxy. You didn't stop like what I told you to. That weren't very friendly, now, was it?'

'I couldn't stop, Creechy. That's the honest truth,' said Cox, his voice wavering. 'Not with the revenue aboard.'

'You should've left that to me, Coxy. I make the decisions, not you. What you done with them, anygate?'

'Who? The revenue?'

'Who else, you addlepated coxcomb?' said Creech pointing his cudgel at Cox's face.

'They's below, Creechy. Sleeping, like.'

Creech hesitated, his gaze turning towards the hoy's closed hatch covers. He waved impatiently at the two men with him and the mooring lines were quickly withdrawn. 'You get yourself to the Royal Oak. Be there in an hour. D'you hear me, Coxy? An hour.'

Forty minutes later, Cox left the house in Cinnamon Street and walked down towards the river, his mind consumed by what lay ahead. He had meant to confess everything to Mr Horton, the owner of the *Sisters*; to tell him about the plot to seize the silk and the ostrich feathers that presently lay in her hold. In the end, his courage had again failed him.

He crossed the Thames and turned down Bridge Yard, towards the Royal Oak and his meeting with Creech. It was a place he'd visited many hundreds of times in the past, a place which, until recently, he'd regarded with affection, a kind of second home in which to while away the hours, waiting for his next assignment.

But not any more. Things had begun to change when Creech had taken a fancy to the place. He and his cronies had quickly taken over a corner of the taproom and made it their own. Thereafter it had rapidly acquired a name as a den of thieves it was best for honest folk to avoid. The change was more than old John Davy, the landlord, had been able to resist – not at his stage in life. Years ago it might have been different. Then he had run things his way and people knew where they stood. He'd been as hard as iron then. But always fair. That was the real difference between him and Creech. Fairness; or rather the lack of it, in Creech's case.

The Royal Oak was also where Cox had first laid eyes on Tom

Pascoe. His face creased into a lopsided smile as he recalled the occasion. There had been nothing remarkable about that evening in late July of '98 – except, perhaps, that it had been an usually hot day. Tempers had become increasingly frayed throughout the afternoon and, by late evening, were threatening to boil over. Even so, a few tables overturned and a bloody nose or three were no more than could be expected on most Saturdays in every tavern on the waterfront. So he hadn't been unduly concerned when the first insults were exchanged and the first punch was thrown. He had heard and seen it all many, many times before.

Yet on this particular evening matters did not progress along their usual course and expire under the weight of the physical activity required. Quite the reverse. Before long the confrontation had spilled onto the neighbouring benches, gathering increasing numbers as it swelled in sound and fury.

Cox had been standing by the front door, strategically poised for a fast exit, when it burst open to admit the six-foot-two-inch frame of a man wearing what he suspected had once been the uniform of an officer in the King's Navy. The stranger had stood there for a moment, his eyes travelling round the mêlée before the roar of his voice brought the room to silence. Not a man there had dared to question the voice of the quarterdeck. Each had dusted himself down and sat back on the few benches that had not been broken.

'You don't know him?' one incredulous, blood-splattered figure had asked when Cox had inquired as to the stranger's identity. The fellow had shaken his head and moved away as if afraid such ignorance might be catching.

Cox sniffed the scent of the river, a delicate tangy odour that had always had the effect of soothing him in times of stress. He felt its calming influence now as he neared the front door of the tavern and heard the tide lapping the foreshore. They were the smells and sounds of his working life, as much a part of his existence as the Kent marshes where he lived and the village church at which he worshipped.

He pushed at the tavern door and watched it swing open, the hinges squealing in protest, alert to every shadow, every movement, every sound. The taproom was dark and seemingly deserted, the dozen or so candles dotted about the room failing to lift the gloom. He was conscious of their flickering light depositing dollops of darkness here and there, great black shapes rushing to and fro across the ceiling and along the walls. It crossed Cox's mind that it was strange for the candles to be lit with no one in the room. He wondered where the landlord had got to.

'Come here, Coxy, you infamous dog.' The grating voice made Cox jump. 'You got some explaining to do, ain't yer? Didn't I tell you what I wanted?'

Cox spun round. Creech was seated in his usual corner, his upper face in shadow, his mouth twisted in rage. He did not get up. Behind him hovered his two acolytes, the same ones who'd been with him on the Thames half an hour before. Cox had time to wonder if the scrub ever did or said anything without his bully boys at his side.

There was no warning of what followed. With a speed and force that belied his age, Creech leapt to his feet, his fist sinking into the soft folds of the sailing master's stomach. Cox, already weak from his previous beating, doubled up and fell to the floor.

'You've cost me, Coxy. That silk were mine.' Creech was screaming now, spittle flying from his open mouth, his face red. 'How
am I going to get me hands on it now, you worthless scrub? I told
you what would happen if you crossed me, didn't I?'

Cox felt a boot strike his shoulder, a shaft of pain shooting
down his arm. He would have cried out, but his breath had yet to
return. Another kick, this time to the small of his back. Then
another, to the base of his skull. Cox felt drowsy. The blows kept
coming. An image of his wife came into his mind. She was sitting
alone by the hearth, crying. His eyes fluttered open, alarmed by
the sight of her distress. Then they closed again, the image fading. Creech was still screaming at him. His voice seemed far away,
not as loud as it had been a moment before. Someone was holding him by the collar of his coat and was dragging him to his feet
but he couldn't stand. His legs weren't working. He tried opening
his eyes again, but they wouldn't respond. A hand struck him
across the mouth, once, twice, a third time. It made no difference. God, how sleepy he felt. He was beyond caring. Now he was
being pulled across the floor, through a door and along a passage, was conscious of a sudden rush of cold air and the familiar
smell of the river, the scent of fish and rope and tar. Perhaps a
door had been opened. He struggled to think. The tavern had no
door leading directly onto the river, only a hole in the floor and
even that was hardly ever open. Again he tried to open his eyes.
Again he failed. The flesh of his face had swollen, reducing his
vision to mere slits of hazy light. He wondered when the beating
would stop. When he'd be allowed to sleep.

It would soon be over. He was sure of that.

*

Tom rubbed the tiredness from his eyes and blinked at the ships' lanterns arrayed on either side of Limehouse Reach. They were a welcome distraction after the unremitting gloom of the journey up from the coast, the task of navigating in the pitch dark difficult enough without the added requirement of searching every creek and inlet for the *Sisters*.

He was conscious of an overwhelming sense of disappointment. Away to the east, the first glimmerings of a new dawn were visible, the skyline tinged with grey and black. He'd failed in his task. Somewhere along the thirty or so miles of river that separated the Medway from the Port of London, the *Sisters* had, in all probability, been plundered of her silk, not to mention the documents of such immense value to the war effort.

He thought back over the night, wondering where he'd gone wrong. There had been any number of locations where it would have been possible to hide the *Sisters* and take her cargo. Some, particularly those on the marshlands of Kent and Essex, he'd ignored. It would have been difficult, not to say impossible, to unlade the silk and carry it away over the soft, bog-like terrain that stretched for miles on either shore. Carts, and the horses that drew them, would surely have sunk under their own weight without the added bulk of the skeins. Yet there had been other places where the chance of discovering the hoy had been sufficiently high as to warrant a search. And still there had been no trace of it.

But what if he'd not missed the sailing hoy? What if the plan had been to plunder the silk after it had arrived in the Port? Tom glanced up again at the hundreds of ships' lanterns and dismissed the idea. It made no sense for anyone bent on thievery to choose to do so where the risk of detection was at its highest. Every ship had its nightwatchmen, any one of whom might see what was happening and be able to give evidence of what happened. Even so, he had to make sure; he had to continue his slow and laborious search.

'The silk was bound for the vicinity of the legal quays,' said Tom, looking at his exhausted crew. 'There's just a chance it got there. We'll have a look and see. If the hoy ain't there, well . . .'

# CHAPTER 13

It was risky. If there had been any other way, he would have taken it. But there wasn't. If he wanted the silk, he would have to get the *Sisters* away from her present berth to somewhere less public.

'You planning on coming with me, mister?' whispered Creech.

'I'm here, ain't I?' grumbled Gott.

The two men slipped over the edge of the quay and climbed down onto the deck of a lighter. Lashed to it were another half-dozen barges, hoys and sloops, all waiting for the coming dawn and their turn to be unladed at the King's Beam. Quietly, the two crossed over the succession of decks until they reached the outermost vessel. A quick check confirmed she was the *Sisters*.

Creech moved to the hatch leading down to the single cabin in the forepeak and listened. Someone was snoring. He thought of going below and making sure whoever it was didn't wake up, but changed his mind. He'd deal with any interruption if and when it came. He picked up a lantern he'd been carrying and examined its long tapering spout. Across its mouth was an iron gate held in place by a small catch. He raised the lantern to eye level and, pointing it across the river, opened and closed the gate in quick succession – once, twice, three times.

A minute later, a skiff appeared out of the darkness and fetched alongside the hoy.

'Everything ready?' said Creech.

'Aye, we got the barge anchored in mid-channel,' said the figure in the skiff. 'Not more than thirty yards yonder.'

'Good. Give us them lines and then get back there. You know what to do. Wait for me signal and then tow us out,' said Creech, taking two thick hemp ropes that were being handed up to him. Passing one to Gott, he hitched the remaining rope round the forward mooring post. Suddenly, he was aware of a scraping noise coming from below, as if someone were moving about in the cabin. It was followed by the clumping sound of boots on the companion ladder. 'Someone's coming,' he hissed.

'What's happening?' said a sleepy voice. 'Is that you, Cox?'

'Aye, it's me all right,' said Creech. 'We're moving to the middle of the channel. The owner wants us up Queen Hythe Dock first thing in the morning. Go back to sleep.'

He was too late.

A tousled head had appeared through the hatch and was looking round in the pitch darkness. 'Don't sound like you, Cox. Where are you, anygate?'

Creech drew a knife from his belt, knelt down and held the blade to the man's throat. 'Get below, mister, and keep your mouth shut. The less you see, the better. Same goes for your mate.'

The head slid obediently back down the ladder and out of sight.

'Gott,' whispered Creech. 'Get yourself forward. I want the skylight and scuttles sealed. I don't want no more interruptions, see?'

'Creech!' Creech looked down into the skiff. The man was pointing downriver.

'What?'

'Someone's coming.'

'Where away?' Creech spun round, searching the river.

'Southwark side. Looks to be travelling this way. See the light?'

A moment or two passed before Creech saw it. He watched the dim glow of a lantern separate itself from the blur of ships' lights stretching the length of the Pool. It was close to the south bank and travelling quickly – too quickly for a rowing boat. Most probably under sail. If it kept to its present course, it would be opposite them in the next five minutes.

'Damn the scoundrel.' Creech's jaw muscles tightened. There was no way of telling who the newcomers were, or the nature of their business. He glanced up and down the reach. There was nothing else moving. Nor would there be for a least a couple of hours. He thought for a second. There was a chance the boat belonged to a waterman returning a captain to his ship. He dismissed the idea. It was travelling too fast for that. His stomach lurched as he considered the alternatives – customs or the police. Neither was welcome. Both would, for different reasons, insist on knowing what his barge was doing in the middle of the river. After that it wouldn't take them long to find the lines linking the barge to the *Sisters*. Creech swallowed noisily. The end of that particular story had the kind of inevitability he didn't care to contemplate.

'Watkins,' he said, leaning over the side of the hoy, an urgency bordering on panic in his voice. 'Get back to the barge, you hear me? You make sure there ain't nothing on board what'll hang us. And take them lines with you.'

He watched the skiff disappear into the night and then turned towards the approaching light. It was almost opposite Hays Wharf, barely a hundred yards downstream from the *Sisters*, the dark outline of a sail billowing in the wind, just visible. Then she appeared to change course and head diagonally across the river towards them. Creech swore and ducked out of sight behind the roof of the cabin. The new arrival would pass too close for comfort.

Cautiously, he raised his head above the roof line. He could see the oncoming craft more clearly now. She was slowing, spilling her wind. He shrank back out of sight and waited for what seemed a long time. There was no sound except the gentle gurgle of the tide and the occasional squeal of the hemp lines under strain. Then he heard what sounded like a sail flapping in the breeze. He waited a little while longer, willing the sound to go away. The flapping noise continued. The urge to look grew too strong. He poked his head up. The sloop was motionless in the water, her boom let loose, her sail whipping back and forth in the wind. Creech was aware of a powerful sense of being watched. He felt trapped, unable to move and yet compelled to do so. He considered the possibility of the watchers belonging to a rival gang. He tried to gauge how many there were likely to be on the boat; what chance he and Gott would have in the event of a fight. It would take Marr and the others on the barge a few minutes to come to their assistance. Too late to be of any help.

He eased his cramped body away from its hiding place and crawled to the neighbouring barge. Pausing, he glanced back. The sailing boat was still there. He could see Gott following him. He started crawling again, a slow, painful journey over and around coils of rope, mooring posts, boathooks, rolls of canvas and the rest. It was five minutes before he and Gott finally reached the ladder leading up onto the quayside.

At the top, Creech glanced back. The sloop had gone. There was no sign it had ever existed. The relief that swept over him was short-lived. He still didn't know who the strangers were or what they wanted. The possibility of arrest and its inevitable consequences was not something he care to contemplate. Nervous as seldom before, he tried to make sense of a situation that had little to commend itself. The silk was within his reach. Another hour and it would all be over. Nothing had succeeded in standing in his way. Until now.

Creech paused, the memory of the sailing sloop haunting him. He shook his head, willing himself to believe its presence didn't matter; those on board had not interfered with him, their presence no more than a passing coincidence. He had come too far and taken too many risks to stop now. Beckoning to Gott, he returned to the ladder and made his way back to the hoy. The tide was still making. Another hour, perhaps an hour and a half and it would turn. They had to get through the Bridge before then. He risked another two flashes with the signalling lamp.

'Gott, grab ahold of them lines,' said Creech when, a minute later, the hemp ropes were again handed up to them. 'We ain't got no time to lose.'

He bent over the forward mooring line and sliced through it with his knife. Then he ran aft and did the same there. Immediately, the tide caught the hoy and propelled her clear of the barge road, towards the solid edifice of the Bridge, less than a hundred yards away.

'Can't hold her, Creech.' Gott was leaning back in a vain attempt to control the hoy. The vessel gathered speed as it moved out into the faster-flowing current and began to turn broadside to the flow.

'I'm coming,' said Creech, running to the bow and picking up the second line connecting them to the distant barge. It made little difference. The tide was too strong, was continuing to carry them towards the Bridge.

'Watkins,' he shouted at the man who'd brought the lines across. 'Damn your eyes, if you don't get yourself aboard, and quick. We're losing the hoy.'

The man leapt onto the *Sisters'* deck and caught hold of the line, adding his weight to Creech's. Gradually, the slide towards the Bridge was slowed and then reversed, the hoy pulled against the tide to come alongside the waiting barge.

Still sweating, Creech looked at the shoreline. The night stars had dimmed and the velvet black of the sky was a little lighter. He could see the outline of the buildings and the ships at anchor, their tall masts rising into the greying sky. Soon, the first of the lumping gangs would arrive for their day's work and the grinding sound of the treadmills would signal the awakening of the new dawn. Time was running out and they had yet to begin transferring the silk bales out of the *Sisters* and into the barge.

Tom Pascoe glanced longingly at the twin lanterns shining above the police pontoon at the Wapping police office. He'd have given a lot to be able to fetch alongside and go home for some much-needed sleep. He looked at the faces of his crew. They, too, were exhausted, their shoulders slumped forward, their red-rimmed eyes barely open.

He looked up the crowded reach towards London Bridge. A few small boats were on the move in the early morning light, scurrying between the ships or ferrying passengers from one side of the Thames to the other. Through a gap in a line of brigs, something else caught his eye. A dark object – possibly a barge of some kind. It appeared to be stationary in the centre of the navigable channel, a little way short of the Bridge. Tom raised himself an inch or two off his seat for a better view. The barge, if that's what it was, was in a damn-fool position and would shortly be in everyone's way. He continued to stare at it for a moment or two. It was probably nothing – nothing that could justify the added strain to an already tired crew. And yet . . . and yet there was something about it that had stirred his policeman's mind.

Creech watched the men bring up silk bales from the *Sisters'* hold and carry them to the sailing barge, their sweat-soaked shirts clinging to their bodies, their backs bent with exhaustion. Another ten or fifteen minutes and they'd be done. He glanced at the black mass of the river below him. The tide had stopped running. Shortly, the long lines of barges in their various roads would begin to swing round and face downriver and the ebb would gather strength. He crossed over to the barge and dropped the bale he was carrying through the open hatch.

'Creech.' It was Marr, his face turned towards Limehouse. 'There's a galley what's coming our way. If I'm not sadly mistook, it looks to be the officers.'

*

'D'you hear there?' said Tom, staring up towards London Bridge. 'The cullies on those barges have seen us. Give way together. Smartly, if you please.'

'Mr Pascoe, sir.' A voice was hailing him from the police pontoon. Tom looked across to see the night duty waterside officer waving at him.

'What?' he yelled.

'It's begging your pardon, your honour, but his worship Mr Harriot wants to see you, sir,' said the man.

'Please be good enough to present my compliments to Mr Harriot and inform him that I will report to him in about an hour,' said Tom, wondering if the bloody man ever went to bed.

'I regret, sir, the magistrate said I was to be sure to tell you he wants to see you right away. He's waiting in his room, sir.'

Tom breathed deeply and resisted the urge to utter a few well-chosen words of advice about what the resident magistrate could do with his inquiry. He glanced back up the reach. The dark shape was still where he'd first seen it, partially hidden by the intervening ships riding at their moorings. The sky was lighter now and he could see it wasn't a single vessel, as he'd first imagined, but two.

Then he noticed something else that was odd. There were several figures moving about the vessels. Barges were normally in the charge of one man. Occasionally, he might have a boy along as his assistant, but that was the limit. Tom had counted a total of six on the two craft. He considered ignoring the summons. He could be back at the police office in an hour at the most. It would surely make no difference to the magistrate.

The waterside officer was calling again. 'His honour were most particular, sir.'

Tom sighed angrily. It would not be sensible to keep Harriot waiting. Ten minutes more or less was not going to make a penny-worth of difference in his search of the two barges or, for that matter, the missing silk. In all probability he'd passed the *Sisters* in the dark. And if he had, then it was certain the silk, and the documents the Foreign Office was so desperate to get their hands on, were gone for good.

With that, he altered course and took the galley alongside the pontoon.

# CHAPTER 14

Creech's nerves were as taut as backstays, his face running with the sweat of his fear. He was staring at an empty stretch of water where, a moment or two before, there'd been a police galley travelling towards him. It had now disappeared behind some brigs lying in the Wapping Tier. Had they seen him? Were they now creeping up on him? His stomach somersaulted at the thought, his eyes darting from one shadow to the next, his capacity for rational thought deserting him.

He glanced at the *Sisters* lying alongside. The men were still bringing bales up from her hold and carrying them across to his barge. He leapt across the narrow strip of water separating the two craft and peered down through the *Sisters*' hatch. The last of the bales were being brought up.

'About bleedin' time,' he muttered. Then, louder, 'Marr? Where are you, you scabby villain?'

'Here,' said Marr from behind him. 'What d'you want?'

'Cast the hoy loose. We've got to go.'

'What about them revenue cullies what's still below?'

'Leave them where they are,' said Creech, his finger jabbing at the other's chest. 'Unless you want to introduce yourself. Make friends, like.'

'Just asking, Creechy, that's all,' said Marr, gesturing to the others to help him.

Creech stood for a moment, watching the *Sisters* sheer away and begin to drift downstream, twisting round and round as she went as if in the grip of a giant hand. It reminded him, as if he needed reminding, that the tide had already turned. Every minute he delayed made it less likely he would make it through the arches of the Bridge.

He needed to reach Clink Dock, about half a mile west of the Bridge. It was quieter there, away from the prying eyes of the port. He'd arranged for carts to be there, to carry the silk to his yard off the Ratcliff Highway. And there was another reason why he wanted to be upriver from the port. It was only a matter of time before the drifting hoy and the two tide waiters locked below her deck were discovered.

When that happened . . . He glanced at the ebbing tide. When that happened it would be virtually impossible for Pascoe, or any-one else, to pass through the arches of London Bridge. He shifted his gaze to the tumbling *Sisters*. She was on a collision course with a barquentine, close to the St Catherine foreshore.

'Make sail,' he snapped. 'Get ready to weigh anchor. Look sharp about it.'

The barge heeled gently to the same north-easterly wind that had been blowing all night. Creech ducked his head and peered under the boom. In two or three minutes they'd reach the Bridge. In theory, it was a simple procedure – drop the mast so the vessel could pass safely beneath the arch and then raise it on the other side before the tide carried the boat back the way it had come.

Success largely depended on having enough speed under the keel to ensure the vessel got to the other side. The problem was that he'd only ever done the manoeuvre once before, and then he'd been with others for whom it was child's play. Creech bit his bottom lip. There was much that could go wrong, even without some two thousand pounds' worth of stolen goods on board and the threat of pursuit.

The Bridge was coming up fast. Then, without warning, the wind died. Almost immediately, Creech felt the barge begin to yaw. He struggled to hold her course, but couldn't. Panic seized him. Only a miracle would now get him through the Bridge. He looked over his shoulder. Still no sign of the police galley. Suddenly, the barge lurched as if struck, heeling drunkenly to a sudden squall. Creech looked up at the gaff sail, now bowed taut. Behind him, he was aware of a howling sound, the noise of the wind racing through the rigging of nearby ships. On either side, white flecks had appeared on the surface of the water. Abruptly, he remembered the Bridge. He ducked below the boom and stared ahead. It was less than twenty yards away.

'Drop the mast,' he screamed. He watched it crash to the deck with more force and noise than was good for it. He hoped they hadn't broken it, but dismissed the idea. There'd be time enough to worry about that once they'd cleared the arch. The moments dragged by, the barge losing her forward motion, slowed by the gathering force of the tide. Creech held his breath and waited.

Then they were through.

'Up mast. Quick as you like,' he said, euphoria pulsing through him as the wind caught the sail and propelled them on their way. He glanced over his shoulder. There was no sign of any pursuers.

In another five or ten minutes it would be nigh on impossible for anyone to get through. The tide would see to that.

They ran before the wind in silence, Creech staring at the Southwark foreshore, the deserted wharves and jetties playing host to a jumbled fleet of old barges, sloops, yawls and ketches, each of them awaiting their crews and their day's labour. Opposite the Bankside Barge Road, Creech picked up a signalling lamp and, pointing it towards the shore, shone it twice. At once there was an answering flash of light from further up the river. He leaned on the long paddle oar and took the barge through a gap in the road and up past the half-built skeletons of a dozen ships, towards where he'd seen the answering flash of light. Soon the black mouth of the Clink Dock opened on their larboard bow.

'You see that, Creechy?' murmured Gott.

'Seen what?' said Creech, concentrating on getting through the dock entrance.

'Thought I saw something. A light.'

'Where? Damn you, man, speak up,' said Creech.

'Behind you. On the north shore.'

There should have been nothing unusual about it. Elsewhere, the quays were slowly coming to life, a treadmill cranking into motion, a few small boats emerging from their night's inactivity. On another day and in other circumstances Creech might have let pass what Gott had seen. But not tonight. Tonight was not the time to be taking unnecessary chances. He felt his pulse quicken, his eyes searching the north shore.

But there was nothing – no light, no sound, no movement.

'What did it look like? This light you saw?'

'Just a light, Creechy,' said Gott. 'It's gone now.'

'I can see it's gone, you bracket-faced villain,' said Creech, his eyes glinting dangerously. 'What *sort* of light was it?'

'Like one of them navigation lights, it were,' said Gott, shifting from one leg to the other.

Creech remembered the sloop that had stopped opposite the *Sisters* a few hours before. He'd not seen where she went. She'd vanished as if by a trick of light. At the time he hadn't considered the possibility of her passing through the Bridge. There had been too much else on his mind. But now? A cold hand gripped his heart.

'You wanted to see me, sir,' said Tom, walking into John Harriot's room on the first floor of the Wapping police office.

'Good lord, man, you look exhausted,' said the resident magistrate glancing up from his desk. 'Help yourself to a coffee and come and sit down.'

Tom hesitated. Time was passing. He wanted to complete the search for the *Sisters*, to have a look at her usual berth at the Galley Quay Road in case she was there. And he wanted to check out the two vessels he'd seen close to London Bridge.

'I won't, if you don't mind, sir. There's still something I need to do.'

'Do I take it, Mr Pascoe, that you had no success in tracing your silk?'

'Yes, I'm afraid so. By the time we got to the *Velocity*, the silk had already gone. According to the captain, the sailing master was in possession of the necessary papers and there was no reason to refuse him the cargo. We missed the handover by less than an hour.'

'What a pity,' said Harriot, picking up his pipe and filling it. 'I'm afraid that since last we spoke, the situation has got a little more complicated.'

'How so?' said Tom, struggling to stay awake.

'You know, of course, of the existence of a highly confidential document that is supposed to have been hidden inside the silk skeins?'

'Yes, the Under Secretary of State told me. What of it, sir?'

'According to the Foreign Office there is reason to believe there are foreign agents in London with instructions to intercept it.'

'Did they say any more about these people?' said Tom.

'The note from the Under Secretary doesn't say a great deal about them,' said Harriot, picking up his pipe and lighting it with a spill from the fire. 'I rather gather that their identities are, for the moment, unknown. I'd hazard a guess that the information came from someone on the French side who might have been reluctant to say any more. I can't say I blame the fellow, particularly having regard to what happened to his colleague. Didn't you tell me the man had been arrested?'

Tom nodded. 'That's what I was told.'

'In which case the existence of the report would quickly have become general knowledge within the Directoire. After that I warrant it would only have been a question of time before others got to hear of it.' Harriot paused, blowing a mouthful of tobacco smoke into the air. 'I'm sure the importance of us securing this document has already been made clear to you, Mr Pascoe. And if we are to believe the intelligence coming out of the Foreign Office, then we must assume the French and possibly the Americans are equally determined to stop us getting it.'

'I don't intend to let them,' said Tom, rising to his feet, his joints still stiff from the long hours of inactivity. 'For the moment I'm expecting to find what we're looking for up at the Galley Quay Road. If it's not there, then I'll start worrying.'

On the north side of the river, close to Bull Wharf, two men sat in the stern of a sloop, their faces turned to the Southwark shore watching the progress of a slow-moving barge. There was nothing remarkable about them. In their dress and general appearance they were no different to the thousands of others who spent their lives in and around the Port of London. But a listener might have remarked on the manner of their speech and come to the conclusion that neither man was from these parts

'I reckon that's them,' said the larger of the two men, nodding in the general direction of the barge. He climbed to his feet, opened the gate of the navigation lamp hanging from the top of a short pole, and blew it out. 'No point in drawing attention to ourselves. Ready?'

'Aye.'

'Then it's time we was at work.' If Second Lieutenant Milton Brougham of the United States Navy had had time to think, he might have wondered how he'd managed to get mixed up in this affair. He had, until two months ago, been tolerably content with his life on board the thirty-eight-gun frigate, the USS *Constellation*, when he'd received orders to repair aboard a packet boat bound for England. Once there he was to report to the Minister Plenipotentiary for the United States at the Court of St James, London.

In some respects, he was an unlikely choice for the delicate mission his government had seen fit to send him on. A sandy-haired Bostonian with the leathery features of a seaman and the blue eyes of his Irish forebears, Brougham's outward appearance of geniality was deceptive. While his loyalty to his country was never in any doubt, he had a tendency to the unorthodox. When this was coupled with a liking for hard liquor it was apt to get him into more than his usual amount of trouble. But for all his faults, Brougham usually – if not always – managed to complete whatever task he was given without too much embarrassment to the uniform he (sometimes) wore.

He was grateful, therefore, that the minister chose not to touch on his many failings when the latter had briefed him in his office on Tower Hill. Brougham smiled to himself. He could almost hear the old man now.

'The United States government has received information from a reliable source that requires our immediate attention if we are to avoid the possibility of war with the British,' Mr Rufus King had said to him. 'You are, of course, already aware from your previous involvement in the case, of the negotiations which have taken place between our government and Monsieur Talleyrand of the French Republic, designed to put an end to attacks on our shipping. Unfortunately, it now seems that a report disclosing the existence of those negotiations is on its way to London. Should it reach the British government it will undoubtedly lead to a serious rift in our relationship and might lead to renewed hostilities between our two nations. I regret that is as far as our information goes, except for one small detail. Our sources have indicated the strong possibility that the papers will be hidden in a consignment of silk being brought to this country. Unfortunately, we do not yet know the name of the ship concerned or its current whereabouts. As far as we know, however, the silk has not yet reached its intended destination and it is therefore fairly safe to assume that the documents are also still out there somewhere. Find the silk, Mr Brougham, and you will have found this rather troublesome report. But in doing so you are to bear in mind the sensitive nature of your task. This operation is designed to protect our relations with His Britannic Majesty's government, not destroy them. You come highly recommended, Mr Brougham. Don't let us down.'

Brougham's mind travelled back over the last year to when it had all began, to the night a gentleman had been ushered aboard *Constellation* under a veil of secrecy. The frigate had sailed from Boston that same evening, out into the north Atlantic swell. It was only then that he'd been summoned aft to meet Mr Elbridge Gerry and told he was to be the gentleman's bodyguard on a mission of the utmost delicacy. For the next six weeks, they had sailed on a course that took them north-east across the Atlantic, away from the usual trade routes and the prying eyes of the French and British men-of-war, before turning south, to the coast of France.

He had grown to know and admire Gerry well over the time they'd spent together and learned from him a little of the purpose of the mission to put a stop to French attacks on American shipping. When, ultimately, no resolution had been possible, and the mission was recalled, Gerry and Brougham had remained behind in a hopeless attempt to see what could be salvaged from the endeavour.

Brougham waited for the sloop's keel to touch the hard on the south bank of the Thames before slipping noiselessly into the shallow water. 'Wait for me here. Not sure how long I'll be.'

Wading ashore, he found some rusting iron rungs set into a quayside up which he now climbed. At the top, he made his way past a number of warehouses, each one heavy with the scent of timber or wine or hemp, stored within their respective walls. Turning the corner of the last building, he found himself overlooking a dock approximately sixty yards wide and about one hundred and fifty yards in length. Along each side were a number of vessels undergoing repair, their masts and rigging removed, their decks covered with discarded paint pots, wood shavings, lengths of timber, coils of rope and much else. On the other side of the dock a number of men were carrying heavy packets up from the hold of a barge and loading them onto some waiting carts.

Brougham watched the activity. He was far from certain that the barge he'd followed from London to Stangate Creek and back again was the one involved in the plunder of the particular silk bales in which he was interested. While there was no doubt the men he could now see were engaged in some kind of villainy, he was still a long way short of knowing exactly what they had stolen. He'd not seen what was unladed from the brig *Velocity*, and had been forced to make a judgement based on rumour. The thought depressed him, given the number of hours he'd spent getting this far.

People had been reluctant to talk to him. The drink had helped, of course. It always did. With a jar or two inside them and another on the table in front of them, men's tongues had at last been loosened, much good that it had done him. Most of the time the information had been garbled accounts of half-remembered conversations heard through the haze of alcoholic stupor and repeated with all the conviction of a self-evident truth. The conflicting barrage of stories had raised more doubts than they'd solved.

Yet despite this, two names had come to the fore. The first was Rob Cox, a sailing master from Erith who, it was said, was in desperate need of cash. The second name had been whispered over and over again. Dan Creech was not a man to be crossed, people had said, fear lurking in their exhausted eyes. A mean curse of a man, they'd said, capable of every depredation.

What no one had been able to tell him was where the silk could be found.

It had been a passing remark by an especially inebriated lumper that had suggested both men would be leaving London at dawn the following day. With his time running out and nothing to lose, Brougham had made the decision to follow up the information and wait for the two men on the legal quays, close to London Bridge. It was on such flimsy evidence that he'd followed them to the Medway and back and now found himself watching Creech and his men transferring anonymous bales from a barge onto waiting carts.

He looked up at the sound of cartwheels rumbling over the surface of the dock. The bales were, it appeared, being moved to a more secluded spot, less obvious to anyone passing along Clink Street and, coincidentally, out of his own line of sight. He moved a yard or two to his right and then regretted it. His foot struck a tin bucket that toppled over, clattering noisily over the cobblestones. Brougham ducked behind a bollard, but he was too late.

Faces had turned. He'd been seen. Men were running towards him.

Brougham turned to run, tripped over an unseen length of timber and fell to the ground. Dazed, he scrambled to his feet. He could hear men shouting and the sound of running feet close behind him. He shook his head, trying to clear the dizziness. It made no difference. He looked back. Three men had rounded the bottom of the dock and were almost upon him. He stooped, picked up the length of wood and darted round the corner of a building. Seconds later, the first of his pursuers appeared at the end of the warehouse.

Brougham swung the heavy bludgeon, aiming for the man's head. There was a dull thud as the club found its mark and the man crashed to the ground. Almost immediately, the second of the pursuers appeared at the corner, saw his outstretched friend and stopped, a look of astonishment on his face. Before he could react, Brougham's fist had sunk into his stomach, winding him.

Suddenly, Brougham was aware of the click of a pistol being cocked. He crouched low and waited. He knew his range of options were limited. If he waited much longer, others would come to the gunman's assistance. If he tried to run for it, he'd be shot. He reached for the piece of timber by his feet and tossed it a few feet. It landed with a clatter.

The barrel of a pistol appeared round the corner, followed by an arm. Brougham grabbed the gun barrel and twisted hard. There was a cry of pain followed by an explosion as the weapon fired. Kicking the gun into the Thames, Brougham ran to the steps up which he'd come, dropped to the foreshore and sprinted across to the sloop.

'What happened?' asked his companion as Brougham reached the vessel and pushed it out into the tideway.

'Just go,' yelled Brougham, clambering aboard. He looked back at the small knot of men gathered on the quay, their faces contorted in rage, and wondered if he would ever again have the chance of finding the document he'd been sent to get.

# CHAPTER 15

Creech swore under his breath. He knew he should have done something about the light Gott had seen on the north shore, although exactly what, he couldn't say. It seemed obvious now that it and the presence of the stranger on the dockside were connected. And they, in turn, were linked to the sloop he'd seen by the legal quays. If he was right – and he was sure that he was – someone knew what he was doing.

He glanced behind him where the carts stood waiting on the quay, each fully laden with the bales of silk taken from the *Sisters*. He had to get them to the safety of his own yard as quickly as possible and certainly before the strangers could return. He peered up into the eastern sky and wondered how long he had before the roads became clogged with the usual herds of cattle, sheep, pigs and sundry other livestock being driven to the slaughterhouses north of the river.

'Move yourself, George,' he said, turning to the lead cart man, his name painted in large letters on boards on either side of the carts. 'Jim here will show you the way. I'll be along later.'

He considered telling the fellow to remove the name-boards but thought better of it. The less the cully knew about the operation, the less likely he was to be suspicious. Doubtless it was, for him, just a job for which he would be paid. All the same, Creech felt a nervous twinge about the journey.

He watched the carts disappear round the corner into Clink Street and head towards Borough High Street, the shriek and clatter of their iron-clad wheels receding into the distance. If all went well, it would take them about an hour – perhaps a little more – to reach his yard, the last part of the journey in full daylight. But there was nothing he could do about that. Of greater concern was the stranger.

Creech turned his eyes to the river. The sloop had long since gone, disappeared behind some barges on its way towards London Bridge and the relative anonymity of the port. He thought for a moment. The stranger clearly hadn't been from the revenue or the police and he doubted it was another villain. He knew most of them – certainly those from around Wapping and Shadwell, and quite a few from Southwark.

'Who was he, Gott? That cully in the sloop.'

'Seen him once or twice in the Harp,' said Gott. 'Couldn't find nobody what knew his name.'

Tom walked to the edge of the pontoon and gazed up towards the Bridge. His view was obstructed by the slight curve of the river and the wooden walls of the ships lying close to the north foreshore, their tall, dew-covered masts glistening in the cold light of an autumn morning. The dark shapes he'd earlier seen anchored in mid-channel would almost certainly have gone. It was a pity. He would have liked to have seen what they were up to. He felt a rising sense of irritation. There had been nothing urgent about anything Harriot had told him. Nothing that couldn't have waited another hour or two.

He glanced at the tired faces of his crew. They were close to the end, their bare hands blue from the cold, their shoulders hunched, dark circles under their eyes. It had been a long night. He thought about calling a halt and asking one of the early-turn crews to check out whether or not the *Sisters* had arrived safely. And if the two vessels were still in the middle of the channel, the relief crew could look at them as well. He took out his pocket watch and realised the early-turn patrols were not due for another forty-five minutes. He sighed, stepped into the galley and sat down at his place in the stern sheets, the ache in his calf muscles still throbbing.

'We'll have a look round the Upper Pool. See if we can't see the *Sisters* and then it's home,' he said, trying to sound cheerful. It was all so pointless, searching for something he didn't believe still existed. He ran his tongue over dry, cracked lips. When this was over he'd think about a drink. It would help him sleep.

The ebb tide was flowing quickly, its strength growing by the minute. It was going to take longer than he'd supposed for them to get to the Galley Quay Road. Tom pushed the tiller a fraction to larboard and brought the galley close in shore, avoiding the worst of the pressure. A double-handed skiff moved away from St Catherine's Stairs and headed for a collier moored opposite Griffin's Wharf. It was swiftly followed by a second and then a third boat, each one filled with silent, ragged-clothed men, their faces blackened with ingrained coal dust. He could see others waiting their turn at steps further along. It would, he thought, be many a long hour before they returned to the shore. They didn't last long, these men of the river. Disappointment, exhaustion and a pick-led liver would see them to their graves quick enough.

The murmur of voices was swelling now to a crescendo of noise as the day's work got under way. A few lighters drifted past, on their way down towards the ships in the lower reaches. Tom glanced at each one before dismissing them as of no interest.

Then he saw her. A little short of the fish market at Billings-gate. The *Sisters* was lying athwart the bows of a barquentine, swaying precariously as if at any moment she might be torn free by the force of the tide and sent headlong into the next ship that lay in her path. Getting her off was going to be tricky. Tom would have to take the galley upstream and drop her down, stern first, towards the stricken craft. Getting close enough to allow him to put a line aboard was fraught with danger. But he had no alternative.

'Steady. Steady,' he shouted over the general noise of the port, the galley's tiller more trouble than it was worth as he fought to keep the boat on her course. 'Away starboard. Enough. Now lar-board oars. Steady. Steady. Give way both.'

The rapid stream of orders went on, instantly obeyed, expertly executed, the galley keeping her line to the tide, slowly dropping closer to the hoy.

'Keep her there,' said Tom, when the stern of the galley had reached the *Sisters*. He leaned over, slipped a line over one of the stout timber mooring posts in the bows and tied it off.

'Take up the strain,' he said, as the tide caught the *Sisters* and threatened to spiral her away. He looked up at the barquentine. Men were lining the rail, watching him. 'Lay along there,' he shouted, cupping his hands to his mouth, 'I'm fetching the hoy alongside. Stand ready to make her fast.'

Half a dozen men slid down the ship's companion ladders and leapt across the narrow strip of water that now separated the hoy from the barquentine's massive timber hull. Others threw them lines and these were used to make the *Sisters* fast alongside.

Tom stepped across, noticing as he did so the open hatch and the discarded covers. It told him all he needed to know. The hoy was empty. She'd been plundered of her cargo. He walked to her larboard side and examined the collision damage. It wasn't as bad as it might have been – a few planks stove in above the water-line, but no more. He turned his attention back to the hatch. Dropping to one knee he peered inside the hold. It was empty, but for a few scraps of brown paper.

Suddenly, he was aware of someone shouting. He stood up and listened. The muffled sound was coming from below the forward hatch, a hatch that had been battened from the outside. Tom made his way over and kicked away the battens before lifting off the wood cover. Two pairs of frightened eyes stared back at him.

'Thank the lord you're here,' said a man's voice. 'I thought we was going to die.'

'And who might you be?' said Tom.

'We is revenue,' said the same man. 'My mate and me was posted to look after the cargo on this 'ere barge until it could be took to the King's Beam . . .' He stopped, his eyes travelling over Tom's mud-stained coat, an anxious expression on his face. 'Who are you, anygate?'

'Marine police,' said Tom, drawing his tipstaff from his pocket, its gold crown flashing in the early sunlight. 'What happened?'

'Don't rightly know,' said the man. 'All I can tell you is that we is lucky to be alive.'

'Go on,' said Tom.

'We was ordered to go to Stangate Creek where a ship out of Gibraltar what were under quarantine were due to unlade her cargo for it to be taken to London. Everything were all right and we got to the legal quay last night. The sailing master – Cox, he were called. I don't recall his first name—'

'Rob?'

'Aye, that were it. Anygate, he told us he were going to see the owner. We turned in for the night and it weren't until later that I heard someone moving about on deck. I came up the ladder what I'm standing on now and looked out. There were a cully there but it were too dark to see his face. I think it were Rob Cox – leastways, that were who he said he was. All of a sudden he has a knife to me throat. I were proper frighted, I can tell you. He tells me to go below and I did what I were told.'

'But you never saw his face?'

'No.'

'Are you sure it was Cox who you were speaking to?'

'That's what he told me.'

'But you're not sure?' said Tom.

'It didn't sound like him.'

'Anything else?'

'No.'

'When you travelled up from Stangate Creek, did you notice if anyone was following you?'

'Can't say as I did, your honour.'

Tom looked at the second tide waiter who, until that moment, had said nothing. 'What about you? Did you see or hear anything during the night?'

The man hesitated and glanced at his colleague as though unsure of what he was expected to say. 'I didn't see nothing, your honour. I were asleep until me mate woke me. We tried to open the scuttles and the skylight, but they'd been shut tight. Then I heard noises on deck like we were being pulled out into the middle of the river.'

'Anything else?'

'After a few minutes there were a nudge like we'd fetched alongside a wharf or something. After that there were a lot of running around. It seemed to go on for close on an hour. I didn't know what it were about. It seemed like they was taking away the silk bales.'

'Could it have been a lighter or barge, rather than a wharf?' said Tom, remembering the dark shapes he'd seen in mid-channel earlier in the day.

'Aye, it could've been,' said the second man, his eyes widening a fraction as though considering the possibility for the first time.

'How long ago was all this?'

'Maybe an hour since.'

'Then they cut you adrift?'

'Aye.'

Tom clenched his teeth. An hour ago Harriot had required his presence for what amounted to no more than a chat – a chat that had cost him the chance of catching the men he'd rowed sixty-four miles to find. He shook his head and looked down at the fast-flowing river. An hour ago the tide would just have been on the turn. Rob Cox – or whoever else was responsible for plundering the silk – would have had the choice of going up- or downriver. Now it would be impossible to row through the narrow arches of the Bridge where the racing waters swept through in a wild and dangerous torrent. He knew which path he would have taken had he been them. Beyond the Bridge a sailing vessel could quickly lose itself amongst the numerous hulks that littered that part of the Thames and be safe from pursuit until the next flood tide.

'Anything else you remember?' he asked.

'Don't know if it means anything,' said the first customs officer. 'But after me and me mate were forced below, I heard a noise like a sail were flapping in the wind. I thought it a bit strange on account that it were too late for folk to be sailing around the port. It sounded as if it had stopped right opposite where we were. It stayed there for about a minute and then it were gone. I thought it were you lads come to see what were going on but I heard nothing more until we was towed out into the tideway.'

'Might be important. I'll bear it in mind,' said Tom, turning to the galley. 'Sam, get yourself aboard this brig. See the master and tell him I want to know what happened this morning. Talk to any crew members still on board. The lumpers, too. Somebody must've seen the hoy before it hit the ship. With any luck they might also have seen what happened in the hour or two before that. Meanwhile, I'm taking these two customs men back to Wapping for a few questions. I'll send the early-turn boat for you.'

'Aye, sir,' said Sam. He paused for a second. 'You think this cully, Rob Cox, is involved?'

'I can't think who else,' said Tom.

# CHAPTER 16

Milton Brougham was not in the best of moods as he gazed at the dreary prospect of the Rotherhithe shoreline through the rain-lashed windows of the Devil's Tavern. Behind him, he could hear the raucous banter of a bunch of sailors, doubtless celebrating their return to shore from weeks or months of shipboard life. Their jollity added to his sense of isolation and gloom. His distinct lack of progress in the job he'd been sent to do offended his self-esteem, his pride in an ability to get the job done even in the most difficult of circumstances. The reality of the situation was that he had comprehensively lost all trace of the *Velocity*'s cargo and, with it, the intelligence report it was supposed to contain.

He picked up his tankard and took a long, soothing draught of ale. He might have done better if the inquiry had been in Waterford or Dungarvan or even Cork where at least he would have been amongst his own. He'd never had much time for the British. What little time he might once have had for them had been swept away when news reached Boston two years ago of the uprising in Ireland and its suppression by the British.

Brougham had long carried with him memories of the harsh reality of life in his homeland. He'd left there many years ago but could not forget the suffering his parents had endured, the hunger and the destitution, the constant threat of eviction from the hovel they had regarded as home. And while it was true that many of the worst excesses had been foisted on them by the land-owning Irish, it was the English that he blamed.

Yet while the sentiments of hostility still existed, the old memories were no longer as acute as once they had been and, if he was honest with himself, he would admit that whatever anger he now felt was based on a life that, for him, no longer existed. He had built a new life in the United States. His loyalties were to his new nation.

But . . . Brougham thought of his mother and father, his five brothers and three sisters still living in the old country, and wondered if life for them had moved on.

'All right, shipmate?' Brougham turned to look at the man settling himself onto the bench next to him. He was a big cully, but no bigger than himself, a long, vertical scar running down the right side of his face, his yellow hair tied back at the nape of his neck. There was little doubt he was a seaman – the way he carried himself, his dress, his manner. Everything about him pointed in that direction. Brougham's eye fell on the man's blue coat with its white lapels and brass buttons. They had, he thought, seen better days.

'You Navy?' he asked, more in disbelief than curiosity.

There was a long pause as the man appeared to ponder the question, his upper body swaying from side to side, his breath smelling of drink.

'I was,' he said, at last. 'You?'

'No, not Navy, I just got in on the *Sally-Jane*,' lied Brougham, jutting his chin at a barquentine riding at her moorings in the Lower Pool, the Stars and Stripes fluttering from her mizzen.

Tom Pascoe nodded. He raised a hand and signalled to the pot-boy. 'Want a drink?' Then, 'Two Hammond's, George, quick as you like.'

Brougham shrugged. He had nothing else to do, nothing that was going to make any difference. He studied his new drinking companion with interest. Probably one of the hundreds of naval officers the British had put ashore for want of ships for them to sail in. He sympathised with the man's plight, would struggle to find other work himself if the same fate were ever to befall him. He finished his drink just as the pot-boy returned with fresh mugs. He regarded them for a moment. He'd never been averse to drink, could put most men under the table, but he needed to keep a clear head until he'd found the silk he was supposed to be looking for. He looked across at his new companion. It didn't seem right to let the guy drink on his own and besides he might know something about the silk. He picked up the fresh mug and drained it. Perhaps it would, after all, be best to save the questions for another occasion

'Have another one, sir,' he said, tapping the table with the tip of his index finger.

'Don't mind if I do, sir.'

Two hours passed in contented yarns about the sea and shipboard life, eased along by yet more ale and much back-slapping, the enunciation of the language growing ever more slurred as the time ticked by. Brougham could not remember when he'd last spent such an enjoyable interlude when, finally, he parted company, swearing undying fealty to the man whose name he knew only as Tom.

Brougham's memory of where he'd been and who he'd met did not survive the day, still less the name of his new friend, as the effects of the alcohol faded and died. He had more important things to worry about.

'Did you find anything?' he said, when he had rejoined his assistant. His head felt as though it had got in the way of a recoiling cannon.

'Not much.' Chief Petty Officer Bill Hawkes was, like Brougham, a Bostonian. Now twenty-three years of age, he had spent much of his early life in and out of the town jail on Court Street, put there for a variety of offences ranging from burglary to larceny simple. At the age of eighteen, he had been one of hundreds of men who had been tipped out of the jail into the arms of the United States Navy. Rated a topman on the USS *Constitution*, he had quickly learned that behaviour which, in Boston, might have warranted a few months of incarceration was, in the Navy, likely to have him tied to the ship's grating and flogged to within an inch of his life. But he had never forgotten the skills he'd acquired in his youth and, perhaps for this reason, he had been chosen to accompany Brougham to England. 'But there was one thing.'

'What was that?' said Brougham, doing his best to catch the eye of the particularly attractive barmaid who'd made the mistake of glancing in his direction.

'We're not the only ones looking for the silk. There's a guy called Pascoe asking questions. They tell me he's a constable. Could be trouble, from all accounts.'

'What's his name, again?'

'Pascoe. Tom Pascoe.'

Brougham shrugged. The name meant nothing to him. 'I guess

we'll just have to make sure he don't find anything before we do. Where does he live?'

'Don't know,' said Hawkes. 'Want me to find out? They say he lives with his kid brother.'

'Aye, do that. It could be useful.'

Tom walked up Old Gravel Lane towards Cinnamon Street, conscious of a hammering sensation in the back of his head. He had, over the months, developed a considerable capacity for drink but was fairly sure he'd overdone things when he'd gone into the Devil's Tavern earlier in the day. Why he'd done so was a complete mystery to him, particularly as he had thought himself free of his demons. Perhaps that was the problem. The details were, to say the least, hazy.

He should have gone to bed. He'd not slept since leaving London for the Medway and was still no nearer finding the missing silk skeins. No one was talking. Except the two merchants whose property had been stolen. And what they had to say was of no help. It was as if the incident had never happened. Nor were the constant inquiries from an increasingly anxious Foreign Office helping matters. But he knew the longer it went on, the greater the risk that the document would never be found.

Nor had anyone seen or heard of Rob Cox, the sailing master of the *Sisters*. What little information there was about him had come from one of the lumpers on board the brig across whose bows the hoy had been found. Even then it had not related directly to Cox himself. All the witness had seen was a hoy moored alongside a sailing barge about a hundred yards east of London Bridge, probably the same two vessels Tom had witnessed.

He turned right into Cinnamon Street and came to a halt outside a neat terraced house, its front door freshly painted.

'Mr Horton?' he said, when the door was opened by a man in his late sixties. 'My name is Tom Pascoe. I'm—'

'I know who you are, Mr Pascoe,' said Horton, running a hand over his bald scalp. 'I doubt there's anyone in this part of London who's not heard of you. Welcome to my house, sir. Do come in.'

'I understand, sir, that you are the owner of the sailing hoy, the *Sisters*,' said Tom, following Horton into a small parlour at the front of the house.

'Yes, I am. I heard her cargo had been plundered and have been expecting you to call.'

'The hoy was, I believe, in the charge of Mr Robert Cox.'

'Yes.'

'Have you seen Mr Cox since his return to London?'

'I saw him last night, shortly after he arrived. He told me the goods were in the hold under the protection of the revenue. But I've not seen him since.' Horton looked surprised, his voice rising. 'I assumed, sir, you had him in custody for stealing the silk and the feathers.'

'What, sir, makes you think that?'

'I naturally thought . . . That is . . .'

'No, sir,' interrupted Tom, pressing his fingertips against his temple and wishing the man would quieten down. 'Cox is not with us although I would certainly like to ask him a few questions. Where does he live?'

'He comes from Erith, sir. I don't know exactly where, but doubtless somebody from there will know.'

'What can you tell me about him?'

'Not much. He's worked for me these five years since and, for the most part, he's been a reliable sailing master. He's been before the magistrate at Shadwell several times in the past. Nothing too serious, mark you. The most he ever got was a week inside. But . . .' Horton paused and looked down at the fire burning in the grate. When he looked up, there was a sombre quality to his eyes. 'Just of late I could see something was troubling him. He had changed.'

'In what way?' Tom rested his hands on the back of a chair. He was struggling to concentrate.

'There are those who say he was in debt and had been threatened by the people he owes money to,' said Horton.

'Enough to cause him to steal the silk?'

'It's possible. I hear the sum of money he owes is considerable.'

'Do you know who these people are?'

'I regret it extremely, sir, but I do not.'

'Pity,' said Tom. 'Do you know if Cox was involved with anyone else?'

'No, not that I recall . . . No, wait . . . there is a man that he's been seen talking to of late.'

'And he is?'

'Dan Creech, one of the most unpleasant men I've ever come across.'

Dan Creech leaned on the bar of the Royal Oak in Bridge Street, Rotherhithe, his brow creased into a frown. He'd be lying if he said he wasn't concerned. He wasn't used to being wrong-footed; had always been able to deal with any problem which came along with a word or two in the right ear. Sometimes, it was true, he had had to go a little further. But then some people were just slow.

This time it was different. The business of the sloop off Clink Dock and the subsequent appearance of the stranger on the dock itself had unsettled him. It was as if the cully had known where to come and exactly what he would find when he got there. Why else would he be there? He thought for a moment, wondering if it were possible he'd been followed all the way down to Stangate Creek and back again. It seemed unlikely, but if he had been, the scrub would know all there was to know.

A shiver passed up his spine. If the infamous rogue knew all that, why hadn't he shown himself? Creech had seen no sign of him on the journey across London Bridge to the yard he owned at the back of Shadwell Market. Of course, it didn't mean they definitely *hadn't* followed him. The roads had been busy for the last part of the journey and it would have been easy enough to stay out of sight. He clenched his fist and brought it down hard on the bar. He might have to think of moving the bales to somewhere safer.

But the strangers were not the main problem. He'd sort them out in his own good time. No, the main problem was coming from another direction.

He knew Tom Pascoe by repute and that was as close as he ever wanted to get to the villain. He especially didn't want him asking questions about the plundering of some silk from a sailing hoy in the Upper Pool.

Beads of sweat formed along the top of Creech's forehead. He would have a quiet word with Marr and Gott and the rest of the lads. Pascoe needed to be dealt with. His thoughts drifted. He remembered the mate of the *Sisters*. A young lad. Hardly more than a boy. How much did he know? Had Coxy said anything to him? Then there was the Jew, the merchant he'd approached as a potential buyer. The list of people was getting longer. He couldn't silence them all. Then again, maybe he could.

Creech's thoughts returned to Pascoe. Everything he'd heard about the scrub worried him. But getting him would be difficult, even dangerous. He pushed himself away from the bar and stood upright as something Blind Jack had said to him entered his mind. It had been something to do with Pascoe, but he hadn't been listening. He struggled to recall the words, but they remained frustratingly out of reach. He walked into the back parlour and stood looking out of the window. The Thames was shrouded in a low-lying mist, the buildings on the Rotherhithe shore poking through the soft white carpet as though floating above it.

Rotherhithe. The name jolted Creech's memory. He had the sense that it was connected in some way with what Blind Jack had been saying about Pascoe. The details drifted away as though on the wind. It had something to do with a young lad.

He put it to one side. It would come to him in time.

# CHAPTER 17

It was the Sabbath and, as it happened, the last day of the Jewish feast of Sukkot. Sam stood to one side of the tabernacle, close to the front of the synagogue in Duke's Place, his eyes closed in prayer. He wasn't sure of the exact moment he became aware of someone standing close beside him. He opened his eyes. Jacob Emden, the merchant he'd been to see a few days previously, was standing a few feet away, staring at him.

'Master Emden,' said Sam. 'I would not expect to see a Sephardi here. Is there something I can help you with?'

'Meet me at my shop. There is something I have to tell you.'

An hour later Sam sat facing the merchant in the same room where he had first seen him.

'The man I spoke of?' said Emden, seemingly on edge. 'The one who approached me and asked if I was interested in a quantity of silk?'

'Aye,' said Sam. 'What about him?'

'I saw him yesterday in Rosemary Lane. He told me he'd heard the silk had arrived and the men who possessed it were looking for a buyer.'

'How much are they asking for it?'

'I hear they want twenty shillings a pound.'

'Is that the usual price?'

'About the same. But that would be for something *kosher*. If this is stolen . . .' Emden shrugged. 'It is too much. They will have difficulty selling at that price.'

'Did your friend say where the silk is now?'

'No. I don't think he knew. He had only been offered a sample.'

'Did he have a name, perhaps?'

'I asked him that question. He told me he knew the man only slightly. He believed his name to be Marr. A Gentile, he said, a man ugly enough to keep the Messiah from coming.'

'And your friend's name?'

'You must know, Master Sam, that I cannot give you his name,' said Emden. 'Already I have said more than I should. But there is . . .'

'What is it?'

'Nothing.'

'You were about to say something. What was it?'

'Please, Master Sam, I have said enough.'

'Tell me,' urged Sam.

'I have a friend, a synagogue knocker. He has some clients in Market Hill, close to the Shadwell Market. He was on his way to visit them early yesterday morning when he saw some carts pass by in the Highway. Each was laden with bales. He thought no more of it until he reached my house. We spoke and he happened to mention the carts to me. I have more knowledge of these matters than my friend and I knew at once that what he was describing were bales of silk. It seems, also, there was a name painted on the side of each cart. Alas, my friend cannot read so could not tell me what it said.'

'The devil take him for a fool,' groaned Sam, burying his face in his hands.

'Later, I was returning from the synagogue when I saw three carts travelling along the Ratcliff Highway.' Emden paused and wiped the back of his hand over his mouth. 'They were empty but I guessed they were the same ones my friend had seen. The name on the sides of the carts was George Andrews. There, I have told you. I pray God that the Mahamad never comes to hear of my transgressions.'

'Anything else?' said Sam, oblivious to the merchant's concerns.

'Nothing,' said Emden.

Sam breathed out, trying to assess the value of the information he'd received. It might be something or it might be nothing. He had two names and a vague location of where the silk might have been seen. The names meant nothing to him and without some knowledge of where the men lived or worked it would need a miracle to find them. And even if he were to succeed, there was no guarantee that they were concerned with the silk.

Forty-five minutes later he turned in through the main entrance of the Wapping police office.

'Mr Pascoe wants to see you, Sam.' Sam turned to see the gaoler walking across the hall towards him. 'He's been calling for you every ten minutes for the last hour.'

'I'll be there directly,' said Sam. 'Did he say what it was about?'

'He reckons he knows where the silk is. He's upstairs with the rest of your crew and some others.'

Sam Hart mounted the stairs three steps at a time and ran along the short corridor to the constables' waiting room where Tom and the others were waiting for him.

'There you are, Sam. I thought we'd lost you. You know everyone here, of course.' Tom's arm swept the room. 'We've got information that a man named Creech may have been involved in the plundering of the *Sisters*. Don't know the cully myself, but Kemp here tells me he frequents the Royal Oak on the south bank and it's possible he may be keeping the silk somewhere on the premises. He's a bit of a handful by all accounts and likely to have some bully boys around him, so we'll be going in mob-handed, just in case. That's why the crews of the upper and lower boats have joined us. When we get there I want to go in hard and fast before anyone has a chance to react. Kemp will grab Creech, assuming he's there, and get him back to one of the galleys. The rest of us will stay behind and search the premises under the authority of a warrant I have here. As you all know, the Royal Oak is a rough place that's likely to turn nasty. For that reason sticks will be carried, as will firearms. All clear?'

A murmur of assent ran round the room.

'Very well, let's go.'

The twelve men from the three patrol galleys filed out of the waiting room and made their way quickly out of the police office, down to the waiting galleys.

Moments later, they had left the pontoon and begun their sweeping turn into the ebb tide, the rays of the late-afternoon sun dancing on the surface of the river. Eight minutes later they were closing on a flight of wooden steps that led up the side of the Royal Oak, on the south bank, their view of the tavern obscured by the choking pall of coal dust that hung above the dozen or so colliers moored close by.

Tom sprang ashore as soon as the boat pulled alongside, Sam,

John Kemp and Jim Higgins following close behind. Then the other two boats swung in, their crews tumbling ashore and racing up the stairs after the others.

'You two take that side door,' whispered Tom, pointing to the last officers ashore and indicating an entrance off the narrow passage. 'The rest of you, follow me.'

Ten seconds later the main door of the tavern crashed open.

'Stand fast in the name of the King,' roared Tom. 'D'you hear there, I'll knock down the first man that moves, so help me.'

For a moment there was absolute silence. From out of the corner of his eye, Tom could see Kemp lumbering towards a fit-looking man of early middle age seated on one of the benches at the far end of the room. He guessed it was Creech. With him were a number of others. They'd risen to their feet as soon as the tavern door had opened and were now fanning out in front of Creech.

'Higgins. Come with me,' said Tom, moving swiftly up behind Kemp. 'Stand aside, lads. Any trouble and you'll find yourselves before the beak so fast your feet will burn.'

'Anything you say, your honour,' said the nearest of the men, a bull-necked, barrel-chested fellow of about thirty-five. He turned away, only to swing back, his balled fist sinking into Kemp's stomach. The waterman constable doubled up and would have fallen but for Tom grasping his arm and steadying him. The man came in again, this time aiming his blow at Tom's face. Tom swayed out of the way before ramming his tipstaff into the other's throat. A strange gargling sound came from the man's mouth, and he fell back, his skull striking the corner of a table, sending jugs of ale clattering to the floor. More men had put down their drinks and were joining the fight. Tom could see Creech standing at the back of the group, his face red with rage.

Tom tried to force his way through. In front of him stood a small, whippet-like man, crouched as if ready to spring, a hard, mirthless smile on his face, his body swaying slowly from side to side. In his right hand was a knife, its blade pointing at Tom's stomach. For a second, nothing happened. It was if the world had stopped, the noise and clatter of combat falling away. Tom's whole mind and being focused on the ice-blue eyes of the man in front of him, waiting for the telltale movements that would give him the split-second advantage he needed. Gabriel Marr's eyes flicked down to Tom's midriff and then up again. It said all that needed to be said. Tom saw the blade coming in, hard and very fast. Judging the moment, he used his left hand to sweep the knife out of harm's way, while his right fist ploughed into Marr's face.

A shout from his right drew Tom's attention. He glanced over. Sam appeared to be surrounded, his fists pounding like the pistons he'd seen on one of the new steamboats on the river. Why his friend was there, he could only guess at. He'd told him to stay out of harm's way. A movement to his front made him turn away. Two men were coming at him. One of them was Marr. The other he didn't know. This time neither man was armed. Before he could act, Kemp was beside him and had lifted Marr, his feet dangling a foot from the floor. A fast jab of the fist from Tom put a stop to the second man's activities.

'Thankee, Kemp. I'm much obliged,' he said. 'Where's Creech?'

'Went through that door, your honour,' said Kemp pointing to a door to one side of the bar. 'Want me to get him?'

'No, stay here and take care of these two. I'll look after Creech.'

Tom forced his way through the mêlée, slipped through the door and found himself in a corridor, off which lay two further doors. A third, at the end of the passage, appeared to lead out onto the river passage. Suddenly, he heard a groan coming from the other side of the nearest door. He pushed at it. Something was in the way, stopping it from opening. He put his shoulder to it. The door moved. Tom drew his pistol and squeezed through the gap.

One of the two waterman constables he'd instructed to enter the tavern by the side door was lying on his back, blood seeping from a wound to his head. The second officer had his back propped up against the left-hand wall. It was his groan that Tom had heard.

'What happened?' said Tom crouching by the man's side.

'Walter and me came in through yon door like what you told us, your honour. When we got in, we see an old hag with a face like . . . begging your pardon, sir. Anygate, she wouldn't let us pass. Told us to go and mind our business. Neither me nor Walter wanted to hurt her so we tried to talk to her. It were then that this cully comes up from nowhere and whacks Walter on the head. Before I knew what had happened, another villain had clobbered me from behind. Then we was dragged in here. I see the two of them drop down through that trapdoor, your honour. Didn't see them no more after that.'

Tom got up and hurried over to the second constable. He was still breathing. Tom removed a clean kerchief from his coat pocket and tore it into several shreds, the first of which he used to wipe away the blood from around the wound. The remaining shreds he used to bind the hurt. Then, leaving him, he walked over to the open trapdoor.

'What did they look like?' he asked the first officer.

'Didn't get a proper look at them, sir. They was always behind us. Only time I saw them were when they dropped down yonder hatch and then it were only their backs what I saw.'

'Pity,' said Tom. 'I could have done with some evidence against that villain, Creech.'

John Harriot stood up from behind his desk and waited for the pain in his thigh to subside before limping over to the fireplace. The warmth helped alleviate the throbbing pain of the old bullet wound he'd sustained in India some years earlier. He looked tired. There were dark circles under his eyes and his grey skin appeared positively unhealthy.

'How are the two men who were attacked?' he asked, turning away from the fire.

'Nothing serious. A bit shaken, but they'll live.'

'Good. Any trace of the silk?'

'No, sir. We searched the tavern, of course, but I don't think it was ever there.'

'I'm not entirely clear why you thought it might be. I seem to remember you considered it probable the silk had been taken with the connivance of the *Sisters'* sailing master. What was his name again?'

'Robert Cox,' said Tom, sensing the whiff of criticism in Harriot's words. 'He's still of interest to me, but he's gone to ground somewhere. No one knows where. In the meantime Creech's name has been mentioned by several people. He's been seen talking to Cox on a number of occasions. On the day the silk was taken from the *Velocity*, Creech was missing from his usual haunts. I think he followed Cox down to the Medway, perhaps to make sure the fellow didn't cheat on him. Either way, I think he's involved.'

'If that were the case, why on earth did they bring the silk all the way back to London?' said Harriot. 'Surely it would have made better sense to offload it on one of the lower reaches.'

'I agree, sir. That's puzzling me too, but the fact of the matter is that the silk *was* brought into the Pool and that's where the transfer took place. Since Creech is known to frequent the Royal Oak and we have no other address for him, it seemed a good starting point.'

'So, what now?' asked the magistrate, turning away from the fire and tucking his hands beneath his coat-tails. 'You cannot have forgotten the seriousness of the situation. We must find those secret documents before anyone else does.'

'If Cox is involved, he will know where the silk is. His home is in Erith. I'm going down there to see what I can find. I've got some people keeping a lookout for Creech and as soon as we find him, he'll have his collar felt. Meanwhile, Sam Hart wants to see me about something. Says he's got a name that's worth following.'

'Very well. Keep me informed, Mr Pascoe. It might help in keeping the Foreign Secretary at bay.'

# CHAPTER 18

Dan Creech threaded his way through the crowded bar of the Harp public house, the air thick with tobacco smoke and the pungent odour of unwashed bodies. Not that he noticed. His hands were trembling and he could feel sweat seeping down his body. What had happened at the Royal Oak was the last thing he'd been expecting. He'd recognised Pascoe as soon as the scrub had barged his way in through the door – him and the other one, the officer Kemp. He knew Pascoe mostly by reputation although he'd also had the misfortune to see him once or twice, albeit from a safe distance. That was enough. The same applied to Kemp. Their paths had crossed several times since Creech had first learned of the existence of a new police.

The sailmaker caught the eye of the pot-boy and ordered a drink. Then he found himself a vacant seat on a bench under one of the windows and sat down. Apart from the Royal Oak, on the Rotherhithe side of the river, the Harp was where he felt most at ease. Here, no one knew who he was. He could come and go as he pleased and folk minded their own business. Yet he still insisted on sitting with his back to the wall and his face to the front door. Only a fool would knowingly hand the advantage to others and allow them to approach unseen.

Someone had talked. Of that Creech was absolutely certain.

He'd taken every precaution to ensure that his involvement with the silk was known only to those most closely involved. But already he was a suspect, to be hunted down and arrested by that unpardonable villain Pascoe. Blind Jack had told him as much, had warned him that Pascoe already knew what had been planned and how it was to be executed. He looked up as the pot-boy placed a mug of Hammond's ale in front of him and held out his hand for payment. Fishing out a coin, he gave it to the boy and returned to his thoughts. If Pascoe had known about the plundering of the *Sisters*, knew who was involved and where they drank, he probably also knew about the yard where they'd hidden the silk. Creech scowled. He'd already considered the possibility that the stranger on the sloop had known of the yard. On that occasion he'd decided to risk leaving the silk where it was. But Pascoe was a different proposition. This time he would have to move it.

A thought drifted into his head. It was something he'd been trying to recall for some time, something Blind Jack had said to him. Creech picked up his drink and swallowed a mouthful. The blind beggar had mentioned a boy recently arrived in London. Pascoe, it seemed, was now responsible for the care of his young brother. He started to his feet, the significance of the information only now apparent to him.

Creech rushed to the door, colliding with a man who was, at that moment, entering the premises.

Sam Hart paced up and down the entrance hall of the Wapping police office. Every so often he would stop and gaze up the stairs leading to Harriot's office on the first floor. He was growing impatient. He'd meant to tell his honour Mr Pascoe about the sighting of some carts in Market Hill sooner. Unfortunately, the raid on the Royal Oak tavern had pushed the thought from his mind. By the time they got back, charged the last of the prisoners and taken them before the court, the sun had sunk below the western horizon and the matter had escaped his mind.

Sam turned towards the stairs and began to climb, stopped, changed his mind and returned to the bottom. He could hardly knock on the magistrate's door and ask to speak to Tom. He would just have to wait. Around him he could sense the stares of the two dozen or so men and women waiting their turn to go into court, his impatient muttering offering some light relief to what was, for everyone else, a stressful wait for the administration of justice.

He looked up at the sound of voices coming from the first floor. Tom was standing in the doorway of Harriot's office, listening to some last comment from the magistrate. A moment later he had closed the door and was coming down the stairs.

'May we speak, sir?' Sam didn't wait for Tom to reach him.

'Why, yes, of course,' said Tom. 'Here?'

'No. Outside.'

Sam led the way out of the police office, to the head of the river stairs. As soon as they got there, he told Tom of his meeting with Jacob Emden and what the merchant had told him about the sighting of the carts in Market Hill, including the name that had been painted on the sides.

'What else did he tell you?' said Tom, looking down at the turbulent waters of an ebb tide, scattered with flotsam.

'That Marr – one of the scrubs what we arrested in the Royal Oak had approached one of Emden's friends with a sample of silk.'

'Did he, now?' mused Tom, tucking his chin into the folds of his coat as a sudden chill wind blew across from the Rotherhithe marsh. 'Might be a coincidence, of course. It might have come from some other depredation altogether, but it doesn't seem likely.'

'It don't seem likely to me neither, sir,' said Sam. 'He's one of Creech's bully boys.'

'True enough,' mused Tom. For a moment longer he continued to stare out over the Thames. 'Did you say the carts were seen in Market Hill?'

'Aye, so I did, sir.'

'Then I think it's time we had a look up there.'

Two men turned right off the Ratcliff Highway into Market Hill and walked down past Shadwell Market, their shoulders hunched against the lashing rain beating a noisy tattoo on the earthen road surface. They moved slowly, hampered by the darkness of the night, their eyes scanning the buildings on either side of the narrow street, searching for anything which might provide the clue they needed.

A cart appeared out of the gloom, travelling in the opposite direction. It was being led by a man, his hand resting on one of the shafts. Milton Brougham let his fingers wind round the hilt of a knife hidden in the waistband of his breeches. He'd not expected to see anyone here. Not at this time of night and not in this weather. The vehicle drew level, its pace momentarily slowing as the driver appeared to see them for the first time. Then it was gone, the rumble of its wheels and the clopping of the horse's hooves drowned by the falling rain.

'This is the place,' said Hawkes, suddenly, his voice muffled by the collar of his coat. He pointed to a pair of dilapidated wooden gates that appeared to have been built between two houses. *Daniel Creech. Master Sailmaker* was dimly visible, painted in large letters across both gates. 'Want me to light the lantern, sir?'

'Not till we get inside,' said Brougham, looking in the direction the cart had taken.

Nearly forty-eight hours had elapsed since he had stood on a quay close to Clink Dock and watched the unlading of a sailing barge with what he hoped were the bales of silk in which he was interested. He'd been far from sure on that point and needed to find out one way or the other as quickly as possible. The stakes could hardly be higher. He stared at the gate and thought back over events.

His escape from Clink Dock had come at a price and by the time he'd been able to return there, the carts and what they carried had gone. He'd spent several fruitless hours searching the area around Clink Dock before giving up and going to the Devil's Tavern for a drink. By late that evening, he was still no closer to discovering the whereabouts of the silk and had retired for the night.

It wasn't until earlier this evening that someone had mentioned that Creech had been seen drinking in the Royal Oak. Brougham had immediately made his way there only to discover that the premises had, in the past hour or so, been raided by Pascoe. Creech, he was told, had probably gone to the Harp, a tavern in the City, not far from the Custom House.

It was luck that finally brought them together. Brougham had arrived at the tavern at the very moment Creech was leaving. The two had collided but if Creech had recognised the American, he gave no sign of it.

Following at a safe distance, Brougham had watched the sail-maker as he made his way east to the Ratcliff Highway, his head constantly turning to look back as though aware he was being trailed. He'd seemed in a hurry, almost as if he were frightened by something, his eyes scouring the people in front and behind him. Brougham had thought it sensible to drop back, leave a greater distance between them.

It was to prove a mistake.

The Highway had been at its blowsy best with barely enough room to move, the stench of cooked onions, spices and stale meat filling the air as Brougham fell further behind. Soon he'd no longer been able to see his quarry and had tried to close the gap which separated them. A young girl – she can hardly have been above twelve or thirteen – had thrust herself in his way, her rouged cheeks like those on a Punch and Judy doll. 'Want a good time, mister?' she'd said, her empty smile not enough to cover her tears. He'd pushed her aside, but the damage had been done. By the time he'd reached the place where he'd last seen Creech, the man had disappeared. It was not until nearly an hour later that he'd again seen the fellow as he emerged from Market Hill and began to retrace his steps towards the City.

It was now well past midnight. Brougham crossed the street and examined the large padlock and chain with which the gate in Market Hill was fastened.

'What d'you reckon, Billy?'

'Should have it open in less than a minute, sir,' said Hawkes, whose nefarious and often colourful life had allowed him to acquire certain skills in the lock-picking department. Withdrawing from his pocket two thin metal rods, each of which had been bent through a right angle close to its tip, he inserted first one and then the other into the padlock and, with a deft twist of the wrist, released the locking mechanism. A minute later, the two men had passed through the gate and closed it behind them.

'You can light the lantern, now,' whispered Brougham.

The oil lamp fired into life, spilling its golden glow onto a passageway about ten feet wide and not more than fifteen feet in length. Apart from some sacking, a few coils of hemp and a spare cartwheel propped against one of the side walls, the passageway was empty.

'Over there,' muttered Brougham, waving down the length of the passage. 'Looks like it might open up a bit.'

Reaching the end of the passageway, they found themselves standing in what appeared to be a yard, perhaps eighty feet square and occupied at one end by a large wooden shed with a shallow-pitched roof.

'See if you can't get us inside, will you, Billy?' said Brougham, gesturing towards a pair of heavy locked doors guarding the entrance to the shed. 'I'm going to see if there's another way out of this place. Just in case we need to leave in a hurry.'

It didn't take Brougham long to find what he was looking for. A door had been set into the back wall of the yard, its timbers rotting from want of attention, its twin bolts rusted firmly into position. It was clear it hadn't been used in a considerable time. He looked round for something with which to loosen the bolts.

To the right of the door, under a crude lean-to shelter, he could see a workbench on which lay a number of large needles, some tarred thread, a wooden mallet and a sheet of canvas, run through with red cotton. Brougham tut-tutted, reasonably sure the presence of the thread meant the canvas had been stolen from a naval dockyard.

He lifted the lantern and continued his search. On a shelf below the bench he found a hammer, partially hidden by a second roll of canvas. He picked it up and walked back to the door where, aiming a blow at the top bolt, he released it from its rusty grip. A second blow to the bottom bolt and that, too, slid back. He stood still for a moment and listened, but no one came. Blowing out the lantern, he inched the door open and peered into the gloom beyond.

In front of him and on the opposite side of a narrow path was what seemed to be the backs of a row of houses, each one of which had a door corresponding to the one at which he was standing. He looked to his left and right but could make out nothing of interest. Quietly he closed the door and returned to the shed where Hawkes was still standing.

'Anything?' said Brougham.

'Not been inside yet, sir. Only just got the lock off.'

Pulling open one of the doors, they entered the large shed, the dim light from Brougham's lantern sufficient to illuminate only a section at a time of the interior. From what he could see, Brougham supposed the place was used as a storeroom of sorts. Shelves along one wall were stacked with rolls of canvas. On a table next to them were a number of open boxes containing bundles of sewing thread. Another box contained spare sewing needles while a third was filled with large scissors.

'You start that side,' said Brougham. 'I'll do over there. We're looking for bales of silk wrapped in brown paper. If you see anything that looks about right, give me a shout.'

# CHAPTER 19

Tom Pascoe didn't hold out much hope of success. Too many hours had passed since Creech had made good his escape from the Royal Oak. If the scrub possessed a grain of intelligence in his head, he'd have cleared out any silk he might have stored in the place. He turned into the Ratcliff Highway and headed east, weaving in and out of the late-night crowds. The pace of the last few days was catching up with him. He'd not rested properly since the beginning of this case. What had started as a vague allegation concerning the possible theft of some anonymous quantity of silk had rapidly assumed the proportions of an international incident with the potential to bring the United States into the war on the French side.

Tom's eyelids began to droop. He breathed deeply and immediately wished he hadn't, his lungs filling with the sharp stench of burning coal from a nearby food stall. There was a part of him that hoped he'd find nothing in Market Hill and could go home for some sleep. He also needed to check on young William and find out how he was settling in to his new school. The issue of the boy's safety troubled him. He knew he'd been guilty of dismissing the reality of life in and around the port. The boy was safe enough while he remained in the schoolroom, but how safe was the brother of Tom Pascoe outside the hours he spent there?

It was common enough. There was hardly a man at the Wapping police office who'd not faced the threat of retribution for acts done in the execution of his duty. Mostly they were idle threats designed to unsettle. But occasionally they would be carried through into acts of violence. He thought of Peggy and of how she must have suffered in the moments before her death for no reason other than a desire for revenge. The thought brought to mind the man responsible. Tom's hatred for him had known no bounds, his desire for revenge all-consuming.

All the more strange that he now regretted the loss of his self-control which had resulted in Dubois' death. In the months that followed the fatal shooting, he'd often lain awake thinking about the circumstances of that morning, wondering if there had been some other course of action he could have taken. Certainly he had drawn no satisfaction from his actions. They had not brought Peggy back.

At the junction with Market Hill, Tom and the others turned south, the road empty, silent and dismal, a stark contrast to the highway he was leaving. Soon he'd passed through a deserted Shadwell Market, his nostrils filled with the lingering smell of slaughtered meat. The lane was narrow, the houses on either side small and decrepit, the paint long since stripped from their windows and doors, the foul stench of human waste hanging like some unwelcome haze in the public space through which he must pass. Tom walked on, trying to limit his breathing, his eyes searching for anything that might suggest the presence of a yard.

He and Sam saw the partially open gate at the same moment. It looked as though someone had forgotten to lock it, a chink so slight that Tom had very nearly missed seeing it. He waved Sam, Kemp and Higgins into the shadow of an adjacent building.

'Looks like Creech has beaten us to it, sir,' said Sam.

'Aye, you could have the right of it, Sam,' said Tom. 'He's had plenty of time to get here and clear the place out. Even so, I reckon he'd have locked up after himself.'

'Someone else, sir?' asked Sam. 'You think they could still be here?'

'It's possible. I'm going to assume they are.' Tom looked up and down the street. Twenty yards further on he spotted what looked like the entrance to a path. 'You see that gap between the houses, Kemp? Get yourself down there. I reckon the path goes up the back of this lot. If it does, I'll warrant there's another entrance to this yard. Find it and stay there. We'll give you a minute and then the rest of us will go in through the front gate.'

They stood silently, alert to every noise, while Kemp vanished behind the buildings.

'Ready?' said Tom, barely a minute later. 'Follow me.'

Hawkes was the first to hear a soft scraping noise, like that of a sagging gate being pushed open. He touched Brougham's shoulder and pointed. Brougham nodded and, beckoning Hawkes to follow, crept to the door at the back of the yard. Easing it open, he peered into the alley.

'Someone's there,' he whispered, drawing back into the yard and closing the door.

He ran to the shed and climbed onto one of the tar barrels he'd seen stacked on one side of the double doors. Gripping the edge of the roof, he hauled himself up and lay down on the shallow pitch. From here, he could see the front gate. It was being pushed open. A moment later the dim outline of a man appeared, followed by a second and then a third. Once inside, they stopped as if waiting for some signal. A moment of silence passed. Then he caught the sound of a low whistle coming from the direction of the passage door. He looked back at the men by the front gate. They had started moving towards the main part of the yard. In a few seconds they would round the corner and be able to see the shed with its doors wide open.

'They're coming,' he whispered. 'Get up here. Quick.'

'I'm trying to.' There was panic in Hawkes's voice. 'I can't get ahold of anything. Got grease on me hands.'

Brougham looked up. The strangers were rounding the corner into the main part of the yard. He reached for his pistol. If someone had to die he'd prefer it if it wasn't him or Hawkes. He'd worry about the political fallout later. He glanced down. Hawkes had made it onto the first barrel and was trying to keep his balance as it rocked from side to side.

Brougham felt his heart beating painfully against the wall of his chest. Another few seconds and the newcomers would reach the shed. Brougham drew back the hammer of his pistol and aimed it at the leading figure. Who he was and what he looked like, Brougham couldn't see. Nor did he much care. Thieves were thieves whichever side of the Atlantic they came from and these three were no different to any he'd seen before. He felt, rather than saw, Hawkes drop down beside him, his breathing seemingly loud enough to wake the neighbourhood.

'Start with the shed. You know what to look for.' The English voice was crisp, sharp and confident. Its tone caught Brougham by surprise. If he had expected anything at all, it certainly had not been the voice of authority. He risked peering over the edge of the roof. He could see little beyond the blur of an outline in the yard below.

A lamp flared into life. Brougham ducked out of sight and listened to the sounds of movement as the strangers entered the shed. It sounded as if benches were being dragged across the dirt floor and the contents of the shelves moved around. Now and again, something would fall to the ground with a crash and be followed by a muttered oath. Then one of the strangers emerged from inside the shed, carrying a lamp, the light falling on a wide, rugged face, a scar running down its right side.

Brougham stared. The face meant nothing. If they had ever met, he could not now remember. What had caught his attention was the man's dress. Old and heavily soiled though it was, there could be no mistaking the blue coat with its broad white lapels or the double row of brass buttons that ran down the front. He lowered the hammer of his gun. They were both men of the sea.

Hawkes look inquiringly at him. 'Recognise him?' he whispered.

Brougham shook his head.

'Tom Pascoe,' said Hawkes. 'I told you about him. He's with the marine police. Used to be in the British Navy. Master and commander, from what I hear.'

'So that's him,' breathed Brougham. 'The guy we got to beat.'

He dropped his head out of sight as two other men came out of the shed and stood next to Pascoe.

'It ain't in the shed, sir. Me and Higgins is sure of that,' said the smaller of the two.

'Thankee, Sam. If it was going to be anywhere, it would've been in there,' said Pascoe. 'It wouldn't have made sense to hide something like silk where the rain could get to it. The question is, if it isn't here, then who's got it?'

'Cox, maybe?' said Sam.

'Not sure about him,' said Pascoe. 'If he's involved, he and Creech would have to find another boat to get the stuff down to his place in Erith. On top of that, Creech and his friends need a buyer and they won't find one down where Cox lives. No, I reckon it's still somewhere in London. Come, it's time we left. We'll start again in the morning.'

Brougham watched the men walk out of the yard, closing the gates behind them. He lay in silence for a minute or two, waiting for his heart-beat to slow, glad he'd not had to shoot. He might not like the British but that didn't mean he wanted to kill them, more especially a fellow seaman.

'That cart that passed us in Market Hill, sir,' Hawkes's voice drifted into his consciousness.

'Aye, what about it?' snapped Brougham, unwilling to be dragged back from his thoughts.

'You don't suppose it could've been Creech or one of his bully boys?'

Brougham's eyes widened. 'What makes you say that?'

'Just a feeling. There was nothing else moving in the street. There was a name on the side. I could only read part of it. The rest was hidden by a sack.'

'What was the name?'

'Andrews.'

*

The house stood alone, its front door facing out onto the little-used lane that ran north out of Bow. Its nearest neighbours were about a quarter of a mile away but might as well have been in the next county for all the single occupant of the house had to do with them. The old lady rarely went out except for the purpose of buying the few provisions she needed to keep body and soul together. She preferred watching the geese that swam in the River Lea, a few yards from the back of her house. The less she had to do with the rest of the world, the better.

The presence, therefore, of a horse and cart outside her front door was not only a source of irritation but – and she wasn't sure which she disliked more – was also likely to rouse the interest of anyone passing along the heavily pitted lane. Such passers-by would remember the other occasions in the last twelve hours that the same cart had made a similar appearance. And they might have remarked on the quantity of bales that had been offloaded on each of those occasions.

Mrs Josephine Gott was not best pleased at the interruption of her day, even though her visitor was there at the express invitation of her son, Joe. Nor was it just the interruption that she objected to. She had taken an instant dislike to the driver of the cart with his cold, empty eyes and mirthless smile. The cant scrub – Mrs Gott had a tendency to say what she meant – the cant scrub had begun offloading the bales into her barn yesterday afternoon. It was now late morning as she watched the last of the load disappearing into what was otherwise a cavernous empty space. A day – two days at most – the driver of the cart had said, and then it would be gone. She would, she thought, believe that when it happened. It had been the same with her late husband.

He, too, had brought home all manner of things that he'd no business having in the first place. It was a wonder that he'd survived long enough to die in his own bed rather than dancing at the end of a rope, as she'd expected. It worried her that her son was going the same way and wouldn't be so lucky.

'I'll be leaving you, missus,' said Creech, touching his hat and turning away. 'Don't you worry about a thing, now. Me and the boys will be back for them bales before you know what's what.'

Mrs Gott leaned heavily on her stick and walked back into the house, an unpleasant churning sensation in the pit of her stomach that she couldn't altogether explain. There was no doubt in her mind that the bales now residing in her barn should not be there. Long exposure to her late husband's thieving ways convinced her that they meant trouble. But it was what was below her floorboards that was really worrying her. She felt helpless. If she spoke to anyone about it, she would risk her son's life. Her face softened. Joe had promised to come by before nightfall. He would take care of it. He was the one joy of her life.

# CHAPTER 20

Sam Hart was a few minutes late reaching the police office. There had been something about the raid on Dan Creech's yard in Market Hill which was puzzling him, a feeling that they had been watched the whole time they were there. It was impossible, of course. They had searched every inch of the yard. Yet still the feeling persisted. He tried to rationalise it. Both the main gates and the doors to the shed had been unlocked. So, too, was the gate into the back passage. It was as though someone had either left in a hurry or had still been on the premises when it had been raided.

The principal suspect had to be Creech himself. He, above all others, would have known the police would come looking for him and would have wanted to remove any evidence of his involvement in the plundering of the silk. But he wasn't the only one thought to be involved in the theft. Others in his group of bully boys could equally well have removed the bales. Sam ran through the names of Creech's known associates. Marr was still in custody and could safely be ruled out. Then there was Gott, of course. And finally, there was Cox, the sailing master of the *Sisters*. It was strange that no one had seen or heard of him since the night the hoy had been plundered.

Sam rubbed the tiredness from his eyes. He was finding it

difficult to think. He should have gone to bed when he had the chance. Instead, when he and the others had got back to Wapping after the raid, he'd taken it into his head to go and see Jacob Emden to find out if the merchant was able to add anything to the story of the three carts. And if, in the process, Sam should happen to see Adina, then so much the better.

He felt his cheeks redden. He'd been able to think of little else since meeting her. He knew he wasn't being sensible. Nothing could ever come of the meeting. He'd tried to forget her, but couldn't. Worse, he suspected her father knew how he felt. There had been a curious look in the old man's eye when Sam had called.

He walked in through the main door of the police office and turned towards the stairs. Mr Pascoe would be waiting to begin his briefing at the start of the late-turn patrol.

'Sam.' It was the gaoler calling. 'Best you get yourself up them stairs to Mr Harriot's room as quick as you like.'

'Mr Harriot?' Sam's face paled. 'What's he want me for?'

'Everybody's in there: the crews of the upper and lower boats, the supervision boat and even the waterside officer as well as the night duty crews what've been recalled. There's a big flap on.'

'What's happened?'

'It's on account of his honour, Mr Pascoe's young brother. He's disappeared. They reckon he's been taken. Kidnapped, like.'

Tom stood next to Harriot, his face grey, his eyes red-rimmed and exhausted. He'd not been to bed. He had discovered his brother's absence as soon as he walked in to his room on Burr Street. Now, he looked up at the sound of the door opening and saw Sam sidle in and take his place in the corner. Harriot's office was crowded. There were at least twenty present, men squashed up against the large mahogany desk, others perched on the windowsills or leaning against the sideboard.

The magistrate was speaking. Tom could hear the words but they meant nothing to him; disjointed sounds that had no relevance for him. He was thinking of what had happened. He remembered walking home from the police office and turning into Burr Street just as the first light of the new day was filling the sky. It had been quiet. The sort of quietness that will sometimes make the hairs on the back of the neck rise in anticipation of an unwelcome event.

He didn't notice the sou'wester lying on the front steps of the house in which he lived. That came later. It was a filthy, sweat-stained specimen that was at once common among the thousands of river workers and fishermen of the Thames and yet oddly distinctive.

He had passed it by, going in through the front door and climbing the wooden staircase that led to his room. He could still hear the hollow echo of his footsteps as he dragged his tired feet one tread at a time. The first real sign that all was not well had come with the sight of the door to his room standing open. He'd felt his stomach turn over and he'd run the last few feet to the threshold.

When the first rush of fear had come and gone, he had begun to hope the boy had simply gone out for a walk as he had done in the past. He couldn't blame him, much as he might have wished otherwise. The lad had been cooped up for days, from late afternoon onwards.

But then he noticed the boy's trunk had gone from its place by the door. He'd stared at the empty space in disbelief. Could he have decided to return home? There had been that brush with Blind Jack that had so terrified the boy and which had resulted in Tom shouting at him. It was possible that that might have prompted him to flee of his own accord. It didn't seem likely but he would have to check the stage post in Fleet Street.

He had gone back down to the street. A woman – Tom couldn't recall her name – a neighbour who occupied the room opposite his own, had come out onto the landing and spoken to him. She had heard a commotion coming from Tom's room during the night but had thought no more about it. Seeing him now, she wondered if all was well. Tom had thanked her and run down into the street.

It was then that he'd seen the hat lying to one side of the front steps.

Even then, it had meant nothing to him beyond an odd sense of its familiarity and a feeling that it might somehow have some connection with what had happened to William. It was, he knew, a foolish thought, one born out of desperation for some explanation of what might have occurred. And yet . . .

'Oh, sir, I do believe that sou'wester belongs to me husband.' The voice had come from somewhere behind him. Tom had turned to see a young woman, her hand held out, her fingers stretched towards him. She was smiling.

'What . . . ?' Tom had looked from the woman to the hat in his hands, and back again.

'He lost it on his way to work,' offered the woman. 'He sent word for me to find it. He reckons he must have dropped it.'

He had watched her walk away, the hat dangling from one hand and he'd wished he'd thought to question her, find out who she was and where she lived. But he'd given it to her without another word, unable to think of a single reason why he should refuse.

Harriot was still speaking, the magistrate's voice clearer now. '. . . it was only then that one of Mr Pascoe's neighbours stated that she had seen two men carrying something from the house before putting it into a cart waiting outside. No description of either man is presently available, but I think we can assume the bundle they were carrying was young William Pascoe. I think we have to accept that the boy has been kidnapped, possibly for reasons connected with Mr Pascoe's work as an officer of this court. Needless to say, we need to find the lad quickly. I will be briefing the surveyors on our course of action in more detail. They, together with Hart, are to remain behind. The rest of you are to wait downstairs.'

Sam stood aside while the men exited the room leaving him with Harriot, Tom and the other five river surveyors who'd been called in.

'I've asked you to stay behind, Hart, because of your close involvement in the investigation into the theft of the silk from a hoy in the Upper Pool. There is a suspicion that one or more of the men involved in that case might have been responsible for this kidnapping. At the same time, it is important that we don't overlook the possibility that William was taken by someone else of whom we know nothing.'

Sam nodded, but said nothing.

'Am I right in thinking that it was as a result of your information that Mr Pascoe learned of the location of the yard that you raided last night?'

'Yes, sir,' said Sam, looking uncomfortable with his sudden status as the centre of attention.

'Your informant indicated that he'd seen three fully laden carts in Market Hill on the night the *Sisters* was plundered. Yes?'

'Yes, sir. That is, no, sir. It were a friend of my informant what saw the carts.'

'But was your informant able to give you a description of the men in the carts?'

'No, sir. He weren't. But he told me they all had the name of their owner painted on the sides. The name were George Andrews.'

'Has the man been spoken to?' said Harriot.

'So far we've been unable to find him,' said Tom, interrupting. 'But inquiries continue.'

'What about the man you've got in the cells? Marr, isn't it? What's he got to say about any of this?'

'He's refusing to speak, sir,' said Tom, his voice flat and barely audible. 'If Creech is involved in taking my brother, I don't think Marr will know anything about it. Creech would not have taken this step before he knew we were looking for him. If that's the case, he wouldn't have had the opportunity to speak to the man in the cells.'

'No, I suppose you're right, Mr Pascoe. What about other suspects? Do you have anyone in mind? Someone with a grudge against you?'

'That probably covers half the lumpers and coal-heavers in the port,' said Tom, a weak smile crossing his lips.

For a moment or two there was an embarrassed silence in the room.

'Your worship?'

'Yes, Hart, what is it?' said Harriot, turning to look at him expectantly.

'It's just a thought, your worship, but ain't there some talk of some secret documents what's hidden in the silk?'

'What's your point, Hart?' said Harriot, a hint of impatience creeping into his voice.

'Well, sir, Mr Pascoe were saying there's talk of foreign agents what's looking for the documents. If I were them and I knew Mr Pascoe were looking for the same thing, I'd want to give him something else to think about, if you get my drift, sir.'

'It's a possibility,' said Harriot, lacing his fingers behind his head and leaning back in his chair. 'The Foreign Office seems to think it likely that the French know about the document and either they or the Americans might already be here and be intent on finding the papers before we do. What are you suggesting we should do about it, Hart?'

'Let me talk to the prisoner what's in the cells, your worship. He won't know about the secret papers but if there's anyone what's been showing an interest in the silk, he'll know. My guess is that them foreign agents will have been asking questions and might even have been following Creech and the others. You can't do that without half the villains in London knowing what you're up to. It'll give us something to go on, sir . . .' Sam's voice trailed away as he remembered where he was and the seniority of his audience.

'Do that, Hart, and let me know how you get on,' said Harriot.

'In the meantime I don't want us to lose sight of Creech. I want you, Mr Pascoe, to pay a visit to the Royal Oak. See the landlord. He could well have information on the fellow's present whereabouts or that of other members of his gang of rogues. The sooner we find him, the sooner we might be able to get your brother home.'

Harriot turned his attention to the other river surveyors in the room, giving each of them responsibility for a specific area in which to search for the missing boy. It was a sombre group that left his room half an hour later, none of them in any doubt about the likelihood of finding the boy alive.

Few things in life bothered Joe Gott. His philosophy – if such a term could be used to grace his general outlook – was based on the idea that so long as you weren't caught, you could do what you liked. He had grown up in a time when his misdeeds seldom, if ever, came to the notice of the law. The threat of the gallows or a lifetime of servitude in a far-off land were distant prospects that had rarely troubled his mind.

But things had changed of late and the old certainties could no longer be relied upon. He had, it was true, been late in coming to this conclusion, remaining oblivious to the risks of his freewheeling violence and acts of criminality. But even he had baulked at the idea of what he'd been told to do. The risk had seemed a step too far, the consequences too severe to contemplate.

He, like most men of his acquaintance, was only too well aware of Tom Pascoe's reputation for doling out summary justice. It made no difference to Gott that Pascoe's victims might have richly deserved their fate. Or that the officer was also known for his honesty and compassion. So far as Gott was concerned it seemed foolhardy in the extreme for anyone to go out of his way to invite such a man's attention.

But that was exactly what he had done.

He walked past the few cottages and the church that together made up the village of Bow and turned left onto the lane that led past his mother's house to the waterworks beyond. His mother was someone else he wasn't looking forward to meeting. She'd made her views perfectly plain when he'd arrived at the house on the previous day and told her of the intention to store some bales in her barn. He'd not told her what they were or why it was necessary to keep the stuff out of sight where they'd not be seen by strangers. There didn't seem to be any point. It would only have made her even more cantankerous than usual.

Gott had gone along with the idea of using her house, principally because he'd had no say in the matter. Only with the passage of time had it begun to dawn on him that using his mother's house to hide stolen property would, if it were found, result in his and his mother's arrest, rather than Creech's. And the more he thought about the whole business, the more nervous he became. He had recently become convinced that Creech was planning the alibi he might eventually need to escape the clutches of the law, an alibi that did not include Joseph Michael Gott or his mother or, indeed, Marr. It wouldn't be the first time that villainous scrub had sought to sidestep the consequences of his actions and leave someone else to take the blame. Gott wasn't even sure Creech had been telling him the truth when he'd announced that he'd found a buyer for the silk.

Gott stopped and gazed out over the River Lea to the desolate sight of the marshlands beyond. Few went that way, except perhaps the two or three hundred armed men, their mules laden with contraband, who regularly came up from the Essex coast in the dead of night. There were times when he wished he could join them, their lives seemingly less complicated, less burdened with the troubles that beset him. He wasn't sure how much more he could take of his own existence.

# CHAPTER 21

Sam Hart walked down the steps to the cells below the police office. It was always damp down there. The spring tides would often creep in below the overhanging building and lap against the cell walls. Often the smell of dampness would be added to by the stench of a rotting carcass deposited on the foreshore by the falling tide or by the presence of a cadaver awaiting identification. But the smell was far from Sam's mind as he opened the small wicket gate in the cell door and peered in.

'Wake up, Marr,' he said, unlocking the door and walking in. 'I want to talk to you about some silk.'

'Don't know nothing about no silk.' Marr rolled over on his iron cot and faced the wall.

'No, of course you don't. That's why you were seen on a hoy in the middle of the tideway, moving bales of the stuff onto a barge what was fetched alongside.'

'You're lying.' Marr swung back to face him. 'You ain't seen nothing.'

Sam smiled. It was true he'd seen nothing but the shadowy outline of two vessels anchored in the middle of the river. But he was not about to admit it. To do so would spell an abrupt end to the interview and nothing to show for it.

'You sure about that?' he said. 'How else would I know what

happened? I saw you cut the *Sisters* adrift and then you and the others took your barge upriver. That's where you unladed the silk onto some carts what belonged to a cully called George Andrews. Sound familiar? Of course it does. We've got enough evidence to hang you, Marr.'

Sam waited for his words to sink in before going on. 'It don't have to be that way. I know none of this was your doing. It were Creech what told you to do it. I want you to tell me about him and the other men what were involved in the depredations.'

'What other men? I ain't got a clue what you're talking about.'

'Let's start with the name Gott. Or Cox? What about the men who followed you and Creech and Gott down to the Medway? Mates of yours, were they?'

Marr's eyes widened a fraction.

'No, I didn't think so. Want to tell me about them?'

'He's a dead man; him and his mate. He—'

'Seen him before, have you?'

Marr stared at the opposite wall of the cell, his mouth twisted in silent rage. 'It were the sloop what we saw first. It were off Custom House Quay. We thought it were the revenue but then it were gone. Disappeared, like.'

'But you saw it again?'

'I ain't saying no more, Mr Hart.'

'Please yourself, mate. You ain't going anywhere, aside from the Old Bailey. And Creech won't be far behind you. But the others? The cullies what followed you? Why, it wouldn't surprise me if they didn't take all the silk for themselves. Is that what you want?'

Again, Marr stared at the wall of the cell. Once or twice he opened his mouth as if about to say something and then appeared to change his mind. Sam waited. Silence was sometimes a powerful weapon. Sooner or later, Marr would want to fill the vacuum.

'He were watching us at Clink Dock,' said Marr, his face impassive. 'Me and some of the boys tried to catch him, but he were too quick.'

'Too quick?'

'Aye, well,' said Marr, his fingers touching a bruise on the side of his face that Sam had not previously noticed. 'He were just lucky.'

The questioning went on, but it was clear Marr had said all he was going to say, his answers increasingly monosyllabic and morose as if contemplating the probable outcome of an appearance at the Old Bailey.

Sam left him, disappointed at the outcome. He had hoped to learn something about the occupants of the sloop: who they were, what their interest was in the silk. Mr Pascoe had mentioned the possibility of others being involved in the search for the silk for reasons far removed from the intrinsic value of the bales themselves. He wondered if their presence at Clink Dock meant they were at least one step ahead of Tom and might yet win this particular race.

Tom was standing by the first-floor window of Harriot's office, looking down at the crew of a patrol galley busily lifting something out of the water. It was one of those rare autumnal mornings when the sun shone out of a clear blue sky, the light reflecting off the surface of the river, blinding in its intensity. The crew on the pontoon stood back a little and Tom was able to see the shape of an adult human being, the skin of its bloated face a black and grey mottle. He turned away from the window.

'When, sir, did this arrive?' he said, holding out a torn scrap of paper that Harriot had given him.

'About an hour ago. I'm told it was handed to Hart by a young urchin,' said Harriot. 'But because it was addressed to you, he didn't read it and by the time anyone did so, the child had gone. He probably wouldn't have been able to tell us a great deal anyway.'

Tom looked down at the paper and read it again. *Your brother is safe. If you want to see him again, stop looking for the silk.* He felt sick, emotionally drained, blaming himself for what had happened. He thought of his mother and how she would take the news. He had to think. The reference to the silk probably meant he could ignore all the other cases he'd had dealings with in the last twelve months. He could assume whoever had taken the boy was also involved with the silk.

'. . . it's probably best if I take you off the case.' Tom struggled to listen to what Harriot was saying to him. He tried to concentrate, to put thoughts of William to one side, and listen to what the magistrate was saying. 'Go home and get some rest. You're in no state to deal with this.'

'I can't stop, sir, not while my brother is still out there,' said Tom, suddenly animated. 'Whoever's got him is involved in some way with the silk inquiry. Even if you take me off the case and send me home, I shall continue to search for him and, in the process, continue to work on the case.'

'Every man I've got is looking for your brother. All normal patrols have been suspended for this week in an effort to solve the matter,' said Harriot. 'Do you think you can add anything? You've barely slept for days and this inquiry needs a clear head.'

'I've been longer without sleep,' said Tom, thinking of his days at sea. 'As for whether I can add anything to the inquiry, there is no one who knows more about this case than me, no one who is more likely to see the relevance of a detail than me.'

'Very well,' said the magistrate. 'If you think you can add something. Where will you start?'

'Blind Jack,' said a relieved Tom. 'He knows more than most sighted men about what's going on.'

A pall of soot-filled smoke hung low over the streets north of the Thames as Milton Brougham turned in through the entrance of the Harp public house. A day had passed since he and Hawkes had searched the yard in Market Hill; a day in which the two of them had visited every drinking house in the port in their search for the man named Andrews. If anyone knew, he wasn't saying, and Brougham was beginning to wonder if there wasn't a quicker way of finding the silk skeins and the documents they were supposed to contain.

The talk in the port was all about Pascoe and his search for his brother. The officer was tearing everything apart in his efforts to find him. It didn't surprise Brougham. He'd do the same. What did surprise him was that Pascoe was continuing to ask questions about the stolen silk. It wasn't at all what the American had expected. The boy's disappearance should have kept the officer off the case, left Brougham a clear run at the silk and the documents hidden there unless . . . Brougham paused as a thought struck him. Unless whoever had taken the boy had also taken the silk.

It was the only explanation that made sense. The problem was that Pascoe's activities were making it more difficult for Brougham to perform his own task. He'd already been called to the American embassy where the minister had made clear his concern. 'The situation in France is extremely volatile,' Rufus King had said to him. 'The ruling Directoire is said to be in a sorry state and unable to form an effective administration. If the British see that missing report they'll know we and the French have been talking. It could lead to serious difficulties between us, particularly given the anti-British sentiments back home.'

There had not been much that Brougham could say. Creech had gone to ground and taken the silk with him. Of the others thought to be involved, Gott was also missing while Marr was in custody. A fourth man, Robert Cox, had not been seen since the night of the attack on the *Sisters*.

Brougham called over the pot-boy and ordered drinks for himself and Hawkes. The bar was unusually quiet. At the next bench a group of porters from the fish market on Upper Thames Street were in unusually high spirits. Over by the main door, another, smaller, crowd was gathered round the entrance of one of the booths. No one appeared the least interested in the presence of the two Americans.

A sudden loud smack of a cane striking the surface of the deal table at which they were sitting made Brougham start. He looked up to see a man standing close behind him, his head turned towards the ceiling, a foul stench pervading the air around him, his clothing notable only for its filthy and ragged state.

'Well, if it ain't our Yankee cousins,' said the man. 'Blind Jack

188

at your service. Going to buy me a drink, is you? I'm much obliged, I'm sure. I'll have a Hammond's, same as what you've got.'

Brougham looked round the room, weighing up the wisdom of telling the man to lose himself. Several men had turned and were looking in his direction. Much as he favoured his initial thoughts on ridding himself of his unwelcome visitor, he knew it was likely to prove counterproductive.

'A drink it shall be,' he said. 'Now what else can I do for you?'

Jacob Emden left his house on Aldgate and hailed a passing hackney cab. It was late evening and he was lucky to find one so quickly. Before long he was moving swiftly along Houndsditch, the rhythmic beat of the horse's hooves accompanied by the encouraging crack of the driver's whip. Soon, the carriage had turned into Bishopsgate Street and, shortly thereafter, come to a halt outside Henry's Coffee House, an anonymous narrow-fronted, red-brick building at which the Jew was often to be found. Usually he would be surrounded by friends and business associates at the same table on the ground floor, and the conversation would be laced with references to the price and availability of various commodities in which there was an interest. Emden had always found it an enjoyable and profitable way to spend an evening. But tonight, he climbed the stairs to the first floor where there were a number of small rooms available for those who wished to conduct their affairs in private.

He was nervous at the prospect of what lay ahead. He'd given the matter some thought and while the risks were considerable, he'd considered them worthwhile. At least, he had at the time. Now he was no longer quite so sure. He reached into his coat pocket, drew out a handkerchief and wiped away the perspiration gathering on his brow. He had committed himself to a course of action. But that didn't make it any easier now that the time for its execution had arrived.

The door to the room he'd hired for the meeting was the second on the left. He opened it and went in. It was bare but for the presence of a small circular table and a few chairs. A single candle had been lit and stood on the table. Emden consulted his pocket watch and sat down. He was a little early. He turned his mind to the purpose of his visit, ticking off the list of hurdles that would need to be overcome, and considering the rewards against the consequences of failure. It didn't look good. He thought of walking away, sighed and remained where he was. Taking risks for the sake of a profit was what he'd spent his life doing. This was what had made him wealthy. It was in his blood.

He looked up as the doorknob rattled and Creech walked in. Emden did not get up, the muscles in his legs refusing to obey him. He managed a half-smile and waved Creech to the chair opposite.

'You got the money?' Creech was staring at him with cold, expressionless eyes.

'It's safe. Where's the merchandise?'

'I'll see the money first.'

'The price is too high.' Emden shrugged apologetically. 'I have expenses. There are risks. I have people to pay. If the quality of the goods is right, I'll give you fourteen shillings a pound.'

'Don't waste my time, mister. The price is twenty shillings,' said Creech. 'If you don't want to pay, there are others who will.'

'Come, my friend. Is it not written on your face that you have no one else who will trade with you? We both know where the merchandise comes from. For every hour that you delay, the risk to your neck increases. I have already had the officer asking questions of me.'

'What?' Creech's face paled. 'Who've you been talking to?'

'I told you. The officer. He came to see me from the Wapping police office.'

Creech moved with surprising speed, leaping to his feet and drawing a knife from his belt. He caught hold of Emden by his blouse, the knife blade to his throat. 'What did you tell him, Jew boy?'

'Nothing. Upon the life of my child, I swear it,' said Emden, his eyes wide with shock.

Creech let go and strode to the window overlooking the street, his head turning from side to side as though searching for any indication he'd been betrayed. Finally, he turned and walked back to where Emden was still sitting. 'Be outside St Mary's Church, Bow, tomorrow night at eight o'clock with the money.'

With that, he was gone.

# CHAPTER 22

She was waiting for him when he returned to the police office, sitting amongst the rogues and vagabonds in the entrance hall, her head bent forward, her eyes staring at her feet. She had, according to the gaoler, been there since early morning refusing to talk to anyone but his honour, Mr Pascoe.

'I were told you would help me, sir,' she said, when he'd gone out and introduced himself. Her voice had no strength to it, her head stretched forward as though to help her cause. She had the appearance of someone in the final stages of exhaustion, her sunken eyes pleading for help. 'It's about me husband, Rob – Robert Cox.'

'I regret it extremely, Mrs Cox,' said Tom, gently, 'but no one has seen your husband for several days. We know he reached London. But nothing since then. Do I understand from what you've told me that he didn't return home from his trip to Stangate Creek?'

'No, he didn't. He's never been away from me this long. Something must have happened to him.'

She began to cry.

Tom steeled himself. He had little experience of women and those of whom he did tended to hide their unhappiness if for no other reason than the adverse effect it usually had on their earnings. He wondered if it was sensible to rely on what the woman was saying. If her husband was involved in the plunder of the silk, then would she not make every effort to throw his pursuers off the scent?

'You live in Erith, I believe. How did you travel here?'

'A friend of my husband's brought me up. He returns to Erith tomorrow.'

'What of your children? Are they with you?'

'No, it were not possible. I left them with a neighbour. We've not eaten for three days, Master Pascoe. We eat when my husband brings home the few pennies he earns as a sailing master. Otherwise we go in want.'

There were times when Tom hated the work he did. The woman was telling him the truth. He felt it in the core of his being. Yet he knew that was never going to be good enough. Sooner or later, someone was going to have to go down to Erith and search this woman's house – for her husband, for the silk, for whatever might be there. Suddenly, he realised that neither he nor anyone else at the police office had ever seen Cox; would be unable to recognise him if he were to walk past in the street.

'What was your husband wearing when you last saw him?' he asked.

'What he always wore, Master Pascoe. Long canvas coat, boots and a sou'wester.'

'Anything distinctive?'

'Can't say as he did.' Mrs Cox thought for a while. 'Only his rosary. He never went anywhere without that in his pocket.'

Tom's eyes widened a fraction as he remembered something. 'Wait here, Mrs Cox, will you?'

He left her and went through to the gaoler's office. There, in one of the drawers, he found what he was looking for. It was a rosary. He bit his lip, remembering the floater he'd seen being dragged up onto the pontoon. There had been nothing by which to identify the body, only this object he held in his hand.

'Is this your husband's rosary?' he asked, when he'd rejoined her.

She took it from him, her hands trembling, hope flooding her eyes. 'Is my husband here, sir? Can I see him? What's he done wrong? I'll kill him when I gets him home.'

'Mrs Cox . . .' The woman's head jerked up as if she recognised something in the tone of Tom's voice. 'Are you quite sure that rosary belongs to your husband?'

'Aye, it's my husband's right enough. You can see where the crucifix has been bent. He did that a year or so ago when he fell down the ladder into his cabin.' She avoided Tom's eyes, her fingers gently caressing the olive-wood beads. He could hear her breathing quicken.

'Will you come with me, Mrs Cox?' said Tom. He led her through a door to the gaoler's office where he turned to face her.

'He's dead, ain't he?' she whispered, not waiting for him to speak, the blood draining from her face, her hands leaping to her mouth. 'My Rob's gone, ain't he?'

'I can't be absolutely sure. I need you to confirm that for me. Will you do that? Will you come and see him?'

The woman began to shake violently. She reached out a

hand and supported herself against the wall as her eyes met Tom's. She shook her head. 'What am I to do, Mr Pascoe? I got two little girls at home what's expecting to see their father. But he ain't coming home. How's we going to live with no food in the house and no hope of none, neither? Tell me that, Mr Pascoe.'

She said nothing for a minute or two, her long, heaving sobs seeming to reach up from deep inside her. Gradually, they faded away and she sat down on one of the nearby chairs. 'What happened to him, sir?'

'Shall we see him first? It's best we make sure.'

Tom led the way out of the building and down a flight of stairs to the basement where they turned towards the river and descended the few steps to the foreshore. The body lay on the shingle, below the overhang of the police office, covered by a canvas sheet.

'Are you ready?' asked Tom, doing his best to ignore the stench of death.

Mrs Cox nodded, her hands again in front of her mouth. She moved closer as Tom folded back the body sheet. The face of the cadaver was turned to one side, its bluish-black skin sunk around the jawline, its teeth protruding beyond the shrunken lips. She gasped and shrank back from the sight, the sleeve of her dress covering her nose.

'Is this your husband, Mrs Cox?'

She nodded mutely, her eyes fixed on her dead husband's face. 'What happened to him? How did he die, sir?'

'I'm not certain,' said Tom, leading her back towards the police office. 'All I can tell you is that he was sent to collect a cargo of silk from the Medway for delivery to a merchant here, in London. I know he got back to London and, at that time, the cargo was still in his hold. At some point during that night the silk was stolen and your husband disappeared. His body was found yesterday by a police patrol and brought here. I'm so very sorry for your loss.'

She looked back over her shoulder at the shape beneath the canvas cover, her eyes wet with tears. Then she followed Tom up the steps from the foreshore.

'Did your husband ever say anything to you which might explain what happened to him?'

'What can you mean? Was his death not an accident?'

Tom hesitated. The woman had clearly not seen the injuries her husband had suffered about his face and neck. He could only speculate that Cox had, shortly after his beating, been tossed into the Thames, where he had died. 'I don't yet know,' he replied. 'I'm trying to find out. Did he say anything to you? Was he worried about something?'

She thought for a while.

'He were in debt, Mr Pascoe. He told me he'd been gambling and owed a man a lot of money. He were worried sick about it. One day I sees him talking to two men outside our house. I'd seen them before. They live in the village and work on the wharves in Stangate Creek. I never liked them and told Rob so, but he didn't take no notice. It seemed like he suddenly had hope for the future, so I said no more. But now . . .'

'Perhaps you could give me the names of the two men you saw, Mrs Cox. I'll need to see them in due course.'

'I only knows their Christian names. They live next door to the blacksmith, in the high street.'

'And the name of your husband's mate on the *Sisters*? Do you know?'

'Yes, I know. He's a good lad, Mr Pascoe. Sailed with Rob for several years now. His name is Stevie Lyons.'

'What about a man named Creech? Does that name mean anything to you?'

'No. Who is he?'

'Nobody you need worry about, Mrs Cox. It was just a thought. If you think of anything else, please send word.'

Tom walked with the woman to the front door of the police office and bid her goodbye. It seemed improbable that Cox's death was not somehow tied up with the theft of the silk and ostrich feathers. Whether he'd been a willing participant or not was now largely academic. What was of greater interest was who had killed him.

He had the feeling he already knew the answer.

Night had fallen and lamps shone above the doorways of the shops in Narrow Street, Shadwell, as Tom walked east towards Horse Ferry Road for a meeting he'd arranged with Blind Jack, at the Swan and Duck public house.

The street wasn't busy. The evening crowds had yet to make their nightly appearance, and those whose work had finished for the day were already departed. From across the Thames, a soft breeze carried the scents that were so familiar to Tom and which so reminded him of the small fishing harbour at Seahouses on the Northumberland coast where he'd grown up.

It was strange how infrequently he thought of those far-off, carefree days of childhood. So much had happened in the inter-vening years that the two halves of his life might almost have been separate existences. And then some small, insignificant event – the smell of the river, the sight of a tern wading in the shallows, or a word overheard – would trigger something in his mind and bring the memories back.

Tom walked on. Now and then a figure would appear in the street ahead of him, look in his direction and quickly melt away or cross the street to avoid him. Others tipped their hats or called a greeting as he passed by. Few ignored him or failed to move aside on his approach. All of them knew him, for better or worse.

Unusually, he saw nothing of all this, his mind fixed on Wil-liam and what might have happened to him. Harriot had been right. He'd been unable to concentrate on his day-to-day duties since the night of his brother's disappearance. Initially, he had dared to hope the little fellow had simply gone for a walk and would shortly return. But as the hours had passed with no news to help him keep alive his hopes, Tom had grown more fearful. It was the note that had finally extinguished in him any hope that the boy would return of his own volition.

He turned left by the tar yard into Horse Ferry Road. The Swan and Duck was a little way ahead. He slowed his pace and thought about the questions he wanted to put to Blind Jack. It seemed odd that a blind man might know things that other men did not. Yet the beggar had, more than once, confounded expectations. More than anything else Tom hoped the man would do so again and tell him where he might find his brother.

'Evening, Master Pascoe,' said a beaming landlord when Tom

entered the tavern. 'It's been a while since we saw you in these parts. You'll be wanting to use the private room upstairs, no doubt. The other party is waiting for you, sir. You'll not be disturbed.'

'Thankee, Master Landlord, that's most kind.' Tom strode over to a door at the back of the taproom. It was a risk being in a tavern again so soon after his bout of drinking in the, admittedly convivial, company of a stranger. He'd agreed to the arrangements for this meeting today without considering the implications. The smell of the place was enough to cause his mouth to dry. He clenched his teeth, went through the door and mounted the stairs behind. At the top he found himself in a short corridor, on one side of which were a further two doors. The first led to more stairs while the second opened onto a small, sparsely furnished room. A single tallow candle sat in its sconce on the windowsill.

Blind Jack was sitting by the fireplace gazing at the empty grate, the deep shadows cast by the candle flickering over his face and the wall behind him. He did not look round as Tom entered. 'Expected you before this, Master Pascoe. Ain't you interested in what Blind Jack has to tell ye?'

Tom closed the door and leaned against it. He was in no mood for an argument.

'I want to know about my brother. What've you got for me?'

'All depends on what you want to buy, Master Pascoe,' said Jack, a slow smile crossing his lips and exposing a row of blackened teeth. 'I've got a living to make, same as what you have.'

Tom felt his anger rising. He closed his eyes for a second, willing the mood to pass. Blind Jack was his best hope of finding William. He couldn't afford to throw it away. 'I'll not be paying for nothing, Jack. Not till you tell me what you know about my brother. Then we'll talk about the price.'

'A man's got a right to live, ain't he?' said Jack. 'And didn't old Jack warn you this might happen? Didn't he tell you to look after that poor little brother of yours? Come now, Mr Pascoe, all I want is a few coppers. For me breakfast, like.'

'Talk first. I want to hear what you've got.'

The smile faded from the beggar's face as he seemed to consider the proposal. Finally, he shrugged and said, 'I'd heard he'd been taken but no one knows who's got him or for why. There's been talk, of course. Some say it were them cullies what robbed the silk. Others say it were the Americans what have been asking questions.'

Tom's head jerked up. He'd known of the probable involvement of American agents in the search for the stolen silk, but had never subscribed to the notion that they could have taken his brother and be holding him to ransom. Yet he knew better than to dismiss the collective opinion of those for whom information often meant the difference between a meal and going hungry.

'What do you know about the Americans?' he said, settling himself back against the door, his arms folded.

Jack turned towards the sound of Tom's voice. 'I've seen them, in a manner of speaking. They was in the Harp. One of them. The cully what did all the talking. I reckon he were Irish. Could hear it, all mixed up in that Yankee voice. He wanted to know about you.'

'What did you tell them?'

'He already knew who you were and what you did. Mostly he wanted to know what you were doing about the silk what was plundered from the *Sisters*.'

'Did they know about young William?'

'Aye, they knew him, as well.'

'Whoever's got my brother sent a letter to the police office. Was it them?'

'If it were, Mr Pascoe, they didn't tell me.'

The candle by the window began to gutter and Tom looked round for a fresh one, lit it and jammed it on top of what remained of the old stump. The description of an American with an Irish accent stirred a memory in Tom's mind that he struggled to identify.

'What about the silk? Where's that being hidden?'

'What about a few coppers, Master Pascoe? Like what you promised.'

Tom reached in his pocket and threw some coins onto the table. He leaned forward and covered them with one hand. 'The silk, Jack. Tell me about the silk.'

'Don't know nothing about that, Mr Pascoe. Except . . .'

Tom waited.

'I were in the Royal Oak minding me own business when I over-hears some cullies talking. At first I didn't know any of them. Then I heard a voice I knew. It were Joe Gott what's a bully boy for Dan Creech. He said he'd been at his mother's house for longer than he wanted and were happy to be back. I thought it were strange cos he's always said he never saw her.'

'Did he say anything else?'

'Only that he were going to be busy for a day or two. I didn't hear the rest on account of some sailors what were singing in the taproom.'

'Where does Gott's mother live?' said Tom, his hand still covering the money.

'Can't help you there, Mr Pascoe. He don't normally talk about her. By-the-by, them Yanks wanted to know the same thing. Seems like you got a race on your hands, Master Pascoe.'

# CHAPTER 23

The boy stood at the entrance to Queen's Head Alley where it emerged into Wapping Street. He was no more than ten years old, thin and short for his age. He'd been there since early morning, despite the cold east wind and the driving rain that had turned the surface of the road into a sea of mud. Few others had chosen to brave the elements and the street was largely empty of the comings and goings that he might have expected to see. He shivered, pressing his body against the protective wall bordering the alley. He was here because he'd been paid – half now and the remainder when he'd delivered his message.

A man emerged from a passage on the other side of the street, some fifty or sixty yards from where the boy was standing. The youngster hesitated. He'd seen the man for whom he'd come only once before and then only for a moment. He couldn't be sure this was him. He waited until the figure had stepped down into the street and turned east, towards Shadwell. Still the boy waited. He didn't want to make a mistake. Then, his mind made up, he ran after the fast-disappearing figure.

'Mister?' he piped as he drew alongside the man.

Sam Hart looked at the bedraggled collection of rags trotting along beside him, and stopped. 'Yes?'

'Are you Master Hart, the officer?'

'Yes, my name is Hart,' said Sam, looking closely at the boy as if he felt he ought to know him. 'What can I do for you, son?'

'There's a cully what wants to see you, sir. He were most particular that it were you and none other. He said I were to be sure to fetch you to the place where he's waiting for you.'

'Oh, aye? Did your friend say why he wanted to see me?' said Sam, a wary look in his eye.

'He said you might ask,' said the boy, his head nodding vigorously. 'He said it were to do with Master Cox and the *Sisters*.'

'Did he, now? And what's the name of your friend?'

'Begging your pardon, mister, but he ain't my friend. He told me to wait for you. I never seen him before in me life. Will you come, sir? I ain't had nothing to eat today and the man won't pay me if you don't come.'

'Why did he not come himself?' asked Sam, doubtfully.

'Don't know,' said the boy. 'But he looked proper frightened to me, sir.'

'Then best we find out what your friend wants.'

'But—'

'I know,' said Sam. 'He's not your friend.'

The rain was still falling and puddles had formed in the pitted surface of the track off Old Gravel Lane into which Sam and the boy now stepped. The houses here were few, their condition more pitiful even than those in the neighbouring streets, their roofs sagging under the weight of their tiles, the doors and windows cracked and broken by walls that seemed on the point of collapse. None appeared to be occupied, but that might simply have meant the occupants had seen no reason to show themselves. To the right of the track, behind the row of houses, Sam could see an area of wasteland covered with gorse, brambles, wild grass and birch and sycamore saplings that had sprung up unchecked.

Almost immediately, the boy turned into this wasteland and crossed to the far corner where a pile of brushwood appeared to have been gathered at the base of a large beech tree. Approaching the place, the boy gave a low whistle. Almost immediately Sam saw a pair of frightened eyes staring out at him from under the tangle of twigs and broken branches. Then a tousled head appeared and a hand beckoned the two visitors forward.

'You got me money, mister?' said the boy, holding out a filthy hand, clearly anxious to be away. A coin was passed and the boy turned to leave.

'Wait,' said Sam. 'I remember now where I've seen you before. You brought a message to the police office a few days since.'

The boy looked startled and seemed on the point of running. 'Not me, mister,' he said.

'Don't be afraid,' said Sam. 'You've done nothing wrong. Do you remember who gave you the message?'

The boy stared at the ground in front of him, saying nothing.

'Come now. A shilling for your answer,' said Sam, delving into his pocket.

'It were Blind Jack, mister. Can I have the money now?'

The next moment he was gone, running barefoot across the field to the lane beyond. Sam watched him go. If what the boy had just told him was right, it was a shilling well spent.

'Master Hart?'

Sam looked back to where the dishevelled and grime-encrusted young man was looking at him. 'The boy said you wanted to tell me something about Master Cox.'

'Not here, sir.' The young man's eyes were darting around the field as though afraid they'd be seen. 'Come inside.'

Sam hesitated before dropping to his hands and knees and crawling in through a small opening in the brush. Inside, he found himself in a cramped space largely occupied by a single blanket and a rolled-up article of clothing that was evidently being used as a pillow. He glanced up at the low roof. It was impossible to do more than squat with his shoulders hunched and head bent forward. It reminded him of the shelters he and his friends used to build in the forest outside his village in Poland when he was a boy. They would use them for a day or so before growing tired of the adventure and thinking of something else to keep themselves amused.

'The boy who brought you told you I wanted to speak of Master Cox,' said the young man when they had both settled.

Sam nodded.

'My name is Stevie Lyons,' said the young man. 'I am . . . I was the mate of the sailing hoy, the *Sisters*. It's—'

'I know of the *Sisters*,' said Sam. 'Tell me about Master Cox.'

'I know that he's dead,' said Stevie. 'Ever since I heard, I've been living in mortal fear of me life.'

'Who told you he was dead?' said Sam, surprised.

'A mate of mine told me. He said he'd heard some cullies talking about it in the Royal Oak, over on the south bank.'

'Did he say who these cullies were?'

'No.'

'You say you've been living in mortal fear. Why? Have you been threatened by anyone?' said Sam.

'I've heard that villainous swab Creech is looking for me,' said Stevie, his eyes wandering to the entrance of the shelter. 'It's on account of the fact that I were with Coxy when he were sent to Stangate Creek. He told me Creech wanted to plunder the silk we was to collect. Coxy refused and sailed back to London.'

'You know Creech?'

'Aye, in a manner of speaking. I've seen him around and I seen him when he followed us down to the Medway.'

'Did you hear him tell Cox he wanted him to plunder the silk?'

'No. It were only what Cox told me.'

'Why would Creech be looking for you just because you were with Master Cox?'

'They say it were Creech what killed Coxy for what he knew. And what Coxy knew, I did too.'

'Did you see anyone else with Creech when he followed you to the Medway?'

'Aye. There was Gabriel Marr and Joe Gott and some others what I didn't know.'

'Anybody else? Another vessel, perhaps?'

'I only saw Creech, and the cullies with him on his sailing barge. Later, when we was on the *Velocity*, I saw a sloop what seemed to be watching us.'

'Did you see any of the crew?'

'Not proper, like. And that were the only time.'

'What happened when you got back to London?'

'Coxy told me to go home. He said I was to stay away. That were the last I saw of him.'

'Did he say why you should stay away?'

'Not in so many words. He told me he were going to see Creech and tell him why he'd not driven the hoy onto the hard like he'd been told to. He knew he'd be given a flogging but that were all. He didn't expect to die.'

'Does anyone else know you're here? Your mother or your father? Anyone?'

'No, I don't think so. Except that nipper what were here just now.'

'If Creech is looking for you, you ain't safe here,' said Sam. 'Somebody will see you and when they do, it's likely Creech will find out.'

'What can I do, sir?' said Stevie, his lips quivering. He seemed on the point of tears.

Sam thought for a moment. He would have liked to have helped, but the fact of the matter was that there was little he could do. Stevie's information, while useful in confirming Creech's involvement in the plot to steal the silk, fell a long way short of the evidence necessary to prove his guilt. Even the supposed risk to the young man's life was, at this stage, speculation, unsupported by any facts. He couldn't justify asking Harriot to treat him as a witness deserving of special protection – but he would try.

'I'll see what I can do,' said Sam. He couldn't leave the lad without hope.

# CHAPTER 24

It was an unusually warm afternoon when Sam removed his *kippah*, left the synagogue in Duke's Place and headed down towards Aldgate High Street. Turning into the busy thorough-fare, he heard the noise of a disturbance further along the street. A young woman was screaming and pointing at a youth running in Sam's direction. The young man appeared to be carrying some-thing. Whatever it was, Sam doubted that it was his. He waited for the boy to draw level with him and then nudged him with his shoulder into the path of approaching cart. The next moment the youth lay sprawled in the roadway with Sam's knee pressing down on his back.

'Is there something you want to tell me about that bag you're holding?' said Sam above the stream of abuse coming from the boy's mouth.

'He was stealing my bag,' said a female voice behind him.

Sam turned and at once felt a hot flush rising to his cheeks as he recognised Jacob Emden's daughter standing by his shoulder.

'Do you wish me to call the constable?' he stammered.

'No,' she said, taking her bag from his hand and smiling. 'I'll warrant he has learned his lesson and I must return home. I am late.'

'Perhaps you will allow me to escort you?'

'You are very kind, but I think not,' said the girl, hurriedly looking at the small crowd that had gathered to watch.

'Then at least permit me to walk behind you,' said Sam.

Adina's eyes appeared to dart nervously from one onlooker to the next, the tips of her fingers resting on her lips. Then she caught sight of the youth still pinned to the ground by Sam's foot. 'Very well, but it would not be right for you to speak to me.'

Sam took his foot off the boy's neck and pulled him to his feet. 'This time you go free. If I catch you again, it'll be the police court for you.'

He looked round. The girl was already on her way. He followed her, careful to keep his distance as she weaved through the hurrying mass of black-clad figures. She had nearly arrived at her father's house when she stopped, seeming to admire some object on a stall. He waited, but she didn't move. After a minute or so, she glanced back at him and smiled.

'I'm nearly home,' she said. 'I wanted to say thank you for what you did.'

He didn't have time to reply before she had turned and run the final few yards to the Emden shop. He walked to the entrance and stared at the place where he'd last seen her. A small piece of paper protruded from under the door. Without thinking, Sam stooped and picked it up, feeling its rough brown surface with his thumb, his mind taken up with thoughts of Adina.

'Any news of your brother?' John Harriot waved away the plume of tobacco smoke and looked across his desk at Tom.

'No, nothing positive.'

'I'm sorry to hear that.'

An awkward silence followed. Harriot stared out through the window. Tact had never been his strong point and he'd often suffered agonies of embarrassment at the all too frequent slip of the tongue. He'd known perfectly well there had been no movement on the search for young William. He coughed, looked down at his desk and started again.

'The silk case. Where have we got to on that? You won't be surprised to hear that I've received another note from Hookham Frere chasing me for some news. Apparently the Home Secretary is on his back.'

'We've still not found the bales, sir,' said Tom, wrenching his mind away from his missing brother. 'We think they were taken from Clink Dock to a yard owned by Daniel Creech. As you know, we raided his yard but found nothing. We think the silk was moved shortly before we got there. I've reason to believe it was taken from there to a house owned by the mother of one of Creech's associates. Unfortunately, we've been unable to discover the address. But inquiries continue.'

'What associate is that?' asked the magistrate, cradling the bowl of his pipe.

'Joseph Gott,' said Tom. 'He's been before you on a number of occasions, mostly for assault.'

'You've had a look through the court records? If he's been before me, we'll have an address for him.'

'Yes, I've checked. The address he always gives is the Royal Oak, Rotherhithe. Landlord says he's never spent a single night there.'

'I see,' said Harriot. 'So what now?'

'We'll keep looking,' said Tom. 'Incidentally, I was speaking to one of my snouts earlier today. He said two Americans have been asking questions about the silk. As far as he knew, they haven't yet found it but they must be getting close. There is also some suggestion they might have been involved in my brother's disappearance.'

'How so?'

'The note, sir. The one telling us William had been taken. It was, you may remember, brought here by a small boy and given to Hart. At the time we didn't know who'd given it to the boy. It now transpires that it was Blind Jack.'

'Are you suggesting Blind Jack is involved?'

'No, sir, but we do know that Blind Jack was seen in the company of the Americans shortly before the note was delivered. There can't be more than a score of men in the entire port who can read or write but I'd be surprised if an American agent couldn't.'

Tom fell silent, his eyes glazing over as if deep in thought.

'There's something else on your mind, Mr Pascoe,' said Harriot. 'Talk to me, sir.'

'It's probably nothing, sir,' said Tom. 'But on the morning I discovered William was gone, I found a sou'wester on the steps of the house where I have my room. At the time I had the feeling that I'd seen it before.'

A puzzled frown crossed Harriot's brow. 'Those things must, sir, be worn by every other man in the port.'

'Yes,' said Tom, 'I agree. But there was something else about this particular hat that struck me as odd.'

'And that was . . . ?'

'A needle threaded into one side. It was of the type used by sailmakers. For a time, I thought it might have belonged to Creech

212

since he is himself a sailmaker, but the descriptions of the men seen in the vicinity of my home that night don't fit him.'

'Pity,' said Harriot. He paused and then, as if anxious to move the interview along, said, 'What about this fellow Marr we've got in the cells? What's happening about him?'

'I'm confident he's involved in the plundering of the silk. I'd like to keep him in custody for another few days while I try and find Creech. I don't want them talking before I've had the opportunity of questioning them both.'

'Do you have any evidence to justify Creech's arrest? Beyond mere suspicion, I mean,' said Harriot.

'Sam Hart has met with the mate of the *Sisters*, a young man by the name of Stevie Lyons who has been in hiding ever since he got to London with the silk. He's quite clear about Creech's involvement in the depredation. He saw the cully following the *Sisters* down to the Medway and all the way back again. It seems that Cox, the sailing master, was coerced by Creech into an agreement to plunder the silk and some ostrich feathers. Unfortunately there is no direct evidence of this – only what was said by Cox to young Stevie Lyons – but it does show Creech's involvement. We also think that some carts seen in the vicinity of Creech's yard in Market Hill may have been loaded with the silk.'

'But no one has actually come forward to say he saw Creech in possession of the silk or that the carts in Market Hill were, in fact, loaded with silk?' said Harriot.

'The evidence is, at the moment, circumstantial and is likely to remain so unless I'm able to interview all three suspects – Marr, Creech and Gott. I'd like to do that before they speak to each other and can sort out their stories. I also need to find out where

Gott's mother lives so we can have a look to see if the silk is there. We need to do all this quickly if we're to have any hope of getting to those papers before the Americans.'

Harriot put his elbows on his desk and clasped the bowl of his pipe as he puffed, watching Tom through the clouds of smoke.

'Marr is still in the cells. Do you know where Gott is?' he asked.

'He's been seen in the Royal Oak. If the silk is at his mother's house, he'll want to get back out there sometime in the near future. I've instructed Sam Hart to follow him wherever he goes.'

Brougham brought the sloop up into the tide and fetched alongside one of the lighters moored in the Battle Bridge Barge Road, close to the south bank of the Thames. From here he had a clear view of the Royal Oak and the side door that was occasionally used to enter the premises. It was just unfortunate that the main door – and therefore the one used by the majority of patrons attending the premises – was at the front of the building and out of his line of sight. If he wanted to be sure of seeing who was entering the place – and he did – he would either have to wait inside the tavern itself or stand in some doorway further up Bridge Yard. On balance, he thought he might prefer the comfort of the tavern.

He'd already wasted most of the morning and the whole of the previous day in his search for Joe Gott. He would not normally have bothered with the man. It was Creech he really wanted. But it had been something the blind beggar had said that had caused him to pause and think. The beggar had made an oblique reference to the time Gott had been spending at his mother's house in the days immediately after the raid on the Royal Oak. It had meant nothing to the American at the time. He'd regarded most of what Blind Jack said as the ramblings of a boastful fool who was not to be taken seriously. Yet, of late, he'd been forced to reconsider what had passed between them. He'd begun to see it in the light of the fruitless visit to Creech's yard in Market Hill.

It had surprised him not to find the silk at the yard. It had seemed such an obvious place for Creech to have kept it. And yet it had not been there. It was only afterwards that he'd begun to reconsider the value of Blind Jack as a source of information. Looking back now, it all made sense that Creech should want to move the silk from his yard immediately after the police raid on the Royal Oak. His problem would have been to find somewhere suitable. In his haste, it was entirely possible that he had settled on the home of the mother of one of his bully boys.

'Wait here for me, Hawkes,' said Brougham. 'I'll not be long. If Gott is in the tavern, I'll call you over. If he's not, I'll have to wait for him.'

He slipped over the side, into the sloop's gig. A moment later he'd shoved off and was sculling towards the river stairs at the side of the tavern.

# CHAPTER 25

Sam hoped this assignment wouldn't last long. He had other plans for later in the day and he had no intention of delaying them any longer than was absolutely necessary. He smiled at the thought as he crossed London Bridge to the south bank and turned down into Tooley Street. He'd done his best to put Adina out of his mind, but it hadn't worked. He found himself walking up and down the street where she lived at every opportunity.

He reached the junction with Bridge Yard and turned in, the smells of the river coming up to meet him. A minute later and he was able to glimpse the brown rush of water in a gap between the buildings. The Royal Oak was in front of him. Next to it was Cotton's Wharf and between the two lay the path to the river stairs.

A man had come ashore and was presently climbing the stairs towards the Royal Oak. Sam watched him walk to the side entrance of the premises and turn in. Behind him, on the river, he could see a sloop moored to one of the lighters, its mainsail spilling the wind. It seemed out of place, as though it had no business there, a solitary figure sitting in the stern sheets, his head turned towards the shore. Sam watched him for a while before making his way down to the tavern. There was nothing special about him, no reason to watch him. Besides, Sam had other things to do.

The Royal Oak was, as usual, busy. Sam pushed open the door and looked to his left, to the spot where he'd seen Creech and the others sitting on the night of the raid. The bench was unoccupied. It was as though it had been reserved for a party who had yet to arrive. He looked round the rest of the bar, the air thick with the odour of human sweat, the walls stained a brownish yellow from years of tobacco smoke.

Old John Davy, the landlord, nodded and waited for Sam to come across. 'All right, Master Sam. What'll it be?'

'Thankee, John, I'll have a quart of your best.'

'Coming right up. No trouble, I hope?'

'None that I know of,' said Sam, looking round the room. 'Still no sign of Dan Creech, then.'

'Ain't seen him since you lads came in the other night.'

'Ah.' Sam paid for his ale and found a seat by the main door from where he could see most of the room. The man he'd spotted going in through the side entrance was seated in the opposite corner. He was on his own, a pewter tankard on the table in front of him. Sam looked at him from under his eyelashes. He was nothing like the usual run of lumpers and coal-heavers who frequented the waterside. True, his hair had an unkempt appearance and he did not look as though he'd shaved in more than a month, but that couldn't hide the well-fed features or the tolerable state of his teeth, only a few of which were missing. And there was something else: an aura of quiet authority that Sam had only previously seen in Tom Pascoe. He suddenly realised the man was staring at him. He turned away and took a long swig of his beer, conscious that he too must have been staring.

When he looked back, the man had gone, his tankard left

behind on the table. Sam shrugged. The cully was probably a ship's captain come ashore for a drink. He understood how the man must have felt, his sense of isolation in the company of strangers whose behaviour he did not entirely understand. Sam had often suffered the same himself. He looked quickly round the room, hoping to see Gott, but there was no trace of him. He sighed. This job was going to take longer than he would have liked.

It was another hour before the front door of the tavern opened to admit the heavily built frame of Joe Gott, his bald head perched uncomfortably on his broad shoulders, his small eyes almost buried behind folds of skin. He shuffled to the empty bench and table Sam had previously noted, and sat down. He seemed nervous, his body shifting in his seat, his head constantly turning to the door as though expecting someone to come through. At length, he got up and left, the door banging closed behind him.

Sam waited a moment and then sauntered out into Bridge Yard. He stopped and looked round. A number of carts were trundling slowly up the lane from Cotton's Wharf, their drivers shouting encouragement to the exhausted-looking beasts as they laboured under the strain. From the wharf itself came the dull rumble of men's voices mingled with the clank of the treadmills. On the opposite side of the lane, two young women lounged against a wall, their vampire stares and raucous invitations directed at every male that passed.

Of Gott, there was no trace.

Sam ran to the bend in the lane and was in time to see him turning into Tooley Street. He sprinted to the junction and followed as Gott climbed the steep incline to London Bridge. At the top, the man stopped and looked back. His apparent nervousness had given way to irritation, his gaze sweeping both sides of the street. Apparently satisfied that whoever he was searching for was not there, he hurried across the Thames.

Milton Brougham followed the two men up Tooley Street. He'd suspected Joe Gott would be followed. It had seemed too much of a coincidence that one of Pascoe's men should have come to the Royal Oak for no reason other than a drink. Initially, he'd taken little notice of him, relegating his face to one of the hundreds of men he'd spoken to and drunk with over the last few days while he'd searched for information about the cargo of silk. Why he had begun to take note of him, he couldn't say. Perhaps it was because the man had been staring at him. Whatever the reason, he suddenly remembered the night he and Hawkes had lain on the roof of a shed in Market Hill and watched Pascoe and his men search the yard below. One of them had been the stranger who'd been at the table opposite. Pascoe had addressed him as Sam.

He hoped Hawkes had understood his hand signals. There hadn't been time to row back to the sloop and tell him what had happened or what he now planned to do. He glanced over the bridge parapet. The sloop had gone. He felt a jolt of apprehension in his stomach. It wasn't that he was afraid of the consequences of being caught in the act of espionage. That came with the job. But if there was value to what he had been asked to do, some point to it, then it seemed to him that it ought to be given the best chance of success. And that, in his mind, could be better

achieved by two men rather than one. He hoped nothing untoward had happened to his colleague.

Once over the Thames, he saw Sam Hart turn right into Lower
Thames Street, walk past the Custom House and skirt round the
Tower of London. From here he continued into Rosemary Lane,
filled with hundreds of stalls, each with its own canopy of coloured canvas under which the traders did their best to outdo one
another with their shouts of encouragement.

Brougham had little idea of where he was and even less of
what he would do if Gott were to lead him to the silk. His orders
had seemed straightforward. He was to locate the compromising
documents, believed to be hidden in a consignment of silk,
extract them and pass them to the Minister Plenipotentiary for
the United States government.

The reality was turning out to be a great deal more involved,
not to say time-consuming. It was bad enough that the silk had
been plundered, without the additional problem of dealing with
the likes of Pascoe and his men. He studied the small, slightly
built man ahead of him, walking as though in some sort of pain,
weaving around the multitude of young and old. He was an
unwanted complication that Brougham hadn't expected and one
he would eventually have to deal with.

They walked on into Back Lane, shortly followed by the rope
walks of Sun Tavern Fields. The day was slipping by, the sun
already beginning to dip towards the horizon. In an hour it would
be dark. Brougham wondered where he was and whether, when
this was over, he would be able find his way back to the room he'd
rented in Oxford Street. Then he caught sight of a flag flying
from the bell tower of St Anne's, Limehouse, a mile or so to the

east. He'd seen the flag before, the white ensign of the British Navy, as he'd travelled up Limehouse Reach in the packet boat that had brought him over from America. He felt better. It was a reference point by which he might find his way back. He would make for that church and from there travel west along the banks of the river to London Bridge. He was confident he'd find his way to his room from there.

It was dark by the time the three of them reached the Lea Cut and began to follow the towpath along the side of the canal. Brougham had no warning of what happened next. The first indication of trouble was the sensation of a knife blade being held against his throat. He felt, rather than saw, the two men who had come out of the dark. For a moment Brougham considered retaliating. He could probably get one of the men, but what then? The knife was pressed harder against his neck, He felt the warm trickle of blood running down his neck.

A hand was going through his pockets. He felt his pocket book being removed. Then it was the turn of his knife. He regretted that. It had been with him ever since he was a lad in Ireland.

'That ain't playing fair, my boys.' The voice came from behind him. Perhaps five paces away. The accent was difficult to place. More European than English.

Brougham strained his neck to see the speaker and was aware of a short, slim figure standing to his left, all but invisible in the darkness. He felt the grip about his neck loosen and the hands which had so lately been in his pockets quickly removed. He seized the chance and brought his elbow back with all his considerable strength, feeling it sink into the stomach of the knifeman.

There was the sound of air being forcibly expelled and the dull thud of the man dropping to his knees.

Brougham turned to face the second man only to find him stretched out and unconscious on the towpath. Standing over him was the slim figure he'd seen moments before. He was flicking his right hand up and down as though in an attempt to ease the pain in his knuckles.

'Why, sir, I'm mighty pleased to see you,' said Brougham.

'It were only fair,' said Sam, clutching at his chest with his free hand. 'I saw them rogues as I passed and I thought to myself, they're trouble. Then I heard them attacking you. Is you hurt?'

'No, thanks to you,' said Brougham, suddenly recognising Sam. 'But you, sir. It seems you are in some pain.'

'It's nothing. An old hurt.' Sam glanced down at the unconscious figures. 'There'll be no more trouble from them. I warrant they'll think twice before they do this again. Where are you heading?'

'I . . .' Brougham searched round for a suitable answer. 'I were looking to join my ship, but got lost. She lies in Limehouse Reach.'

'Best you turn about, my friend. You'll not find the river up this way. Now I must leave you. I've work I must do.'

Brougham watched Sam go quickly away, one hand still clutching at his chest. He knew the encounter had complicated matters. He couldn't risk being seen again without rousing suspicion. Yet he still needed to trace the silk. No amount of regret was going to alter that. If he was quick he might just catch up with Sam and Gott and still remain out of sight.

After that he'd consider what needed to be done.

*

At the eastern end of the village of Bow, past the squat outline of the church of St Mary, Joe Gott turned left, along the lane that ran parallel to the River Lea. He'd had no contact with Creech or any of the others for some time. He'd hoped he'd see them at one or other of the taverns where they usually gathered – the Harp, or the Royal Oak. Perhaps then Creech would favour him with news of whether or not a buyer for the silk had, at last, been found.

But the villain hadn't been in either of those places and Gott was growing increasingly sceptical about the man's motives. He'd already considered the possibility that Creech had moved the silk from his own yard so he could safely deny all knowledge of it should it ever be found. Now, it seemed, the man himself had gone into hiding. How else could his absence from their usual haunts be explained? In the meantime, the silk remained at his mother's house where he and she stood at constant risk of arrest.

Gott reached the house and went in. His mother was asleep in a chair by the fire. He left her and, picking up a candle, crossed the room to where a chest of drawers stood against the end wall. Pushing this to one side, he pulled open a trapdoor and descended some steps to a large, low-ceilinged cellar.

The boy was sitting on the earth floor, his back propped against a pillar. He was trembling, his eyes wide open and staring, a strip of cloth tied over his mouth, his hands and feet bound with cord. Gott looked at him with something approaching regret. He bent down and removed the gag.

'Want some food, boy?' he asked, roughly.

William Pascoe shook his head, saying nothing, his eyes still staring at his captor.

'Water?'

Again, the shake of the head.

Gott replaced the cloth and stood up. Taking the lad had been another of Creech's ideas. 'Pascoe will be too busy looking for the boy to worry about us,' Creech had told him. 'The boy walks to school. Best you catch him on his way home.' But the moment had never seemed quite right. There had always been too many people about for him to snatch the boy without being noticed. In the end, an irritated Creech had agreed to another plan. The boy was to be taken from his bed while Pascoe was away.

Gott surveyed the boy, unsure of what to do. Creech had said he'd remain at the house for no more than a day or two, until some more permanent solution could be found. But that time had now passed. He remembered his earlier doubts about Creech. The scrub was quite capable of selling the silk and cutting every-one else out of their share of the profits. Once the silk had been disposed of, the boy would be of no further interest to him. Creech would leave the others to deal with the matter. He, Gott, would be the sole suspect if anything untoward happened to the boy. It was him, after all, who'd taken young William from his bed. He alone would hang for his trouble.

He decided he would have to deal with William before anyone knew where he was. It was the only safe way. He climbed the steps and looked across at his mother.

She was still asleep in her chair.

# CHAPTER 26

Sam stood facing the old stone bridge over the River Lea, undecided about where to look next. Gott had disappeared. The bridge led only to a towpath on the opposite bank. Beyond the path lay the empty wastelands of the Abbey Marshes, stretching away into the night. It was unlikely the scrub would have gone that way. To his right was another street with houses on either side. Sam had already been down there, checking each one for any sign that someone might have recently arrived. There'd been nothing, not even candlelight in any of the windows. It was as if the village had been abandoned. Then he remembered seeing another turning that had appeared to run north, parallel to the river. It couldn't be any less promising than where he was.

He retraced his steps and turned onto an earthen track. Within a few yards he found himself in open country with nothing to check the biting north-easterly wind blowing into his face from across the marshes. He turned up the collar of his coat and tucked his hands under his armpits, listening to the faint whistle of the wind and the slapping of the river amidst the reed beds. It seemed an unlikely route for Gott to have taken. There were no houses to be seen, nowhere to which he might be heading. Sam was about to turn back when he caught sight of a faint light in the near distance. It was gone in a second, so quickly that he thought he'd imagined it. Then he saw it again, more clearly this time.

He hurried towards it before dropping into a ditch at the side of the track and crawling the last few yards to the house. Reaching a point opposite the building, he stopped and peered over the lip of the road. The light was still burning in the window. He stayed where he was for a minute or two. Then, satisfied he'd not been seen, he crept out of the ditch, crossed the track and approached the lighted window. An elderly woman was sitting alone in front of the fireplace, apparently asleep. Sam ducked out of sight and thought about what to do next. There was nothing to suggest this was the house for which Gott had been making. All he'd seen was the elderly woman.

He was on the point of crawling away when he heard a scraping noise, as though something heavy were being dragged over floorboards. He risked another look through the window. He could see nothing that might have accounted for the sound. Then Gott appeared, crossed the room to the old woman and turned towards the window.

Sam inched away and crept back to the other side of the lane. For the first time he noticed a barn, partly hidden by a stand of trees, a little distance from the house. It was, he thought, an unlikely place for the silk to be hidden, but it was worth a look. He's taken a few steps when the front door of the house opened and Gott came out carrying a heavy object on his shoulder.

Sam dropped to the ground and watched him disappear from view round the back of the house. A short time later there was a splash as if something had been dropped into the Lea. A minute later Gott reappeared empty-handed, and went back into the house.

Sam sprinted across the lane and, skirting the house, ran towards the darkened river and began searching along the bank for any evidence that the reed beds might have been disturbed. There was nothing. He turned about and retraced his steps. It was then that he saw that some reeds had been crushed as though by someone forcing a way through. Sam waded into the shallows hoping he might see anything that would point to where the heavy object had been thrown in. But there was nothing – no floating object nor stream of bubbles rising through the water. Whatever it was had now gone. He made his way back to the lane and again looked at the barn. If the silk was there, it was unlikely to move before morning.

By then he'd be back with the others – and a warrant.

Sleep was impossible. Tom turned over in his bed and looked out at the clear night sky, the velvet blackness littered now with a million stars that blinked and sparkled in their heavenly solitude. He closed his eyes and tried not to think about what Sam had told him on his return from Bow, earlier in the night.

'There is something else I should have told you, sir,' Sam had said to him at the end of his report about finding the likely location of the bales of silk.

'What? What should you have told me?'

'When I were outside Gott's house, I saw him—'

'Yes, I know—'

'No, you don't understand. What I didn't tell you, sir, is that I saw him carrying something on his shoulder. Whatever it were, Gott carried it to the Lea and threw it in.'

Tom wished he hadn't been told. His mind had been in torment ever since. He'd gone over what might or might not have happened; considering the possibilities of who or what had been pitched into the river, a thousand times in the intervening hours. He would have gone straight to Bow had it been possible, but Sam had persuaded him that nothing good would come of it. Better to wait for a warrant and a local constable to accompany them, he'd said.

Tom rolled over onto his side, his hands covering his face. He was as far from sleep as ever. He got up, put his coat on and paced the room, willing the hours away before he could leave for Bow. A bound sheaf of vellum caught his eye. It was lying on top of his open sea chest. He'd forgotten the existence of his old sketch-book, long abandoned amongst the detritus of his life. He stopped and eyed it for a moment before stepping over and running his fingers over its battered linen cover.

His drawings had often sustained him through the troughs of his life, allowing him to step aside for an hour or two from whatever difficulties had beset him. In those moments he'd sit alone and sketch the world that he saw around him, his troubles temporarily forgotten. He flicked through the pages, each one reminding him of a particular episode in his life – the early years around the Holy Isle off the Northumberland coast, his time at sea in war and in peace, his burgeoning love affair with Peggy, so savagely cut short. He sighed, replacing the book in his chest, his thoughts abruptly returning to his missing brother and the raid he hoped would bring an end to his misery.

But the application for a search warrant would be for the stolen silk, not for William. There was no evidence of the boy being held at the house, only a vague suspicion. It would not be enough to support an approach to a magistrate for a warrant. It would be refused. Tom knew that as well as anybody. Not that it mattered. If the boy was there, the absence of a warrant specifically mentioning him would not prevent his rescue. But the absence of evidence, the sheer lack of any information that the boy might be there, was a forceful reminder that this might not be the end of Tom's search. Then he recalled Sam's words: . . . *Gott carried it to the Lea and threw it in.*

Tom wandered back to the window and gazed over the silent rooftops of Wapping to the winding Thames, bathed now in the silver light of the moon. He turned back to his sea chest, picked up his old sketchbook and a sliver of charcoal and returned to the window. Almost without thought he began to draw, his hand moving swiftly over the page, a line here, a smudge there, his eyes roving the scene before him, noting the slant of light and shadow, the occasional wisp of smoke and the tiers of ships upon the Thames.

For a while he was at peace.

The cold dawn light filtered through the first-floor window of the constables' waiting room at the Wapping police office. There was a smell of damp from the sodden clothing draped over chairs or left hanging from nails hammered into the walls. The smell barely registered with Sam as he watched the door open and Tom walk in. The crew – himself, John Kemp and Jim Higgins – had been waiting for some time.

'All correct, sir,' he said, snapping to attention.

'Stand easy. You all know why we're here,' said a tired-looking Tom. 'I dare say Sam will already have told you where he went last night. We think there's a good chance the silk skeins that we're looking for may have been hidden there. We're about to find out if that's the case or not. Since we will be operating outside the area for which we're authorised to act as constables, we'll be taking a local officer with us who will be in possession of the necessary search warrant. I'm not anticipating much opposition but we will be carrying firearms and the usual pikes and hangers.'

Tom paused and looked round before going on: 'Just two other things. The first is that the Americans may also have found out where the silk is hidden. It seems that one of them followed Sam to within a mile or two of the house. Sam assures me that he lost the fellow before reaching Bow, but we won't know that for certain until we get there. If he did find the house, he would have been faced with the same difficulty as Sam. He was on his own and would have been in no position to remove the silk. The second thing I want to draw to your attention is the possibility that my brother, William, may be held captive at the same location. I don't think I need say any more on that subject.'

'We'll find him for you, sir,' said Sam a few minutes later as the four of them made their way up New Gravel Lane towards the Ratcliff Highway, the street already filling with men trudging wearily towards the river and another day's work.

'Thankee, Sam,' said Tom, a distracted look in his eyes. 'I've not been able to sleep, thinking of him, hoping he's all right.'

Sam didn't reply. There was nothing he could say, nothing that would make any difference. He knew how much hope Tom was investing in this raid. The emotional toll of the last few days had cost him dear. They reached the Ratcliff Highway and crossed over into Cannon Street.

'The American . . .' said Tom. 'The one you helped. D'you think he recognised you?'

'Can't see how he could have. He's never seen me before.'

'You can't be sure of that, Sam. But if he didn't know you, he would have to be following Gott.'

'I don't follow you, sir. Why would he follow Gott?'

'For the same reason he followed Creech down to the Medway and later turned up at Clink Dock. He knows as much as we do about this silk and there is every chance he and his friends might get to it before us.'

Joe Gott threw off the fetid blanket, climbed groggily to his feet and yawned, conscious of an unpleasant niggling sensation at the back of his mind, something that he knew he should be worrying about – if only he could remember what it was. He bent down and put his boots on. The leather had cracked and split long ago, exposing his toes and the soles of his feet to the elements. They hadn't been in much better condition when he'd acquired them several years before.

He stopped in mid-action as he remembered what was troubling him. It was the silk. If anyone came snooping round here, they'd find all the evidence they needed to hang him – and probably his aged mother as well. He had to get rid of the stuff. He wasn't about to hang for Creech. He finished tying his boots and walked into the yard.

It was then he noticed the big double doors were open. He ran to the entrance and stopped, waiting for his eyes to adjust to the gloom of the interior. The barn doors should have been closed. They always were and always had been. It had been an iron rule in his father's day when the old man had cause to put things in there he didn't want seen by anyone else.

Gott stepped inside. The barn was a large, oak-framed, oak-clad structure that smelt of warm hay. It was empty but for a four-wheeled hay wain and, next to it, a smaller cart which had been tilted onto its rear gate. On the wall to the left a dusty harness hung from a wooden peg, while below it a stack of oak planking lay on the earthen floor. Gott's eye ran down the length of the building to where a line of haystacks stretched across the width of the building, forming a barrier to whatever lay behind. He could see, even from this distance, that several of the stacks had been tossed aside, leaving a clear path to what lay beyond – the place where the bales of silk had been hidden.

He could feel his heart pounding. He approached the line of stacks and passed through. The space behind was empty. The skeins had gone. He remembered a second hiding space, behind the pile of oak planking against the wall. He ran over. They, too, had gone. He stood gaping at the place where the bales had been, sweat streaming down his face, the dust churned up by his frantic search now choking him. Not a single skein remained.

He rushed to the house and shook his mother awake.

'The bales,' he shouted. 'They've gone. Who took them, Ma?'

'What?' The woman looked up, her eyes blurred with interrupted sleep.

'Who took the bales from the barn, Ma? The ones what Creech put there.'

'How would I know? Nobody tells me nothing these days,' grumbled his mother.

'You must have seen something. Was it Creech?'

'Who?' The old woman blinked away the last vestiges of her slumbers. 'Don't know nobody what's called Creech.'

Her son swore under his breath and walked over to the window overlooking the lane. Then he sprang back in alarm. Men were approaching the house. He recognised Pascoe but not the others. He didn't need to. He felt the blood drain from his face as he backed away and waited for the knock on the door.

'Don't say nothing, Ma,' he managed, his mouth dry. 'They got nothing on us, see?'

The loudness of the knock startled him. He flinched, as though surprised by the sound. For a second or two there was utter silence. No one moved. He considered running; opening one of the windows at the back of the house and bolting. Yet where would he go? How far would he get? He couldn't swim and even if he could, he'd not run more than five paces at a time in the last ten years.

He moved slowly to the door and opened it.

'Joseph Gott?' Pascoe's voice sounded like the last call from Hell. Gott nodded. 'I've reason to believe you were concerned, with others, in the larceny of a quantity of Valencia silk. My colleague here has a warrant to search these premises and any outhouses within its curtilage.'

'Suit yourself. There ain't nothing here,' said Gott, sounding a great deal more confident than he felt.

'Good. We'll start with the barn,' said Tom. 'I want you with us.'

# CHAPTER 27

The scene inside the barn was much as Tom might have expected: a couple of carts, some pitchforks, a double-ended saw that had seen better days and, at the far end, some stacks of hay, some of which appeared to have been thrown aside.

'Looks like someone's been careless,' he said. 'What happened there?'

'No idea, cock,' said Gott, a bored expression on his face. 'It's me mother's place. Don't come here much.'

Tom strolled to the end of the barn and looked behind the wall of hay. The space was empty. He turned to go.

'Sir?' said Sam.

'Aye, Sam, what've you got?'

Sam was pointing at a scrap of paper that had become snagged on a splinter of wood, close to the floor. Tom picked up the fragment and examined it.

'This yours?' he said, looking up at Gott.

'Never seen it before in me life.'

'So you can't tell me what a piece of wrapping paper is doing in your barn.'

'No idea what you're talking about. Anygate, it ain't my barn, it's me ma's.'

'Nor, I suppose, do you know what this letter means?' said Tom, pointing to a letter 'M' on one side of the paper.

'Not the foggiest.'

'Please yourself,' said Tom. 'I think it's from the paper used to wrap some bales of silk skeins that were stolen from a sailing hoy in the Upper Pool. I think this piece of paper will help to prove that fact. If I'm right, it's enough to send you to the Bailey. That would be a pity, don't you think? Especially as your mates Creech and Marr will walk free. Doubtless they'll enjoy spending your share of the money they get from the silk. What d'you think, Sam?'

'Aye, sir. Can't see how our friend here can escape taking all the blame. Unless he talks to us. Still, I reckon Creech will give him his share of the money, won't he?'

'What about it, Gott? You reckon Creech will give your share of the money to your mother to look after?' Tom paused long enough to let the implications sink in. 'Of course, it could all be very different . . .'

Gott's eyes flickered and looked away. It was not the reaction Tom had expected. 'You thought the silk was still here, didn't you? You're as surprised as we are that it isn't. That's it, isn't it? Creech or someone else took it without you knowing. Either way, you're likely to swing unless you start talking to me.'

Gott chewed his bottom lip but said nothing.

'Come with me.' Tom took hold of the man's elbow and guided him out of the barn and across the yard to the old single-storey stone building that was his mother's home. It had clearly seen better days. Ivy adorned the walls and covered the windows while a thick layer of moss had colonised much of the slate roof. They were met at the entrance by Kemp.

'Any trace of William?' asked Tom, taking his crewman to one side, an anxious look on his face.

'Nothing, sir,' said Kemp. 'But we ain't searched the house yet. We've been talking to the old lady about what she knows.'

'Anything?'

'Claims she knows nothing about the silk and has never set eyes on anyone apart from her son for days.'

Tom turned back towards the front door. 'We're going to search the house, Gott,' he said. 'Anything you want to tell us before we start?'

'I told you, I ain't got nothing to hide.'

The floor of the front room was almost entirely covered with discarded rags, broken items of furniture, a cartwheel that was missing several of its spokes and sundry other articles. In a corner to the right of the front door lay a heavily stained flock mattress on which an elderly woman reclined. Next to her were some items of unwashed clothing, while in the middle of the room, next to a cheap wooden table, a second mattress was partially covered by an old blanket. To one side of the front door, an ancient musket was propped against the wall.

'This yours?' said Tom, picking it up and examining it. It wasn't loaded.

'Belonged to my father,' said Gott.

Tom put the gun down and looked round at the rest of the room. At the far end, standing to one side of a second door, was an old and battered chest of drawers. He stared at it for a second or two. It seemed oddly out of place. Alone of the contents of the room, it was tolerably clear of dust. He let his gaze move on. There was no sign that his brother William had ever been here. He walked towards the back of the house and into a second room as squalid as the first, the presence of a few cooking utensils and a small range serving as the only clue to its probable use.

He turned and walked back into the front room, the weight of disappointment heavy on his mind. Coming out here had been about finding the stolen silk. But it had also been about finding his brother. He had long suspected that whoever had taken William from his bed was also involved directly or indirectly in the plundering of the silk.

'You're coming with me, mister,' he said, turning to Gott. 'You've got an appointment with the magistrate.'

At the front door he paused and looked back, his eyes again straying to the chest of drawers by the back wall, conscious of a powerful feeling that he was missing something.

Tom stood at the window of Harriot's room at Wapping New Stairs, and stared at the afternoon sky dotted with puffs of white cloud. Occasionally his eye would drift to the river below him where the reflections of sunlight danced and shone on the heaving surface of the water. Harriot was speaking. Tom half turned to listen.

'. . . I've not the slightest doubt of Gott's guilt but that is neither here nor there,' said the resident magistrate. 'You will need to produce substantive evidence in support of your case before I can even consider allowing a charge to be laid. At this moment there is nothing.'

'I understand that, sir. But I'm confident that will be remedied as soon as I've spoken to Mr Horton. He is, you will doubtless recall, the agent responsible for delivering the silk to its new owner. I believe the piece of brown paper we found at the barn comes from a larger sheet used to wrap the skeins. The letter M that appears on that paper may, I believe, be the first of Mr Horton's two initials and was used to identify the owner of the bales.'

'You've had the whole morning to do that, sir,' said Harriot. 'Is there any reason why you haven't yet seen him?'

'He wasn't at his usual table at Jerusalem's nor was he at his house in Cinnamon Street,' said Tom, rather more brusquely than he'd intended. He wasn't used to criticism and Harriot's question had all the hallmarks of that. 'Perhaps you, sir, could tell me where I might find him?'

Harriot's eyes flared with anger. He pointed a finger at Tom. 'Find him, sir. And when you've heard what he has to say, please be good enough to let me know. In the meantime, I have little option but to release both Gott and Marr from custody.'

'If, sir, we do that, I doubt we shall ever find the silk,' said Tom, struggling to retain his composure. 'No one will talk to us with those two roaming the port.'

'Didn't you tell me there is every possibility the silk was removed from the Gott house by others? I think you mentioned the Americans had been seen in the area.'

'Sam Hart was certainly followed by an American who, we think, was looking for the silk. Hart tells me he lost him well before the house was reached.'

'But he can't be sure?'

'No,' said Tom, wearily.

'So it's entirely possible the Americans could have taken the silk?'

'Yes.'

'That could be serious.'

'I do know that, sir,' said Tom, irked by the statement of the obvious.

'What about the French? There was some talk of them being involved in the search for the documents smuggled out of Paris.'

'There was a time I thought they were here,' said Tom, 'but if they were, I would have expected to have heard something by now. My feeling is they're not involved.'

'So we're left with Creech and his friends, or the Americans, or some third party we know nothing about,' said Harriot.

'There is another potential witness, in addition to Mr Horton, whom I've not yet seen and who may have some useful information for us. If we've finished here, I propose to talk to him as soon as I've seen Mr Horton.'

'Certainly,' said Harriot. 'Who is it?'

'Do you recall a note that was delivered to me warning me not pursue this case?'

'Yes, I do. It mentioned your brother.'

'That note passed through the hands of Blind Jack. I think he may be able to tell us who gave it to him.'

# CHAPTER 28

It was late evening when Tom left the Wapping police office, the autumnal bite in the air helping to clear his mind. He regretted his spat with Harriot earlier in the day. It was not like him to lose his temper quite so easily. The absence of rest had taken its toll on his ability to think and act with the clarity he should have shown. That said, the release of Marr and Gott had been difficult to come to terms with. Doubtless they would be celebrating in a tavern somewhere. He tried to put the setback behind him and concentrate on what lay ahead.

He felt in his pocket for the shred of brown paper that Sam had found in the barn and which he intended to show to the agent, Horton. He'd already spent much of the afternoon looking for him, without success, and was now on his way to the man's house.

Expecting the fellow to positively identify the paper was, he thought, probably asking too much. The most he could hope for was that Horton would confirm the use of similar paper in previous consignments. He might also be able to confirm the use of his initials on the wrapping as normal procedure. It would be a start.

Tom strolled east down Wapping Street, hardly aware of the tuneless singing of a group of inebriated seamen, or the plaintive calls of a legless beggar sitting at the side of the street. Even the bawdy comments of the hatless, bare-armed women who leaned from doorways with their inviting smiles failed to attract a response.

His thoughts drifted and, for a while, no longer centred on his missing brother, or the silk, or even the consequences of any failure to find and secure the intelligence document. He didn't often let himself think of the Lady Annabel. He'd not seen her for nearly a month. There had been no reason for him to have done so, much though he might have wished otherwise. Usually resident close to the south coast, she only occasionally visited her house in London.

But he thought of her now, her slim figure sheathed in a cream-coloured satin dress, her auburn hair worn high on the back of her head. She was standing to greet him in her home in Rye, overlooking the Romney Marsh. They had met under difficult circumstances – an inquiry into the circumstances surrounding the violent death of her brother.

Tom had been acutely conscious of the social gulf that separated them, a feeling made more acute by the state of his own appearance. That meeting, more than any other, had persuaded him of the need to visit his old tailor in Conduit Street, if only to improve his sense of self-esteem. He doubted she would notice but he had gone ahead anyway and ordered some new suits. They would, he remembered, be ready in the coming weeks. Perhaps, then, he would summon the courage to call on her on some pretext or another. Perhaps . . .

Recollecting himself, he turned north, into New Market Street, the bustle of Wapping's main thoroughfare left behind, a sudden stillness surrounding him. He slowed his pace, his eyes probing the evening shadows, the hair at the back of his neck rising. He brushed aside the sudden feeling of anxiety, the feeling he was being watched.

When it came, there was no sound, no warning.

A pair of arms encircled his chest, pinning his hands to his sides. A second man appeared out of the night, his face hidden by a mask, the knife in his hand glinting in the moonlight. Tom felt the blade press against his throat. Adrenalin pumped through his body, his tiredness forgotten. He brought his knee up into the knifeman's groin and heard the fellow's yelp of pain as he reeled away. Behind him the grip around his chest loosened as Tom jabbed backwards with his elbow. He spun round, his fist connecting with someone's jaw, the sound of bone on bone loud in the still air of the night. Suddenly he felt a sharp pain at the back of his head. He couldn't focus, felt dizzy, his legs no longer able to support him. He put out his hands to save himself, saw the ground rushing up to meet him.

He could only have been unconscious for a few seconds. He awoke to find his arms tied behind his back and a sack being pulled over his head. He was dragged to his feet and a hand pushed him in the small of his back, propelling him along the street. He had no idea how far he went. Perhaps twenty yards, perhaps fifty. He was brought to an abrupt halt and heard a gate opening. They passed through and the gate was closed behind them.

'That him?'

Tom forced himself to stay awake and take notice of what was happening. The voice was muffled, yet vaguely familiar.

'What d'you want us to do with him?' asked a second voice.

'What d'you think I want done with him?' Again, the half-remembered voice. Tom struggled to listen, twisting his head, hoping to clear the hemp sacking from his ears. It didn't work. 'When's high water?'

There was a pause, then, 'About three hours from now.'

'Wait for that. Then throw him in.' This time there was no doubting the voice. It was Creech. 'He were warned but he were too stupid to listen. Put him in the cellar until then.'

A hand gripped Tom's shirt and pulled him through a nearby door and down some wooden steps into a musty-smelling room. The rope around his wrist was passed through what sounded like an iron hoop in the wall and made fast. Then he heard a door slam and the key turn in the lock.

Alone, Tom felt his knees giving way from under him. He sank to the floor, trying desperately to stay awake, to make sense of what was happening. He had to think. He'd told Sam where he was going. Sooner or later his friend would realise something had happened and come looking for him. He had to hope he was in time. His eyelids grew heavy. He'd think some more in a moment. He had to rest.

'On your feet, cully,' said the same rough voice Tom had heard earlier. He felt his shoulder being shaken. 'Time for your swim.'

New Market Street was quiet but for the occasional growl of a stray dog in search of food and the rustle of rubbish disturbed by the gentle night breeze coming up from the river. Far above, in the black vault of the sky, the moon still shone, its ghostly light deceptive in what it revealed.

The emaciated form of a cat emerged from the shadow of a court and crossed the street, its head stretched forward, its belly close to the ground, alert to its surroundings, its tail twitching. It made for a doorway directly opposite and rubbed itself against the body of a youth, purring as it did so.

Stevie Lyons didn't move. He was asleep, lying under the bulk of a bow window. He'd not rested nor eaten properly since he'd left his shelter in Farthing Field, constantly moving from one place to another in his attempt to keep out of Creech's way. Several times he'd seen the scrub in the distance and been forced to hide until he judged it safe to continue on his way. He no longer had a job. That would have risked exposure. And without a job he'd been unable to buy food. He'd had to resort to begging for whatever people could afford to spare, which wasn't much.

He'd hoped his meeting with Sam Hart might have resolved his difficulties and led to Creech's arrest for the murder of his old sailing master. But as time passed and nothing happened, his hopes had faded. In spite of that he had, earlier in the evening, gone to the police office at Wapping with the intention of again asking Sam for his help. His courage had failed him at the last minute and he'd abandoned the idea.

Stevie hadn't meant to spend the night so close to the river, where the risk of discovery was at its highest, but hunger and exhaustion had got the better of him. This was the first vacant spot that offered any protection from the wet and the cold, and he had taken it.

He woke with a start as the cat jumped onto his shoulder and nuzzled its wet nose against his face. He opened his eyes, forgetting for a second where he was. Then he stiffened. Some men had appeared from the shadows of the court opposite. They were carrying something long and heavy, wrapped in some sort of material. He suspected he knew what it was. He'd seen the attack on Mr Pascoe earlier in the evening. He'd recognised two of the men involved. They were the ones who'd followed him and Coxy down to the Medway. He wished he'd listened to his own advice and moved away to another, safer place for the night. He watched the men walk down the street in the direction of the river. Mr Pascoe – if that was who it was – was struggling violently.

He was about to follow when he saw a man emerging from the same court that the others had come from. He slipped back into the shadows, stifling a gasp as a shaft of moonlight fell on the face of Dan Creech. Silently, he watched him follow the others, always thirty or forty yards behind them.

At the junction of Wapping Street, the men turned left, shortly followed by Creech. Stevie set off in pursuit and reached the corner in time to see the men disappearing down an alley leading to the river. One man remained behind in the road. It was Creech. Stevie stared at him. Why he had chosen to remain behind, Stevie could not fathom. What was certain was that he had done so for a reason.

Stevie leaned against the corner house and closed his eyes.

There was nothing he could do.

Sam Hart paced up and down the length of the constables' waiting room, a worried frown on his forehead. For the fourth or fifth time in as many minutes, he strode to the door and peered along the corridor to the stairs. Tom had been due back at the police office an hour ago. It was unlike him to be late. Sam vaguely recalled being told his honour wanted to see a witness about something. He'd not been paying much attention; had been thinking of Emden's daughter. He cast around for the name of the witness but if it had ever penetrated his head, it had now vanished without trace.

He flung open the door and hurried down to the pontoon where Higgins and Kemp were cleaning the galley before handing over to the night-duty crew.

'Seen Mr Pascoe?' he asked.

'No,' said Kemp. 'We thought he was with you.'

'He's not returned from seeing the witness he was telling us about.'

'Horton? The agent what owns the *Sisters*?'

'That's the man.' Sam snapped his fingers. 'Can you remember where he lives?'

'Cinnamon Street, somewhere,' said Kemp. 'Where are you—'

Sam didn't hear the question. He was already running up the river stairs and past the police office into Wapping Street. With luck, he'd meet Tom on his way back. Then he could be off home. He was looking forward to some sleep.

The route to Cinnamon Street was fairly straightforward. It ran parallel to Wapping Street and could be reached by any one of a number of connecting streets. But that was the problem. Tom could use any one of them for his return journey. Sam chose one at random.

'Mr Pascoe?' said a surprised and sleepy Horton, answering the door in his nightshirt. 'I've not seen him at all this evening. You say he was on his way here? No, he never arrived.'

Sam thanked him and hurried to the corner of Market Hill. A group of men were approaching up the hill from the river. Sam stopped, suddenly alert. The men seemed ill at ease, in a greater hurry than he would have expected at such an hour, seemingly furtive, as if anxious to remain out of the public gaze. Several times, one of them looked over his shoulder, towards the Thames, a quick, nervous twist of the head.

They drew level with him, on the other side of the street, and turned into a court. Sam thought of Tom and hesitated. His friend was missing. Finding him was more important than chasing shadows. He turned away. A nagging doubt pulled him back, a vague suspicion born of experience. He'd follow the men for a minute or two. But no longer. If nothing transpired, he'd return to the task of finding Tom. A gate was opening, the harsh scraping of its bottom edge on the road surface, not far from where he stood. He crept towards the sound. In the darkness he could just see the outline of the men. They were entering a small yard. The next moment the gate was being pushed shut.

Sam was aware of a sense of disappointment. It was possible they'd done nothing wrong although he doubted that that was true. There was an inexplicable sense of dread in his stomach. His instinct rarely let him down.

He turned towards Wapping Dock Street. Tom might have taken that route.

Slack water, that period of calm while the tide turns, was over and the ebb flow had begun. Soon the barge roads would swing through a hundred and eighty degrees and trail downriver of their mooring buoys. Shortly after that, the first of the ships ready to depart would weigh their anchors and begin the long journey to the sea. Slowly, the ebb would build in strength and speed, and carry with it everything that had not been made fast.

Stevie stood at the top of Wapping Dock Stairs and gazed out over the black waters of the Thames. He knew the job was all but impossible. Even from a few feet and in broad daylight it was difficult to see an object floating in the water, let alone the almost wholly submerged body of a human being. At night and without a light to help him, the chance of success was even more remote, the body carried further and further away with each passing second.

Stevie's mind raced. He couldn't stay where he was. Creech might return at any moment. He bit his lip and forced himself to think. A man's life was at stake. Yet he knew that finding him was only the beginning. Somehow he would have to get the sodden dead weight out of the water.

From further upriver there came the sharp bark of an order. He looked up to see a boat's navigation light moving swiftly through the water. The craft would pass close to him. Already, he could see the foaming bow wave and hear the dull thud of its sweeps striking the thole pins. For a second he thought of calling for its crew's assistance but something stopped him. He had a shrewd idea the men in the boat were police. What could he say to them without arousing their suspicions of him? How would he explain his presence on the riverbank in the middle of the night? A passer-by would not have heard what he had heard and lived to tell the tale. For all he knew, he might already be a suspect in the death of Rob Cox, his sailing master. If he was, he doubted the police patrol would believe his story about Mr Pascoe being thrown in the river. As like as not he'd be arrested and Pascoe would drown for want of help.

Stevie waited for the galley to pass on down the reach and looked round for a boat. He checked the nearest mooring poles. Two had lines attached to them. He caught hold of one and pulled, feeling the drag of something heavy at the other end. A skiff came into view. He fetched it alongside the bottom step and got in. The oars had been removed. It was standard practice. Watermen were choosy about who used their boats. Stevie got out and tried the second line. This time he had better luck. The owner must have been in a hurry and had forgotten to take his sweeps with him. Stevie picked one up and hefted it over the stern. Casting off, he let the craft drift with the current, guiding it first this way and then that with a gentle figure-of-eight sculling action, while he searched for the impossible.

Suddenly his oar snagged something. Stevie cursed and tried to lift the blade clear of the water. It wouldn't move. Irritated by the delay, he drew the sweep towards him, feeling the heavy drag. Then something collided with the hull. Stevie's heart jumped when he saw the long, thin object wrapped in a sort of blanket. He leaned over the gunwale and hauled it inboard. He was young and strong but still the effort left him breathless. He took out his knife and quickly cut through the cords holding the blanket in place, letting the material fall away. A hemp sack hid the face of the inert figure. Quickly, he cut this free.

Tom Pascoe lay limp and still, his face pale, his eyes closed, his mouth partially open. There was no sign of life. Stevie stumbled to the stern, unsure of his next move but knowing he had to get ashore. No good could possibly come from being found in possession of a dead body, particularly the body of an officer of the police court. There was little doubt he'd be blamed for the death. The sensible thing was for him and the body to part company; either take it ashore or tip it back into the Thames.

Pascoe's death wasn't his affair.

# CHAPTER 29

Sam reached the bottom of Wapping Dock Street. There was no one in sight. He considered checking Tom's room in Burr Street to see if his friend had simply gone home. But Tom had specifically said he wanted to see Horton before he finished for the night. Sam doubted he'd have changed his mind in so short a time. He crossed the main road onto the riverside and turned towards the police office a few hundred yards away. Passing the mouth of the passage leading to Wapping Dock Stairs, he heard a low squeaking sound. He listened for a moment and then dismissed it. It had sounded like two boats being pushed together by the tide. Then he heard a gasp, like the sound of a man exerting himself.

He walked back to the passage and peered in. It was too dark to see anything. He waited. Then he heard a grunt, followed by the smacking sound of a boat rocking in the water. Sam drew his pistol and crept down the length of the passage.

He was almost on top of the man before he saw him, bent double over what appeared to be a dead body dressed in the blue and white uniform coat of a naval officer.

'Stand away,' Sam hissed, drawing back the hammer of his pistol and pointing it at the youth's head. 'And be quick about it.'

'Don't shoot,' said the young man, getting slowly to his feet, his eyes widening in fright, his hands held above his head. 'It were me what fished him out of the tideway. He looks like a goner . . .'

'I've seen you before,' said Sam, lowering his gun. 'At Farthing Field, if I'm not mistook. You're Stevie Lyons. What happened to Mr Pascoe?'

'I—'

'Never mind. You can tell me later. Is he dead?' said Sam, dropping to one knee beside his friend.

'Don't rightly know, Master Sam. It looks that way but I ain't had a chance to see to him.'

'Move out of the way,' ordered Sam, taking his coat off and laying it on the ground beside Tom. 'We need to try and warm him up. Help me move him onto my coat, then take yours off and spread it over him. He needs it more than you do. Look lively.'

The boy nodded.

'As soon as you've done that, lift his legs into the air and keep them there. D'you understand?'

'Aye.'

Sam knelt and turned his friend's head to one side while the boy raised Tom's legs into the air.

'Good,' muttered Sam, as water began to trickle out of Tom's mouth. 'Keep them like that.'

Sam rocked back and forth on his knees, the palms of his hands pressing down on Tom's chest. Four minutes went by. Then five, then ten minutes. Suddenly Tom retched. A moment later, his eyelids fluttered and opened. For another minute no one spoke as Tom coughed, spitting out mouthfuls of foul water.

'Now you can tell me how you come to be here,' said Sam, turning to face the young Stevie.

'Master Pascoe got took by a bunch of bully boys. He stood no chance,' said Stevie. 'They brought him down here not fifteen minutes since, and flung him in.'

'And you just happened to see them?' said Sam, a sarcastic edge to his voice.

'Aye, I did,' said Stevie. 'It were like this . . .'

Joe Gott leaned against the wall of the taproom at the Blind Beggar, close to St Saviour's Dock, Southwark, and gazed at the ceiling timbers with unseeing eyes. His future did not look good. Some men at the next table were discussing the Pascoe incident. He'd apparently drowned; fallen into the Thames by accident when he was drunk. Gott scowled. Aye, he might have drowned but it hadn't been no accident. And he should know. He'd been there with Creech and Marr and some others and helped to throw him in. It hadn't been his idea, though. Turning off a man like Pascoe was never going to be sensible. If he'd had his way they'd have made it look more like an accident. That sort of thing happened all the time especially if the cully were a drunk – like his honour Mr Pascoe. But Creech had insisted on doing it his way. He'd wanted Pascoe to suffer before he died.

Gott paused as he remembered a detail he'd almost forgotten. Creech hadn't actually been present when Pascoe had gone in. He'd stayed away and waited for them in the street. It had seemed odd at the time but he hadn't questioned it. But now he felt his stomach turn over. It confirmed what he'd suspected for some time. Creech wanted to distance himself from the killing. He knew the cloud of suspicion would hang over all of them and he wanted to make sure of his alibi.

Gott thought of the boy he'd snatched from his bed on Creech's instructions. He was still at his mother's house on the outskirts of Bow. He'd meant to get rid of him, had already thrown his trunk into the River Lea and intended to follow it with the lad himself. For some reason he couldn't now recall he'd decided to leave the boy until morning. But then Pascoe had arrived and he'd found himself on the way to the police office. It was a miracle Pascoe hadn't found the lad.

The boy still had to be dealt with. When the officers at Wapping found out what had happened to Pascoe they would be certain to want to come and talk to him about it. They might even search the house again. He couldn't rely on them missing the boy a second time.

He glanced at the tavern door. He'd arranged to meet Marr but the fellow was late. He signalled the pot-boy to fetch him another mug of ale. He had no money to pay for it, but that didn't matter. The landlord ran a tick for men like him. When the tick was big enough, Gott would have to work it off, unlading a ship or two without pay. He knew it was an expensive way to get a drink but what else could he do? The tick was too big for him to pay for in one go – always assuming he could get a job which actually paid cash. Most of the men on the river worked for the opportunity it provided to take what they needed.

The street door opened and several men walked in. Gott had seen one of them before. He was one of Pascoe's men. The scrub was staring straight at him. There was no doubt who they were looking for.

Gott sprang to his feet, ducked behind the bar and ran through a door leading to another part of the tavern. He found himself in the landlord's private quarters, his wife sitting in front of the fire, knitting. She looked up as Gott came in, fear in her eyes.

'Which way leads out, lady?' he asked. For a moment the woman went on staring at him, her hands covering her mouth. 'Quickly, woman.'

'That one,' she stammered, pointing at one of the three doors in the room. 'Leads to the dock.'

Gott rushed over, pulled the door open and ran outside. In front of him was the long tapering stretch of St Saviour's Dock. A dozen or so hulks lay moored alongside. He ran to the nearest vessel, a brig shorn of its masts and rigging. On its upper deck, twenty or so men hammered, sawed and planed new timbers into place. He paused, looked back at the tavern and then ran up the gangplank, his sudden arrival attracting curious stares. He ignored them and ran to the fo'c'sle break from where he could see the back entrance of the tavern.

The man he'd seen in the taproom was standing at the door with three others. The group split into two, the first walking down his side of the dock while the second took the east side. Gott knew that if he stayed where he was, he'd be seen. Slipping through a door below the fo'c'sle, he ran down the starboard ladder to the main deck and from there dropped to the damp surroundings of the orlop. He'd hoped there might be something down there that would hide him, some leftovers from the brig's last voyage; a bale of hay, perhaps some sacking. But there was nothing. Only the droppings of rats and the dank stench of decay. He could do nothing now but wait.

The men were not long in coming. Gott marked their progress by the sound of their boots on the decks above his head and the clatter as they descended the companion ladders. He remembered the name of the cully who he'd seen entering the tavern. It was Officer Kemp. He wondered if they'd found Pascoe and if that was the reason they were looking for him. He backed against a bulkhead and waited, trembling. Of all things, he didn't want to hang. He'd only done what Creech had told him to do.

'There's somebody wants to see you, Gott.'

Kemp's words seemed very loud.

# CHAPTER 30

Tom opened his eyes. He was in a strange bed. He moved his head to one side. There were other beds, each of them occupied. Some way down the long room, he could see a lantern perched on a table. Someone was sitting there, not moving. He closed his eyes and tried to think. Nothing came to mind. He felt sleepy.

When next he woke, the sun had risen and light streamed in through the windows opposite. He remembered the light on the table and someone sitting there. He turned to look. The table was deserted. He heard the rustle of a dress behind him. The face was indistinct, out of focus. The woman – he was sure it was a woman – was speaking to him.

'. . . been waiting for you to open your eyes all morning, sir. You was nearly a goner, so they say. Weren't too pretty when I saw you, and all.'

The voice. He'd heard it before.

'Where am I?' Tom put his arm over his eyes, shielding them from the bright sunlight.

'You's at the London, that's where,' said the voice. 'You got your friend to thank for that. And Dr Hamilton, of course. Don't know how you got to be in the river but it near killed you. Your friend – what's his name – Sam, ain't it? He brought you here.

Tried to stay but I told him he could bugger off and I'd look after you.'

'Miss Squibb? Miss Charity Squibb?' said Tom, dropping his arm away from his face and squinting up at her. 'Is that you?'

'Ain't nobody else, Captain,' said Charity, bending down and tucking in the bedsheet, her breath heavy with the smell of rum. 'Lord, sir, you didn't half give me a fright when I came onto the ward this morning and found you here.'

'Fear not, Miss Squibb, it will take more than a ducking in the Thames to get rid of me,' said Tom, conscious of slurring his words. He remembered Charity as Peggy's room-mate. Not a friend exactly, but a companion to whom she'd felt able to confide in times of need.

'You might think so, Captain,' said Charity, wagging a finger at him. 'But it'll be a day or so before you is fit to be discharged. Wouldn't surprise me none if Dr Hamilton wants you kept till Monday.'

'Monday?' Tom raised his head off the pillow, his face aghast. 'What day is it today? Friday? Saturday? I can't stay here for another two days. I've work to do.'

'I don't know nothing about that, Captain. But I'll tell you what I do know. You won't be the first to keel over after being in the water. I seen it happen with the girls I knew. Weren't unusual for them to be thrown into the Thames when they asked the client for money. Lots of them died. A few came out alive and thought they was all right. Two days afterwards they'd be dead, Captain. Same thing might happen to you. Best you stay put. That's what Dr Hamilton reckons.'

'I can't. It's a risk I've got to take,' said Tom. 'Where's Sam?'

Charity Squibb raised her hands in a gesture of mock despair. 'Said he'd be back to see you this morning,' she said. 'Shouldn't be long.'

'Seems I owe you my life.' Tom lay back on his pillow in the men's general ward on the first floor of the London Hospital, and looked up at Sam. 'How did you find me?'

'It's not me, sir, you have to thank. It's young Stevie Lyons what I told you about. He was the mate on board the *Sisters* when she went down to get the silk off the *Velocity*.'

'How did he come to be by the river? Was he following me?'

'No, but it were a good job he were there. He saw everything from the moment you was attacked to the time you was taken down to the Thames. It were him what fished you out.'

'So he knows who did this to me?'

'Aye, he does. Leastways he knew three of them – Marr, Gott and Creech. There were another three cullies he didn't know.'

'So we've got enough to bring them in.'

'You'd have thought so,' said Sam. 'We found Gott and brought him in. He were found hiding in a brig on St Saviour's Dock. But his honour, Mr Harriot, said we couldn't be keeping the scrub in the cells without we had the evidence. Seems Stevie didn't actually see who threw you in. So we had to let him go. Same goes for Creech. There weren't no evidence against him, neither.'

'Good grief,' said Tom. 'I sometimes wonder how anyone ever gets charged. By the way, I've still not seen Horton with that piece of paper you found in Gott's barn. It's in my coat pocket.'

'Not any more, it ain't, sir,' said Sam. 'Miss Squibb found it in your pocket first thing this morning, soaking wet. She gave it to me and I went round to see Master Horton. He thought it were the paper used to wrap his silk but he ain't certain. Said it were normal for his initials to appear on the packaging.'

'Pity he can't be certain,' said Tom. He thought for a moment. 'Of course, if we ever manage to find Gott again, we don't have to tell him that Horton wasn't sure about the packaging. He won't know one way or the other but if you tell him the truth, he won't say a word.'

'No, I don't suppose he would.'

'What about Marr? Is he inside?'

'Not yet, sir. The lads are still looking for him.'

'Where's Stevie Lyons? We need a statement from him about what he saw. And I want you to make sure nothing happens to him.'

'That might be difficult, sir,' said Sam. 'He's in hiding on account of Creech might do him some harm.'

'He's probably right about that. Find him, will you, Sam? As quickly as you can.' Tom's face suddenly clouded. He turned to look at his friend. 'Speaking of finding people, is there any news of William?'

'I regret not, sir. We're still looking.'

Tom lay back on the pillow. He felt helpless, wondering if there was any more he could have done, anything he might have missed.

'Do you think the Americans took William?' he asked, suddenly. 'It would make sense if they thought it would force me to stop the search for the missing document.'

'They could have taken him,' said Sam, slowly. 'But how would taking your brother help them get the document?'

'I suppose I was thinking that William might have been taken as a hostage. They would release him in return for the document.'

'It still don't make no sense,' said Sam. 'They don't know what's in the document. If we get it first – which we will – all we'd have to do is produce another paper saying whatever we liked, and give it to them. By the time they worked out what had happened, it would be too late.'

'Then what about Creech? Could he have taken William?'

'Creech's too clever to do it himself,' said Sam, seating himself on the end of Tom's bed. 'If he's involved, he'll have got one of his bully boys to do it for him.'

'Like Marr?'

'Or Gott,' said Sam.

An image of Gott's fleshy face and pig-like eyes popped into Tom's mind. He could see him standing in the front room of the house at Bow on the morning it was searched for the missing silk, the floor covered with rubbish of one description or another and, at the far end, a chest of drawers. He'd thought about that chest more than once since that day. It had seemed to him an oasis of calm midst the general squalor.

He turned to look at Sam. It was strange that he should be thinking of the chest now, as though it mattered in the least.

He didn't hear the man coming across the field towards him. It would have been impossible for him to have done so. The little sound he made treading through the long grass was hidden by the rain beating against the canvas sheeting that covered the tangle of gorse and bramble that Stevie Lyons had fashioned into a shelter of sorts.

The lad turned over onto his side, his head resting on his arm. As soon as the rain stopped he planned on going to the Ratcliff

Highway where the opportunities for begging were greater than elsewhere. And if he couldn't beg, he'd steal. He'd felt guilty taking what didn't belong to him, but that had soon passed. Near-starvation did that to people. He would have gone to his mother and father for help but for the risk that entailed. His only real contact had been with Master Hart when the latter had been brought here to this hiding-place on Farthing Field.

After that meeting, Stevie had meant to move on, make a new hideout for himself somewhere else where no one could find him. For a night or two he'd moved around, sleeping wherever he could find a shelter, but the close encounter with Creech had frightened him and he'd moved back to Farthing Field. He felt safer here, despite the fact that the urchin knew where he was and had doubtless told all his young friends.

In the meantime, he had hope for the future. He felt sure Master Hart would repay him for saving the life of his honour Mr Pascoe. That had to mean something, didn't it?

A shadow fell across the entrance to the shelter. Stevie raised his head a few inches and looked to see what had caused it. He paled at the sight of the face staring in at him.

'You Stevie?'

Stevie could only nod. He knew exactly who it was. He'd seen the scrub recently, down by Wapping Dock Stairs, helping to carry the body of his honour Mr Pascoe to the river. And he'd seen him before that, on the barge that followed the *Sisters* down to the Medway. Coxy had once told him his name. He'd known to keep out of Gabriel Marr's way.

'On your feet,' hissed Marr. 'You're coming with me.'

Stevie crawled out from beneath his shelter and stood up. He'd been dreading this moment since the night of his and Coxy's return. For a brief second he wondered how his old sailing master had met his end and considered the possibility that he might be about to suffer the same fate. It was more than possible. There was a man with Marr, standing a few feet behind him. It was Gott, another of the men he'd seen carrying Pascoe. Stevie thought of running. Neither of them would be able to outpace him. But what then? Sooner or later they would find him again and then he would pay the price of his defiance. Better that he go quietly, at least for now.

It took them about half an hour to reach their destination. The hamlet of Ratcliff lay on a bend in the river at about the point where the Lower Pool ends and Limehouse Reach begins. It was distinguishable from its neighbours to east and west only by the extreme squalor of its inhabitants and the soot-blackened face of its tumbledown buildings. Turning off the main street, they entered an alley which could not have been more than four feet in width, the upper floors of the buildings on either side seeming to meet over their heads. A foul-smelling stream, swollen by the rain, ran down the centre of the alley towards the junction. A gaggle of small, barefoot children stopped what they were doing and stared in silence as the three men passed along. A little further on Marr came to a halt and pointed to the half-open door of a house.

'In there,' he said, shoving Stevie in the back.

The powerful stench of human waste rose to meet them as they went in. A woman was sitting on the bottom step of a flight of stairs, an infant at her tiny breast. She glanced up as Stevie and the others approached, looking at them without interest.

'Is he in?' said Marr.

The woman jerked her head at the upper floors and waited for the newcomers to pass. Stevie shot her a look. She was probably about fourteen or fifteen, skeletal-thin, her long black hair tangled and shining with grease, her face a mass of bruises. She was shivering from the cold. He kept walking. They reached the first floor, deserted but for a drunk stretched out on the landing apparently asleep, an empty bottle in one hand. Stevie looked back over his shoulder and saw Marr motioning him towards the next flight of stairs, many of whose treads were either missing or rotting. He stepped over the inebriate and continued his ascent. At the top he stopped in front of a closed door.

'Move,' spat Marr.

Stevie hesitated, then went through. There were three people in the room, only one of whom could he recognise. Creech was sitting at the head of a small table. To his left was a large, heavy-chested woman with a rubicund face and bleary eyes with which she now regarded him. Opposite the woman sat a blind man, his head tipped back as though looking at something on the ceiling. He was holding a stout stick with which he beat the floor at regular intervals while muttering threats and curses to no one in particular. He, like Creech and the woman, had a pewter mug in front of him from which he took the occasional swig.

'You two can hop it,' said Creech, looking from one to the other of his companions. 'Me and the lads have some business to attend to.'

'No, Creech. Not the boy,' pleaded the woman, screwing up her eyes and pawing at Creech's arm. 'Not again, Creech. He's so young.'

'Get yourself out afore I clout yer,' said Creech pulling the woman to her feet and shoving her towards the door. 'And that goes for you, too, Jack.'

'All right, all right,' said the blind man. 'Keep yer hair on. I just wanted me drink.'

The door slammed shut behind the two, and was immediately followed by a loud string of oaths and the beating of a stick on the walls as Blind Jack and the woman made their way down the stairs. Stevie waited. Out of the corner of his eye he could see Marr and Gott leaning against a wall, eyeing the proceedings. In front of him, Creech was still seated, the table between them. He weighed up his chances of escape. If he was quick, he might make it to the door before anyone could react.

But what if he failed? He felt his resolve waning. Creech might only want to talk to him, warn him to keep his mouth shut. At worst he might threaten him with the consequences of a loose tongue. Why risk the cully's wrath before he knew what he wanted?

'Stevie, Stevie, my son. Where've you been these past few days?' Creech poked a finger into his mouth as if to dislodge some particle of food that had become stuck. Removing it, he examined the tip with exaggerated care and waited for an answer to his question.

Stevie said nothing. To his left Marr sniggered. He could feel the dampness in his armpits spreading, a trickle of sweat running down his sides. Creech was playing with him. Soon the empty smile would fade.

'The thing is, Stevie boy, I've got a problem.' Creech flicked the particle of food onto the floor. He watched it land and then turned to the boy. 'You know too much. If you was to open your mouth, me and my boys here would end up in all sorts of bother. And we all know what happens to folk what gets into bother.'

It was clear where this one-sided conversation was going. It didn't require much imagination to see its outcome. If Creech had been responsible for Coxy's death, why would he stop now? Stevie slid another glance at the men by the wall. They were still there, still lounging. He calculated it would take them a second or two to react if he was to run. Marr was the real problem. He looked as if he could move quickly. Creech and Gott he wasn't so bothered about.

Creech was talking again, his voice a distant drone in Stevie's ear as he continued to think about escaping. There were two flights of stairs he would need to negotiate. He remembered some of the treads were missing and others had felt as though they were rotting. He would have to be careful. If he reached the street he was confident he could get away. He hoped the girl with the baby was no longer sitting on the bottom step.

Creech had not finished talking when Stevie made his move. He turned and sprinted for the door, opened it and had reached the head of the stairs before a bellow of rage told him that his departure had not gone unnoticed. The next moment he heard a loud explosion, and a bullet sang past his head. He made it to the landing and was on the second flight of stairs when his foot sank through a rotten timber. He tried to stop his forward momentum, his arms flailing the air, searching for anything to break his fall. There was nothing.

From behind came the sound of heavy footfalls. Rough hands caught him round the neck and carried him back to the room he'd just left.

# CHAPTER 31

Sam Hart crossed over London Bridge and turned down Tooley Street towards the Royal Oak on Bridge Yard. He was looking for Stevie Lyons. The mate of the *Sisters* hadn't been at the shelter in Farthing Fields where he'd had last seen him. Nor had he been at any of the other places he was known to frequent. The tavern on the south bank of the Thames was close to the bottom of his list of places to visit and Sam's expectations of success were not high.

He put his hand into his coat pocket, his fingers coming into contact with a scrap of paper. He drew it out and looked at it without interest. Doubtless, he'd put it there in an absent-minded moment. It meant nothing to him. He was about to throw it away when something stopped him. He looked at it a second time. Then he delved into another of his coat pockets and withdrew a larger scrap of paper, a scrap he remembered finding in a barn on the outskirts of Bow and which he had subsequently shown to Mr Horton, the agent. He placed it alongside the first piece. They appeared identical in colour and texture. He frowned, wondering if he'd simply torn the larger scrap.

Then he remembered where he'd found the smaller piece.

It had been poking out through the front door of Jacob Emden's shop in Aldgate. Sam felt physically sick. If the two were connected there was a high probability that Emden had, at some stage, had sight of the stolen silk. Sam recoiled from the idea, its consequences too painful for him to think about, his future happiness in the balance. He wrestled with his conscience. He knew what needed to be done. Carefully and deliberately, he put the two scraps together and returned them to his pocket.

He walked in through the front door of the Royal Oak. The interior was its usual dingy self, a pall of tobacco smoke hanging like a permanent cloud over the whole room. Even on a sunny day, little daylight was able to penetrate the thick layer of grime covering the windows. Sam paused and let the door swing closed, the shriek of its hinges like that of a stray cat caught off guard. There were, he guessed, no more than fifteen or twenty men present, most of them barely awake, exhausted by the hours of hard labour on empty stomachs, their heads drooping over their half-drunk tankards of ale. He glanced to his left, at the table usually occupied by Creech and his friends. It was deserted. No one would be foolish enough to sit there while there was any prospect of the man himself coming in.

'Afternoon, John.' Sam walked over to the bar and nodded at the landlord.

'Afternoon, Master Hart. Very nice to see you. What'll you have?'

'Why thankee, John. Let me get this one. A Hammond's, if you please, and one for yourself.' Sam propped himself against the bar while his drink was brought. When it came, he said, 'I'm looking for young Stevie Lyons. You ain't seen him around, have ye?'

John Davy started as if he'd been struck in the face. He looked quickly round the taproom and jerked his head at the door behind him. 'Go through. First door on the left. I'll follow in a minute or two.'

Sam nodded imperceptibly. A moment later he levered himself

away from the bar and strolled through the back door into a corridor, turning left into the first of several rooms. A minute later John Davy entered and waved him to a chair.

'Sorry about that, Master Hart,' he said, turning to face Sam. 'Truth is, I can't say nothing without someone hearing. And that ain't healthy, if you know what I mean.'

'I can guess,' said Sam. 'D'you know what's happened to young Stevie Lyons?'

'Last I heard he were keeping his head down on account of Creech is looking for him.'

'Yes, he told me. But he's gone from where he was hiding. I was hoping you'd be able to tell me where he went.'

'You think Creech might have got him?' asked Davy, a concerned frown creasing his forehead.

'It's possible,' said Sam.

'He's the very devil, is that cully. The sooner you catch him, the better, Master Hart.'

'We'll do our best, John,' said Sam, his mind returning to the scrap of brown paper he'd found in the doorway of Emden's shop. He had the sense that finding Stevie – and young William, too – was bound up in the search for the stolen bales of silk. Find the silk and the rest would follow. There was little doubt that the paper pointed to Emden's involvement with the silk and, whatever his private motives for keeping silent about it, he could not now do so. He looked across at the landlord. 'If you want me to deal with Creech, I'm going to need your help.'

John Davy's eyes narrowed, his brow creasing into a worried frown. 'I can't help you none, Master Hart. I've a wife and family to look after. What'll happen to them if I get myself turned off?'

'What d'you know about the silk what was plundered?'

'They say a Jew's interested in it.'

Hart felt his stomach wrench. 'What Jew?'

'Don't know his name.'

'Do you know anything about him? Where he lives? Where he has a shop?'

'Can't help you no more, Master Hart. Honest, I can't.'

'Very well,' said Sam. 'I'll not ask you any more questions.' He turned towards the door and pulled it open.

'He's still got the silk,' said Davy.

Sam spun round and stared at him. 'Who has?'

'Creech.'

'What makes you say that?' said Sam, staring.

'Marr were in here yesterday morning. He were in his cups, shouting and cussing. He reckoned Creech were going to see a Jew about the silk and weren't going to share it with them what helped him get it.'

'When? When and where is he going to see this Jew?'

'Marr didn't say. Could be today. Could be tomorrow.'

Stevie Lyons tried to move but a sharp pain to his left thigh stopped him. He closed his eyes and let the pain subside before opening them again. His hands had been tied behind his back and he was lying on his stomach. He looked about him. It was dark and the air smelt of damp earth. For a moment he was puzzled. Then he remembered being taken to see Creech, his attempted escape and his tumble down the stairs. After that he must have lost consciousness. Why he'd been spared, he could not imagine.

Suddenly he tensed, could hear the faint rustle of clothing. He rolled onto his back, his teeth clenched against the pain in his leg. He could see nobody. Directly above him, thin strips of daylight filtered through cracks in what he assumed were floorboards.

'Who's there?' he said in a hoarse whisper.

There was no answer. The rustle of clothing stopped. Stevie felt his chest constrict and his breathing quicken.

'Who's there, I say?'

'Me.' It was a child's voice. A boy. He guessed he was no more than eleven or twelve years of age.

'What's your name, lad?' Stevie felt his breathing return to normal and the pressure on his chest lessen.

'William.'

'What are you doing here, William?'

'I don't know, sir.' There was a catch in the boy's voice. 'My brother is Tom Pascoe.'

'Pascoe, the officer?' said Stevie, unable to keep the surprise out of his voice. 'How long have you been here?'

Again there was a silence. Stevie tried again.

'How long have you been here, William?'

'Don't know.' The voice sounded close to tears. 'A man took me from my bed and brought me here. Said it were all Tom's fault and he should be ashamed of himself.'

'Was that all he said?'

'I think so.' There was a pause, then, 'Please, sir, will you help me escape?'

'We'll see what can be done,' said Stevie.

*

'You'll be the death of me, Captain and that's the truth,' said Charity Squibb turning her back on Tom as he rolled out of his bed at the London Hospital and pulled on a pair of filthy breeches. 'Dr Hamilton left strict orders that you was to stay in bed until he sees you on Monday. What's Charity going to say to him, then?'

'I'm sure you'll think of something,' said Tom, retrieving a silk blouse from the foot of his bed and pulling it over his head. 'Tell him I was kidnapped by Master Sam. That'll do.'

'Very funny, Captain,' said Charity, her arms folded over her ample bosom, her feet planted wide apart as if to bar the way. 'You can't leave without no certificate. You know the rules.'

Tom paused. He'd forgotten about the certificate, without which he'd not again be treated at this hospital. But that meant waiting until Monday and he couldn't do that. He sat on the edge of the bed, fished around for his shoes and put them on, feeling suddenly nauseous.

'There, didn't I tell you you ain't fit to leave?'

'Dear Charity, you're a real friend but do stop fussing,' said Tom looking up at her and smiling. 'Sam will take care of me as soon as he gets here. Now, about that certificate . . .'

'No, Captain, I'm not going to ask the doctor to give you one. What will you think on next?'

'Not even for an old friend?'

'No.'


It was dark by the time Sam arrived at the London to see Tom. Ten minutes later they were both in a chaise heading west along the Whitechapel road as Sam reported his conversation with the landlord of the Royal Oak a few hours earlier.

'And you think the Jew being referred to is Emden?' asked Tom.

'I'll warrant there's a good chance of it, sir. Emden knew about the planned depredation before we did. He once told me a friend had been offered the silk a week before it was put aboard the *Sisters*. I think it was him what was offered the silk, not his imaginary friend. But there's something else you should know.'

'What's that?' said Tom.

'I found this piece of paper in the doorway of Emden's shop. It looks as if it came from the same sheet that was used to wrap the silk.'

'I think you're right, Sam,' said Tom, examining the paper and the second scrap that had also been handed to him. Changing the subject, he asked, 'Didn't the landlord of the Royal Oak tell you Creech still had the silk?'

'Aye, so he did.'

'And he was due to meet with a Jew, who you believe may be Emden?'

'Aye.'

'Then it don't look as if we've a minute to lose. Best we get ourselves down to Aldgate and see what we can see,' said Tom.

# CHAPTER 32

A man emerged from the side door of a house next to the Blue Boar Inn and looked up and down the moon-dappled High Street. It was late and London was as quiet as it ever could be. A carriage rumbled up from Whitechapel towards him, the clopping sound of the horses' hooves loud in the still night air. The man stepped back into the shadow of the building and waited for it to pass into Fenchurch Street and the City beyond. Jacob Emden took out his watch and checked the hour. He was in good time.

He had decided to walk for the first part of his journey. He was less likely to draw attention to himself that way and would be able to slip in and out of the shadows as the situation demanded. A thrill of excitement passed down his spine. He was reminded of years gone by when he'd often ventured out at night in pursuit of some deal of dubious legality that might otherwise have slipped through his fingers. He had always been fortunate in that regard, making money where others failed. But that was then. He was older now, less physically able to look after himself in the hurly-burly of his chosen way of life.

But there was another reason for Emden's caution: Adina, his daughter, had told him about the attempted robbery. It had, she said, only been foiled because Master Hart had been in the area and had come to her rescue. Emden's sense of gratitude had quickly turned to suspicion. The officer had already made it clear that he thought Emden was involved in some way with the plundered silk. Could it be that his presence was no mere coincidence, that he was, instead, watching the Emden residence for evidence of criminality? He hoped not but had decided on a greater degree of caution than he had exercised hitherto. He could no longer afford to take chances.

A while later, he turned into Lower Shadwell, close to the north bank of the Thames, and saw the men standing close to the entrance of the dock. There were about six of them; big lads who looked as though they could handle themselves. His eyes scanned the street beyond them. There was no one in sight. It was the same behind. He crossed the road and approached them.

Tom had seen Emden standing in the shadow of the Blue Boar Inn on Aldgate, watching the carriage's approach. As soon as they had passed him, he'd ordered the driver to turn into the Minories from where he and Sam had walked back to the corner of Aldgate.

'He's still there,' whispered Sam, retreating out of sight. 'He's walking away from us towards the Whitechapel road.'

They slipped in behind him and followed him as he turned down through the maze of side streets, stopping every now and then as Emden turned to look back. But if he saw anything of his pursuers, he gave no sign of it and continued his journey south towards the Thames.

'What now, sir?' whispered Sam as, sometime later, he and Tom stood at the corner of Lower Shadwell watching Emden talking to a huddle of men by the entrance to a dock. 'We can't take on that lot. You ain't in no fit state to fight and neither am I.'

Before Tom could reply, the group moved off and turned into a small court leading off the Lower Shadwell.

'Wait here,' said Tom. 'I'm going to see what they're up to. It don't lead anywhere so they'll have to come out the same way they went in.'

He crept to the corner and peered down a short, gloomy space bordered on one side by a high wall and on the other by a series of stable-like buildings, each of whose doors appeared firmly locked and bolted. Emden's group were standing outside one of these while Emden himself pulled open its doors and went in, followed by two of the group. A minute later, he emerged with a large, four-wheeled hay wain that was being drawn by the two young men.

'If I ain't mistaken, that cart is for the silk,' said Tom. 'Emden must have the money with him. I can't see Creech, or anyone else, handing over the goods without the payment.'

They watched the group leave the court and turn left along Lower Shadwell. Suddenly there was a shout and the cart came to a halt in the middle of the carriageway. An elderly man had stepped into the road and was walking towards the group, carrying a lantern and a long stave.

'Ye Gods,' muttered Tom. 'It's the watch.'

'You want us to help him, sir?'

'Not unless we have to. If we go now we'll lose the silk, *and* Emden *and* Creech,' said Tom. 'I just hope the old fool doesn't try and do anything stupid.' He drew his sea service pistol and checked it as snatches of conversation reached him. 'We ain't . . . nothing . . . home.' The old man raised his lantern and walked round the cart and asked a few more questions. Finally, he stepped back and waved them on. Tom breathed a sigh of relief, unsure of what he would, or could, have done if things had turned ugly. A minute later, Emden's group moved off, travelling west, towards Wapping, the streets still silent and shrouded in darkness, the only sounds those of the river and the rumble of the iron-clad wheels of the hay wain.

It was some time later when a large sign appeared to suggest that the journey might be over. *Morgan's Wharf*, it read, the name painted in large black letters on a board that arched over the double gates of a yard on the Thames side of the street. The cart slowed to a halt and turned in through the gates.

'I'm going to have a look. See what's going on in there,' said Tom, as soon as the gates had closed again.

'With respect, sir, you bloody ain't,' spluttered Sam. 'Not in your condition. If anyone's going, it's me. Someone's already tried to kill you once. If you get caught in there, who's to say Emden won't do the same?'

'I'm going in alone,' said Tom, firmly. He pointed to a gap in the houses about twenty yards away. 'There's some steps onto the foreshore over there. I'll go that way.'

Leaving Sam at the side of the road, Tom made his way to the passage leading to some river stairs. The tide was out, the shingle still damp from the receding water, a trove of mussels hiding beneath its slippery surface. Some barges had begun to swing. The tide was turning. He reckoned he had thirty minutes – forty at the most – before the rising water level made his route back impassable.

Feeling his way in the dark he saw the dark shape of a barge, moored alongside a wharf. He looked up at the signboard.

*Morgan's Wharf*, it read. He climbed up the wooden struts supporting the quay and peered into the yard beyond. It was cluttered
with sawn lengths of timber of varying lengths and thickness,
piled high and occupying every available space.

Tom searched for any sign of movement, but could see nothing
of interest. Then he heard voices and the rumble of cartwheels.
The sounds were getting closer. He ducked out of sight, wedging
himself between the struts, and waited.

'Put the box in the hold.' The voice had a nasal quality to it.

'Tide's turned,' said another voice. 'Be about half an hour
before she floats.'

'Good,' said the nasal voice. 'You know where we're going?'

'. . . Dock, you said.'

Tom tried to listen. It was difficult. Suddenly, he felt faint. He
knew he'd taken a risk. He'd thought himself cured of his near-
drowning. Had refused to listen to those who knew better. He
looked down at the rapidly disappearing foreshore. The flood
tide had almost reached the bottom of the wharf. Another few
minutes and he would have to wade back to the stairs down
which he'd come. Any more than that and he'd be forced to
swim – if he had the strength.

His head was spinning. He looked up. The men were still there.

'Have you eaten?'

'Aye. The lady brings me food every evening.'

Stevie Lyons considered the boy's answer. If the woman was
alone it should be an easy matter to overcome her and make good
his and William Pascoe's escape – if only they could free themselves from the bindings.

'She carries a pistol,' said William, as if reading Stevie's thoughts. 'She undoes the rope for me to eat. When I've finished she ties me up again.'

Stevie nodded as he assimilated this new piece of information. The gun certainly made a difference, although how willing the woman would be to use it was another matter. He dragged himself over to the nearest wall and leaned his back against it. Gun or no gun he didn't think he was in any state to try and get out of here. Not for the next day or two, while he recovered from the flogging Creech had given him.

'Does the cully what brought you here ever come to see you?' he asked.

'No,' said William. He thought for a second. 'My brother were here once. I heard him talking to someone. He were just there.' He jutted his head at the trapdoor. 'Leastways, I think it were him.'

'Why didn't you call out?' said Stevie, staring incredulously at the boy.

'I weren't sure it were him. I were afraid.' He stopped at the sound of something heavy being drawn over the floorboards. The next moment there was the rattle of a bolt being drawn back. Then daylight flooded the basement as the trapdoor was lifted. A woman's face appeared in the opening. She was probably in her early sixties.

'Don't want no trouble out of you boys. Any trouble and you get this, see?' she said, waving a pistol in air.

'We ain't going to be no trouble, lady,' said Stevie.

The face disappeared for a moment. When next she appeared she was carrying a plate with some food on it. Descending the steps, she put it down on the ground next to William, undid his bonds and waited while he ate. When he'd finished she again tied his hands behind his back. Returning to the hatch, she brought a second plate and gave it to Stevie, repeating the process she'd followed with William. When he, too, had finished, she left the basement, closed the trapdoor and drew the bolts across. Finally, there was the sound of something heavy being dragged across the floorboards.

'Told you,' said William. 'Didn't I tell you the woman's got a gun?'

'Aye, so you did, lad,' said Stevie, a faraway look in his eyes. 'So you did.'

The sound of their boots on the wooden surface of the wharf receded into the distance. How long he had before they returned, Tom didn't know. What he did know was that the tide was swilling round the base of the wharf. In a few minutes he would find it impossible to walk along the foreshore. His strength was not up to it. He had to make a move.

He eased himself out from between the struts and climbed unsteadily down to the riverbed. He felt the wet stones beneath his feet crunching noisily as he made his way to the stairs. Suddenly, he heard voices behind him. Darting behind a large timber support of a house, he looked back. A couple of Emden's men were crossing from the wharf to the barge, a bare five yards away. If they looked in his direction they could hardly fail to see him. He slid behind the timber support of a house and waited. Five minutes passed. The tide was rising fast and was now swirling round his ankles. He couldn't see the steps from where he stood. Wisps of fog had appeared but not enough to hide him.

The sudden clatter of boots and the muttered conversation of the two men drew Tom's gaze back to the barge. They were crossing the gangplank back to the wharf. He looked at the rushing water and wondered if it was not already too late for him.

Silence returned to the wharf. Tom stepped back into the water. If he was quick he might just do it.

'You do that to me again, sir, I'll flatten you as sure as I'm standing here,' hissed Sam as he helped Tom up the steps. 'I were half dead with worry.'

Tom sat down in the passageway.

'I just need a couple of minutes to recover,' he said. 'I think Emden is meeting someone at one of the docks further upstream. He didn't say who, or why, but I'll warrant it'll have something to do with the silk. Come, we ain't got a minute to lose.'

Hitching a ride on the night-soil cart had not been the ideal mode of transport back to Wapping, particularly as there had been no room on the driver's seat, but it had been the best Tom could have hoped for as he and Sam hopped off the tailgate and walked up the steps to the police office.

'All correct, sir,' said John Kemp, as Tom walked in through the door of the constables' waiting room on the first floor of the police office. 'Christ, the smell . . . Begging your pardon, sir.'

'We've had a busy evening,' snapped Tom. He wasn't in the mood for further explanations. 'Where's Higgins? We got work to do.'

'He's down the chophouse, sir. Getting us some victuals. Won't be a minute, sir.'

# CHAPTER 33

Tom had known it was coming. The greyish white cloud of fog tumbled and swirled over the surface of the river, reducing the ships and lighters in the Lower Pool to ghostly apparitions that fleetingly appeared and disappeared in the light breeze.

'Give way together.' Tom was sitting in the stern sheets of the police galley, his gaze probing the central channel into which they were now edging. 'We'll not be showing any light. No sense in telling the world where we are.'

It was harder to row against the tide out here, in the middle of the river, where the flood was at its strongest. Tom would not normally have considered doing it. But he didn't want to miss Emden and mid-channel was exactly where the merchant was likely to be.

A dark shape appeared ahead, coming straight for them. Tom altered course. It was a lighter. 'Stand by to go about,' he whispered. The galley curved round and, within a minute, was alongside the slow-moving vessel.

'Police. I'm coming aboard,' said Tom.

He eased himself off the arms' chest that doubled as his seat and clambered up onto the high-sided barge.

It was no more than a routine search. He'd known it from the moment there had been no reaction to his challenge. No one had sworn or threatened him, waved a cutlass or pointed a gun. The lighterman was on his own. A few questions and it was over. Tom got back into the galley, pushed the tiller hard over and was soon back on his course downriver.

'Barge on the larboard beam, sir,' said Higgins, quietly. 'He's tucked in on the shore side of the Wapping Road.'

'Thankee,' said Tom, craning his neck to see the dull outline of a lighter opposite the King's Stairs, moving upstream with the tide. It was, he thought, a stupid place to be. The lighterman would have no steerage, no ability to determine the course of his vessel. Only a fool would be there – or someone anxious not to be seen. 'We'll have a look at him. See where he goes.'

'Ain't we going to stop her, sir?' asked Kemp.

'No, not for the moment,' said Tom. 'There's a good chance that it's Emden. And if it's him, he won't have got the silk yet.' He paused as he caught sight of the Goodwyn brewhouse coming up on the larboard bow, the smell of fermenting yeast drifting across the water. 'He's got to be making for Hermitage Dock. If he goes any further he's got to pass the Tower. Then there's the Custom House. I doubt he'd want to be seen there.'

The fog was thickening. He could no longer see the barge and would have to close with it, increasing the risk of being seen. The alternative was to go ashore and hope he was right about where Emden would land. Tom swore under his breath. He didn't much care for either option.

'Make it Parson's Stairs,' he said.

A few minutes later, the galley drew alongside some river stairs positioned a little way upstream of Hermitage Dock where Tom jumped out and ran to the main street. Behind him he could hear Sam's hoarse whisper.

'You ain't in no fit state for this, your honour. Let one of the others go.'

'Thankee, Sam, but I'll be all right. You stay here in case I need the boat in a hurry.'

Leaving Sam behind, Tom hurried to the edge of Hermitage Dock. To his right, he could see a wooden bridge arching across its narrow mouth and guarding the approaches. To his left was the dock itself, one side used by the Goodwyn brewhouse, the other for the repair of small vessels. It was to this second side that he now looked and where he could see a number of huts set back from the water's edge and separated from each other by a narrow gap. In front of one of them and tied up at the quayside, was the barge Tom had seen coming up the river.

He was about to cross the bridge when he saw a shadow moving along the deck of the barges. He crouched and waited. A man clambered out of the vessel and went into one of the huts. He was too far away for Tom to see his features but he doubted it was Emden. He'd been too thin for that.

Tom ran to the bridge, crossed it and, keeping close to the boundary wall, crept towards the hut into which the man had gone. From inside there came the sound of raised voices. He couldn't be sure but he thought one of them was Emden's. He decided to check. Drawing his pistol, he checked it was loaded and primed. Then he crept forward.

He was still about five yards away when the door to the hut swung open and a man appeared in the opening. Tom froze. He'd never make it back to safety before he was seen. He waited for the inevitable, his thumb drawing back the hammer of his pistol.

*

Dan Creech turned back into the room, closed the door and looked at the merchant with ill-disguised annoyance. He didn't trust Emden. Nothing in his experience of life had ever suggested the need or even the value of trusting someone and he certainly was not about to begin now. Trust was for the weak. It was what one did when there was no alternative. The fact that he was, himself, very nearly in that position merely accentuated his deep sense of being played for a fool. He and the Jew had been talking for close on ten minutes and were no nearer to closing the deal than when they'd started. In fact they were so far apart that the subject of where the silk was at that precise moment and what the expected price was to be had not yet been mentioned.

Creech had taken a risk in arranging to meet Emden at the very place where he'd hidden the silk. Yet, in truth, he could have done little else. The merchant had already seen a sample of the silk and had expressed an interest in buying. As far as Creech was concerned, that should have been an end of the matter – pay the money, take the silk, and go. But it seemed the Jew had other ideas. Creech was rapidly losing patience. If it hadn't been for the fact that he needed to get rid of the stuff, he'd have kicked the scrub and his friends out a long time ago.

'I ain't got all night, mister,' said Creech. 'Either you want what I've got or you don't. You can please yourself but I ain't standing here talking to you for the sake of me health. You understand me?'

'I am sure you understand the need for care, my friend. I have not seen the merchandise; only a sample. I must be satisfied as to the quantity and quality of the goods on offer. After that I will make my decision.'

'Then come and look,' said Creech. He strolled over to a door at the back of the hut and pushed it open. It led into a small, windowless room almost entirely filled with large bales covered with brown paper, each one of which bore the letters MH. 'This is what you wanted to see, weren't it?'

Emden followed him in and removed a small knife from his coat pocket and cut through the paper wrapping. Drawing out a few strands, he examined them minutely while rolling them between thumb and forefinger.

'What are you're doing?' said Creech, pushing the Jew away. 'You've seen the goods already.'

'I've no wish to buy a cartload of paper, my friend,' said Emden. 'How do I know these bales contain the same thread as the sample?'

Creech fell back, grinning in spite of himself. The Jew had a point.

'Satisfied?' he said, when the merchant had finished.

'I regret it extremely, sir, but you play with me. This silk is of the lowest quality. It has not been cleaned nor combed. I'm not interested in a purchase.' He paused and appeared to reflect. 'But as a favour I am prepared to offer you twelve shillings a pound and not a penny more.'

'It's worth twenty shillings, you thieving scoundrel,' shouted Creech, his earlier, grudging respect, evaporating.

'No, my friend. Twenty shillings is what you are asking. I tell you it is too high. If it had been of the highest quality, I would have paid you fourteen. But not for this.'

'It's worth more than that and you know it.'

'You might be right,' said Emden, spreading out his arms. 'But who is going to pay you more in the circumstances? As true as the Law of Moses, you would not do better than twelve shillings. Whoever buys must also make a profit and it has taken a good deal of my time to come here. Also, I must pay these men for their time. Then there is the small matter of the washing and combing that must be done before the skeins can be given to a weaver. Where is my profit, sir, if I give you what you ask?'

'Twenty shillings or nothing,' said Creech, pointing a finger close to the merchant's face.

'Then, sir, I shall bid you goodnight.' Emden turned away.

'Wait,' said Creech, aware he'd pushed Emden too far. He needed this deal. Then he could disappear for a while. Let the dust settle. 'Do you have the money?'

'Of course.' Emden crooked a finger at one of the men standing behind him who now came forward with a small metal box. 'The money is in here. My men will remove the bales as soon as you are satisfied with the payment. I will— What was that noise?'

'I heard nothing,' said Creech, staring at the window.

'Somebody is there. I heard a noise.'

Tom dived into the narrow gap separating the hut from its neighbour just as the door of the hut was flung open and someone emerged onto the quay. For a moment there was utter silence. Tom waited, trying to control his breathing, his back pressed against the wooden wall, wondering if he'd been seen. The seconds ticked by. He guessed that whoever it was was waiting for him to make the first move.

A footfall. Barely audible.

Tom tensed, raised the barrel of his gun and drew back the

hammer once more. He rolled his shoulders, attempting to rid himself of a niggling pain at the base of his skull. It didn't work. Another footfall, closer than the last. Tom pushed himself away from the wall and stood to face the approaching threat, his sea service pistol ready to fire. He wasn't about to risk someone else shooting first.

'I ain't got all day.' Emden's voice sounded far away.

'I'm coming. There's no one here.' Tom recognised the voice. It was the same one he'd heard when trussed and blindfolded in a house off Old Gravel Lane. He listened as the footsteps retreated. He heard a door close and the muffled sound of men talking. Then the silence of the night returned. Tom crept to the front corner of the hut and looked at the closed door.

He still had a job to do.

He moved to the window.

The glass was covered with dirt. It was difficult to see what was going on but he recognised Emden. The merchant was standing with his back to the window, his head turned to one side as though listening to someone Tom couldn't see. Next to Emden were two or three others standing in a semicircle. They were all looking at someone or something just out of Tom's view. It had to be Dan Creech.

Tom slipped away. He'd seen all he was likely to see from where he was. He'd wait for the men to leave the hut. Then he would know whether or not he was right about it being Creech. He crept back to the bridge and crossed over to the brewhouse. He could watch developments from there.

He didn't have long to wait.

# CHAPTER 34

Lieutenant Milton Brougham felt strangely relieved to hear of Pascoe's recovery. He didn't know the fellow; had only seen him once before and could hardly be expected to feel any sense of fraternal kinship. To make matters worse, the man was English. But the feeling persisted, perhaps inspired by their common background in the sea. It was, in its way, highly problematical given his visit, yesterday afternoon, to the American ambassador's office on Tower Hill.

He'd been ushered into a large room, warm with the smell of polish, its high windows looking out over the Thames, the autumn sunlight streaming between the heavy drapes. The ambassador had wasted no time, his questions starting almost before Brougham had reached the large mahogany desk at which he was sitting. It seemed the way with busy men. Their time was valuable and not to be wasted. Mr Rufus King had wanted a detailed account of Lieutenant Brougham's progress in tracing the present whereabouts of the intelligence report.

It had not been a comfortable half-hour.

'You are to consider, sir, the very serious embarrassment that will result for the United States government should it become known that we were, albeit unofficially, engaged in discussions with the French,' the Minister Plenipotentiary had said. 'It will undoubtedly be seen as an unfriendly act by the British. You make darn sure you get hold of that document, sir. We don't want another fight with the British.'

Now he sat in the Harp tavern watching the front door through a haze of tobacco smoke. He shifted uneasily in his seat. The trail for the document had gone cold and the man who might have helped him, and for whom he was waiting, was worryingly late. He removed a pocket watch from his waistcoat and glanced at the time. He'd give it another ten minutes. After that . . . well, after that he would have to begin looking for the fellow in his usual haunts and hope he wasn't too late. He was putting the watch back into its pocket when Hawkes tapped him on the arm. He glanced at him and then at the front door towards which his colleague was peering.

Joseph Gott was pushing his way through the press of drinkers, his face pink and running with perspiration. He stood for a moment, wiping his forehead with the sleeve of his coat, his eyes nervously sweeping the room. Apparently giving up the search, he found himself an empty seat and ordered himself a drink.

Brougham got to his feet and ambled over. He knew Gott only by repute although he had seen him once – from a distance. Tonight's meeting had been arranged through a long and complicated chain of intermediaries. As is the way in such cases, each stage had required an ample slice of the American's rapidly diminishing supply of money provided to him by the taxpayers of the United States.

'Gott?' he said, standing over the seated figure.

A pair of hostile eyes peered up at him from deep within the folds of facial skin. 'Who's asking?'

'Henry,' said Brougham, catching the sour reek of the man's sweat. The fewer people who knew his real name, the better. 'Drink?'

Gott shook his head and pointed to the quart mug on the table in front of him. 'What d'you want to see me for? I were told you'd make it worth my while.'

'Could be,' said Brougham. Conversation, except of the shouted variety, was proving well-nigh impossible amidst the din of the taproom, and he was not inclined to shout about the sort of things currently on his mind. 'Where can we talk?'

Gott looked round the bar and shrugged. 'Ain't nobody here what's interested in anything you say. Wouldn't matter to me if they were. I ain't leaving me drink what I just got.'

The American sighed. 'They tell me you know a man named Creech?'

'What of it?' said Gott, his eyes narrowing.

'I hear he's got something of yours.'

Gott didn't answer but looked carefully around the room before returning his gaze to the American. Finally, he said, 'He might have. What's it to you?'

'I can help you,' said Brougham.

Gott looked down at the table in front of him, a finger tracing patterns on the rough surface, his forehead creased into a frown of concentration. 'Why would you want to do that?' he said, without looking up.

'The way I hear it, Creech ain't dealing straight. Where was he when the officers felt your collar at the Royal Oak? I'll tell you. He ran, didn't he? Didn't stop to help his mates, did he?'

'It were a fight. Ain't unusual. Happens every Saturday. It don't mean nothing.'

'Except that it was the officers you were fighting. And they were after Creech, not you. But let's talk about something else. Let's talk about the night Creech wanted you to catch Pascoe. Did he go out with you? Or did he leave you to take the risk? And then, when you did catch Pascoe, who was it that threw him into the Thames? You or Creech? Let me guess. It was you. Creech was nowhere to be seen, was he?'

'No.' Gott's whispered answer was almost lost in the welter of noise inside the tavern.

'So when the time comes, who'll be standing in the dock at the Old Bailey? You or Creech?'

Brougham waited for an answer. When none came, he said, 'He's playing you for a fool, isn't he? And you're letting him.'

Gott's face reddened and his eyes narrowed into mere slits. He opened his mouth. Seemed about to say something, but no sound came.

'Where's Creech put the silk? You know you want to get back at him. I can do that for you.'

'Aye, I want what's rightfully mine,' said Gott suddenly banging the table with a clenched fist. 'The thieving villain promised me a share of what were taken. I'll not be cheated.'

'Where is he?'

'Hermitage Dock. He's found a buyer what he's going to meet there.'

# CHAPTER 35

Tom didn't hear him coming. He was still watching the hut door from his vantage point on the other side of the Hermitage Dock. There had been no movement in the last quarter of an hour and he was beginning to wonder if he should not again have a closer look at proceedings when a voice at his elbow made him jump. He spun round, his hand closing on the butt of his pistol.

'Lord, Sam, did you have to frighten me like that?' said Tom, recognising his friend in the half light. 'What are you doing here, anygate? I thought I told you to stay with the others.'

'You ain't well, sir. I keep telling you but you won't listen. You should be in the accident hospital, like Miss Charity told you.'

'Well, that makes two of us . . .' Tom stopped. He knew Sam was right. Neither of them had any business getting involved in potentially violent situations. He'd rest as soon as he could. 'Where are the others?'

'By the stairs, where you left them.'

Tom looked back at the hut through the drifting fog. After a moment's silence, he said, 'What d'you suppose has happened to my brother?'

'I don't know, Tom,' said Sam. He rarely used his friend's first name, even when they were alone together, choosing to reserve it for those occasions when the two of them spoke about personal matters outside the sphere of their professional lives. 'But there ain't no point in thinking the worst when none of us knows what's happened to the little fellow.'

'No, you're right, of course. I try not to think about it but I do. Every waking moment I'm thinking of him and hoping he's all right. I feel it was my fault he was taken. If I don't find him soon, I'm going to have to go home and tell his mother. It will break her heart. I know it will.'

'We'll find him,' said Sam, putting a hand on Tom's shoulder.

'You remember the house out Bow way?' said Tom, a faraway look in his eyes.

'Aye.'

'Did you notice anything odd?'

'You mean apart from the smell and the filth that were everywhere?'

'Yes, apart from that. Did you notice the chest of drawers?'

'Aye, I saw it, right enough.'

'There were some marks on the floor as if it had been moved.'

'I don't understand.'

'I think it's possible it was hiding something.'

'William?' said Sam, staring at him.

'I dare not believe that, Sam. But I intend to have a look as soon as we've finished here.'

Sam nudged him into silence and pointed to the hut. Some men were coming out carrying bales. They walked to the lighter moored at the dockside and dropped the packages into its hold before returning to the hut and repeating the process. It didn't take them long to complete their task.

'Someone else coming out, sir,' whispered Sam.

'It's Creech,' breathed Tom.

'What d'you want to do, sir? said Sam.

For a long time Tom said nothing. He just stared at the villainous wretch who had tried to kill him; would have done so but for the intervention of young Stevie Lyons. Every fibre of Tom's being shrieked for revenge, an overpowering desire to end Creech's life.

'Sir?' Sam was shaking him gently, a hand on his shoulder.

Tom looked at his friend, stony-faced, his eyes devoid of humanity, his fury fuelled by a sense of impotency.

'What do I want to do?' he said. 'What I'd really like to do is rip Creech's head off. But I'll settle for seeing him standing in the dock of the Old Bailey facing the certainty of his own death.'

Sam nodded sympathetically.

'And you know the worst of it?' said Tom, staring across the narrow strip of water that separated him from Creech. 'It's the fact that we still don't have evidence of his involvement in any offence. We don't know for certain that he stole the silk, we don't know what's in that barge over there or what Emden is here for. We can only guess. If we go in now and find nothing, my brother's life might well be forfeit. I've little doubt Creech – or whoever has got him – would turn him off rather than let him go. The risk is too high, Sam. All we can do is follow the silk in the hope that we learn something.'

'I can follow Creech. See where he goes, like,' said Sam. 'Leave you free to go after Emden.'

'Just do what you're told for once,' snarled Tom, his pent-up fury spilling out. 'We'll stay with Emden and the silk.'

'Very good, sir,' said Sam, turning away, a hurt look in his eyes.

'Emden's coming out now,' said Tom, angry with himself for the pain he'd caused.

Milton Brougham was less than happy with developments. Gott had decided against providing him with any information beyond naming the location where Creech was expected to meet a buyer for the silk. The scrub's explanation – that he doubted Creech would look kindly on his treachery – while impeccable in its logic, had done nothing to improve Brougham's mood. He was now in the position of attempting to find his way to Hermitage Dock through unknown streets and without a guide. The journey which, on foot, might have been expected to take around forty minutes, was now likely to take very much longer. And it was time he didn't have.

A little way past the Tower, he stopped at a junction and debated which of two routes he should take. He could see a group of men approaching from the southern fork. He thought of asking for directions but decided against it. They looked to be in a hurry. All but one were in their twenties. The last was older, perhaps in his mid forties with a thin face and a strong, aquiline nose. Brougham had seen him before but couldn't remember where. The group drew abreast of him, their stares boring into him. Then they were gone.

A breeze drifted up the street along which the men had come, carrying with it the scent of the river. Brougham turned and walked in that direction. It was as good a choice as any. He reached the mouth of an alley which appeared to lead directly to the river. A large wooden signboard at its entrance announced the presence of the Goodwyn brewhouse. He recalled Gott's instructions: *Take the alley down to the brewhouse. The dock is there.*

A few minutes later he leaned against the passage wall, staring at the black expanse of water, and knew he was too late. The row of huts on the far quayside were in darkness. There was no movement and no sound, save the lapping of water against the barges moored on the brewery side. Silently, Brougham made his way to the first of the three huts and tried the door. It was locked, as was the second. He put his face to the window but could see nothing. Going to the third hut, he found the door open and went in. Inside, it was dark, the grey light of early morning barely able to penetrate the lingering fog.

A candle sconce stood on a table in the middle of the room. He picked it up and lit it. The hut's interior sprang into view, rolls of canvas resting on wooden brackets from floor to ceiling, a long workbench running almost the entire length of the hut, coils of hemp heaped on the floor beneath it. There was nothing here that was unusual. It was, self-evidently, a sailmaker's shop. Then he saw a second door. He went over and pulled it open. It was empty, aside from some torn sheets of brown paper and some twine that lay discarded on the floor.

'It was here,' said Brougham, clenching his fists in frustration. 'It must've gone in the last half-hour or so.'

He walked to the door and breathed in the cold morning air while he tried to decide his next move. Then he caught the faint sound of a splash. He'd nearly missed it amid the bumps and creaks that could be heard on the river at any hour. He guessed the sound had come from the other side of the bridge spanning the mouth of the dock, perhaps a lighterman going about his business. Brougham wanted to be sure. He ran to the bridge. Through the fog which had blanketed the river for much of the night he saw a barge heading away from the dock, into the tideway.

There was hardly a ripple on the surface of the Thames as the galley appeared out of the remnants of the fog and drew alongside Parson's Stairs where Tom and Sam were waiting.

'Make it Hermitage Dock,' said Tom, settling into his place in the stern. The bows of the sleek, twenty-seven-foot cutter sheered away into the channel, its presence soon hidden from the shore by a jumble of small craft. There was little else moving. It was still too early for the port to have been roused from its slumbers. 'When we get to the mouth of the dock, I want absolute silence. The tide's due to turn in the next few minutes. I make no doubt Emden's waiting for that. Then he'll come out.'

The galley glided through the last of the flood tide and, a few yards west of the dock, pulled alongside the solid bulk of a barquentine. Almost immediately, a lamp appeared on the upper deck and a querulous voice called out, 'Who's there?'

'In the King's name, be quiet,' growled Tom. 'We're police.'

The lantern promptly disappeared from view and the silence returned. Tom looked towards the north shore. The bridge over the entrance to the dock was only just visible. He debated going in closer to the shore, concerned about the possibility of Emden slipping out, undetected. He was still considering the matter when Kemp's voice cut into his thoughts.

'Something moving, sir. Looks to be a barge what's coming out of the dock.'

A white ripple of a bow wave appeared in the mouth of the dock. On its present course, the barge would pass uncomfortably close to the galley and could hardly fail to see it. Tom thought quickly. It would be a simple matter to board the lighter. He doubted the opposition would amount to very much. And yet . . . He again thought of his young brother and the harm that might befall him as a result of his actions. There was no question that Creech would hear of any action against the barge and be enraged by it.

'Heave back on the hitcher, Higgins,' said Tom. 'Jump to it, man. Get us out of sight, amidships of this barquentine. The rest of you, ready cutlasses and stand by to board. If they see us we won't have a moment to lose.'

Suddenly, it was there, its broad, bluff bow churning the water, the shadowy outline of several men standing on her deck, another leaning on a long paddle-oar at the stern, controlling her course.

'Down,' said Tom. 'Onto the bottom boards. Now.'

Creech continued up Nightingale Lane before turning towards the Tower, a thoughtful look in his eye. The stranger he'd passed in the street had seemed vaguely familiar. Not that that was, of itself, unusual. He knew a lot of people and even those he didn't know by name, he would have seen in or around the port area. He shook off the feeling. He was being unduly suspicious. It was natural enough. He knew he was already suspected of involvement in the plundering of the silk. Why wouldn't he be suspicious of someone out at this unusually early hour?

He turned off the main street. It wasn't safe to return home. Not with Pascoe still alive and looking for him. He consoled himself with the thought that, with the silk now gone, there would be little or no evidence left to link him with the theft.

'Tell the lads they can go home,' he said, glancing at Marr. 'I'll see them at the Royal Oak later. That goes for you, too.'

He walked on alone, his thoughts returning to Pascoe. The villain was becoming a nuisance and would need to be dealt with. He thought of the boy, Pascoe's young brother. The original idea of warning Pascoe off the case had obviously not worked.

Something more drastic was necessary.

A solution formed in his mind.

# CHAPTER 36

Tom raised his head over the gunwale and watched the barge pass under the bows of the barquentine, before swinging round to face downstream. There were no shouts from those on board, no indication that the police galley had been seen, the men's attention caught instead by something on the shore. He let the barge drift away. He'd catch up with it later. He knew where she was going. In the meantime he wanted to see what, on Hermitage Dock, had so exercised the attention of its crew.

'Wait for me here,' he said, glancing up the side of the barquentine. Without waiting for a reply, he got to his feet and ran up the companion ladder and onto the vessel's upper deck.

'You again, young feller?' The elderly face of the nightwatchman shook his head and waved him through.

Tom thanked him and walked quickly to the ship's rail, his eyes scanning the foreshore. A man was standing at the mouth of the dock seeming to stare downriver at the departing barge. For a fleeting moment Tom wondered if it could be Creech. But the cully was too tall and broad in the shoulder for Creech. Mentally, he ran through the list of Creech's bully boys but drew a blank there as well. It was nobody he knew.

Tom shook his head, walked back across the deck of the

barquentine and climbed down to the galley. He had other, more urgent matters that had to be attended to.

'Cast off,' he said. The narrow hull of the police galley sliced easily through the water, a north-easterly wind catching the spume and sending it down the length of the boat, drenching the crew. Yet they'd passed the Wapping police office and were approaching Shadwell before Tom caught up with the barge. He'd nearly missed her, the constant spray almost blinding him to his surroundings. He'd wiped his face and caught sight of her beginning her long, lumbering turn into the tide, the lighterman's body leaning into his paddle oar with all the force he could muster.

Tom drew down on the starboard tiller guy and took the galley behind some lighters on the south bank, by the King and Queen Road. He knew he was taking a risk being so far from the barge but there was little alternative. Remaining in mid-channel would mean he'd be seen. He needed a vantage point from where he could watch and not himself be watched.

But it was a mistake.

The fog had lifted, but from this distance he could see nothing save the lights of the ships on the north shore. Emden's barge had gone, vanished from sight as surely as if she'd never existed.

'Give way together. Put your backs into it.' Tom felt the galley surge forward, cutting across the flow of the tide. He searched a river seemingly devoid of life. Nothing was moving. Perhaps he'd been wrong to assume Emden would want to unlade the silk at the same wharf from which he'd set out. Perhaps he meant to go on further downriver. Or perhaps he'd stopped earlier than Tom had anticipated. His doubts grew as the possibilities multiplied.

'Way enough.' The bow of the galley sank back into the water as she slowed to a halt. Soon they were wallowing dead in the water while Tom searched a foreshore dotted with dozens of barges and lighters, each one as near identical to its neighbour as made no difference. Most were moored alongside the wharves, quays and docks that stretched, almost without interruption, from London Bridge to Limehouse and beyond.

Then he saw her.

She was in the shadow of a high building and moving slowly downriver. She'd almost completed her turn into the tide, her black hull virtually indistinguishable from the shoreline. He'd have missed her were it not for the white shirt worn by one of the men on board. The next moment it slipped out of sight behind a brig.

The dark outline of the Shadwell waterworks came into view and slowly slipped astern. Morgan's Wharf was now less than two hundred yards away. Tom took the galley through a gap in the moored line of ships, anxious not to lose the barge a second time; equally keen not to be seen. The barge was lying at a slight angle to the tide, being pushed gently towards the north bank. Tom scoured the shoreline astern of her.

'They're fetching alongside Morgan's Wharf,' he said. 'We'll stay put for a while. No point in rushing in.'

'Where d'you reckon they'll take the bales?' asked Sam. 'There's nowhere safe on the waterfront.'

'Somewhere secure,' said Tom, watching the crew of the barge make her fast to the wharf. 'I want to be ready for whatever Emden decides to do. Sam, you and me will go ashore and watch the front gates of the wharf. I want you, Kemp, and you, Higgins, to stay on the galley and watch things from the river side. Sam's right. Emden won't want to keep the silk where it is now. He'll be too concerned about Creech, or someone else, nicking it. As soon as we know what his plans are, we can think again.'

A few minutes later, Tom and Sam were standing at the corner of a house in Lower Shadwell, a little way short of Morgan's Wharf. The fog had cleared now, dispersed by a cold north-easterly wind that nipped at the tips of their ears. Tom cupped his hands and blew into them. The cold reminded him of the endless days and nights spent pacing the quarterdeck of a man-of-war in the south Atlantic, with only his thoughts to keep him company.

'They're coming out, sir.'

Sam's voice cut short his musings and he looked expectantly towards the wharf. A chink of light appeared in the crack between the two gates. It got larger as first one and then the second swung open. A face appeared. It looked up and down the road before disappearing again. For a minute or two there was silence. Then a hay wain drawn by four men and laden with bales rumbled into the street and turned left towards the two officers.

'Emden ain't with them,' whispered Sam, leaning back into the shadow of a building. 'He must have stayed behind.'

'Get yourself down there and have a look. If he's there, stay with him,' said Tom, his eyes fixed on the approaching cart. 'I need to stay with those scrubs. I don't want to lose the silk now we've found it. If you get a chance, tell Kemp and Higgins what's happened and tell them to come and find me.'

They waited until the men and their cart had passed. Then Tom stepped out and followed the vehicle along Lower Shadwell and into Wapping Wall before turning right at the Shadwell waterworks. He walked to the corner and peered round. The cart had come to a halt less than forty yards from the junction, in a little-used lane, its heavily pitted surface rising steeply away from the river. Tom leaned back against a wall, his elbow catching a loose brick that tumbled to the ground with a clatter. He saw one of the men stop and look round. He said something and the cart came to a halt.

The next moment three of them had begun to walk down the hill towards him. Tom drew his pistol. He had no illusions about what would happen if they caught him. The law counted for little in this part of London, where the threat of the hangman's noose was but a distant prospect. He looked round for somewhere else to hide. Houses lined both sides of the street, their doors leading directly onto the roadway. He retreated ten, then twenty, yards along Wapping Wall, could hear the men's footsteps approaching the corner. Another few seconds and they'd see him. He tried to run but couldn't, still weak from his near-drowning. He looked back. Still no sign of the men. He felt a sharp pain shooting across his chest. He had to find somewhere to hide and rest for a moment, the sound of the footsteps behind him like drumbeats in his head.

The door of one of the houses was missing. Either that or it was wide open. He wasn't sure which. Nor did he care. It offered sanctuary. He stepped inside. The roof had collapsed and with it several of the interior walls, the rubble lying where it had fallen. He could not have gone any further even if he had wanted to. Flattening himself against what was left of the corridor wall, he waited.

Footsteps approached, stopped outside the house, moved on, stopped again and returned to the house. Tom could hear the murmuring of a conversation. It seemed to go on for a long time. Then silence. He wanted to look, to see what they were doing, had visions of them creeping towards him. But the risk of moving was too great. He would undoubtedly be seen. The silence continued. At last the footsteps began again. They were leaving, returning the way they'd come. He expelled a lungful of air and listened to the sounds fading away. Easing himself out of his hiding place, his gun cocked and primed, he moved stealthily to the front door and peered into the street. Satisfied that it was clear he walked quickly to the corner of the lane up which the men had gone.

The hay wain had come to a halt opposite what appeared to be a small warehouse. Tom crept closer. A dog barked, the sound deep-throated and aggressive, coming from somewhere close by. Tom dropped to the ground, his pulse racing. The barking grew louder, more insistent. He crouched lower, watching to see the men's reaction, unsure if he was the cause of the commotion or not. The men had turned and were staring in the dog's direction. Carefully, Tom pulled the front of his coat across the lower part of his face, twisting the white lapels so they would not reflect the ambient light and give away his position. Slowly the animal's yelps became less persistent, the silence between them longer.

Seemingly satisfied, the men resumed their work. The doors of the warehouse were pulled open and the wain pushed in. Minutes later, the men re-emerged, closing and bolting the doors behind them. Tom's eyes widened in surprise. The locks and bolts fastening the doors seemed hardly up to the task of protecting the silk. It had to be a purely temporary arrangement. That might also explain why Emden hadn't accompanied the men. There

would have been no point. The deal with Creech had been final-
ised. There was nothing for him to do until morning.

Tom waited for the men to leave. Then he, too, left. He would
return with his crew and seize what he hoped was the silk. In the
meantime he needed to speak to Sam and find out where Emden
had gone.

# CHAPTER 37

Sam could see the oval shape of her face in his mind's eye and hear the soft murmur of her voice as she spoke. He'd seen her many times since the day of the attempted robbery; passing her house at every opportunity or standing at the corner of the street in the hope of speaking to her. Yet only once had she noticed him. Then she had blushed and smiled before hurrying on her way.

He'd known, of course, that no friendship was possible between them, yet he continued to hope for the impossible. Now, all was in jeopardy. He buried his head in his hands.

He looked across the street at the open gates of Morgan's Wharf. Emden was still inside. Sam could see him standing at the river's edge, his hands tucked beneath the tails of his coat. He wasn't moving, his head turned to the east where the first hint of the dawn could be seen low down over the Isle of Dogs.

The idea wormed its way into Sam's brain like some hideous sickness, as attractive as it was repulsive, as natural as it was amoral. He would tell Emden about the danger the merchant was in. What harm could there be in that? He would tell him that he must return the plundered silk to its rightful owner and that would be the end of that. Surely that was the way forward, the sensible and honourable way to behave. Was it not written in the

Torah that a man must not spill the blood of another? And if, in return, Emden could find it in his heart to give his blessing to the friendship with his daughter, then Sam, for one, would not complain.

Of course, he could not expect Tom to see things in the same light. It would be necessary to keep the facts from him and from his worship, Mr Harriot. He would—

'Why, Sam, there you are.' Sam looked up, startled. Immersed in his thoughts, he'd not heard Tom's approach. 'What are you doing here? Where's Emden?'

'He's still on the wharf, sir,' said Sam, wondering if Tom had guessed his thoughts, a sense of shame washing over him.

'Good. Get the others over here. As soon as Emden makes a move, I'll want you to follow him. The others will come with me.'

Milton Brougham sat in the stern sheets of the sloop and looked at the dark shoreline of the Thames. A signalling lamp flashed twice, the light coming from a point about sixty or seventy yards west of Morgan's Wharf, on the north shore.

A little under two hours earlier, Hawkes had arrived at Hermitage Dock with the sailing sloop and he and Brougham had set about searching for the barge Brougham had seen leaving the dock. It had been a slow process. There'd been hundreds of similar vessels to choose from.

It was pure chance that Brougham should have seen the police galley fetched alongside a brig. He guessed Pascoe was there because the silk was in the vicinity and he'd taken the sloop to the opposite side of the river from where to keep watch.

A second lantern flashed. This one came from the police galley.

He watched it sheer away from the brig and make its way to the north shore.

'Time we had a look,' said Brougham when, ten minutes later, the galley had still not returned to its former position. 'I reckon they've gone ashore.'

'There's a fellow standing on the edge of the wharf,' whispered Hawkes.

'Aye, I've seen him,' said Brougham. 'You think he's seen us?'

'Wouldn't surprise me none. Didn't look to be Pascoe, though.'

'Who then?'

'Don't know. Not seen him before.'

Brougham was quiet for a while. He'd known for some time that Pascoe was searching for the silk. He wondered if he had been told about the documents as well. Probably he had. Why would the British government keep such a detail secret from the man tasked to find it? And given its importance, would they not have insisted on the job being given to the most capable officer available? Everything Brougham had learned about Pascoe suggested they had done just that – in spite of his reputation as a man who drank more than was good for him.

His thoughts returned to the silk. It was clear, from everything he knew, that the bales had now passed out of the hands of the original thieves and into the possession of others. 'He's found a buyer what he's going to meet . . .' Gott had said when he'd seen him at the Harp. It was the reason the skeins had been moved from Hermitage Dock and were now apparently at an almost identical location less than a mile downriver.

He looked at the distant wharf. It was too far away for him to see anything useful. He had to assume the men from the police galley had gone there and might, at this moment, be taking possession of the silk. If he went ashore now and was caught, it would cause a diplomatic firestorm, not to mention displeasure at his failure to get hold of the intelligence papers. There had to be another way.

Tom watched the police galley draw alongside Parson's Stairs and tie up. 'You two, come with me,' he said, addressing the remaining two members of the galley's crew. 'Sam, you'll be staying close to Emden. The rest of us are going to search the silk for the papers the Foreign Office want so badly. If Emden's crew come back while we're there, things could get a little rough and you ain't properly recovered for that.'

'And you are?' spluttered Sam.

Tom held up his hand for silence. 'I want you to stay close to Emden. Find out where he goes. If he meets anybody, I want to know about it. Clear?'

Tom waited until Sam had taken up his position opposite the gates of the wharf and then set off with Kemp and Higgins, retracing the route he'd taken earlier. Reaching the narrow lane that led past the waterworks, he turned and walked up the still-dark incline to the warehouse into which he'd seen the silk-laden hay wain driven.

'Want me to see to the padlock, sir?' said Higgins.

'Think you can do it?' asked Tom.

'Shouldn't be a problem, sir,' said Higgins. 'If I can get past them wards, of course.'

Lapsing into silence, Higgins fished a couple of narrow L-shaped blades from one of his coat pockets, and inserted them into the keyhole. Twisting them first this way and then that, he was rewarded, a minute later, by the metallic click of the lock springing open.

'Well done,' said Tom, pulling open the warehouse door. 'You got the lantern, Kemp? Light it and bring it here, will you?'

The light shone on the hay wain standing in the centre of the warehouse, its worn shafts resting on the earth floor, several spokes missing from two of its four wheels. Tom carried the lantern closer. The wagon was loaded with bales wrapped in brown paper. He took a knife from his belt and cut through the covering.

'It's the silk, right enough,' he said, his mind already on how to search the bales in such a way as to leave no trace of their having been there. He would have taken them away if he had thought it possible to do so without alerting Emden, and through Emden, Creech. He glanced at the open doors of the warehouse.

He knew there was every chance that Emden's men might return at any moment. If they did, he was in no fit state to do much about it.

'Don't look like the document's here,' said a perspiring Higgins, sometime later.

'No, it doesn't look that way.' Tom frowned and looked round at the bales neatly stacked on the floor of the warehouse, their paper wrapping bound with twine. 'You've searched every bale?'

'Aye. Gone through them twice.'

'How many have you searched?'

'All of them, sir.'

'No, I mean how many bales were on that wagon?'

'Nineteen.'

'Are you quite sure? Count them again.'

'Nineteen, sir.'

'Then there's two missing,' said Tom. 'Either they were left behind at Morgan's Wharf, which doesn't seem likely, or Creech has kept two for himself. I wouldn't put it past a villain like him.'

'And no clue about—' Kemp's sentence was cut short by a loud voice from the door of the warehouse.

'Well, well, well. What've we got here?'

Tom spun round. Six men stood at the entrance. He noticed all of them were carrying bludgeons.

'Police,' said Tom, holding up his tipstaff. 'And who are you?'

'Never you mind who we are, cully,' said the same man who'd spoken before. 'You ain't got no business snooping round other people's property. Isn't that right, lads?'

There was a growl of agreement.

'On your way, lads, before I decide a night in the cells would be good for your manners,' snapped Tom.

'We ain't going nowhere, mister,' said the man, swinging his bludgeon from side to side. He took a step forward.

Tom's hand went to the hilt of his sword but he wasn't quick enough. His weakened state had made him vulnerable. He felt a savage blow strike his arm, sending him crashing into the side of the cart. He looked up, feeling dizzy. The image of a man came into view, blurred, indistinct, and coming towards him. He had something in his hand, raised above his head. He could hear shouting. Didn't recognise the voices. His knees buckled beneath him and he sank to the ground. He had no strength left. He felt sleepy, the pain in his arm slipping away.

# CHAPTER 38

Sam Hart followed Emden from Shadwell back to his house on Aldgate High Street. Several times during the long walk Sam had thought the moment right to approach the merchant and warn him of the danger he was in. But each time something had stopped him. He thought of his friendship with Tom and of the oath he had taken when he'd joined the new institution shortly after its formation in July of last year. He thought, too, of the moral code instilled in him by his mother and father and what they would make of his intention to betray his friend and the law he had sworn to uphold. But then again, the opportunity that had presented itself to him might be his only chance of winning the hand of Adina. With each step he took it seemed his temptation grew stronger and his resolve to hold back was weakened. Who would know of his actions, except Emden himself? How would anyone find out?

What held him back, Sam didn't know. He wished he did. Loyalty to Tom? An innate sense of what was right? Perhaps. He thought of Tom and what he was doing at this precise moment. A sense of shame at what he had proposed washed over him. In that single moment he knew what he had to do.

He watched from across the street as Emden reached his front door, opened it and went inside. A candle suddenly burst into life and moved about the front room as though Emden was searching for some lost article. Then it appeared to mount the stairs to the first floor.

Sam must have dozed off. The sudden noise of a watchman's rattle, a yard or two away, woke him with a start. He stared at the fellow for a moment, trying to remember where he was. It was still dark. He could not have slept for long. He stared at the retreating figure of the watchman, the sound of his rattle gradually receding. Abruptly, the noise stopped. The quiet of the night returned. He checked the building opposite, wondering for a moment if he'd missed Emden; if the cully had slipped out while he dozed. It was unlikely. The house was in darkness. If anyone in there was awake, there was no sign of it.

He looked up at the windows and thought of Adina and wondered if she ever thought of him, whether her father had ever mentioned him in her presence and, if he had, what her reaction had been.

The sharp crack of a bolt being drawn put a sudden stop to his musing. The sound had come from Emden's house. Sam melted back into his doorway and waited. Almost immediately, he saw the Jew emerging from a side passage. The merchant paused for a moment as though unsure of himself. Then he stepped into the highway.

'Wake up, sir.'

Tom's eyes fluttered once or twice and then opened. He could see Kemp's enormous bulk kneeling at his side. Next to him was someone else. Tom closed his eyes and opened them again, as if to focus more clearly. He knew it wasn't Higgins. The cully was too big for that.

'Who's that?' Tom flicked a pointed finger at the stranger.

'Don't rightly know, sir,' said Kemp. 'But it were a good job he showed up – after you went down, like.'

Tom looked at his crewman, sighed and raised himself up onto his elbow, wincing as he did so. 'Did they get away? The scrubs who attacked us?'

'No, sir. This gentleman's friend is looking after them with Higgins. They're over there, sir.' Kemp jerked his head towards a sorry-looking bunch of men being overseen by a grinning Higgins and a wiry-looking man Tom didn't recognise. 'They've been secured.'

'I'm much obliged to you, sir,' said Tom turning to look at the stranger. His face clouded as a thought occurred to him. 'How did you happen upon us?'

'We heard a noise, loud enough to wake the dead,' said the stranger, casting a long look at the hay wain, and the bales of silk on the floor. 'We came to see what the fuss was about. But I see that you are now quite recovered, sir, so we shall leave you.'

'My thanks to you and your friend, sir.' Tom climbed unsteadily to his feet and supported himself against the side of the cart. 'Forgive me, but have we not met before? I seem to recall your face from somewhere.'

'I think not, sir. I would surely have remembered.'

'My mistake, sir,' said Tom. He watched the two men leave, his shoulder throbbing with pain. He shook his head, trying to clear his mind. Events had unfolded so quickly, he needed a moment to think them through. The stranger had appeared to glance in the direction of the silk bales. Had it just been idle curiosity, or was it something more? And why hadn't the stranger asked who they were and what they were doing? Tom put the matter to the back of his mind. He had other things to worry about.

He had wanted the search of the warehouse to pass unnoticed. It would have left him free to look for his brother, safe in the knowledge that neither Creech nor Emden would be aware of how close they were to arrest. But now? The noise created by the fighting would, without doubt, have attracted the attention of the neighbours. Before the day was out the incident would be common knowledge on the waterfront, even without the assistance of the two strangers who'd just left.

Tom felt his stomach tighten. He needed to find his brother before word of the silk's discovery got back to Creech. But first he had to get the prisoners and the silk back to Wapping. He couldn't do both at the same time. It would need more than the three of them to achieve that. He went to the door of the warehouse and looked out into the cold glint of the dawn. It was difficult to see much beyond the vague outlines of the houses opposite. If the strangers who'd come to his assistance were still in the area, he doubted he'd see them.

He thought of leaving Kemp or Higgins behind to guard the place but dismissed the idea. He needed both of them for escort duties. Besides, of what good would one man be if there were another determined attempt to steal the skeins?

He thought again of the two strangers. Had their arrival on the scene been simply fortuitous or was there some other explanation? The image of the bigger of the two men flashed through

Tom's mind. The fellow reminded him of someone who he'd seen sitting at a table, opposite to him. But where? And in what circumstances? The image faded.

And what of the missing intelligence document that was so exercising the minds of the Foreign Office? If it really was in one of the missing bales, had it now been found by either Creech or Emden? He doubted it. Neither man would have been remotely interested in the skeins for their own sake. For them, what mattered was its intrinsic value, the profit that could, with the least amount of effort, be made on the sale. They would have no reason to open the bales; still less to search through them.

So where were the missing two bales? He was reasonably sure the wooden hut at Hermitage Wharf was empty. It followed, therefore, that they had been separated from the main batch prior to this point. It was likely that when the split had been made, those bales that had remained would still be in the original hiding place. Creech would have known of the risk of unnecessarily moving stolen goods around London. And only a fool took risks he didn't have to. It meant there were only a limited number of locations available to him. Tom ran through three of the ones he knew about – Creech's yard in Market Hill, off the Ratcliff Highway, the Royal Oak tavern in Bridge Yard and the house at Bow. Tom had already searched all three and come up with nothing. But . . . once more he recalled the chest of drawers he'd seen at the house outside Bow and how odd it had seemed to him. He had intended to return to the house anyway, his suspicions aroused by the absence of any dust in the area of the chest.

The prisoners were shuffled out of the warehouse and made to stand while their bindings were again checked, the door of the warehouse locked, and the surrounding area inspected for any trace of the strangers – or anyone else showing undue interest in the goings-on of the last hour. Then they moved off, Tom's thoughts returning to his brother. It was not knowing that was so difficult. Again and again his mind strayed back to the house in Bow. If, as he now believed, the house was where Creech had hidden the missing two bales of silk, was it not also possible that it was where William was being kept?

He would go there as soon as humanly possible. He had to hope it would be several hours before either Emden or Creech discovered what had happened to the rest of the silk.

'What now, sir?' Bill Hawkes looked expectantly at his superior.

Brougham didn't answer immediately. He glanced up the lane along which Pascoe and his little gang of prisoners had travelled less than five minutes before. He'd known they would pass this way. Even with his limited knowledge of the streets around Wapping and Shadwell, it had seemed self-evident that Pascoe would have to use this route to reach the police office. Nor, Brougham had thought, would he have any option but to abandon the silk and deal with his prisoners.

'We're going to have a look at those bales in the warehouse,' he said, at last.

'With respect, sir, we can't do that sir,' said a horrified Hawkes, fully aware of the realities of prison life. 'We ain't got time before Pascoe gets back. He'll catch us for sure.'

'I reckon we've got the best part of half an hour,' said Brougham, stepping out from behind the wall of a house where they'd been keeping watch and heading back towards the warehouse. 'It's the only chance we're likely to get and I'm not about to lose it.'

'You don't think Pascoe has searched the bales, sir?

'I'm certain he has,' said Brougham, remembering the sight of the bales arranged on the floor of the warehouse. It was highly unlikely that Pascoe would have left the warehouse before he'd done everything to find the document. And although the need to guard his prisoners would have slowed him down, it wouldn't have stopped him. 'But that don't change anything. We still need to get in there and have a look.'

'Reckon they jammed the lock, sir,' said Hawkes, when they had reached the warehouse. 'One of the wards is broken. Can't spring it, sir.'

'We'll have a look round the back,' said Brougham. 'There might be another way in.'

A quick inspection revealed a second, smaller door along the right-hand wall of the building, above which was a small window hardly big enough to allow a man to squeeze through.

'It's worth a try,' said Brougham. 'You stand on my shoulders. You should get through without too much difficulty.'

Before long, Hawkes had succeeded in forcing the window and wriggling through. Moments later he had dropped down inside the warehouse and opened the side door. They found an oil lamp hanging from a nail by the main doors, which they lit and carried over to the cart. As Brougham had suspected, all the bales had been opened and repacked.

'Check them again, will you, Hawkes. I don't suppose you'll find anything but I want to be sure. I think . . .' Brougham squatted down and, holding the lantern close to one of the bales, carefully examined it. 'Have you seen this?' he asked.

'What's that, sir?' said Hawkes bending down next to Brougham.

'This writing. D'you see the letters MH? And below them, in smaller lettering, two numbers separated by a forward stoke? What d'you make of it?'

'Means nothing to me, sir,' said Hawkes, staring at the script.

Brougham moved his gaze to a second bale and then a third. 'You notice how the first of the two numbers on each sheet remains the same?' he said, pointing.

'Aye.'

'And the second one is different in each case?'

Hawkes peered at each of the three bales in turn. 'Aye, I see it now.'

'What would you say if I was to suggest that the first number tells you the number of bales in the consignment while the second number identifies each bale within the consignment?'

'Never thought of it that way, sir.'

'If I'm right, there should be twenty-one bales here but I can only count nineteen. Did you see Pascoe or any of his men carrying a bale when they left?'

'No, sir.'

'Nor did I. It means there are two missing— What was that?' Brougham sprang to his feet and listened. He could hear a faint rasping noise coming from the far side of the main doors. It was followed by the sound of the bolts being drawn back.

'Someone's coming,' whispered Brougham. 'Quick. Get out.' He blew out the lantern and ran for the side door, closely followed by Hawkes. Once outside, he pulled the door closed and stumbled through some undergrowth towards the back of the building. A moment later, the side door burst open and three men ran out.

Sam kept quite still, his eyes following Emden as the Jew turned right out of his house and walked along the Aldgate towards Houndsditch. He pushed himself away from the door and dropped in behind the man as he entered Houndsditch and travelled north. Fifteen minutes later he turned off the main road and stopped outside a large, terraced house in Spitalfields. The door of the house was opened almost immediately by a bearded man dressed in an ankle-length kaftan who appeared to have been expecting his visitor. Within minutes, the two of them left the house and hailed a passing cab.

Fifty yards behind them and on the opposite side of the road, Sam did the same. Down Houndsditch and across Aldgate, the two carriages rumbled through streets filled with sheep, pigs, cattle and sundry other animals being driven to the slaughter-houses of north London, their cries and bleats competing with the shouts and yells of the herdsmen.

'That'll do, driver,' said Sam, watching Emden's carriage turn into a narrow side street off Lower Shadwell. 'I'll walk from here.'

Sam saw the two men get out of their carriage and approach a small warehouse. Keeping close to the wall, he approached the building. The doors were ajar. Inside, Sam was able to see Emden holding a lantern that he was in the process of lighting. It flared into life and, almost immediately, Sam heard a loud gasp and saw Emden standing at the back of a hay wain, his hand to his mouth.

'It's all gone. The silk has gone.' There was panic in his voice. 'Everything.'

# CHAPTER 39

The dozen or so brigs and barquentines riding at their moorings at the Wapping Tier rocked gently in the fast-moving current of an ebb tide, an ice-cold breeze rustling through their furled sails. Tom pulled the lapels of his coat across his throat, dimly conscious of the sound of the river swirling round the mooring poles adjacent to the nearby Wapping New Stairs. He should have been feeling tired, but wasn't. He doubted he could have slept even if he had gone home. He was thinking of his brother. Time was passing. He needed to get out there, to the house at Bow, as soon as possible and see if his hunch about the presence of a basement was true. If it was . . . He stopped himself, not daring to let his hopes climb too high.

'Are you listening to me, Mr Pascoe?'

The voice broke into his thoughts. Tom's forehead furrowed and he turned to see the resident magistrate looking at him, his face flushed with the cold. Harriot had insisted on meeting Tom on the pontoon. 'Don't get much fresh air these days,' he had said, by way of explanation.

'I beg your pardon, sir. You were saying?'

'Really, Mr Pascoe, I do wish you'd pay attention. I said, what makes you think anyone was in there?'

'I'm sorry, sir, what makes me think anyone was where?'

'In the warehouse. The one you were talking to me about, earlier.'

Oh, that,' said Tom, trying to concentrate. 'We'd left all the bales stacked ready to bring back here. When we next saw them, it was clear they had been disturbed. As we went in, I thought I heard the sound of someone moving about. Whoever it was had gone by the time we got in.'

'But you had a look round?'

'Of course, sir,' said Tom, irritated by Harriot's question. 'The point of entry was a window over a side door. We searched the immediate area but found nothing. We've brought all the bales in. They're in one of the empty cells. Nothing had been taken.'

'And you say there was no trace of the intelligence report the Foreign Office are so keen to get their hands on?'

'The consignment wasn't complete. There should have been another two bales. I think the people responsible for the original theft reneged on part of the deal and kept back the extra bales. I very much doubt they have any idea of the presence of the secret intelligence report. I think they were just being greedy.'

'Well, whatever their motive, they appear to be in possession of something extremely sensitive and of immense potential interest to the Administration, not to mention the Americans and the French. Do you have any suspects in mind?'

'For the larceny? Or the receiving?'

'Both.'

'The original theft is almost certainly down to a gang led by Daniel Creech. He's come up before you on several occasions but there's never been sufficient evidence to convict him. He's not been seen since the day we raided the Royal Oak. He—' Tom stopped suddenly.

Harriot glanced at him expectantly.

'It's nothing,' said Tom. 'I was reminded of something.'

'Anything you'd care to share with me?' asked the magistrate.

'When I was attacked I was taken to a nearby house. While I was there I heard a man giving orders for me to be thrown into the Thames. All of this you already know. What I never told you was that I had the feeling I'd heard that man's voice before but it was muffled by the hood covering my head, so I couldn't be sure. The other night, when I saw the silk being moved from Hermitage Dock, I heard the same voice. It was Creech.'

'Are you sure enough to say so in the witness box?' said Harriot.

'I'm not sure I'd go that far.'

'What about his suspected involvement in the theft of the silk? Is there enough evidence for a committal?'

'To the Bailey? No, sir, not yet. He's rarely at the forefront. Tends to work in the shadows although those shadows can be a dangerous place for his victims. Of the two witnesses who could have placed him anywhere near the scene, one is dead and the other is missing. Stevie Lyons, the mate of the hoy that got turned over, hasn't been seen for days.'

'What about the receiver?' said Harriot.

'I think that's quite straightforward,' said Tom. 'We've got sufficient evidence to arrest and charge a man called Jacob Emden, a merchant living on Aldgate High Street. He was seen in possession of the silk. We think he either owns or rents the warehouse in Shadwell to which the silk was taken last night. Sam Hart is watching him as we speak.'

Harriot nodded and stared out over the muddy brown waters of the Thames, as if in thought. After a moment or two, he said, 'I've not asked you about your brother. I know his continued absence is weighing heavily on your mind. Is there anything I can do?'

Tom shook his head and looked away. He didn't trust himself to answer, his strength deserting him. Finally, he said, 'There's no news, sir. I'm hoping things will change later this morning. I think the missing bales of silk are being kept at a house in Bow. It's possible William is also being kept there. I intend going out there for a look as soon as possible.'

'Mr Pascoe—' Harriot broke off.

'Sir?'

'You mentioned the name of the man you believe to be the receiver of the silk bales.'

'Aye, Jacob Emden.'

'Are you aware of any relationship Emden might have with Sam Hart?'

Tom's eyes widened in surprise. He turned and stared at the magistrate. 'What sort of relationship, sir? I know Sam has seen him at the synagogue from time to time. He has also been to see him at his home in connection with this case. As far as I am aware, that's as far as it goes. Has something happened?'

'Hart has been seen in the vicinity of Emden's house on a number of occasions. I'm afraid that, in the light of Emden's alleged involvement in this case, his actions are becoming a source of concern to me. Do you trust him, sir?'

'He's a first-class constable and a loyal friend,' said Tom, his voice rising.

'Yes, I'm sure he is,' said Harriot. 'But is he someone you could trust under all circumstances?'

Tom fought down his mounting anger. Nothing would be gained

from an emotional outburst. 'I regret it extremely, sir, but I don't think I follow you. Has something happened?'

'It appears that Hart may have formed an attachment to Emden's daughter,' said Harriot. 'And while, in normal circumstances, I could have no objection to such a liaison, the present status of the girl's father as someone under investigation for a felony poses some difficulty.'

'Your fears are entirely misplaced, sir,' said Tom, yet even as he said it, he could understand Harriot's concerns. He hadn't known of Sam's supposed attachment and felt a twinge of irritation that his friend should have placed both of them in a situation that was, to say the least, awkward. 'I will speak to him, of course, but I am absolutely certain that nothing untoward has occurred. May I ask how you came by this information?'

'I have my sources, sir. In the meantime, I'll leave the matter in your hands. For all our sakes, I pray you're right. Now, I think I see two of your crew waiting for you. I wish you luck in finding your brother – and the missing silk, of course.'

Dan Creech started at the sound of hammering at the door of the room where he'd taken refuge. He'd not been there long. It wasn't safe to stay put for more than a few days at a time. Not since he'd discovered that Pascoe had survived the attempt on his life and was looking for him. The early morning light was streaming in through the window but he wasn't about to get up for some fool who'd knocked on the wrong door. He was tired, had not slept well, kept awake by a draught blowing up through the cracks in the floorboards.

His failure to turn off Pascoe had been a serious mistake. So, in hindsight, had taking the scrub's brother. But what was done was done and there was no point in wishing otherwise. Creech turned over and tried to get comfortable just as the hammering on the door started again. Creech heard his name being called and felt the first rush of fear in many a long year. He wasn't expecting anyone. He lay still for a few seconds, his head turned towards the window. At a push he could escape that way. Jump the twenty or so feet to the roadway and run.

'Creech, this is Emden,' said the voice at the door. 'Open the door, will you?'

Creech felt a surge of relief, quickly followed by anger at having his sleep disturbed. 'Clear off, Emden. I ain't got nothing to say to you.'

'Best you open this door, Creech. The commodity I paid good money for has gone. Come, open the door, before I kick it down.'

Creech felt his fear returning. Something had gone badly wrong. Either the Jew was lying or someone had known where the silk had been hidden. He had an unpleasant feeling that it was the latter. Normally, he wouldn't have troubled himself with the matter. He'd been paid. The problem was not his. But some sixth sense was nagging him. How could anyone have known where to look for the silk so soon after it had been put in its new location? Creech's uneasiness grew as he considered the possibility that someone must have followed the Jew. And if the Jew had been followed, it would have been for a reason. Someone had known what he was carrying. And that information could only have come from a person who had seen the handover. But who would have taken that risk – except Pascoe? He felt his heart begin to beat faster and sweat form under his armpits and on his forehead. He levered himself off the floor and stumbled to the door.

'What d'you mean it's gone? I ain't got it.'

'Just open the door, Creech. I'm not standing here for ever.'

Creech clenched his fist. It had been a long time since anyone had spoken to him like this. He opened his mouth to respond and then closed it. He had not, until this moment, considered the Jew in any light other than someone with whom to do business. He'd never looked beyond the empty smile and the fine clothes that the merchant presented to the world. Had he done so, he might have recognised a fellow traveller, a man for whom profit was the objective to which everything else was subordinate, including life itself. Now, the first glimmer of what lay behind that smile forced its way into Creech's consciousness. He paused with his hand on the door handle. He could do without the additional grief of turning the cully into yet another enemy. He already had his hands full dealing with Pascoe.

'Where's it gone, Creech?' said Emden, the moment the door was opened. He was a good four inches taller than the sailmaker and broader in the chest.

'How would I know?'

'Somebody knew,' said Emden, closing the door and leaning against it, his arms folded. 'You were the only person who knew I had the silk. And now it's gone.'

Creech's eyes narrowed, his anger exploding. He took a step towards his visitor, his fists drawn back ready to strike. Before he could act, a long arm had reached out and fingers were closing over his throat. He gasped for air, his own hands trying to free the iron grip around his neck.

'Where is it, you thieving scoundrel?' spat Emden. 'Where's my silk?'

The room began to spin and fall out of focus for Creech. He was dimly aware of a choking noise coming from somewhere and then realised it was him. 'Pascoe's got it.'

The words were out of his mouth before he knew it.

'The officer?' Emden's eyes had widened. He let go of Creech's neck and stared at him in disbelief. 'How d'you know? Did you see him?'

'It's him,' said Creech, standing very still. 'Either he was waiting for you where you unladed the skeins or he's been following you.'

'Impossible. Nobody knew where we were going and nobody knows of my involvement in this except . . .'

'Except who?'

'It's nothing. One of the officers from Wapping came to see me. But I told him nothing.'

'What was his name?' Creech had stopped rubbing his neck. He was staring at Emden, his voice barely audible.

'Master Hart.'

'You fool, don't you know Sam Hart works with Pascoe? He'll have got everything he wanted from you. You just don't know it.' He stopped suddenly. A thought occurred to him. 'Were you followed here?'

'No,' said Emden, turning to look at the door as though it was about to burst open.

'Did you check? No, I didn't think so. You're too stupid for that.' Creech felt his old confidence returning. He was running things again, as he always had done. The Jew might be bigger, but that counted for little without the mental strength to go with it. And Creech doubted Emden had that. He strode to the window and searched the street below. He saw nothing. Then something moved on the other side of the street, about fifty or sixty yards away. His eyes swivelled back to the spot. A gust of wind picked up some rubbish and bowled it down the centre of the carriageway. A second later, a dog emerged from behind a building, its nose close to the ground, its tail in the air. Creech ignored it and continued to stare at the place where he'd seen the movement. Then he saw it again: something pale – a hand perhaps – moving in an arc and caught by the sunlight. He waited a little longer. There was nothing to suggest that the person in the street was there because of Emden. But it seemed likely. Creech bit his lip and turned back into the room. If Emden had been followed, it wouldn't be long before he, Creech, was discovered.

'Is anyone there?' Emden looked nervous.

'Don't you know?'

'I weren't followed, I tell you,' insisted Emden.

'Aye, you've told me. What about when you were on the river? Anyone see you there?'

'It was dark, Creech. I couldn't see anything,' said Emden, his eyes darting between the window and the door.

Creech seldom thought too hard about the decisions that he was, from time to time, called upon to make. He had never felt the need to expend time and energy considering the implications of a course of action that seemed self-evidently necessary. Emden had outstayed his welcome. His usefulness as the purchaser of the bales of silk had ceased the moment the transaction was completed. He should have recognised that simple truth and stayed away. Yet he had not done so and, in the process, had exposed others to risk. Creech sighed. He couldn't pretend he'd ever liked

Emden but, by the same measure, he'd not actively disliked him either. Still, rules were rules and some payment was necessary to atone for his mistake. There was a faint smile of regret on Creech's face that found no echo in his cold, expressionless eyes as he slipped the knife blade deep into the Jew's stomach.

Withdrawing the weapon, he wiped the blade clean and replaced it in the waistband of his trousers. He stood for a moment, gazing at the dying man, listening to the soft gurgling noise coming from his mouth. Then he turned and went out onto the landing. Closing the door, he walked softly down the stairs and out through the rear door of the house into a deserted alley. He had no intention of ever returning. He had paid for the use of the room for a week. When the Jew's body was found, no one would know the identity of the man who'd lived there.

Creech felt alive, his senses excited, invigorated by what he'd done. Emden had been stupid; had deserved his fate. He walked quickly down the alley, his eyes darting from side to side. It was important no one saw him, no one was able to place him at the scene of the killing. He reached the top of the alley where it joined the busy main street. A woman walked past, her head bent, her shawl drawn about her head. She didn't look up. Coming in the opposite direction was a group of young men, coal-heavers by the looks of them, their faces still smeared with the accumulated black dust of months. Creech hesitated. More people were appearing. It was later than he'd thought, the start of another working day. He thought of retracing his steps and finding another way out into the main thoroughfare but quickly dismissed the idea. It would be no different to this. Choosing his moment, he launched out and joined the swelling ranks.

# CHAPTER 40

Sam stamped his feet in an effort to keep warm, his eyes scanning the windows of the house into which Emden had gone. There was nothing to see, no movement behind the glass, no light to suggest anyone might be awake. He glanced up and down the street, surprised by how busy it had suddenly become, people on their way to work or perhaps returning home after a night spent drinking. His eye fell on a woman on the other side of the street. He watched her progress for a minute or so as she passed a group of coal-heavers coming in the opposite direction. She reached the junction of a footpath at the same moment that a man's head appeared round the corner of a building, looking in his direction as though searching for something, his actions furtive, almost nervous. Sam waited, his curiosity awakened. The face ducked out of sight and then reappeared, followed by the rest of him. The man was in early middle age, not above five and a half feet tall with a thin, cruel, aquiline face. He was wearing a blue three-quarter length Richardson coat with a scarlet collar that reminded Sam of the coach drivers he'd seen in Borough High Street.

Yet this man was no coach driver. There was no sign of the weather-beaten features that so characterised the men whose lives were spent in the open air, or the slightly stooped back acquired by years of bending to the reins of a team of horses. And what would a coach driver be doing so far from the coaching routes of Southwark and Fleet Street? Sam felt the hairs on the back of his neck rising. Something was not right. If the cully didn't want to be seen, there had to be a reason for it.

Then he remembered Emden. He was here because of the Jew. Nothing else mattered. He looked back at the house into which the merchant had gone. There was no sign of movement, no light at any of the windows. He considered going in to look for him, but thought better of it. If he found him, what then? Yet if he didn't, the Jew might leave by a back entrance and he, Sam, would be none the wiser.

He glanced back to where he'd seen the stranger. The fellow had turned north, and was walking away from him, towards the Ratcliff Highway. He watched him go. There was still no sign of movement in the house. It was odd. Emden would surely have finished his business and be on his way before this. Something must have happened to detain him. Or perhaps he had, after all, left by a back entrance.

Sam glanced again at the corner of the alley. If Emden had left that way he would have emerged at that junction. If that were the case, Sam would have seen him.

But he hadn't. He'd only seen the stranger.

He sprinted to the junction and turned in, looking down the length of the alley. It passed behind the house Emden had gone into. He raced to the house and found the back door open. He hesitated, undecided about his next move. Searching the house would take time and risk losing the man he'd seen emerging from the alley. Of course, it was more than possible the cully

334

had not come from this house at all; had no connection with Emden.

Sam turned back and ran to the junction. It was more crowded than it had been a few minutes before. He climbed onto a low wall and scanned the street. He saw a flash of scarlet in the distance. It looked to be the collar of a Richardson coat. He jumped from the wall and zigzagged his way through the ever-thickening mass of people moving in the opposite direction. His chest was hurting where the bullet had struck. He wouldn't be able to keep this pace up for very much longer. Again he caught a fleeting glimpse of scarlet and saw it turn right into the Ratcliff Highway. Sam slowed to a walk, breathing heavily. He wondered what he was doing following the fellow, what questions he could put to him if he ever caught up with him. He had no evidence of his involvement in any crime and certainly no evidence that he had come from the house in which he, Sam, was interested. Yet there was still a nagging sensation in the back of his mind that told him that something was amiss. He increased his pace, his chest still throbbing, his breathing laboured. He felt a tug at his sleeve. It was a child, a girl of about thirteen. She wore no shoes or hat, her face filthy with grime, her long dark hair hanging limply about her shoulders. She was smiling, an empty smile that spoke more of grief than happiness. He knew at once what she wanted, this half-starved creature of the streets. Gently, he disengaged himself from her and hurried on. There had been nothing he could have said or done for her. If she didn't offer what she had, she'd not eat, and the first frost of the coming winter would unquestionably carry her away.

He reached the Highway. The barrows and stalls and braziers

were already thick on the ground, offering all that could be imagined from elephant tusks to potatoes, from oriental spices to
coal, from the exotic to the commonplace. If it was available anywhere, it was available in the Highway. The heavy press of people
slowed him down to a shuffling walk, the shouts of the stallhold-
ers and travelling vendors a deafening roar. He could no longer
see his quarry over the shoulders of those in front. The man could
have turned off into any one of a number of taverns, brothels,
coffee houses or early morning breakfast stalls, all of which
would have offered him a place where he might rest unseen. He'd
never find him now.

He walked back to the house. He had a feeling he knew what
he'd find when he got there.

'There you are, Sam,' said Tom, seeing his friend come in through
the door of the constables' waiting room an hour or so later. 'We
were about to leave. How did you get on with our friend Emden?'

'He's dead, sir.'

'Good God, man, what happened?'

'Got a knife in his gut. I followed him home, like you told me
to, but he didn't stop there. He met some cully in Spitalfields.
And the two of them went to a warehouse off Lower Shadwell—'

'That must be the same place we went to,' said Tom. 'The silk
was stored there. Sorry, Sam, I interrupted you.'

'Aye, thankee, sir. After that, Emden and his friend parted company. I stayed with Emden and followed him to a house in Fox's
Lane. After a while I saw a cully come out of the house but there
was no sign of Emden. I had a feeling things weren't right and
when I went in I found him dead on the floor.'

'You didn't see or hear anything?'

'No. There was no noise, no shouting, no nothing.'

'The man coming out of the house; ever seen him before?'

'No. Leastways I don't recall seeing him before.'

'Any idea whose room it was?'

'I spoke to the landlord and he said the cully paid for a week in advance. He only saw him once and wouldn't know him if he saw him again. But I think I would,' said Sam.

'I'd wager it was Creech,' said Tom. 'I reckon Emden knew he'd been short-changed and went looking for the man responsible. What did your man look like?'

'Short, stocky build, narrow face. I reckon he's had the pox at some time. Got the marks on his face.'

'That's the villain,' said Tom.

'What d'you want done about Emden, sir?'

'The body's not on our patch,' said Tom. 'Ask the waterside officer to inform the Shadwell police office. They can deal with it. When you've done that, go home and get some rest. I don't believe you've been to bed for a while.'

'Aye, thankee, sir. I don't deny I could do with a little sleep.'

Tom glanced up, surprised. Sam's reply had been a little too quick. Then he recalled the conversation he'd had with Harriot about Sam's possible involvement with Emden's daughter and thought he could guess what his friend had in mind. If the circumstances had been otherwise he would have done anything to ensure his happiness. But not now. Not like this. He didn't want Sam to see the girl at the moment of her grief. She would want to know the details of her father's death. It was best if someone removed from the immediacy of the event should break the news of his passing and leave the detail until another hour. Sam was too close – not only to the event but to the girl as well – to be able to perform the duty that would be expected of him. Tom struggled to find a form of words that would convey his meaning without the hurt that his opposition would cause.

'Sam?'

'Aye, sir.'

'Go home,' said Tom. 'And promise me you'll leave the officers from Shadwell to do their job.'

'Very good, sir,' said Sam, his face reddening.

Tom waited for Sam to leave and stared for some time at the closed door. He'd seen the hurt in his friend's eyes and would have done much to make it up to him. But, for now, he knew that wasn't going to be possible. He turned back to the other members of his crew.

'Time we were going,' he said, his voice subdued.


The exhilaration that had swept over Dan Creech in the moments after the killing had faded. In its place was something close to panic, born of his certainty that he had become a marked man. It was, for him, a new experience. Gone was the bluster with which he usually faced the world – at least for now. The killing of Jacob Emden – and his attempt on Pascoe's life – marked a new departure for him. It had taken him into a world he didn't understand, where people lived by a different set of rules that had little or nothing to do with his own. Emden's death would unquestionably increase the pressure for his capture and execution.

He'd failed to appreciate the altered landscape in which he now found himself. He had blundered into a situation in which there was only one way out. He had to complete the task he had set himself and deal with the people who knew enough to hang him. There were a few, including Pascoe. You didn't try to kill a man and take his young brother hostage and not expect him to come after you.

The quarrel was now personal. There was no going back.

With an effort, Creech turned his thoughts to the others he'd have to deal with. There was Stevie Lyons, the mate of the *Sisters*, who'd helped bring the silk up to London. And, of course, there was Joe Gott and Gabriel Marr. They'd been useful in their time; had done what had been required of them. But no more than that. He'd no more trust them with his life than he would Pascoe. If it came to a trial – and that was increasingly likely – neither man would think twice about betraying him if it was necessary to save their own necks. Gott, in particular, had begun to show signs of disloyalty.

Then there was the boy.

Creech frowned as he considered the complication. The boy knew nothing. Creech doubted he'd even be able to identify the house where he was being kept, still less be able to identify the person who'd snatched him from his bed. Yet he couldn't take the chance. The boy would have to go the same way as the others. Creech's hand dropped to his waist and he felt for the handle of his knife, a response to the thoughts passing through his head. The knife was always with him, as much a part of him as the clothes he wore.

He turned into the Whitechapel road and headed east towards Mile End, occasionally looking over his shoulder for anyone who might be following. He wanted to be done with this business, to free himself from the anxiety that now dogged him. Once the boy – and Stevie Lyons – were out of the way, he would turn his attention to Gott and Marr.

In the near distance he could see the London Accident Hospital, its imposing edifice partially obscured by a towering mound of rubbish whose stench was rumoured to put back the recovery of the patients by several weeks and, on occasion, permanently. Creech hurried by, the sleeve of his coat held tight against his nose. The hospital was followed by the Jews' cemetery and, a little further on, some almshouses that occupied the approaches to the Old Town at Mile End. He was in open country now. Fields stretching away on either side of the road. He reckoned he'd reach Bow in another twenty minutes and the farmhouse five minutes after that. He wouldn't stay long. He would do what he had to do and leave. He hoped Old Ma Gott wouldn't make much of a fuss. If she did, he would have to deal with her too.

# CHAPTER 41

Stevie Lyons was the first to hear it, the faint sound of a bolt being drawn back on the trapdoor above his head. He nudged William.

'Wake up. Someone's coming,' he whispered, and moved to the foot of the steps that led down from the room above. 'You know what to do.'

William nodded. They had gone over the plan many times in the twenty-four hours since they'd managed to free themselves and inspect every inch of their prison. It was William who'd found the bales in a corner of the basement, bales that Stevie had immediately recognised. He'd known, then, the danger they were both in. 'They won't let us live,' he'd said to William. 'Not now we've seen the bales. They'd be afraid we'd tell your brother about them.'

The hatch cover creaked open and Mrs Gott's face appeared.

'Your victuals is here,' she said, clambering down the steps with a tray in her hands. Halfway down she stopped. 'Where's the other lad?' she asked.

'He's here, missus.' William pointed his chin at the bale covered in Stevie's breeches and jerkin. 'He ain't well.'

'What's the matter with him?' Mrs Gott descended the last few steps. 'You best not be lying to me, boy, else I'll give you a clip round the ear for your trouble.'

She had reached the halfway mark when Stevie crept out from under the stairs and made his silent way out through the hatch. William waited another second or two before springing to his feet and making a dash for the steps.

'Which way?' he asked as soon as he'd caught up with Stevie, the old woman's oaths still ringing in his ears.

'Don't know where we are, Willie boy. We'll have to follow that river,' said Stevie, pointing to the Lea. 'With luck it'll take us down to the Thames. We can find our way from there.'

'What about the men what captured us? Won't they come looking for us?'

'Aye, they'll do that right enough. We'll have to—'

'Look,' said William. 'There's two men coming up the lane.'

'Get down,' said Stevie. 'And keep quiet. D'you hear?'


Lieutenant Milton Brougham dropped to one knee and signalled to his companion to do the same. A face had appeared at the window of the house, a fleeting presence which had gone almost as soon as it had appeared. Brougham wondered if they'd been seen. Not that it would make any real difference. They would still have to do what they had come out here for. His eyes swept over the rest of the house and the surrounding land. He didn't want to be caught by any nasty surprises. A second building, a barn-like structure, lay half hidden amongst some trees, about twenty yards from the main house. He was at the right place.

Brougham had learned of its existence in the same way that he'd learned so much else in his search for the intelligence document. In the crowded taverns close to the river, little was said or done which did not quickly become the currency of common chatter. It wasn't necessary that the speaker should have first-hand, or even second-hand knowledge of the matter under discussion, merely that he should have some rudimentary under-standing of the basic facts. It was on account of one such comment from a semi-inebriated lumper in a tavern on Wapping Wall that he and his companion Hawkes came to be here.

He tapped Hawkes's arm and pointed to the barn. Stooping low, the two men made their way past the house to the barn entrance, the double doors of which stood open. Going in, Brougham pointed to the left side. Hawkes nodded and the men split up.

'Anything?' whispered Brougham when, a few minutes later, the two met up at the far end of the barn.

'Only this,' said Hawkes, handing over some brown wrapping paper. 'Could have been used to ship the silk.'

'But it ain't here any more. We're going to have to look inside the house. Go round the back. See if there's another entrance. I'll cover the front— Wait, someone's coming.'

Brougham shrank back into the barn and looked towards the house as the front door was thrown open and an elderly woman came out into the yard, an ancient musket tucked under one arm. 'She's coming this way. Quick, get to the back, behind that cart.'

They hunched down at the end of the barn and waited. A moment later, Mrs Gott arrived at the entrance. 'Come out, you little vermin. I know you're in there. You wait till my boy gets here. He'll learn you your manners, running off like that.'

Brougham's eyebrows shot up. The woman was looking for someone else. He watched her standing at the open doors, a scowl of annoyance on her face. Then she turned and shuffled back towards the house, muttering to herself. Brougham got to his feet and, with Hawkes at his heels, followed her to the front door.

'Mrs Gott, ma'am?' The woman spun round, a frightened look on her face.

'Who are you? What d'you want,' she screeched, pointing the gun at them.

'We're looking for something, Mrs Gott. We—'

'You looking for them two boys, ain't you?' she quavered. 'I told my son to have nothing to do with them, but he said it were all to the good. What will become of me, sir? That's what I want to know.'

'Nothing for you to fret about, ma'am. Where are the lads now?'

'They's run off, sir. I tried to keep them safe, but they upped and gone.'

'What about the other stuff?' coaxed Brougham.

'What stuff is that, then?' Mrs Gott looked puzzled.

'The bales wrapped in brown paper that used to be in your barn.'

'Oh, them. Is you the revenue, sir?'

'Yes, we're the revenue,' lied Brougham.

'They was taken away.'

'All of them?'

'All except two. You best come in.' She propped the gun against the wall next to the door and led the way to the open trapdoor. 'They is down there, sir. Same place as the boys were until they had it away on their toes.'

'Stay here with the lady, Hawkes. Give me the lantern, ma'am, while I have a look.'

Brougham eased his large frame down through the hatch and descended the steps into a dark, cavernous area smelling of damp. He could see little, the guttering flame of the candle throwing its feeble light no further than the reach of his arm, accentuating the deep shadows that seemed to dance about the low ceiling. He ducked his head and, holding the lantern ahead of him, carefully looked round a basement filled with all manner of jumble. In one of the corners he found a pile of hessian sacks that had probably once contained grain but which had, long ago, been attacked by rats or mice and the contents devoured. Next to them were a couple of wooden boxes that had suffered the effects of the damp conditions and were on the point of collapse. He pulled them away from the wall and peered behind. There was nothing there but a few rat droppings. He moved on. Then, tucked beneath the steps down which he'd come, he saw what he'd come to find.

It was then that he heard the stranger's voice.

The daylight seeping into the cellar dimmed as the bulk of Hawkes's body filled the hatch and tumbled down the steps to the earth floor. A narrow face pitted with smallpox scars appeared in the opening, its coal-black eyes, devoid of pity or humanity, stared down at him.

'You the revenue?' Creech's question was delivered in a monotone, as though the answer, whatever it might be, was of no interest.

'Come down here and ask me that, mister,' said Brougham, looking up from Hawkes's groaning figure, still lying at the foot of the steps. Creech was holding the musket the old woman had propped against the wall by the front door. Brougham wished he'd picked it up as he had meant to do; kept it out of harm's way. He wondered if it was safe to assume it was unloaded and decided not to take the chance. Not yet. His eyes travelled from the gun to the face. He knew who it was, had seen him often enough in his travels around the drinking houses of Wapping, Shadwell and Southwark. His name had been whispered in frightened tones by those he'd met along the way.

'Mind what you say to me, cully,' snapped Creech. 'Where are the other two?'

'If you mean the two boys, you're out of luck. They've gone. Probably talking to the officers at Wapping right at this moment.' Brougham thought he saw Creech flinch. 'What's the matter, Creech? Can you feel the rope round your neck already? That'll never do. Folk round here might think you're frightened.'

The gun barrel pointed down through the hatch, the butt pressed to Creech's shoulder, one eye squinting down the length of the weapon. The house was suddenly quiet but for the sound of his rasping breath. Not for the first time, Brougham wished he'd been allowed his sea service pistol. 'We don't need another diplomatic incident as a result of you being caught with a side arm,' the ambassador had said to him when Brougham had suggested it. But things were rapidly turning ugly. He bent down and began to pull the injured Hawkes out of the line of fire. Suddenly, there was a deafening roar and a sheet of flame erupted from the muzzle of the musket.

For a moment, Brougham could see nothing through the thick, acrid-smelling gun smoke, nor hear anything but a loud ringing in his ears. Surprised that he appeared still to be alive, he groped through the choking fumes to where he'd dropped Hawkes.

'You all right, Hawkes?' He knew he was shouting but couldn't help it, the sound of his voice somehow distant and fuzzy. There was no reply. In the distance he was aware of what sounded like a woman screaming. 'Hawkes, talk to me.'

He shook his colleague's shoulder. It felt wet and sticky. He brought his hand close to his face and looked at it but he already knew what it was. He'd seen and smelt blood before. He fought down a sudden outburst of raging anger. It would solve nothing. For the moment he had to think. He put his cheek close to Hawkes's mouth and felt his shallow breath. He was still alive but for how much longer he couldn't tell. He needed some light, some chance to examine the extent of his friend's injuries. The woman's screams were getting louder. Now he could also hear a man's voice – it sounded like Creech – joining in. Brougham couldn't be sure, but it sounded as if he was trying to quieten her.

He glanced at Hawkes. The dark wet patch was growing in size. He removed the jerkin he was wearing, and then his cotton shirt. Tearing it into strips, he found the point where the bullet had entered. Fortunately, it didn't seem to have penetrated far into the muscle tissue. He could feel the hardness of the skin surrounding the area. He knew he would have to stop the bleeding and, at the same time, avoid pressing down on the lead ball. He folded one of the lengths of cotton in half and laid it gently over the wound. Then he twisted a second length of material into something resembling a rope which he placed in a circle around the outer limits of the wound. Finally he bandaged the shoulder and tied it off with a simple knot.

On the floor above, the shrieking stopped abruptly. It was followed by a strangled cry and the sound of something heavy hitting the floor. A minute later, Creech's face reappeared at the trapdoor. He was breathing heavily and still carrying the musket. He was staring down into the cellar. A door slammed. It made Creech jump and he swung round, the musket pointing at the front door. Brougham guessed the noise had been the old woman leaving the house. He was surprised Creech had not tried to stop her. Then he remembered how isolated the farm was. Even if the woman was fit enough to reach the next house, it would be several hours before any real help arrived – if then.

He toyed with the idea of rushing Creech. It could work. He'd not seen the gun being reloaded. If he could get close enough to the scrub, Creech would be no match for him. But there was a problem. His bulk would make it impossible for him to get through the trapdoor quickly enough to surprise the villain. He heard footsteps moving across the floor of the room upstairs and stop at the hatch. Creech must have temporarily left his post. Brougham cursed. He'd missed his opportunity.

'You down there,' called Creech. 'Come upstairs.'

Two thoughts occurred to Brougham simultaneously. First, that Creech had probably used the time he was away from the hatch to reload his musket, and second, that the scrub could not be sure if he had killed him and Hawkes and wanted to be sure. He waited to see what would happen.

He did not have long to wait.

# CHAPTER 42

Sam Hart hung back as the constable attached to the Shadwell police office approached the front door of the house on Aldgate High Street. He should have gone home. He had no business to be here, particularly as Mr Pascoe had expressly forbidden his involvement and made him promise to stay away. But he hadn't been able to resist coming and, besides, he wasn't about to become involved. The Shadwell constable would do all that was necessary, unless . . . He paused in his torrent of self-justification, his heart beating a little faster than normal, a pleasant tingling sensation in his chest at the prospect of seeing Adina, if only fleetingly. He watched the constable walk past the house, turn and walk back. He knocked, waited a minute and knocked again.

The door of Emden's shop opened and the constable touched his forehead. What he said, Sam couldn't hear but he could guess at the form of words that would be used. They seldom varied in situations like this. Sam had lost count of the number of times he'd been the bearer of bad news. It never got any easier seeing the shock of the unexpected in the other person's eyes.

Adina Emden leaned forward beyond the doorframe and looked up and down the street. Sam thought she saw him but could not be sure. He felt strangely out of place, as though an unwelcome observer to another's private grief. She looked frightened, as if she already knew what the officer had come to say, her hand to her mouth, her eyes wide and staring at him. She stepped back out of sight and was followed by the constable, the door closing behind them.

The wail of anguish, when it finally came, tore through Sam's mind like a sharp knife. He wondered if Emden's wife was at home or if Adina had had to take the news of her father's death by herself. Either way, he was not helping matters by his presence. The door opened again and the officer came out. It was over. Sam turned away and left. He might pay a visit in a day or two. Now was not the time.

The elderly woman was in pain. That much was obvious. She was doubled over and clutching at her stomach as she came down the lane towards him. Occasionally, he would catch a faint cry of pain and she would stop and look back the way she had come, a quick, fearful, darting look as though afraid of pursuit by some unknown enemy.

Tom quickened his pace, his boots sinking into the autumnal mud on the road leading north out of Bow. Beyond the woman, he could see the farmhouse nestling close to a stand of trees. Behind it flowed the River Lea. It was a desolate and lonely place, surrounded by marsh that spread away in every direction for as far as the eye could see, save for a few acres of wheat and barley and the occasional windmill.

'By God, if I'm not sadly mistook, it's Mrs Gott,' said Tom, hurrying up to her. 'What happened to you, madam?'

'It's that villain Creech,' gasped the woman. 'He gave me a whipping. For no reason, sir. Hit me with my late husband's musket, he did. He's nothing but a scoundrel what'll rot in hell, sir, so he will.'

'Are there others in the house?'

'Aye, there's two more cullies what said they was revenue. Don't know if they still live. Creech shot them. That's when he hit me.'

'And Creech is still in the house?'

'Aye, he is. More's the pity.'

'Take care of the lady, Higgins,' said Tom. 'As soon as she's comfortable, come up to the house.'

'Kemp,' he said, turning to the remaining member of his crew, 'I want you to come with me. If I remember correctly, there's a door at the back of the house that leads into a scullery and from there into the main room. I want you to enter through that door and go through to the front room. I suspect Creech will be there. We know he's got a musket and we're going to have to assume it's loaded. That said, I want to take him alive if at all possible which, means not blowing his head off. You got all that?'

'Begging your pardon, sir,' interrupted Mrs Gott. 'But that villain Creech went and bolted the back door, sir. The revenue men told him the boys what were there had escaped and would likely be speaking to the officers. He were proper frightened by that.'

'Boys?' Tom swung round to look at her. 'What boys? Was one of them around twelve years of age, fair hair and pale of complexion? Quickly, woman. Speak up.'

'Might have been,' said Mrs Gott. 'Didn't get a proper look at either of them.'

'You got that, Kemp?' said Tom, glancing at his crewman. 'We're going to have to go through the front door. You know what the room looks like from the last time we were here. As soon as we've secured Creech, we're going to have to search the house for the other two men. After that I want help searching for the two boys Mrs Gott has referred to.'

Leaving Higgins and the woman behind, Tom and Kemp dropped into a ditch at the side of the road and crawled through the thick undergrowth that had long ago taken root. Opposite the farmhouse they stopped and Tom peered through the dew-filled grass at the house opposite. Everything seemed quiet with no sign of movement.

'Ready?' whispered Tom.

Kemp nodded.

They sprinted across the narrow lane and into the courtyard in front of the house. Reaching the front door, Tom put a finger to his lips and listened. He pressed the door latch and pushed. It didn't move. The door seemed to have been locked.

'The door needs your special talents,' whispered Tom.

He watched as the big man took up a position about three feet from the door, lifted his right foot and kicked, hard. Very hard. The door shuddered, creaked and, with a rending crash, fell into the front room. Tom was in first, his long-barrelled sea service pistol cocked and ready to fire. He leapt across the fallen door, his eyes sweeping the room in a single glance, taking in every detail, analysing and sifting the information for the threat it might pose. Creech was by the trapdoor at the other end of the room. He was already on his feet, bending to pick up the musket that he'd lain on the floor beside him, his head turned towards Tom.

'Drop it, Creech. And put your hands where I can see them.'

Creech slowly straightened his back, his eyes on Tom and the gun in his hand.

'Walk towards me. Slowly. Now lie on the floor and put your hands behind your back.' Tom waited while Creech sank to the floor. Then he beckoned Kemp over. 'Tie him up. Hands and feet. Then stay with him. I'm going to look for the two other cullies that are supposed to be here.'

He'd already seen the open hatch and the chest of drawers that had been pushed to one side. Picking up a lantern that stood on a table at the centre of the room, he lit the candle and climbed down the wooden steps.

'Anyone here?' he asked.

'Aye, there's two of us. My friend's been shot. I'm sure glad to see you.'

Tom held out the lantern and let the yellow glow shine on the face of the speaker. 'Why, I remember you, sir. You came to my assistance a little while ago, did you not? Would your presence here have anything to do with those two bales of silk over there?'

'I regret I don't know to what you are referring, sir.'

'Then how, sir, did you come to be here?' said Tom.

'My friend and I were passing. We thought to ask the lady of the house for a cup of water. The man you now have in custody took exception to our being in the house.'

'You surely don't expect me to believe that, sir. According to the lady, you claimed to be from the revenue.'

'Nothing could be further from the truth,' said Brougham. 'The lady assumed, for reasons only she can give you, that we were from the revenue. I did not think to disabuse her. I thought we would shortly be on our way. But I would be in your debt, sir, were you to assist my friend here.'

Tom ducked beneath the joists and made his way over. Kneeling by the injured man, he examined the dressing.

'You appear to have dressed a wound before, sir,' he said, after a minute of silence. 'Am I right?'

'I have watched others, sir.'

Tom helped the injured man up the steps and laid him on the floor. His injury didn't appear to be serious. He turned to look at Brougham.

'Naturally, I shall require a statement from you both concerning the circumstances of your presence here and the shooting which followed. After that you will, of course, appear as a witness at the Sessions House in Old Bailey. Without that, it will not be possible to prosecute the man we've arrested for trying to kill your friend.'

'I . . . I . . .' stuttered Brougham.

'What, pray, is the matter?' asked Tom.

'I regret that what you ask is impossible, sir. No, it is beyond a possibility. It . . .' Brougham floundered into helpless silence.

'I think we both know why you came to this house, sir, and why you are reluctant to become involved as a witness in a criminal trial,' said Tom.

'I regret it extremely, but I don't follow you,' said Brougham. 'I have explained how we came to be in this position. As far as I'm aware there is no law that requires my attendance at court as a witness and I choose not to do so.'

Tom would have liked to pursue his line of questioning but it would have to wait. He thought of his brother, convinced that the old woman's passing reference to two boys could only mean that William was in the area. The desire to search for him was strong, the wish to leave the others to deal with Creech and the two men he'd found in the cellar almost overwhelming.

'You came to my assistance once, sir, and I am grateful to you for that,' said Tom. 'For that reason, I'll not pursue this inquiry. If you will not prosecute for the assault on your friend, I cannot force you. And I dare say that neither my government nor yours would welcome the embarrassment that would result from your appearance in court answering questions on the nature of your business out here.'

He picked up the bales and carried them to the steps leading to the hatch. The brown paper in which they were wrapped was torn. Looking back to where Brougham was still sitting, he said, 'I hear you are an officer in the United States Navy. For that, I salute you, but it would be wise were you to leave the country before too long. Do I make myself clear?'

'Aye, so you do,' said Brougham, a rueful smile creasing his rugged face. 'You are a worthy opponent, sir, whose reputation goes before you. Your country is lucky to have you.'

Tom looked round at the sound of someone coming through the front entrance. It was Higgins. He'd brought the old woman back to the house and sat her down in a chair close to the fireplace.

'Is she all right?' Tom raised a questioning eyebrow.

'Good as she'll ever be,' said Higgins. 'She were badly shaken but she'll recover.'

'Good. There's a cart in the barn which I want brought to the front door. When you've done that, I want the silk bales loaded and taken back to Wapping. With the prisoner. Kemp will go with you. I, meanwhile, will be searching for the two missing boys that were here.'

# CHAPTER 43

The western sky over London Bridge was the colour of burnished copper streaked through with strips of white cloud as Tom walked up the side steps of the police office, his hand resting on the shoulder of a young boy. Behind them walked another lad, an expression of worry and relief simultaneously etched on his tired face. The three turned in through the door and mounted the stairs to the constables' waiting room.

It had taken several hours of searching before Tom had finally caught sight of his brother and Stevie Lyons as they had trudged along the towpath of the Lea Cut, east of Limehouse. They had, they told him, seen Creech's arrival at the farmhouse and had hidden amongst the reed beds of the Lea before travelling south, past Bow to the bridge at Bromley where, unsure of the way home, they'd crossed to the east bank for no better reason than the fact the footpath crossed to that side. It was a mistake they were to regret, and it was some time before they realised they would have to retrace their steps and find a more direct route to Wapping. By that time, Tom had already scoured the banks of the Cut and, failing to find them, looked elsewhere.

'First some food and drink to fill the empty spaces inside you. After that, I've got some questions for you both,' said Tom, smiling. 'I'll sort the victuals out right away, but while we're waiting for that to arrive, I'm going to see Mr Harriot. He'll be wondering what's happening.'

He left them and went down to the gaoler's room and ordered up plates of white bread and butter, some slices of cold beef, a spatchcocked eel and a plate of oysters, the whole to be fetched from the Ramsgate, with two quart pots of small beer. That done, he went back upstairs and knocked on Harriot's door.

'Come in, Mr Pascoe. Take a seat,' said the resident magistrate, glancing up from his desk. 'Did you have any success?'

'If you mean the document, sir, yes, we've got it. It was well hidden in one of the skeins.'

'Very well done, sir. I'm sure Whitehall will be relieved. What about your brother?'

'He's safe too.'

'Excellent. Tell me what happened, will you?'

For the next few minutes, Tom recounted the events of the day, the discovery of Creech at the premises, the finding of the American agents, and the escape and subsequent rescue of his brother.

'You've been busy, Mr Pascoe,' said Harriot, picking up a pipe and filling it with tobacco. 'You say the Americans are refusing to give evidence of their incarceration or even the fact that one of them was shot? I can't say I'm entirely surprised. There would have been the most almighty fuss. Questions asked as to why we weren't hanging them as spies and counter-allegations by the American government that we were hounding innocent men. No, no. I think we'll keep the whole thing under our hats, particularly as we've got the papers they were after. Where are they, by the way?'

'The Americans? We dropped them off at their embassy. I dare say they'll be busy explaining why they failed. I've left Kemp outside to keep an eye on them and make sure they board a packet back to the States.'

'What about Creech? What does he say about the shooting?'

'He claims he was protecting Mrs Gott and her property. He says that he went to the house to talk to her and found our American friends in the act of stealing property. Flatly denies shooting at anybody and says he was merely asking them what they were doing in the house.'

'What about Mrs Gott? What does she say about what happened in her house?'

'She's saying nothing. I think she's afraid of what Creech or one of his bully boys would do if she were to give evidence against him.'

'Hmm, predictable,' said Harriot, cupping both hands round the bowl of his pipe. 'Supposing you tell me what we've got.'

'As you know, sir, there were three men who might have been able to provide the necessary evidence to convict Creech of piracy. Of those three, Cox and Emden are dead. In the case of Cox, he was found floating in the Lower Pool soon after he got back from the Medway. There were signs of bruising on his face and body consistent with a flogging, but no witnesses, apart from the physician who conducted the post-mortem, have come forward to say how he met his end. The second man, Emden, you know about. There is little doubt in my mind that, had he lived, he could have been persuaded to turn King's Evidence. That leaves us with Lyons.'

'How can he help?' said Harriot.

'Lyons travelled to Stangate Creek in the *Sisters*. He was present when Creech ordered Cox to run the *Sisters* onto the hard so the depredation could take place. He also told me about a conversation he had with Cox, his sailing master, in which Cox claimed he was being forced into piracy by Creech. He—'

'I regret that what Cox told Lyons is inadmissible in evidence. Only Cox could have given it and since that is now impossible, the evidence can't be adduced.'

'There is, sir, one other matter . . .'

'And that is?'

'Doubtless you'll recall that the attempts to put a stop to my investigations were not confined to the kidnapping of my brother, but extended to an attempt on my life.'

'Yes. You were fortunate that Master Hart found you in time.'

'I am, of course, extremely grateful to Sam Hart but he wasn't the person who saved my life. Of course I didn't know it at the time but it was Stevie Lyons who found me and pulled me from the river. Later I learned that he'd seen my capture and had recognised the men involved although he did not then know their names. Later, when I was being taken to the river, the men were joined by Creech.'

'Are you sure Lyons will agree to give evidence?' said Harriot.

'Yes, he's as anxious to see the back of these villains as the rest of us.'

Harriot got to his feet and limped over to the window. He stood there in silence for a moment, gazing out onto the river bathed in the golden glow of the setting sun. 'What about your brother? Can Creech be implicated in his abduction?'

'No. The descriptions I've got from William match Gott. But I'm confident we've got the evidence against all three villains in

359

respect of the other offences. I'm getting witness statements from everyone involved, including the captain of the *Velocity* and the two tide waiters who came up with the silk. If they all say what I think they will, we should have no difficulty obtaining guilty verdicts on all three men.'

'Yes, I think I'd agree with that assessment. Let me have the statements as soon as possible. In the meantime, I'll remand all three to Cold Bath Fields until I can make a decision regarding committal proceedings.'

Mr R. Hardwick of Gaby, Gaby and Gaby, attorneys-at-law of Clerkenwell, stared at the heavy wooden gates with an impatient air. He had been waiting some minutes to be admitted to the Middlesex Prison in Cold Bath Fields where his client, Mr Daniel Creech of the Parish of Shadwell, was presently held.

A short man with a round face and an equally round waist, he bore the look of someone who knew his worth and was determined that others should be equally aware of it. He had fashioned his entire career on the basis that he would say and do whatever was required to serve the needs of his clients. Lying, cheating and occasionally suborning the justice system in order to achieve his ends were as one to him. In rare moments of self-contemplation he had felt some sympathy with Pilate's question to Christ – *Truth? What is truth?* – before the Roman governor had handed Him over to His executioners.

Creech was one of his more lucrative clients if not, necessarily, one whom he would have chosen to meet on quite such a regular basis. If the truth were known he was frightened of Creech in a way that transcended his quite natural apprehension when in the presence of violent men. There was something wholly un-predictable about the man that Hardwick could not readily put his finger on. And while, as a general rule, he was able to put aside what remnants of morality still survived within his breast, the demands of his client had the effect of becoming increasingly more perilous to his own well-being.

Hardwick picked up his cane and aimed a fresh blow at the prison door at the precise moment that it began to swing open. He took a step back as the dour face of the turnkey appeared, long greying strands of grease-filled hair hanging down about his ears, a broken tricorn hat perched on the back of his head.

'Yes?' growled the turnkey.

'Ah, there you are, my man.' Hardwick drew himself up to his full five feet four inches and squinted up into the guard's grimy face through a pair of small, steel-framed spectacles. 'Mr Hard-wick, attorney-at-law, here to see my client, Mr Daniel Creech. Please be good enough to tell him I'm here.'

Hardwick followed the turnkey into a large courtyard bounded on three sides by a high wall. The fourth was occupied by the prison building itself, its multiple windows seeming to look down with sorrow at the shuffling mass of humanity below. Groups of perhaps thirty or forty men stood in ranks, marching or halting according to the directions of the turnkeys, their faces uniformly blank of expression. It was, for them, a daily ritual which must be endured without murmur or dissent.

At the edge of the yard, the guard stopped and looked back at Hardwick. 'Your client's over yonder,' he said, nodding at a tread-mill perched at first-floor level above a row of what appeared to be some administrative offices, and extending the full width of the yard. 'I'll tell him you're here when he's finished what he's got to do.'

Hardwick glanced up to see his client engaged in an endless cycle of endeavour that had no discernible purpose, the sweat staining the men's shirts a darkish grey. He looked back at the retreating guard and considered objecting to any further delay in the performance of his important legal duty. But perhaps not. The additional few minutes would enable him to properly prepare himself for the ordeal that was to come.

He walked to the opposite side of the yard and sat on a low wall bordering a garden of sorts. Behind him a small party was at work planting vegetables, overseen by yet another guard. He thought of the instructions an intermediary had brought him from his troublesome client. It had been a departure from the usual threats and arguments he was required to undertake in furtherance of his client's interests, and a great deal more dangerous. He had done it, of course, as he had done everything else demanded of him, preferring not to think about the possible consequences. It was easier that way, less stressful.

The intermediary had arrived at his Clerkenwell office on the same day that Creech had been remanded to the Middlesex, his client's instructions passed on in the convoluted manner so enamoured of the criminal classes and wholly incomprehensible to anyone not well versed in the ways of villains. Hardwick had known at once what was being asked of him, his reptilian mind processing the subtle undertones of every word as it was uttered, marshalling them into some semblance of order. That had been four days ago. Tomorrow, Creech was due before the Wapping magistrate in what was generally accepted would be a straightforward committal to the grand jury at Westminster Hall who would consider the weight of evidence on the indictment. Then – probably after the luncheon break – Creech would find himself in the dock of the Old Bailey along with his two co-defendants, Gott and Marr.

Hardwick knew well enough that his opportunity for effective action lay in that short period between the deliberations of the grand jury and the commencement of the trial. He felt a cold shiver run down his spine as he contemplated the consequences of failure. Doubtless, his client would hang. But his own fate, too, would be sealed.

'You done what I told you?' Creech's rasping voice made him jump. He hadn't seen his client's approach and guessed that Creech had probably done it deliberately to unsettle him; place him at a disadvantage.

'It's all arranged.'

'It had better be. Wouldn't want to be in your shoes else.'

# CHAPTER 44

'I've read through the witness statements concerning Creech and the others,' said John Harriot, as he and Tom took their customary first-floor seats in Jerusalem's Coffee House, on Cornhill. 'I think you've got sufficient evidence to charge all three men with piracy in relation to the taking of the silk. There is also clear evidence against Gott for abducting young William, and a further charge against all three of abducting Stephen Lyons. If you bring them before me this afternoon, I'll deal with the committal proceedings immediately. We should see them all at the Old Bailey before the end of the week.'

'We may have some trouble before we get to that point,' said Tom.

'What d'you mean?' said Harriot, a mug of ale halted halfway to his lips.

'There's been some talk. You know how it is. Whispers, vague chatter based on rumour. It's difficult to know exactly what it refers to, but I've got the feeling it involves Creech.' Tom shook his head. 'It's probably nothing but I think I'll post some men inside the Bailey when the case comes to trial, just in case.'

'Yes, do that,' said Harriot. 'On another subject, I hear you had a meeting with the Under Secretary of State at the Foreign Office first thing this morning.'

'Hookham Frere?' said Tom, catching the eye of a waiter and beckoning him over. 'Aye, he sent a note suggesting a meeting. It seemed the intelligence document we recovered was causing something of a stir in Whitehall.'

'Oh?' said Harriot. 'Did he say why?'

'Shall we, sir, order first? We can talk as we eat.'

'Good idea,' said Harriot. 'Now, what shall we have?'

Tom waited for the waiter to leave with their orders. 'It appears the paper contained some sensitive information not previously known to us.'

'I hope he was grateful,' said Harriot, gripping his thigh, his face twisted in sudden pain. 'Damned leg.'

'Oh, I think he was,' said Tom. 'There was a good deal of background to the ongoing activities of the French Navy in the Caribbean—'

'Against American shipping?'

'Quite so. The Foreign Office had originally thought the French actions would push the Americans into the war on our side but it now seems that despite these attacks, there is a strong body of public opinion in the United States that favours supporting the French on ideological grounds.'

'Meaning what? That the Americans might come into the war on the French side?' said Harriot, his eyes widening.

'Apparently it's a possibility,' said Tom. 'According to the document, American public opinion is still very much against us, principally arising out of the *Baltimore* incident. It's only the President who is holding back.'

'I'd quite forgotten about the *Baltimore*,' said Harriot. 'I imagine if anything could be calculated to raise national fury, having your country's sailors seized from one of your men-of-war and pressed into the service of the Royal Navy would do the trick.'

'Yes.' Tom paused while a cloth was laid on their table. A moment later the waiter returned with plates of food. As soon as he'd gone, Tom said, 'The intelligence paper makes it clear just how far the American president is prepared to go to appease domestic public opinion. At the same time, he doesn't want to risk another war with England. I think he's afraid that if his policy on this becomes known, it will provoke the conflict he's trying to avoid.'

Tom lapsed into silence. He picked up a glass of water and drank it. He had regretted his session in the Devil's Tavern when he and a stranger had drunk to excess. He didn't want to repeat it.

'Did you, sir, get any sense of what the Foreign Office intend to do with the information?' said Harriot, breaking the silence.

'The Under Secretary didn't say a great deal about that,' said Tom. 'I got the impression they'll want to wait and see what happens next. Nobody wants another war.'

'Except the French,' said Harriot.

'Speaking of whom,' said Tom, leaning across the table and forking a thick slice of cold mutton onto his plate, 'it seems General Bonaparte may be planning a *coup d'état*. According to the intelligence report, this business with the Americans has weakened the Directoire and there are rumours that Bonaparte may wish to take advantage of the situation and assume power.'

'Good God.' Harriot stared across the table, his food temporarily forgotten. 'When will all this happen?'

'According to Mr Hookham Frere, Bonaparte arrived back from

Egypt earlier this month. so if he's going to seize power I suspect he'll do it sometime in November or December.'

'What's your assessment of the situation?'

'If Napoleon seizes power?' said Tom. 'I think we would face an enemy vastly better led and more capable than at present. I think it might further encourage the Americans to join the war on the French side. Beyond that I can't say.'

'But a good enough reason for keeping the information from the Americans,' said Harriot, helping himself to another slice of meat and a spoonful of boiled eel.

'It may be too late for that,' said Tom, quietly.

Harriot looked up sharply. 'What do you mean, sir?'

'When Hookham Frere was reading the document to me, I could see traces of dried blood on the back.'

'What of it?'

'One of the American agents we found in the cellar of the house in Bow had been shot and was bleeding.'

# CHAPTER 45

It was one of those situations that was unlikely ever to be satisfactorily resolved. By the time Tom had realised the possibility that the Americans might have seen the secret intelligence report, it was all too late. Of some comfort was the knowledge, extracted from his young brother, that Brougham and his shipmate had arrived at the house in Bow only a few minutes before they were disturbed by Creech. The time available for them to find the report, read it and then hide it again would have been severely limited. All the same, Tom was worried. The probability of war with the United States was real. If the American government should now discover the possibility of Napoleon seizing power in France, they might well take the view that the time was right to settle some scores with the British.

And yet, other concerns were also crowding his mind as, the following morning, he walked up from the Thames, through the late-morning crowds of the Fleet Market towards the Old Bailey. The feeling of apprehension that had dogged him since he'd become aware of the rumours concerning the Creech trial had not left him.

Now he tried to make sense of his concerns. Yesterday's committal proceedings and Creech's appearance before the grand jury first thing this morning had passed without incident. As to the rumours, they had, as he'd admitted to Harriot, been impossible to substantiate. Creech's name had never been mentioned. Tom expelled a lungful of air. He was not being honest with himself. No name had been necessary. Everyone in Wapping and Shadwell, and as far away as Southwark on the south bank, had known immediately who it was that the story related to. Creech was that kind of man. You didn't get in his way. You did what he told you to do or you paid the price. His name – when it was spoken at all – was uttered in quiet and fearful undertones.

Tom walked on, turning right by the Fleet prison into a lane that led into Old Bailey, and the sessions house that lay on the other side of the street. He'd arranged for Kemp, Higgins and several other officers to be present in the courtroom and keep an eye on things. If there was going to be trouble, Tom wanted to be ready for it. It was bad enough losing the two Americans. He shook his head. Brougham and his colleague must have slipped out of the back door of the embassy. Certainly Kemp had not seen them exiting by the front door. But for all that, Tom wasn't unduly worried. It would have been nice to see them safely on board a brig bound for the States but it wasn't to be. And anyway, the intelligence document which they'd been after was now safely with the Foreign Office, albeit that some part of it might have been read by the injured Hawkes.

He put the matter to the back of his mind. The chance of the American having seen anything worthwhile was very slim.

Reaching the session house, Tom showed his tipstaff to one of the doorkeepers and went into the court. It was a large room with a high ceiling and a window which occupied most of one wall. In the centre, and facing away from the window, was the dock, an elevated platform surrounded by wooden panelling about four feet in height and surmounted with a row of iron spikes. At its leading edge, positioned above the heads of the prisoners, was a long, rectangular mirror whose purpose was to reflect daylight onto the faces of the defendants. Unfortunately, it often served merely to blind them to anything that might have proved of interest to them in the proceedings. A court usher was standing close by. Tom made his way over.

'Case of Creech and others,' he said. 'I'm the officer in the case. Do you have him in the cells?'

'Aye, he's there, right enough.' The usher gave a knowing look. 'His mates is there, too. Gott and Marr. Tasty little villains, for sure.'

Tom thanked him and moved away. The court had adjourned for the midday meal and there were no more than half a dozen people in the court, most of them sitting in the area reserved for members of the legal profession. Of the remainder, most were sitting in the public gallery above and behind the jury box.

Tom recognised the attorney Hardwick as soon as he saw him. He'd come across him several times at the Old Bailey and knew him by repute. He walked back to where the usher was rearranging a posy of herbs on the narrow shelf at the front of the dock. Taking the man by his elbow, he guided him to a corner of the court furthest from where Hardwick was sitting.

'That cully sitting alone in the front of the court. Know him, do you?'

'See him in here from time to time. Calls himself an attorney but I don't know so much.'

'Does he have a client here today?'

'Why, bless my soul, I do believe he's in your case, sir. Aye, I'm sure of it. Might be waiting on the barrister what he's instructed. Bit unusual, that. Don't often get barristers for the defence.'

Tom grunted. It was certainly unusual but he wasn't sure he could read anything into the news. There were any number of reasons why Creech might have instructed an attorney, including the fact that he was on trial for his life.

Another thought occurred to him. 'Have the prisoners received any visitors this morning?'

'Only the attorney over yonder.' The usher flicked a finger at Hardwick's rounded back.

'Anybody hear what was being said?'

'Not allowed. Conversation is privileged, your honour.' The man sniffed at the bunch of herbs in his hand and put it back on the shelf. 'Will that be all, sir?'

'Aye, thankee,' said Tom, turning to see the public gallery beginning to fill. He took out his pocket watch. It was almost three. He wondered what had happened to his witnesses, among them William and Stevie Lyons. Both should have been here by now. Tom's brow furrowed in concern. The boys were being brought by Sam. But there was no sign of him either.

A sudden flurry of activity inside the dock caught his attention. A turnkey had arrived in the dock and was looking down the flight of stairs leading to the cells. The prisoners were, it seemed, being brought up. Tom could hear voices, orders being issued and the tramp of boots on the wooden steps. Then, one by one, Creech, Marr and Gott appeared, each of them in turn pushed to their allotted places at the front of the enclosure.

Tom looked away, his eyes running along the seated rows of

men and women in the public gallery, staring, pointing, chatting loudly amongst themselves. There was still no sign of William. Tom's frown deepened, a niggling worry making itself felt in the pit of his stomach. He forced himself to concentrate on other things, studying the faces of the three prisoners. Gone was the insouciant air with which they had habitually faced the world. In its place was the pallor of frightened men and the darting gaze with which they sought, and failed, to find comfort in their fellow creatures. Only Creech gazed straight ahead, his eyes seemingly fixed on the stone sword behind the judge's seat. If he cared at all for his surroundings, he showed no sign of it. Only the occasional moistening of his dry lips gave any hint of the state of his mind.

Suddenly, the loud voice of a second usher cut through the chattering babble and called for silence as the trial judge swept in, magnificent in his red robe, black sash and full-bottomed wig. Immediately, the noise and confusion fell away and eyes alternated between the majesty of the law and the three unfortunates at the bar.

'May it please my lord . . .' An elderly man in a short grey wig and black gown struggled to his feet from his place in the well of the court. 'I prosecute in this case.'

'Do proceed, Mr . . . ah . . . Montague,' said the judge, consulting a sheet of paper he was holding. 'Perhaps you would be good enough to keep it brief. I have a long list this afternoon.'

'I'm obliged, my lord.' Mr Montague adjusted a silver monocle he was wearing, grasped the leading edges of his gown with both hands and turned to face the jury with what some might have described as a strangled grimace. 'This case . . .' he began.

Tom barely heard a word, his eyes straying to the door through which witnesses would necessarily enter the court. Had William's absence anything to do with Creech? Or was he just late? As if from far away, he heard his name being called. He looked up. The usher was looking at him, beckoning him. He jumped to his feet and strode quickly to the witness box. Picking up the New Testament, he was midway through the oath when, out of the corner of his eye, he saw a door open and Sam's head appear, then William's, then Stevie Lyons's. He finished giving the oath and turned to look at the counsel for the prosecution, a sense of relief coursing through him.

'You are, I believe, a river surveyor with the marine police institution based at the Wapping police office,' said Montague, riffling through a large bundle of papers on the table in front of him.

'I am,' said Tom.

There was not a great deal Tom could say about the plundering of the silk skeins. He hadn't seen Creech or Marr or Gott at any stage of the journey to and from Stangate Creek. He could say nothing of the events on board the *Velocity*. Those involved had remained firmly out of his sight and the evidence of their involvement would come from others. His testimony was to be confined to the finding of the bales of silk and the arrest of Creech and his fellow defendants.

Then the questions turned to the attempt on his life.

'On the evening of the twenty-sixth of October of this year you were on your way to see a gentleman in connection with an investigation upon which you were engaged. Can you tell the court what happened to you on that occasion?'

'At about eleven o'clock on that evening, I was on foot in New Market Street, Shadwell, when I was set upon by some men, none of whom I was able to recognise.'

'What happened then?' said Montague, his hands still gripping his gown, his gaze directed at the judge.

'A sack was placed over my head and I was taken to a nearby house where I heard the voice of a man I believe to have been Daniel Creech.'

'Believed? You are not certain, it was the defendant Creech?'

'No, I cannot be certain, but it sounded to me like him.'

'What did this man whom you believe to have been Creech, say?'

'He asked when high tide was and then said, "Wait for that and throw him in." '

'What was your physical condition at this time?'

'I had been beaten and I was firmly bound, hand and foot. The sack was still upon my head.'

'What happened then?'

'A number of men carried me to the riverside and threw me in.'

'During the course of this, did you recognise the voices of anyone else?'

'While I cannot be certain, I think I heard the prisoners Gott and Marr talking as they carried me to the river.'

'But you are not sure about that?'

'No.'

'And I think you were subsequently pulled from the river by a man not known to you at the time.'

'That's correct.'

'Wait there, if you please,' said learned counsel, gathering his gown about him and sitting down.

Tom glanced at Hardwick. He was in conversation with one of the barristers.

'Mr Johnson,' said the judge, peering over the top of his desk and addressing the barrister. 'If it is your intention to join us this afternoon, I should be happy were you to proceed with your cross-examination of the witness.'

The man looked up, the faintest hint of a sneer on his lips, his gaze sweeping the crowded court to rest, finally, on Tom.

' "A sack was placed over my head." That was what you said, was it not, sir?' The sneer became more pronounced.

'Yes,' said Tom.

'And again, "I cannot be certain, but it sounded to me like him." Is that right?'

'Yes.' Tom waited patiently for the questions to follow one another. They were no surprises. He had fully expected an attempt would be made to discredit him, to pour scorn on the evidence he'd already given, to weaken its impact on the minds of the jury.

'How well, sir, do you know Mr Creech?'

'I have seen and spoken to him in the past.'

'How often? Twice? Three times? A dozen, perhaps?'

'Perhaps four or five times,' said Tom.

'And were you, sir, on any of these previous occasions wearing a sack over your head?' A ripple of laughter reverberated around the court.

'No, I was not.' Tom held his irritation in check.

The barrister stared at Tom for a moment or two as though expecting some further response. When none came, his gaze dropped awkwardly to the pile of papers in front of him.

'The truth is, Mr Pascoe, that you cannot be sure of the identity of the men who attacked you on that night. Is that not so?'

'That is what I said, sir.'

'Well, quite so.' The sneer had faded, replaced by the look of a hunted man with nowhere to run. He sank to his seat.

'Do you have any further questions, Mr Montague?'

'No further questions, my lord,' said Montague, rising briefly before dropping back into his seat.

Tom returned to his place and looked across at the dock. The long mirror over the prisoners' heads had caught the rays of the afternoon sun and deflected them down onto their faces. Alone of the three, Creech seemed relatively relaxed. Tom caught sight of a glance passing between the sailmaker and the black-clad attorney. The latter's head had seemed to jerk in the direction of the jury. It might have been nothing, a commonplace look between a prisoner and his attorney. And yet it had seemed to Tom to convey something more than the commonplace. He stared from one to the other, trying to make some sense of what he'd seen. Had some unspoken message passed between the two? And if it had, was there some connection with the twelve men of the jury? The moment passed and the attorney turned his attention back to the witness box where Stevie Lyons was waiting.

'I swear by Almighty God that the evidence I shall give . . .' The oath, the guardian against all perjury, droned on, Stevie's voice nervous and halting. His testimony, when it came, could no more be shaken than Tom's had been. No, there was no doubt in his mind that it had been Creech, accompanied by Marr and Gott who had spoken to the sailing master of the *Sisters* on the harbour wall at Sheerness. Yes, the question of plundering the silk had been talked about and agreed. Yes, he was certain the men he'd seen carrying Tom Pascoe down to the river had included Creech, Marr and Gott. Nor was there any doubt about the identity of the men who had come for him at Farthing Fields and taken him to face Creech, the same three men who then had him imprisoned in the cellar of a house outside Bow.

Stevie was followed into the witness box by William Pascoe who spoke of his terror on the night he'd been taken from his bed by two men one of whom he now knew as Gott. And he spoke of his imprisonment in a cellar and of seeing Creech there on the day of the latter's arrest.

'Members of the jury,' the trial judge had said, less than an hour and a half after the commencement of the trial, 'yours is the solemn duty of deciding the guilt or innocence of the three men who stand before you in the dock. You have listened to the evidence given by the witnesses and you have listened to the defence that each man was invited to make. Upon these facts and no other will you be required to make your decision. In doing so you should weigh in your minds the dread consequences that await these men upon a finding of guilt.'

Tom couldn't remember when he'd last felt so tired. He sat slumped in a chair in Harriot's office gazing at the fire in the grate, his legs stretched out in front of him.

'What d'you think happened?' Harriot blew a cloud of tobacco smoke into the air and watched it rise to the ceiling and curl outwards in a perfect circle.

'It's difficult to say,' said Tom. 'But I thought it odd when the jury decided to retire.'

'They retired?' said Harriot, his eyebrows arching in surprise.

'Aye, I've not seen them do that in a while and, if I'm not mistook, the judge was a little surprised, too. Instead of the usual five or ten minutes to reach their decision, we had to wait for nearly an hour for them to come back.'

'With guilty verdicts against just two of them?'

'Aye. Gott and Marr. They are sentenced to be gibbeted at Cuckold Point at bottom-of-the-water tomorrow morning,' said Tom. 'Creech was acquitted.'

'What makes you think the jury was nobbled?'

'You mean apart from the fact that there was overwhelming evidence against him?' said Tom, staring at the burning embers in the grate.

'Yes,' said Harriot. 'D'you have any evidence of jury tampering?'

'There was an attorney in the court. A man named Hardwick. He has a sham practice in Camberwell. I've known him for some time. Whenever he's involved in a case, you can be sure it smells. He was acting for Creech in this case and was heavily involved in the selection of the jury. He objected to no fewer than thirty potential jurors before accepting the final juror. I saw him nod at the fellow and receive a nod in reply. I'm sure that was his man. After the case, I followed Hardwick into the Magpie and Stump in Newgate Street. I had a suspicion that he might want to meet up with the juror; pay him for services rendered. Sure enough, the cully was there.'

'Did they speak to each other?'

'I can't be sure. They stood very close to one another for a few seconds but I didn't see them talking. Then Hardwick left the tavern.'

'Anything else?' said Harriot.

'After the trial, I instructed Sam Hart to make some inquiries at Cold Bath Fields where, you may recall, Creech was held on remand. One of the turnkeys said he remembered a man who claimed to be an attorney coming to the prison to see Creech. The description he gave of the attorney matched Hardwick. He said he'd been on duty in the garden next to the exercise yard when he overheard Hardwick say to Creech, "It's all arranged." '

Harriot didn't answer for a while, his head turned towards the window, looking out at an overcast sky. 'I'm sure you have the right of the matter,' he said. 'Unfortunately, there is nothing that can be done about it. There was no error in the indictment and even if there had been, the right of appeal belongs to the defence and not the Crown. As for the decision of the jury, there is no appeal, however perverse its decision.'

'So Creech walks free?'

'I'm afraid he does.'

Dawn was still an hour in the future when the man crossed Horse Guards' Parade and walked towards Fludyer Street. There was no one else about, no sound to disturb the stillness of the night save the soft tread of his boots on the hard earth.

At the end of the street, the stranger turned left onto White-hall and, passing in front of the Treasury building, crossed the street into a narrow passage that ran down to the river. For a minute or two he stood on the top step gazing up and down the Thames. Suddenly he put his thumb and forefinger into his mouth and gave a low whistle. A wherry appeared out of the darkness and pulled alongside.

'Where to, mate?' asked the waterman.

'Limehouse Reach, as quick as you can,' said the man, seating himself in the stern sheets.

'You was lucky to get me, mate. Don't normally come out this early. What you doing at Limehouse, then?'

The man didn't answer, his eyes fixed at a point a little above the waterman's left shoulder blade.

'Please yourself, cock. Only being friendly, like.' The waterman lapsed into silence as the wherry headed north and then east at the Liberty of the Savoy, past the Temple Gardens and on to Black-friars Bridge.

'St Paul's coming up, cock.' The waterman's strident tones broke the silence.

The stranger looked up and nodded his thanks. He could see the vast dome of St Paul's rising above the surrounding rooftops of the sleeping city. The sky to the east was lighter now, a kind of inky grey that hid the stars from view. He sat still, gazing into the distance, as if in thought. Then he put a hand into a pocket of his coat and withdrew a single, folded sheet of paper. He opened it and read the contents several times before replacing it whence it had come, frowning as he did so.

Again he looked up. London Bridge was almost upon them, its line of buttresses stemming the flow, forcing the water through the narrow channels of its arches into a deep, silken curve that had seen many a man drowned for want of care. Beyond it, the stranger could see a thin streak of soft pink low down on the horizon.

'Hold on tight, mister.' The waterman braced himself, his head turned over his shoulder watching the fast-approaching bridge arch, steadying his course with first one sweep and then the other.

Then it was on down the length of the Pool, the river filled with a myriad of small craft weaving, cutting, slicing their way between the long tiers of ships, taking lumpers, coal-heavers, coopers and sailmakers to their respective vessels, the din of their presence an unceasing, thunderous roar of frantic movement.

'Some poor devils 'ave breathed their last,' said the waterman, suddenly.

'What?' The passenger looked up, baffled. He'd not been paying attention to where they were, his thoughts elsewhere.

'Over there, mate.' The man jutted his chin at the Rotherhithe shore. A large crowd was gathered on the foreshore, the sound of its excited chatter drifting across the water. At its centre were two thick wooden poles rising vertically and joined by a solid beam that ran horizontally between them. From this hung the bodies of two men, their heads covered with white hoods, lolling to one side, their bodies still. 'Wouldn't wonder if it weren't them two what went down at the Bailey yesterday. Poor beggars. I heard the cully what should have danced were acquitted. Walked out, free as a bird.'

The waterman paused as though expecting a comment. When none came, he said, 'Where to now, guv'nor?'

'Over yonder,' said the stranger, pointing to a trim, freshly painted brig, her snow-white sails tightly furled.

'That one?' The waterman looked curiously at his passenger. He paused. 'If you say so, mate.'

The man didn't answer, his eyes still fixed on the two bodies. Only when they drew alongside did he look away.

'What do I owe you?' His tone was abrupt, almost curt.

'A shilling, mate.' The man held out the palm of one hand, the other gripping one of the lines running down either side of a companion ladder.

The man fished a coin from his pocket, handed it over and, without a backward glance, climbed the ladder to the brig's upper deck.

'Welcome aboard, sir.' An officer had appeared. He saluted, his uniform immaculately cleaned and pressed. 'The captain's been expecting you.'

'Thankee kindly, sir,' said Milton Brougham. 'Is Hawkes on board?'

'He is, sir. Arrived about an hour ago, sir.'

Brougham looked back at the Rotherhithe shore where the crowd was beginning to disperse, streaming back to Southwark along the single track that hugged the Thames foreshore. Close in, he noticed a sleek, clinker-built rowing galley stationary in the water. He thought he recognised some of the crew. The man he was looking for was not amongst them.

'Goodbye, my friend,' he said, raising a hand to his forehead. 'God willing, we'll meet again one day.'

He looked down at the crumpled, bloodstained paper he'd taken from his pocket and read it again.

Tom looked round at the grinning crowd, happy at their morning's entertainment. Long queues had already formed at the food stalls that had, as if by magic, arrived at the Point. People were already sitting at the side of the road, chewing on thick slices of white bread and meat and washing the whole down with quart pots of ale. Most would stay and watch the bodies being taken down to be encased in iron cages. After that, the cadavers would again be suspended from the gibbet and left to rot, as a warning to others who might feel tempted to follow them into a life of crime.

Tom looked round at the sea of eager faces. Some he knew, others he did not. There was a fair smattering of villains amongst them, drawn here by an imperative, an opportunity to meet with former enemies and cement new relationships. It was an imperative based on fear and the need for survival hidden behind a supposed honouring of the passing of old friends.

Tom gave a small shake of the head at the thought. Pragmatism and not honour was what drove the minds and actions of the men with whom his work brought him into daily contact. If some had known Marr or Gott, it would have been at a peripheral level. They had been of little importance in the scheme of things.

For Tom, seeing who talked to who was important. He searched for Creech but couldn't find him. A familiar figure approached him, his stick beating the ground in front of him, his head thrown back. Blind Jack drew parallel to him and was about to pass when he suddenly stopped.

'Why, Master Pascoe. Was you here for the gibbeting?'

'You could say that, Jack,' said Tom, his gaze still sweeping over the crowd. 'What brings you here?'

'You hears all manner of things on a day like today, Master Pascoe. Wouldn't do for old Jack not to hear what's what. Same reason you're here, I fancy.'

Tom smiled inwardly. 'Heard anything interesting?'

Jack's head, which, until that moment, had been in perpetual motion, became suddenly still. 'I've heard talk as you wouldn't like to hear, Master Pascoe. There's folk here what want to do you a mischief. Best you be on the lookout, your honour. It'd be a crying shame if something were to happen, and that's a fact.'

It was nothing Tom had not heard a dozen times before. He could hardly expect to disrupt the lives of men long used to getting their own way and not incur their displeasure. But there was something in Blind Jack's voice that he found unsettling, as if there was more to what he was saying than the usual litany of threats that came his way. He thought of Daniel Creech. The scrub had come as close as anyone to killing him. If there was a threat, was he behind it? Would he want to risk his new-found freedom in this way? It didn't seem credible – except in the context of revenge for what Tom had put him through.

'Got any names to go with the story, Jack?'

'You know how it is, Master Pascoe. You hears these things but most times it ain't from the nag's mouth.'

'You telling me you don't know who wants me dead, Jack?'

'Oh, I knows right enough,' said Jack. 'But it weren't him what was doing the talking. Now I must be gone, your honour, else folk'll think I'm saying what I shouldn't be saying.'

'I just need the name of the cully who's after me.'

Blind Jack turned as if to continue on his way and then stopped. 'I never said it were you, your honour. I said there's folk what want to do you a mischief. You think on it, your honour.'

A tide of fear swept over Tom and he staggered as if struck by a heavy object. It had taken him a second or two to grasp the implication. If it wasn't him who was to be killed, then . . . He raced to the Thames foreshore where the rest of the crew were waiting for him in the police galley. 'Make it Parson's Stairs. Quickly,' he shouted as he waded out through the shallows and heaved himself into the stern sheets.

The ebb tide had turned and they made good speed up Limehouse Reach, past Cherry Gardens and along the Lower Pool. A barque followed them, her fore t'gallant billowing in the following wind, a ripple of water falling away from her bow. Lighters, too, were busy about their work, gliding with the tide towards the Custom House Quay hard by London Bridge. But Tom saw nothing of this. Nor did he hear the bellow of ten thousand voices reverberating up and down the reach, the cacophony of sound bouncing off the wharves and warehouses on either bank and colliding, one into another, in midstream. His mind was shut to everything but the one thing he feared most.

Opposite the Spread Eagle and Crown he took the galley across to the north shore and made for Parson's Stairs.

'We'll go straight in,' muttered Tom, ignoring the following tide. He knew it would be a difficult and uncomfortable man-oeuvre with every prospect of being carried past the stairs. But he was past caring. He leapt ashore, ran along St Catherine's and sprinted up Burr Street.

He saw it from a hundred paces away, the front door of his house standing ajar. He ran towards it, hoping he was wrong, that there was some innocent explanation for it not being firmly shut as it always had been, an irrational paralysing fear clutching at his heart.

He ran through the front door of the house and up the stairs towards his room on the first floor. 'William, William,' he shouted.

# HISTORICAL NOTE

This is, above all, a work of fiction. It does, however, draw inspiration from two events of history which occurred about this time. The first relates to the plunder of a quantity of silk and some ostrich feathers from a ship undergoing a period of quarantine in Stangate Creek in the early years of the nineteenth century. A sailing hoy was despatched to collect the cargo and bring it to London. The facts quickly became known to a gang of criminals and a plot was hatched for the sailing master to run the barge onto a sandbank. The crew, together with the two customs officers, were to be overpowered, locked below deck and the cargo plundered. For the sake of appearances, the sailing master was also to be 'overpowered'.

The plan fell through and the hoy reached London. On the following night it was towed into mid-channel and, in spite of the presence of the two customs officers, the silk successfully removed. All those involved were subsequently arrested and three were hanged for their part in the plunder.

The second incident had its origins in 1798 when, at the invitation of the French Foreign Minister, Charles Talleyrand-Périgord and three American diplomats, including Elbridge Gerry (who later became vice president of the United States), travelled to France to negotiate a peace settlement that would halt attacks on

American merchant vessels by French warships. A demand by Talleyrand for a bribe to allow the negotiations to continue at an official level was rejected by the Americans. Two of the three diplomats returned home leaving Gerry to continue the talks into the following year. Throughout this period there was a strong bias by a significant portion of the American population in favour of France. This was principally due to the fact that France, like America, was a new republic on whose principles the Americans had based their own constitution. At the same time, anti-British feelings were running high following the seizure by the Royal Navy of the USS *Baltimore* and the impressment of many of her crew into the King's service.

In France, meanwhile, opposition to the revolution was in the hands of the Royalists who were an important source of intelligence for the British. I have no evidence that information relating to the Talleyrand negotiations was ever the subject of an intelligence report but it seems highly probable that it was. Similarly, the *coup d'état* by Napoleon on 9 November 1799, shortly after this story is set, could also have been the subject of an intelligence assessment. Any such information may well have persuaded a slice of American public opinion to press for war on Britain. As it was, war with America did not come until thirteen years later.

As for Cuckold Point, this was the place on the Rotherhithe side of Limehouse Reach which, together with Execution Dock and Blackwall Point, was the location for the public execution of convicted pirates and others. Part of the sentence handed down by the court would require the dead bodies to be left hanging in chains (a sort of fitted iron cage) for three high tides as a warning to others.

*

In writing these lines I realise that I have never commented on Mr John Harriot, the resident magistrate at Wapping whose name crops up in all four books to date. He was a real person who, with Patrick Colquhoun, another magistrate based at Queen Square, founded the Thames marine police on 2 July 1798. He was, variously, a sailor who got shipwrecked, a soldier with the East India Company (where he got his thigh wound which was to cause him much distress for the rest of his life), an army chaplain without taking holy orders, a judge-advocate with no legal training, a first-class civil engineer who invented, a farmer (in America) and finally a stipendiary magistrate in Essex and then London.

# GLOSSARY

**Baltimore incident**   On 16 November 1798, fifty-five members of the crew of the USS *Baltimore*, a twenty-gun frigate, were seized by the Royal Navy and pressed into service. While around thirty were later returned, the incident caused uproar in the United States and led to much anti-British feeling.

**Coloured thread**   used by the Royal Dockyards as an anti-theft device. Each dockyard had its own colour. During this period it was a capital (hanging) offence to steal from a Royal Dockyard.

**Fetch**   Thames slang meaning to go alongside.

**Fo'c'sle Break**   that part of the forecastle deck overhanging the upper deck.

**Hangers**   slang for the naval-pattern cutlasses carried by officers.

**Harp Lane**   the present-day Harp Lane is a short cul-de-sac and the Harp public house is long gone. In 1800 it ran between Lower Thames Street and Great Tower Street.

**Herbs**   the fear of 'gaol fever' (typhus) was very real in this period. The disease was known to have carried off several defendants and at least one judge. The herbs were placed in strategic points around the court to purify the air so as to prevent infection.

**Hitcher**   slang term for a boat hook.

**King's Beam**   the point at which goods liable for import duty were weighed. In London that was on the legal quays opposite the Custom House.

**Legal representation**   it was unusual in the eighteenth century for defendants to be legally represented. This was beginning to change by the end of the century, but was still far from routine.

**Lumpers**   men employed to load and unload vessels in port.

**Mahamad**   the guardians of the Jewish Ascamot, the body of regulation providing for every eventuality of Jewish life.

**Pikes**   always issued to Thames officers when patrolling ashore in late eighteenth and early nineteenth centuries.

**Randan**   a rowing formation for three, two of whom carry an oar each (one starboard, one port) while the middle rower carries two oars.

**Schnorrer**   Jewish term for a beggar.

**Sheer**   eighteenth/nineteenth-century Thames slang meaning to depart from the side of another vessel or from the quayside. In naval usage it refers to the upward sweep of a deck towards the bows.

**Spread Eagle and Crown**   a tavern on the Rotherhithe shore of the Thames now known as the Mayflower. It had held its former name since being rebuilt in the eighteenth century, changing to the Mayflower in the late 1960s.

**Stern fetch**   manoeuvring a vessel, stern first, alongside another vessel or quay.

**Synagogue knocker**   usually a beggar who seeks payment for waking the faithful in time for them to attend a service at the synagogue.

**Thwart**   loosely, a seat in a rowing boat, the plank that runs athwart (or across) the vessel.

**Tide waiters**   customs officers whose sole task was to accompany vessels carrying goods on which duty was payable, up the Thames to the King's Beam in London.

**Turn off**   eighteenth/nineteenth-century slang meaning to kill.

**Turn over**   police slang for a search, as in 'His house was turned over.'

**Ward**   an obstruction built into a lock to prevent the lock from opening without a key.

# ACKNOWLEDGEMENTS

Reaching the end of this book, I found myself thinking back over the months and recalling the many people whose precious time I called upon with questions relating to life at the end of the eighteenth century. These would include such obscure matters as pocket watches, shipping movements, quarantine rules and long defunct public houses along the Thames. Then there were other questions on aspects of the English legal system, the negotiations between the French and Americans during the period of my story and, finally, the real events behind the exploits of Creech and his cronies which led to the execution of the latter. Without the full and generous help of these many, many people, books like this one would simply not be possible.

And when, finally, I put down my pen and leaned back in my chair, the real work still lay ahead. My editor, Jane Wood, gave me unstinting time and effort to make sure the story made as much sense as my abilities as a writer would allow. And only after that was the work passed to Liz Hatherell, my copy editor who is wholly without mercy or compassion in her drive to winkle out the least geographical or grammatical error. To them and to my inspirational wife, Sara, I give my heartfelt thanks.

PJE